The Titus Chronicles
Eagle and Wyvern
Book 1

By R.W. Peake

Also by R.W Peake

Marching With Caesar® – Birth of the 10th
Marching With Caesar – Conquest of Gaul
Marching With Caesar – Civil War
Marching With Caesar – Antony and Cleopatra, Parts I & II
Marching With Caesar – Rise of Augustus
Marching With Caesar – Last Campaign
Marching With Caesar – Rebellion
Marching With Caesar – A New Era
Marching With Caesar – Pax Romana
Marching With Caesar – Fraternitas
Marching With Caesar – Vengeance
Marching With Caesar – Rise of Germanicus
Marching With Caesar – Revolt of the Legions
Marching With Caesar – Avenging Varus, Part I
Marching With Caesar – Avenging Varus, Part II

Caesar Triumphant
Caesar Ascending – Invasion of Parthia
Caesar Ascending – Conquest of Parthia
Caesar Ascending – India
Caesar Ascending – Pandya

Critical praise for the Marching with Caesar series:

Marching With Caesar-Antony and Cleopatra: Part I-Antony

"Peake has become a master of depicting Roman military life and action, and in this latest novel he proves adept at evoking the subtleties of his characters, often with an understated humour and surprising pathos. Very highly recommended."

Marching With Caesar-Civil War

"Fans of the author will be delighted that Peake's writing has gone from strength to strength in this, the second volume...Peake manages to portray Pullus and all his fellow soldiers with a marvelous feeling of reality quite apart from the star historical name... There's history here, and character, and action enough for three novels, and all of it can be enjoyed even if readers haven't seen the first volume yet. Very highly recommended."

~The Historical Novel Society

"The hinge of history pivoted on the career of Julius Caesar, as Rome's Republic became an Empire, but the muscle to swing that gateway came from soldiers like Titus Pullus. What an amazing story from a student now become the master of historical fiction at its best."

~Professor Frank Holt, University of Houston

The Titus Chronicles – Eagle and Wyvern by R.W. Peake

Foreword

Once I learned that there were enough people who enjoyed my stories that I could do this for a living, I allowed my imagination to take wing. This is the first product of my imaginings.

There is an apocryphal tale about Pablo Picasso where he said, "Good artists imitate, great artists steal." Setting aside the veracity of this, I freely admit that I'm "stealing" an idea, albeit with my own twist. One of my favorite authors, Edward Rutherfurd, has written a series of novels that are focused on a location, like his *Sarum*, which is one of my favorite books. The idea was to create a fictional genealogy that was then inextricably bound to the location about which he was writing, the immovable object, as it were.

My idea is to essentially flip this around, where the immovable object is this line of men and women that all derive from Titus Pomponius Pullus, born in a hovel in the Roman province of Baetica, and the events of history stream past these characters. Now, what those periods of history are was the first question that confronted me; where would I have the first non-Roman Titus character land?

The answer is here, in the year 878 CE, on the island that was known to the Romans as Britannia, and for those of my readers who are as invested in this series as I am, if you're wondering where the Pullus line might end up…this is your first clue. Now, that's not to say that a Pullus won't be visiting places like Judaea or Dacia, but that's way on down the line at this point. Regardless, my choice of this era is based in my interest with this period of time where the very idea of England was being formed.

More than anything, though, this is a bit more personal a story to me, not just because my roots are firmly founded in the British Isles, and to a lesser degree, Scandinavia, but also because this is another story of the mystical power of blood.

For long-time readers, it's easy to see how the character that I now refer to as Titus the Elder influenced and shaped those generations immediately following his own, from Gaius Porcinus to Titus the Younger, and now to Gnaeus who, while he didn't know the Prefect when he was alive, is still subject to his influence through the scrolls that form the heart of the *Marching With Caesar* series.

But what about later generations? How far does the ripple effect go across the ocean of time? This is where this story becomes more personal to me.

I've spoken of it in my podcasts, but for those who haven't listened to them, my knowledge of my father for the first twenty years of my life consisted of a single sentence: "His first name was Richard, he had red hair, and he was in the Army when he died three weeks before you were born, and he's buried in Virginia."

That's it. No pictures, no letters, nothing more than that. It wasn't a forbidden topic, necessarily; it just never came up. Then, through a series of events, I was introduced to my Aunt Jackie, my father's sister, and it was from her that I got the first pictures of my father, but more importantly than that, an idea of *who* he was. And, to my astonishment, I found a place where I fit in, something that I had never really experienced with my mom's side of the family, through no fault of their own. It was just that I didn't have much in common with them, but suddenly, that all changed, and it was this experience that colors this story about a new Titus, generations removed with absolutely no knowledge of his own personal history.

All of my books have this as a theme, the power of blood that courses through us and why, in ways that we may not ever understand, we exhibit the traits of those who have gone before us. Why was I always drawn to the military? Why did I have a moment, which I suppose was a non-religious sort of epiphany when I was in boot camp, and we were doing our field training where I realized, "I was born to do this." Why have I always had more of a Southerner's outlook when my mother's side of the family, the only side of the family I knew until I was twenty, comes exclusively from the North? Why am I so competitive, and thrive on conflict of some sort? Where did all of this come from?

This, more than anything else, is what drives Titus of Cissanbyrig, a quiet but insistent voice that the path he's currently on isn't the right one for him; it's the same voice that drove me to enlist in the Marine Corps at the relatively advanced age of twenty-three, married and with a family, stepping away from a job that, for that time, paid well, going from making ten dollars an hour to six hundred sixty dollars a month. In that sense, this Titus' journey is much like my own…and that of the son of a poor farmer whose size killed his mother almost a millennium before in the dry and dusty Roman province of Baetica.

Once more, thanks to Beth Lynne for being so adept at shifting gears from the world of Rome to that of Anglo-Saxon England, and to Laura Prevost for a phenomenal cover that has set a record for the quickest turnaround in all of what is now twenty-five books. And, as always, to y'all, the readers of my stories who make "going to work" so much fun for me.

Semper Fidelis,

R.W. Peake

April, 2020

P.S. I'm adding this because the world we're currently living in is, frankly, not only much different than when I began writing *Eagle and Wyvern*, but also scarier than certainly anything I've ever experienced, even after 9/11.

It's my hope that, in some small way, this and the rest of my books help y'all to escape, if only for a time, the uncertainty and worries that have been visited on us by COVID-19. Maybe, by traveling to the Year of our Lord 878, you'll set aside social distancing, wondering if that cough is just allergies or if it's "it," and the cabin fever that comes from this period of isolation, if only for a time. If this book does that, that's enough for me.

Take care of yourselves; take care of those you love, and know that this will pass, and we will endure it.

Historical Notes

I'm of the firm belief that the only way for anyone to improve their craft, no matter what it may be, is to push themselves out of their comfort zone. And, with *The Titus Chronicles – Eagle and Wyvern*, I most definitely did that, perhaps to an extreme, but I won't deny that learning about a whole new period of history, about which I knew very little before, was as exciting as it was challenging. There have been practical challenges, namely that I'm running out of room for all the books!

Normally, I try to rely on primary sources, but as frustrating as it can be writing about Rome because of all the gaps and unanswered questions, I quickly learned something; there is a reason this period is called the Dark Ages. That said, I used *The Anglo-Saxon Chronicles* and Assers *Life of King Alfred* as the primary building blocks for this story, but I also relied heavily on other scholarly works from a variety of sources. I had already learned that as an author of historical fiction, gaps in the primary source material is a double-edged sword, that while it gives us a degree of flexibility, it also puts someone who wants to be as true to the historical record as they can be in an awkward position. Researching this first installment of *The Titus Chronicles*, I learned that this is a matter of degree when comparing Rome to Anglo-Saxon England of the 9th Century CE, so more of this book is based on secondary sources than I'm normally accustomed to.

Before I talk about locations, I want to talk about the social structure, and my use of "Ealdorman" in the manner that I do. I freely confess that I'm new to the Anglo-Saxon world in an academic sense, although my Ancestry DNA test confirms that I am one of the Whitest Men Alive, exclusively from the British Isles and Scandinavia, so I'm either conqueror or conquered, depending on how you look at it. In the social structure of the Anglo-Saxon world, there is the King, the Ealdorman, the

Thegn, and the Ceorl, which was the lowest class of free Saxon, with the Thrall at the bottom of the heap. And, of course, there was the *wergild*, the eminently practical Saxon convention that I suppose could be considered the precursor to the modern insurance industry, where everyone's life had a specific value, and loss of limbs were calculated down to the nearest shilling. For those who are more familiar with this world than I am, let me set expectations; I don't go to a level of detail that might satisfy those who are looking for a richer level than this book offers, but I will also say that while this is the first book, it won't be the last, and as my character grows, so will my knowledge of this world.

As it pertains to my use of Ealdorman when referring to the fictional Lord of Wiltun, Eadwig, early on, I struggled with what made an Ealdorman an Ealdorman, realizing that while all Ealdormen were thegns, the opposite wasn't true. Also, I am working on the premise that not all thegns are equal; some would be richer and more powerful than others, but I was unable to find much information on how thegns were ranked in that society. Consequently, I use the title Ealdorman for Eadwig more as a way to distinguish that he was the senior thegn, although I do use the term "minor" in front of it. For those who are more steeped in this period of history, I ask forgiveness and hope that it doesn't detract from your enjoyment of the story.

Otherwise, I tried to be as accurate as I could be, and to aid me, along with the primary sources, I used a number of secondary sources, ranging from *Anglo-Saxon Thegn 449-1066* from the *Osprey* series by Mark Harrison, to an *Atlas of Anglo-Saxon England* by David Hill, and *Anglo-Saxon Weapons & Warfare* by Richard Underwood, along with several biographies of King Alfred, all of which were very helpful to one degree or another.

However, as long-time readers know, I'm also a bit…obsessive, I suppose, about terrain, and I try to "walk" the ground as much as technology allows. Consequently, I found *King Alfred – A Man on the Move* by Dr. Paul Kelly to be especially helpful. Dr. Kelly is an avid amateur historian who, using the British Ordnance Survey Maps and the primary source material, traces

King Alfred's movements about southern England. Not surprisingly, many of these locations are subject to debate and there are several alternatives for these places, each with their own set of supporters...and detractors, and I will say that it's nice to see that people are every bit as passionate about King Alfred and the Anglo-Saxons as they are about Rome! What Dr. Kelly does is offer each alternative, and while he does rank them according to his own opinion, he offers an argument for each of them. Using a combination of his book, the online version of the Ordnance Survey maps, and Google Earth, I want to briefly touch on the locations that I selected for each of these landmarks, starting with Egbert's Stone, which is mentioned as the assembly point for the fyrd called by King Alfred.

For those interested in such things, you can "see" the location I chose based on Dr. Kelly's argument at 51 07 32N, 2 12 49W on Google Earth, or Grid Number ST 85124 36722 on the British Ordnance Survey Map, in Kingston Deverill in Wiltshire. One clue mentioned in the *Anglo-Saxon Chronicles* is that the spot was "east of Selwood Forest" or depending on the translation "the eastern edge of Selwood Forest". The difficulty is that virtually none of this once vast forest is still there, so like with everything else, this is guesswork, but Dr. Kelly makes a persuasive case for this being the spot.

From Egbert's Stone, the now-assembled army of King Alfred moved to a place called Iglea (or as Asser refers to it *Aecglea*), again from the *Anglo-Saxon Chronicles,* and again Dr. Kelly makes a persuasive case for a place that's now called Southleigh Wood but was once called Iley Oak, west of Sutton Veny at 51 10 30N 2 10 10W or ST 88244 41787, a distance of only four miles from the spot I selected for Egbert's Stone.

Alfred using Battlesbury Hill as a place to deposit his baggage train is of my own invention, as I tried to envision what I would do in Alfred's position. It was a common tactic throughout ancient history for an army on the march to deposit their baggage train before arraying for battle, but I also selected it because by ascending it, it would have brought Alfred and his army up onto the Sarum Plain, where Ethantun (modern

Edington) is located almost five miles north by northeast. As I say in the book, there's an old hillfort on Battlesbury Hill, which is located at 51 12 35N 2 08 58W and ST 89858 45570, so this would seem like an ideal fallback position.

There are several arguments about the actual location of the battle site of Ethantun; naturally, there are those who argue that it's located immediately in or around Edington, along with a suggestion for a spot called Bratton Camp, which is almost two miles west and just a bit south of the modern village of Edington. In fact, the location I selected is within three hundred yards of a large chalk white horse called the Westbury White Horse on the Ordnance Survey map. Unlike the much older Uffington White Horse, this one's history is somewhat obscure, having been "restored" in the 18th century. And while it's often associated with the battle, there's no real evidence that goes back far enough to suggest any connection. But that's not why I picked it as my spot. Using Street View on Google Earth, I was able to "see" that there was a strip of high ground on the Sarum Plain between Combe's Bottom on the east and a dropoff to the west, basically where the escarpment of the Sarum Plain curves from an east/west axis to a north/south axis. For a defending force, it would make being flanked difficult because of the escarpment on either side, or from the north, behind them, although the southern slope, the direction from which I have Alfred attacking isn't very steep. In cycling terms, we would call it a "false flat", meaning that it might look flat to the eye, but does have a gentle gradient. This is located at 51 15 42N 2 08 40W, and ST 90131 51420 respectively. I've included a map that gives a visual idea of how Alfred moves once he assembles his fyrd.

Cippinhamm (modern Chippenham) is obviously still there, although from the evidence the Anglo-Saxon town was south of the Afon (Avon) River, located in the loop of the river, while the village of Aller, where Alfred takes Guthrum after the

Danish surrender is still there as well. Dr, Kelly makes a case that the local church of St. Andrew's there was the site of the church where Guthrum was baptized, and we do know that Aller is mentioned. It can be found at 51 03 19N 2 51 45W and ST 39630 28799. A far as Athelney, that swampland has long since been drained, but there is a small hill located at 51 03 32N 2 56 04W and ST 34605 29250, where there is a small monument located.

Finally, the village of Cissanbyrig is no more, although its name echoes in the modern East and West Chisenbury, at 51 16 25N 1 47 48W and SU 14054 52578, which like Cippenhamm, is along the River Afon.

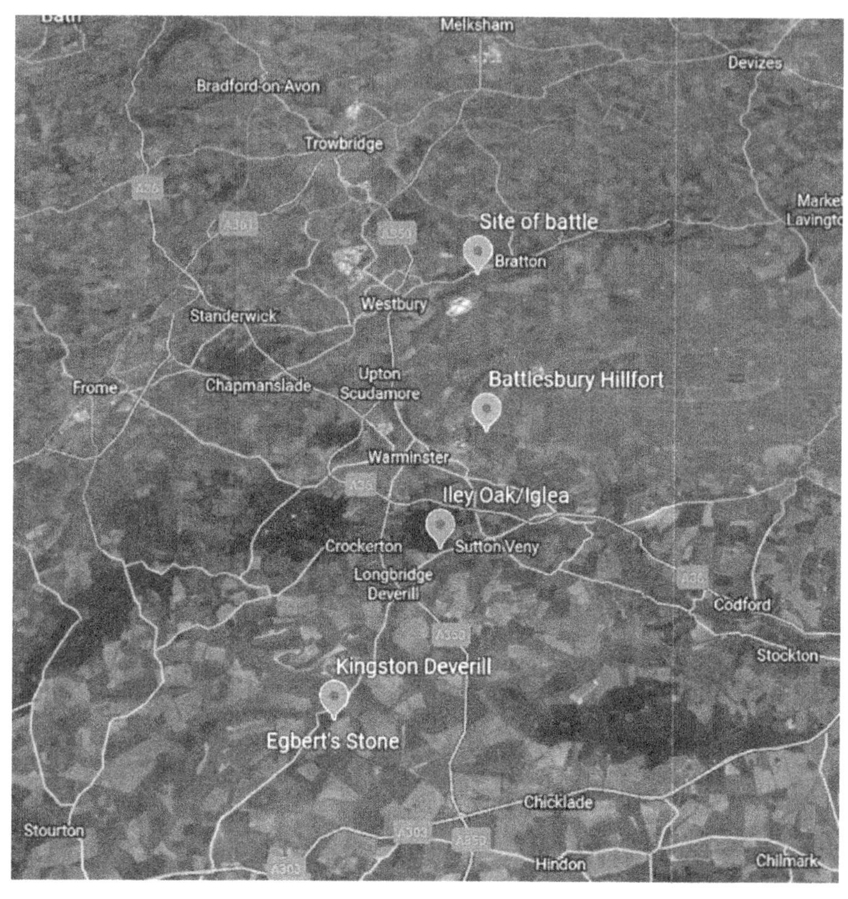

Google and the Google logo are registered trademarks of Google LLC, used with permission.

Table of Contents

Chapter One

The Northmen, the dreaded Danes, were here again, in the Year of our Lord 878, which was how the parish priest referred to it. At the moment, this was all young Titus knew, but it was more than enough to ignite within him a number of intense feelings, some of them in direct conflict with each other. So much trouble with this sentence. Fear, certainly; there was nobody Titus knew who did not have some lurid tale of the bloodthirsty raiders from the frigid northern lands. That, being honest with himself, was the extent of his knowledge, that they were cold and somewhere far to the north. While it was mostly men who spoke of such things, women were not immune, but while women were more circumspect in describing the atrocities for which these fierce barbaric savages were famous, men spoke of things like slow disembowelments, being roasted alive, and "blood eagles," the removal of a man's lungs through his back to be placed on his shoulders to resemble an eagle…while still alive. Now, these despoilers were in Cippanhamm, which they had seized in a dastardly raid during the Yuletide truce, forcing no less than King Alfred himself to flee in the night. Finally, after months of waiting, the King had sent riders out to all the points of Wessex announcing that he was calling the fyrd, the assemblage of every able-bodied Saxon male of fighting age, yet along with the fear that he experienced every time the Danes were mentioned, Titus was excited, and there was a part of him, deep inside from a place he had not even known existed, that was looking forward to whatever these Northmen brought.

Part of this, of course, was because of his youth; Titus was fourteen, but he was already taller than all of his friends and most of the full-grown men in the village of Cissanbyrig, the nearest village to his father's holding. More than that, he was also broader through the chest, with larger arms and thighs, and about this, he had decidedly mixed feelings. Being the largest and strongest of his contemporaries was certainly a fine thing, but the fact that his father Leofric hated him because of that size certainly bothered, and hurt, him. Not that he did not at least understand why his father detested him all that much, because he knew that it was his size that killed his mother bringing him into this world, leaving his father to raise him and his two older sisters, on a *gebur* free holding of one hide that barely fed the family, the minimum amount of land required for a Saxon to declare himself a free man, a ceorl.

If either of his sisters had asked, he would have sworn that this was why he was about to do what he had set out to do, traveling alone to the hall of Ealdorman Eadwig all the way in Wiltun, to persuade the Lord to allow Titus to stand in the shield wall when it was time to face the marauding Danes. The truth was infinitely more complicated, most of which he was only dimly aware, knowing only that there was *something*, a small but insistent voice that kept whispering to him, day and night, that he was not born to the plow, but to the sword. If he had been asked, Titus of Cissanbyrig would have said that he was *Westseaxe* through and through, his roots in this land as deep as anyone's, and there was no questioning his pride in this fact. He had no way of knowing that he was only partially correct about his roots; yes, he had the blood of Saxons running through his veins, but his connection to the land in which he lived could be traced much, much further back, all the way to the people that Titus knew were called the Romans, although that was essentially the extent of his knowledge of them. Certainly, he had heard that in Bathenceaster there were vestiges of Rome that were still visible, although most of it was in ruins, and he knew that the Pope himself lived in Rome, and that Rome was the source of all that was represented by the Church. What he did not, nor would he ever know, was that his lineage ran back for almost a millennium, to a poor farmer's son born in the Roman province of Baetica who, through the only familial connection to survive, bore the same name as this youth, but more importantly, the size and strength that marked him as unique among his peers.

Because Titus' mother had died, he would never learn that it was through her line that, every few generations, a male was born whose introduction into the world often proved fatal to the woman who bore him, and her husband Leofric had only named his son Titus because she had demanded his oath to do so on her deathbed. Nor would he ever learn that, along with the size and strength, there came a combination of more intangible but equally important innate qualities, and it was one of these that caused Titus' feet to be carrying him to Lord Eadwig's hall, that deep, inner conviction that he would be a good warrior. Maybe, he would occasionally think to himself, good enough to wield a sword and not just be a ceorl spearman, another anonymous face in the shield wall, defending his lands against the Northmen. What he *could* say without boasting was that he was already man-grown and man-strong; unskilled as a warrior, yes, but he was willing to learn, and most importantly as far as he was concerned, he was willing to die for his family and his people. Although he would never know it, young Titus of Cissanbyrig was walking down the road to fulfill his destiny.

Otha stood, watching his pupil make another lunge with his blunted training sword, aiming for a scarred wooden pole set in the ground, and it took a fair amount of effort on his part to avoid a string of oaths, accompanied by a quick cuff to his pupil's head, knowing that the boy's father was watching. If it had not been Lord Eadwig's son and heir, Otha would have treated him as he had every other youngster he had trained over the years, but this nobleman was unusually protective of the boy. And, Otha admitted to himself, even as he was walking over to correct the lad, it was not as if the boy was not trying hard; sighing inwardly, Otha thought, I've just never seen a clumsier boy than this one. It did not help that he was scrawny and undersized, although he supposed it was possible the boy would have a growth spurt and be at least as large as his father, who was not particularly tall, nor all that broad in the shoulder, but as Otha knew, did possess a fair amount of strength.

"You're not placing your feet far enough apart, Lord Eadward." Kicking one of the boy's feet out a few inches, he grunted his approval, then said curtly, "Try it again."

As was his habit, Eadward screwed up his face in an expression that Otha knew meant the boy was increasing his effort to please his tutor, causing Otha to turn away so that the youth could not see his smile. Despite not being tied by blood, in his own rough way, Otha held great affection for Eadward that went over and above the normal loyalty that would be expected from the Ealdorman Eadwig's most senior Thegn, which was Otha's role in Eadwig's household. As such, he was responsible for not just assuring that the young lordling attained enough skill with arms that he survived to inherit Eadwig's lands and title, but for organizing the fyrd that was required of the Ealdorman in service to King Alfred. In the ever-shifting and oftentimes treacherous atmosphere that was part and parcel of a royal court, Otha's lord was not one of Alfred's most powerful nobles, but nor was he a minor player, essentially just one rank below an Ealdorman of an entire shire, like Wulfhere, the Ealdorman of all of Wiltscir. And, as Otha knew all too well, Eadwig was an ambitious man, so that, while this was certainly a crisis, he also viewed it as an opportunity to increase his prestige and standing in the eyes of the only man who truly mattered here in *Westseaxe*, Alfred. The truth was that Otha really did not have much time to spare with Eadward right now; there was always much to do when raising the fyrd, especially when it was under emergency conditions, and the return of the Danes certainly qualified.

If it were up to him, Otha would be spending the time this morning inspecting those men who had already answered the summons to assemble here at the Ealdorman's estate, outside the village of Wiltun, which was also part of Eadwig's holding. As a minor Ealdorman, he was obligated to provide one hundred spearmen to the fyrd, drawn from the ceorls of his lands, along with at least thirty sword-wielding warriors, of which Otha was one, and the most senior. Even as he worked with Eadward, men were arriving in the open yard in front of the Ealdorman's hall that was surrounded by a number of outbuildings, all of which was enclosed by a wooden wall with a single gate that was opened, although two of Otha's men were standing guard. Actually, Otha thought sourly, they're leaning on their spears and talking to their friends who are arriving in two's and three's, but he would fix that soon enough.

Titus was tired; he had left his farm three miles outside of Cissanbyrig well before dawn, slipping out while his father was still snoring. Only his oldest sister Leofflaed was aware of his intentions, but while she had objected to what he was doing, it was based on a practical concern.

"Lord Owin is our lord, not Lord Eadwig," she had pointed out during the one whispered conversation they had held the day before his departure. "Father's part of Owin's fyrd and he's remaining loyal to Ealdorman Wulfhere, which means if you were old enough, you would be bound to Wulfhere too."

As he always did, Titus bristled at the mention of his age, but if not the first, it was one of the first that Leofflaed would remember later where he did not offer some sort of retort about his size and strength. Which, she would be the first to admit, was considerable; she was certain that Titus was already stronger than their father, but she was almost as sure that Titus had yet to realize this. Which, as far as she was concerned, was a good thing, because seemingly with every passing day as Titus grew, their father seemed to despise him more, and while she knew this still hurt her "little" brother, she also understood that there was a smoldering, volcanic rage in her sibling that she was positive was growing because of their father's hatred. Scarcely a month before this conversation, Titus had barely escaped serious punishment by the village elders because of a savage beating he had administered to Oswiu, the son of another farmer. He had been saved because of two salient factors: Oswiu was actually seventeen and considered a man, but more importantly, he was a notorious bully, and Titus had actually intervened when Oswiu and two of his friends were torturing a villager's daughter's puppy in front of several witnesses. Ironically, it was Oswiu's two friends and another farmer, Godstan, who saved Titus, because he was so out of his mind with fury that, while she had not witnessed it, Leofflaed had heard from enough people who had, there was no doubt in her mind that her brother would have beaten Oswiu to death. Oswiu's companions had leapt onto Titus' back, but it was not until Godstan joined in before they were able to pull her brother from his now-unconscious and battered victim. She would never be certain because she never asked, but for the rest of her life, Leofflaed would believe that it was this incident that was the impetus for their conversation now, although she was not altogether surprised that Titus was unimpressed with her argument, and she suspected she knew the cause.

Titus confirmed this by snorting dismissively, "Wulfhere is a traitor!" Jabbing a finger in her face, something she detested, he kept his voice low, but there was no mistaking the vehement hostility as he reminded her, "You know that he's the one who betrayed the King to Guthrum and his Danes at Cippanhamm! Why do you think that the Danes haven't raided Cissanbyrig, or our farm?"

This was certainly the widely held belief, but of the family of Leofric, Leofflaed was the pragmatic one and was very clever; that she was a true beauty, and not just in Titus' eyes, made the fact that, at almost nineteen, she was still unmarried a mystery to those outside the family.

"That," she acknowledged, "is what most people believe. And," she hurried to forestall her brother, recognizing the look on his face, "that's likely the truth. That doesn't mean that he'll be punished for it, Titus."

Titus stared at her in astonishment.

"How can he not be punished? King Alfred has been in hiding ever since! When he comes back, Wulfhere will be the first to have his head chopped off!"

Leofflaed knew she was treading on dangerous ground, but she was convinced that her brother was doing the same thing, albeit for different reasons.

"How can you be certain Alfred will prevail, Titus? What if he's defeated?" she asked calmly.

She immediately saw that this had never occurred to her brother, and it was a reminder that, despite his size and strength, he was still young and not very worldly.

"Do you…really think that Alfred might lose?"

Leofflaed was torn between relief that Titus seemed uncertain about this venture and guilt that she had been the one who introduced this seed of doubt, but ultimately, she owed her loyalty to her brother.

"I think," she answered finally, "that it's something to be considered." Thinking to return back to the original topic, she asked, "If you're not going to try and join Ealdorman Wulfhere, where will you go?"

This, at least, Titus had already thought about, because he answered immediately, "Ealdorman Eadwig. I heard in the village that he's raising a fyrd in Wiltun as well."

This caused Leofflaed to look at Titus intently, suddenly suspecting that, perhaps, her brother had thought this through more carefully than she believed. It was, she had to admit, not an altogether horrible idea, because Eadwig's domain was several miles south, and straddled the border between the shire known as Wiltscir and Suthhamtunscir. More importantly, it was common knowledge that Ealdormen Eadwig and Wulfhere despised each other, and it was highly probable that Wulfhere had done exactly what Titus had accused him of; after all, he would not be the first nobleman who chose to accommodate the Danes in order to keep their lands, and Titus was certainly correct that Wulfhere's holdings had been left largely unmolested, particularly in his holdings nearest to East Anglia, the base of Danish power. And, if Alfred did succeed, it would be good for not just Titus, but for herself and her sister Eadgyd, especially since, while Wulfhere had not summoned his own fyrd yet, their father had already announced he would be answering it if he did. Although he would not say as much, Leofflaed suspected that, on the subject of Wulfhere, her brother and father were of a like mind, an exceedingly rare event in itself, but Leofric would not dream of disobeying a command from Lord Owin, since it would indirectly be coming from Wulfhere. We might need Titus fighting for Eadwig, who would be fighting for Alfred to save the family from being punished, she thought to herself, and it was with this in mind that she signaled her acceptance of his plan.

Now, when Titus was within sight of the wooden wall surrounding Ealdorman Eadwig's hall, which, as had been the custom for as long as anyone could remember, situated atop a small hill that, while not high, had a commanding view of the surrounding countryside, it suddenly felt as if his feet had decided on their own to stop moving towards the open gate. Too far away to make out features, he could see two men, neither of them wearing armor but holding spears, while their round shields were resting on the ground and leaned against their legs, looking in his direction as he stood there. This more than anything was what prompted him to resume moving, realizing that a stranger suddenly turning about and walking away would undoubtedly arouse suspicion.

Trying to appear confident, he knew that his size helped his case—the fact that he was cleanshaven did not—but at first, the pair of sentries simply regarded him with idle curiosity, and he was further aided by the fact that not far ahead of him, another pair of men were just climbing the gentle slope up to the gate. He debated for a moment about hurrying to catch up to them, acting as if he was simply rejoining his travel companions after taking a piss, but quickly discarded that. Instead, he tried to mimic their manner, striding up to the gateway with a confidence that he certainly did not feel. The pair of travelers ahead of him were stopped, but their delay was momentary, and one of the guards laughed at something one of the men said, then slapped him on the back as the pair entered into the compound. Taking advantage of their momentary attention on the first two, Titus tried to stride past, his eyes on the cluster of men standing in the middle of the open area, all of them facing a bearded man wearing a boiled leather vest over his tunic. Before he could devote any more attention to what was taking place inside the walls, he was verbally assailed by one of the guards, a stocky man with a black beard at least fifteen years older than Titus.

"*Oy!* What are you doing? You can't just stroll past me and Heard here, can he, Heard?"

The other man, also bearded and slightly taller than his companion, but with narrow features and a countenance that, to Titus, announced a truculent nature, not surprisingly agreed, "No, he can't, Cenric." Glaring at the youth, he demanded, "State your business here."

Trying to sound as if it was the most natural thing he could say, Titus replied, "I've come to join the fyrd Ealdorman Eadwig called."

To his ears, he sounded quite convincing; a mixture of determination and surprise that this would even be a question, and for the briefest moment, he thought he had gotten away with it, because Cenric turned slightly, as if to allow him to pass, but it was the other man, Heard, who spoke up.

"Wait." Titus naturally obeyed, turning to face Heard, who regarded him with obvious suspicion, causing the youth's heart to begin beating more rapidly. "How old are you, boy?"

"I'm seventeen," Titus replied calmly, for the first time feeling more confident; this was far from the first time he had lied about his age, and he could see by the guard's expression that he accepted Titus' lie.

"Why haven't I seen you before?" Cenric suddenly demanded. "You're not from Wiltun or anywhere nearby, I know that."

"I live north of here," Titus answered, hoping this would

suffice; it did not.

"North?" Cenric repeated, then shook his head. "You need to be more specific, boy." Suddenly, his demeanor changed from a wariness to open, hostile suspicion. "Did Ealdorman Wulfhere send you here, boy?" he demanded, but before Titus could say anything, he snarled, "I'll wager that's it! You've been sent here to spy on us!"

Then he reached out and seized the youth's arm, which was a mistake. Even later, Titus had absolutely no recollection of anything that transpired in the ensuing span of heartbeats, but he could clearly recall how it ended, as a terrific force slammed into him from behind, knocking him flat on his face, the impact with the hardpacked dirt driving the wind from his lungs with a great whooshing sound that prevented him from even groaning aloud. He was not knocked unconscious, but he was certainly dazed, and it seemed to take forever before he could suck in enough air to clear away the thousands of pricks of light in his vision. He did manage to roll over, but when he did, he saw that, bare inches from his face was the point of a sword, held by what Titus recognized as the man wearing the vest, although it was the cold expression on his face that captured his attention.

"You better have a good explanation for this, boy."

Otha had been absorbed in counting the cluster of newly arrived men when the incident at the gate started, but like any trained and veteran warrior, his eye was instantly drawn to the sudden flurry of movement, so while he missed Cenric grabbing what appeared to be a young man of a considerable size, he was just in time to see the unknown man react by sending Cenric reeling backward with so much force that he could hear the cracking sound as his guard collided with the open gate. The second guard, Heard, had been slow to react, although to Otha, knowing Heard as he did, this was nothing unusual, but when he tried to tackle the man around the waist, the youngster flung Heard away from him with what appeared to a contemptuous ease. This was what got Otha moving, and he did not hesitate, shoving aside those men in the way, all of whom were as slow to react as Heard, although they did immediately follow him as he went at not quite a run towards the gate. The man was standing more or less in his original spot, but he happened to have his attention on Heard, who had ended up flat on his back and feebly waving his arms when Otha arrived. Without slowing, Otha extended both arms and struck the man in the back with enough power that he had no chance to break his fall, slamming into the ground with a force that, while he had intended it, still made Otha wince. This did not stop him from drawing his sword as the man, whose face was turned away from him, sucked in air with a great gasp, then rolled over on his back, giving Otha a surprise bordering on shock.

"You better have a good explanation for this, boy." Despite his startlement, Otha's voice was as cold as his expression.

"I-I-came to join the fyrd Ealdorman Eadwig called," the supine figure, who, despite his size, Otha was certain was barely a teenager, managed to gasp out. "That's all, I swear it!"

"And you think that knocking around two of my men is a good way to do that?" he demanded. "Especially when nobody knows who you are?" Otha hesitated, then, in a slightly calmer voice, asked, "Let's start with that. Who are you, and where are you from?"

Titus had caught his breath, but when he moved to get up, he was stopped with a simple gesture by the man holding the sword, so he lay back down on the ground, trying to show no fear as he answered, "My name is Titus, Lord. I come from…"

Before he could continue, Cenric, who was rubbing his back and glowering down at the youth, cut him off.

"Titus? That's the kind of name only priests and monks have!" He gave a harsh laugh, but while he addressed Otha, there was no mistaking who his words were intended for. "It looks like we have some priest's bastard here, Lord Otha. Churchmen can't fight, so I don't imagine their bastards are any better."

"I'm no bastard!" Titus snarled, raising up on his elbows, and while he hesitated when Otha prodded him in the chest with the tip of the sword, he did not relent, pressing his chest against the blade as he stared up at Cenric, completely ignoring the man holding the sword to his chest. "My father is Leofric, a free ceorl!"

Despite himself, Otha was impressed at the boy's bravery, although it was just as likely that he was so angry that he was not intimidated by the feeling of the razor-sharp point pressing into his tunic, hard enough that Otha saw a small splotch of red around the tip.

Before Cenric could respond, Otha asked, "All right, Titus, son of Leofric, who's a ceorl. Who," he asked pointedly, "is his Ealdorman? And what's his *wergild*?"

Titus managed to suppress the groan of frustration, but his expression gave him away, as he realized that he had been foolish to think that he could just show up here in Wiltun and talk his way into joining the fyrd of a man who was not his lord. It was more than that, but he realized that what small chance he had would evaporate by being silent.

"My father is Leofric of Cissanbyrig," Titus answered, then added dully, "and his *wergild* is...two hundred shillings, Lord."

Otha's face remained impassive as he pressed, "How many hides does your father hold?"

"One, Lord."

So not only was this boy not anywhere near his home, he came from the poorest class of freeman in their society, but Otha had not missed that Titus had evaded offering what was probably the most important piece of information.

"So, Titus of Cissanbyrig," Otha asked again, "who is your father's Ealdorman?"

"Ealdorman Wulfhere, Lord, through Lord Owin of Cissanbyrig," Titus said, his mouth twisting into a bitter grimace, but before Otha could say anything, the youth added heatedly, "but he's a traitor, Lord! Everyone knows that he betrayed King Alfred to Guthrum! I will not serve him, Lord!"

This, Otha knew very well, was not only the widely held view about the Ealdorman of Wiltscir and his Lord of Cissanbyrig, along with some others in the northern and eastern part of the shire, but it was a view Otha himself held. Still, neither did he put it past the wily Wulfhere to send a fresh-faced lad, no matter how strapping and seemingly passionate about the nobleman's suspected treachery against their king as he appeared to be, to act as a spy. As aware as Titus' sister Leofflaed was about the ongoing tension about this disputed patch of ground between Ealdorman Wulfhere and his own, Otha knew even more about it, and he also knew that Eadwig had been emboldened by the developments that found Wulfhere under suspicion, seeing an opportunity there for his own advancement.

"How old are you anyway?" Otha asked suddenly.

"Seventeen," Titus answered immediately and without hesitation; this was the one question he had been expecting, and he had lied about his age more than once, including just moments before, and he had never been caught.

Otha, however, was not fooled; certainly, this youngster was large enough, and Christ and His Saints knew he had to be strong to throw Cenric and Heard about like he had, but his smooth face and a couple of eruptions that plagued some teenagers told another story. More than anything else, Otha realized he had spent as much time on this as he could afford at the moment.

Sheathing his sword before he turned away, he said casually, "Cenric, Heard, I just watched this lad toss you about like sacks of grain. Maybe he'll take one of your spots." Addressing Titus, "I'm going to let Cenric and Heard see how tough you are, boy. You caught them by surprise, but let's see how badly you want to join this fyrd."

He had already turned about when he heard the first thudding sound, assuming that one of his men had kicked the boy, but he was impressed that there was no cry of pain, and he refused to pay any more attention; there were too many other things to do.

"I'll say this for you," Cenric's tone was grudging, "you can take a beating."

Titus wanted to answer, but he thought his jaw might be broken; besides, drawing breath caused a stabbing pain in his side that, while he had never experienced them before, he thought might mean at least one broken rib. Consequently, all he could offer was a shrug and a mumble that he hoped would suffice.

"And," Heard spoke up, although his voice was muffled by the rag he was dabbing at his split lip, "you hit hard."

The two men and youth were at the well, mostly ignored by the other men who were now being drilled by Otha, and despite the pain he was in, Titus could not seem to keep his eyes off of the proceedings, watching with something more than curiosity. There is, Cenric thought, following the youth's gaze, almost a hunger in him, like this is something that he needs. Although it certainly did not seem to be the case in the moment, Titus had been fortunate that Cenric and Heard were standing guard this day, because while Titus had been correct in his assessment that Heard might have a temper, neither of them were the type to hold a grudge. Oh, they had been angry enough, but they had vented that anger on the boy, and he had not only proven to be tougher than he looked, neither of them could deny that he had gotten a few of his own punches in. The problem was, Cenric had seen, that he relied on his strength too much and knew precious little about how to actually fight, and he shrewdly guessed that it was because he had been the biggest and strongest among his friends all of his life. Someone, he thought, needs to teach him, although it was nothing more than an idle thought.

With some effort, Titus struggled to his feet, while Cenric and Heard held a whispered discussion that ended when Heard turned and went trotting over to Otha, whose back was turned to them at the moment. As Cenric observed, Titus was completely absorbed in watching as, to Otha's commands, the triple line of widely separated men alternately lunged, thrusting their spears while unleashing a shout, then recovered back to their original position, repeating this over and over. This was when Titus realized that Heard had left the well, and he watched with a mixture of dread and anticipation as the guard spoke with Otha, who did briefly glance in his direction. When Otha shook his head, Titus could not stop a groan of despair escaping from his lips, certain that he knew what that shake of the head meant. He was wrong, however, which he learned when Heard came trotting back.

"I asked Lord Otha if we should send the boy on his way, but he said no, he wants to talk to him," Heard told Cenric, ignoring Titus altogether.

The next span of time was an agony for Titus, both in a physical and emotional sense, but he did his best not to betray any of this. It hurt to breathe, his left eye was swelling shut, and it was painful to move his jaw; and yet, it was the inner turmoil he was experiencing that he would remember of this time when he thought about it later. As nerve-wracking as it was for him, it was still informative as he watched Otha intently, not just the exercises and moves he was demonstrating before having what Titus counted was thirty men repeat them, over and over. No, he watched *how* Otha moved; while Cenric had taken notice of how focused Titus was on the Thegn, he did not give it any more thought until, some time later, he glanced over at the youth. To his surprise, the overgrown boy had not moved an inch from where they had left him. It's almost as if, Cenric thought with some amusement, he took it literally that he wasn't supposed to move from his spot. Finally, as the sun's rim was just beginning to touch the horizon, the Thegn declared that they were done for the day, and while Titus could not hear the words, it was made clear when the men walked over and stacked their shields and spears against the side of what was actually the largest building of the Ealdorman's estate, which from the smells and sounds, Titus knew was a barn. He learned what came next when, from out of the Ealdorman's hall, men who were clearly a mixture of servants and outright slaves, one of whom to Titus' eyes was clearly a Dane, carried several long trestle tables out into the yard. These men were followed by several women, who seemed to be equally divided between carrying trays bearing food and flagons of ale, and the sight of it made his stomach growl audibly enough that he actually glanced around to see if anyone might have heard it. Despite his attention, somehow Otha managed to surprise him, using the stone walls of the well to approach the youth from behind, yet at first, the Thegn just stood there, studying the lad. He was aware that this boy had been watching with an intensity that, frankly, was not only unsettling, but fueled his suspicion that he had been sent by Wulfhere for the purpose of spying. And yet, even as this thought crossed his mind, he just could not accept it, not deep down; every instinct was telling him that this boy Titus was telling the truth, at least mostly.

"So, what am I going to do with you, boy?"

Titus was so startled that, without thinking, he leapt to his feet, and he was unable to stop the groan from escaping his lips as he did so, but he said nothing, choosing to stand and face the Thegn in silence. Certainly he was nervous, but he refused to show any fear as he made sure to look Otha in the eye, something that the older man did notice and, while he was equally impassive in his expression, he was also impressed. Perhaps, he thought, this boy has the makings of a warrior after all.

"Have you eaten today?" he asked impulsively, and he got his answer from the boy's expression even before Titus opened his mouth.

"No, Lord," Titus answered. Then, seeing that Otha expected more, he added, "I left before my father woke up."

"Your father?" Otha frowned. "What about your mother? Doesn't she cook?"

"She's dead, Lord," Titus replied, but when he saw Otha open his mouth, presumably to offer the kind of awkward condolence that was expected, he hurriedly added, "She died having me, Lord." Then, before he could stop himself, he blurted, "Which is why my father hates me, Lord. He always has."

Frankly, Otha did not know what to say, but while Titus was ignorant, the Thegn's suspicions about the youth's real purpose were allayed by what he saw in Titus' face. No, the pain he saw there was too real, too raw, and in that moment, he believed that Titus was telling the truth.

"Come with me, boy," he said abruptly, then strode past Titus towards where the other men were already settling down on benches, talking loudly and flirting with the women, most of whom were flirting back. When Titus did not immediately follow, the Thegn called over his shoulder, "You can talk and eat at the same time, can't you, boy? I want you to tell me why I should think you're worthy of standing in a shield wall with me and my men."

For a moment, Titus stood, uncertain whether the Thegn was playing some sort of joke, but then he broke into a trot, his hunger overcoming his worry about being made a fool of, and he caught up to Otha.

"What kind of name is Titus, boy?" Otha asked through a mouthful of roast chicken, and it took Titus an extra moment because his mouth was so filled with saliva, he was worried that he would inadvertently spray the Thegn.

They were seated at the end of the last table, and Titus had noticed that the other men, without being told to do so, had scooted down the bench to give the pair at least a semblance of privacy, but Titus was finding it hard to ignore the sidelong glances thrown his way by the other men.

Swallowing, Titus shrugged and answered as casually as he could manage, "I don't really know, my Lord. All I know is what I heard from my sisters, especially my oldest because she was old enough to remember."

He stopped speaking then, mainly because he was more concerned with filling his stomach, and he tore a huge hunk of bread that he dipped into the flagon of ale that was of a quality Titus could not remember ever tasting.

"Well?" Otha demanded irritably. "What did your sister tell you about it?"

Titus blinked in surprise; he had honestly not thought that the Thegn would care to hear what little he knew, and he had to think for a moment before he answered, "She said that it's a name that my mother's family used for boys who were born…" He trailed off, not really sure how to put it, and Otha finished for him, "…big? Like you?" Titus nodded, mumbling, "Yes, like me."

"Which is why you think you'd make a good warrior, eh? Because you're bigger and stronger than most men who are already fully grown?"

This was certainly part of it, but there was more to it than that; the problem for Titus was that he had no way to articulate what he *felt* in his bones, that he was born to the life of a warrior.

Consequently, what came out was a mumbled, "I suppose so," accompanied by a shrug.

This elicited a snort from Otha, who scoffed, "Boy, I can't count the number of overgrown strong men who aren't worth a fart in a sack when it's their time to stand in a shield wall. Most of the time, they're so clumsy, they trip over their own feet, and they're almost always the first to die."

"I'm not clumsy," Titus countered, ignoring the jibe about dying, and while the words were challenging, the tone was matter-of-fact, and Otha was honest, admitting, "Yes, I saw that you don't move all that badly for someone your size.

Although," he added, "your feet are too close together. That's how Cenric managed to put you on your ass."

Titus felt his cheeks burn, but while he opened his mouth to argue the point by reminding Otha he had been outnumbered, instead, he countered, "Will you teach me those things, Lord?" Before Otha could reply, the words come out in a rush before Titus could stop them. "I swear to you, Lord! You won't regret it! I *know* that I can be a good warrior! A great one, even! If you just give me the chance!"

Otha shook his head and said flatly, "I don't have time to train anyone from the beginning right now, boy. Ealdorman Eadwig has given me less than two weeks before we march, and I need men with experience to be part of the fyrd."

The Thegn would never know the effort it took on Titus' part not to burst into tears, the youth knowing that it would not only be shameful, but the men whose eyes he felt on the pair even now would be unmerciful in their mockery.

Somehow, he managed to keep his voice level as he replied, "That is very…disappointing, my Lord. But," he took a breath, and now Otha clearly heard the desperation, "I *cannot* go back to Cissanbyrig, Lord. Isn't there anything I could do for you?"

Otha actually thought about this for a moment, then he shrugged. "Well, Dudda told me he needed help with the horses. I suppose you can do that."

"But I don't know anything about horses, Lord!" Titus protested, but Otha simply grinned at him.

"You know how to use a shovel, don't you, boy?"

Because of the grin that was missing most of the bottom front teeth, Titus was not certain that Otha was serious, and he hesitated. The smile vanished, and clearly irritated, Otha stood up, slapping the table with a hardened hand.

"If you're too good to shovel some shit, I don't care how

great a warrior you might be. I don't have time for *boys* who can't follow orders."

Titus leapt up, on the verge of panic, holding his arms out as he protested, "I didn't say anything, Lord! Please! I'll do it! And," he tried to hide his disappointment, "I swear that I *will* do a good job."

Otha had stopped walking away, and he regarded Titus thoughtfully.

"Fine," he said finally. "Come with me and I'll give you over to Dudda. I've got more important things to do."

Once again, Titus hurried to catch up to Otha, deciding as he did so that, while this was not what he had had in mind, it was still preferable to returning home to endure his father's scorn.

The beating Leofric inflicted on Leofflaed was not the worst he had given her, but it was still severe enough that, had she known it, she could have been Titus' twin, both in the bruising to her face and the way she was hobbling about their two-room house that, even by the standard of the time, was little better than a hovel. Her younger sister Eadgyd was sitting, with her head bowed and seemingly intent on the sewing work she was doing, but as Leofric was holding Leofflaed's shift with one hand and using his work-hardened hand to slap her, Eadgyd had been anything but passive. She had snatched up the iron rod that was used to stir the fire and was approaching their father from behind when Leofflaed caught her eye and gave her a quick shake of the head, although the moment's inattention on her father was what caused her to fail to turn her head in time, receiving the full force of his blow that split her lip.

"*Where did he go?*" Leofric kept roaring, over and over, timing it so that after he bellowed the question, there was the sodden, smacking sound of his hand striking flesh.

And yet, Leofflaed refused to betray her brother, although

she insisted that she simply did not know. Finally, Leofric shoved her away from him, snarling curses, and stormed out of the hut, slamming the wooden door so that dust shook from the thatch that served as the roof, which was badly in need of repair. There was a long silence between the sisters as Leofflaed dabbed at her lip with a cloth she dipped into a bucket drawn from the well.

"You should have let me hit him, sister," Eadgyd said without looking up from her work.

"Why?" Leofflaed countered. "So he could beat you as well?" She shook her head. "That wouldn't change anything, and it would only have made him angrier. And," she did turn to look her sister in the eye as she finished, "he would have had every right to kill you, Eadgyd. You know this."

"Titus wouldn't let him!" Eadgyd burst out, but Leofflaed saw by her expression that as quickly as the words came out, she realized the truth, which she murmured. "But he's not here."

Deciding this was sufficient, Leofflaed resumed her own chores, which began with taking the family's most prized possession, the milking cow that shared the space under the thatched roof with Leofric and his children, out through the other door that served as the entrance for the animals. Eadgyd finished her task, which had been to drop the hem of what was one of her brother's two sets of trousers, something she seemed to be doing at least once a month, although she did wonder if there was any point to it since he was gone. Setting them down, she walked out to where Leofflaed was perched on the low stool, milking the cow.

"Do you think Titus will ever come back, Leofflaed?" Eadgyd asked plaintively, and it caused her sister to stop for a moment and sit up straight as she considered the question.

"Yes," she answered, and she was being honest. "But," she warned her sister, "it won't be until he's proven himself as a warrior, Eadgyd. And," she offered Eadgyd a grim smile, "*that* is when our father should be concerned."

The idea clearly pleased Eadgyd, who said with a ferocious enthusiasm, “Then I will pray every day to make it so.”

Chapter Two

Dudda had proven to live up to the meaning of his name; he was almost grotesquely obese, and his tunic and trousers, which might have been brown at one time, were black with dirt and grease. Worst of all was his smell, making Titus thankful for Otha's quiet warning when they entered the barn, yet despite this, the stench emanating from the fat man was so pungent that it made the youth's eyes water.

"You said you needed help," Otha spoke abruptly, "so here's your help."

Dudda was shorter than Titus, but so were most men already; what distinguished Dudda to the youth was that he was almost certain that Dudda was as wide as he was tall. He had a beard, also not unusual, except that it was matted and there were objects in it that Titus assumed were remnants of earlier meals, and it was so thick that essentially it appeared as if Dudda was wearing a black hood with an area cut out so that he could see and to shove food into his mouth.

"Does he know horses?" Dudda asked, engendering another surprise; his voice was so high-pitched that, if he closed his eyes, Titus could imagine that it was a woman speaking.

The fact that Dudda was ignoring him completely irritated Titus, and before Otha could respond, he spoke up, "I don't have much experience with horses, but I'm a fast learner, and I'm willing to work hard."

Dudda's response was a dismissive snort, but when he turned away, Otha said sharply, "It's either him or nothing,

Dudda. I don't have time to do your job for you and find a stableboy who meets your approval. So take him or leave him."

Dudda obviously did not like this, but he gave an angry nod, and without saying anything else, Otha turned away and began walking towards the door. Titus opened his mouth, then thought better of it, and he was not particularly surprised when Dudda thrust a spade out towards him, smiling to reveal the jagged, blackened stumps of his teeth.

"You," he said with an obvious relish, "will become *very* familiar with this."

"I grew up on a farm," Titus answered stubbornly, although he was grabbing the spade as he said it. "I've shoveled shit before."

"Oh?" Dudda's eyes, which were barely visible between the black beard and hair that hung over his forehead, widened in mock surprise. "And how many animals does your Lord father have on his farm, boy?"

Titus realized his error immediately, but it was not just this that made him reluctant to answer.

"We have a cow," Titus began, then with a sigh walked over to the first of the series of stalls that Dudda pointed to, but before he could enter the first one, Dudda stopped him with a sharp, almost shrill shout.

"No! Not in there! That's Hama, Lord Eadwig's horse. He doesn't like strangers. If you go in there, he'll probably kill you."

Titus turned to nervously eye the large black stallion, and seeing the animal tear at the straw-covered dirt with one hoof, nostrils dilated as it drew air into its huge lungs, did nothing to soothe him, although he did wonder, Why didn't you tell me that to begin with? And, when he turned to glance over at the stableman, there was no mistaking the malicious grin on the man's face.

Biting his tongue, literally, Titus sidestepped to the next stall, where a brown mare was held, and Dudda called out, "That's the Lady Leofe's mare Freya. You'll be safe enough. Although," he had paused a moment, waiting for Titus to enter the stall, "she has been known to bite people from time to time."

It was at this moment that Titus realized that this would likely be how things would be going for the foreseeable future. Dudda was clearly a disagreeable sort who felt the need to impose what little authority he had and would be needling him in this manner, but in a rare moment of maturity, Titus recognized that this was a test, engineered by Otha, to see if he was truly worthy of being considered to stand in the shield wall. After all, he decided, if I can put up with this dirty fat man playing tricks on me, that will show Lord Otha. This sudden shift in attitude had an unexpected benefit; when Titus began grinning at the thought of how he would prove himself, it clearly unsettled and infuriated Dudda, who restricted himself to muttering under his breath as Titus began mucking out the stalls.

The next days passed in a blur for Titus, but while the work was familiar to him, it was a matter of scale, and he was surprised at how sore he was, over and above the bruises, which were healing quickly. What was even more surprising to the youth was that he was finding that he actually liked what he was doing, and that he enjoyed being around the horses most of all. This did not mean that, whenever he could manage it, he would not sneak away to watch as Otha relentlessly drilled the now fully assembled fyrd, consisting of the hundred spearmen and thirty-seven men at arms who, as far as Titus could see, were mostly left to their own devices by Otha. Instead, almost his entire focus was on the spearmen, which Titus could understand, since despite the fact that they were all older than he was, were essentially farmers like Titus and his father. This was the nature of what would become known as the Anglo-Saxon method of waging war, where there was no standing army, but every ceorl who had a holding on an Ealdorman's lands was beholden to answer the call to fight. And, when that call was because of the Danes, those ceorls were, if not eager to respond to the call, certainly unhesitating in showing up here.

With every passing day, the sense of urgency increased, but Titus only caught occasional glimpses of Ealdorman Eadwig, who did not seem to be all that interested in watching his senior Thegn trying to forge these farmers into a coherent unit that could stand up to the fabled fury of the Northmen. Titus' relationship with Dudda did not improve, and in fact, it got worse because, by the fourth day, and unknown to Dudda, Titus had actually approached Hama in his stall. Part of it was a conscious decision on Titus' part in an adolescent attempt to show that he was not afraid, but he was secretly fascinated and drawn to the black stallion, for reasons that he could not articulate. And, despite some skittishness on Hama's part in the beginning, followed by a period of wary acceptance, the horse and he had seemed to form a bond, enough of one that it led to Titus' first real altercation with Dudda.

While Lord Eadwig was not around and about when it came to the training, there was one thing that he did every day, and that was to ride Hama in the early afternoon. And, as Dudda had warned, and Titus had seen for himself, the Ealdorman was nothing if he was not prompt, and was a stickler for those who served him to have the same standard. Titus had been taught, grudgingly, how to saddle a horse by Dudda, and he had even been allowed to do so with Lord Otha's horse, along with the young Lord Eadweard's, although it was always Dudda who insisted on leading the animals out of the barn to bring them to the spot in front of the hall where they would be mounted by their rider. Titus was not fooled; he knew that Dudda wanted to give everyone the impression that he was the one saddling the horses, which was how Titus got his idea. If he had been asked, Titus would have insisted that his intention was simply to prove that he was capable to perform this task if needed; the simpler and deeper truth was that he wanted to make Dudda look bad by demonstrating that he was the one who had been saddling the mounts and not the fat stableman. Just like Ealdorman

Eadwig, Dudda was a creature of habit, and his early afternoon routine involved waddling around to the back of the hall where the kitchen was located, wheedling the slaves who toiled there to provide him with food. Unsurprisingly, Dudda's appetite was prodigious, and while he received the same portion of food as everyone else, it was never enough for him, which sent him on an almost constant prowl for more.

On the day that he decided to act, Titus waited just long enough to see Dudda disappear around the corner of the hall before he moved quickly to work. Taking the saddle from the top rail of the stall and the bridle hanging from the nail in the wall, Titus tried to appear nonchalant, understanding that, more than most animals, horses responded to the mood of the humans around them. Hama watched him with interest, but Titus was encouraged that he did not seem agitated as the youth approached his stall, and in fact, his ears were pricked forward, which Titus had learned was a sign that a horse was engaged in what was happening. Despite his trepidation, the process went much more smoothly than he had anticipated, as Hama obediently lowered his head for Titus to slide the bridle over his massive head, then fighting the bit, yet in the same way he always did with Dudda, which Titus had determined was more of a formality at this point, and he felt a grin split his face as he adjusted the bit.

"I wouldn't like having a piece of metal in my mouth either," Titus assured him, then with a gentle tug, led the stallion out of the stall, where the saddle lay on the ground.

Quickly, and moving more smoothly than he had even dared to dream, Titus saddled Hama, but he was also acutely aware that time was running short; Dudda would be returning to do what Titus had just done, and the one thing he did not want was to still be in the barn, or even in or near the doorway. While he did not want to rush Hama, he still needed him to move more quickly than the horse did with Dudda, and at first, it appeared that the stallion would balk, but rather than being worried, Titus again grinned at the horse, reaching into his tunic, extracting what he considered his secret weapon, a chunk of bread that Titus had saved. It had been how he gained Hama's trust in the first place, although he had always been careful to do it surreptitiously, not wanting Dudda to see that he was essentially bribing the Ealdorman's horse for his trust, and it was not always bread, but the horse seemed to favor that over apples.

As he always did, Hama stretched out his long neck, showing his big yellow teeth, but Titus shook his head, saying cheerfully, "Not this time. You have to work for it!"

And he moved towards the exit of the barn at a fast walk, with the horse obediently following behind him, still with his neck stretched out as he tried, unsuccessfully, to snatch at the bread. Once they were safely out of the barn and halfway to the hall, Titus displayed the bread, having learned to hold the treat in the palm of his hand after he had received a painful bite when Hama grabbed the bread and included two of Titus' fingers. Now, the normally aggressive, high-strung animal was clearly in the spirit of the game as Titus increased his pace to a trot, which the horse matched, still trying to grab the bread. Timing it perfectly, Titus came to a stop in front of the hall, Hama snatched the bread from his palm and essentially swallowed it whole, just before one of the doors of the hall opened, and Ealdorman Eadwig came out, wearing his mail and cloak.

At first, he continued striding towards Hama, since this was the normal routine, but he was also looking in a downward direction, his bearded face, a chestnut brown that was already liberally streaked with gray, wearing a frown that, to Titus, bespoke a man beset with worries that the youth could barely imagine. It was when he looked up to reach out for the saddle that he stopped abruptly, seeming to notice for the first time that it was not Dudda.

"Who are you?" he demanded harshly. "And why isn't Dudda here?"

From behind him, Titus heard Dudda's angry shout, and he knew that the fat man, waddling or not, would be on them quickly.

Bowing his head, Titus spoke quickly, "My name is Titus, my Lord. I came to join your fyrd, but Lord Otha said I am too young, but I wanted to serve you any way I could, so I am now Dudda's assistant."

"And he let you bring me Hama after he saddled him?" Eadwig frowned and shook his head, "That doesn't sound like something Dudda would do."

"He didn't, Lord," Titus assured him. "I saddled Hama myself, Lord. Dudda was…busy," he finished lamely.

The nobleman gave Titus a hard, appraising look, then shook his head again, his disbelief clear as he countered, "That's impossible. It took Dudda almost six months before Hama would allow Dudda to saddle him, and you say you've done it after being here…" Suddenly, Eadwig looked slightly embarrassed, "How long have you been here, boy?"

"Ten days, Lord," Titus answered.

What happened next was something that, while he was not particularly religious, Titus believed was the work of, if not God Himself, then one of his Angels, because at that moment, Hama turned his head, and using his nose, nudged Titus in the back. It was done in an obviously playful manner, and while Eadwig looked astonished, he also smiled for the first time.

"By the blood!" he exclaimed, then eyed Titus shrewdly. "You clearly have a way with him, boy. So I suppose you're telling the truth."

Before Titus could reply, Dudda's voice cut through the air, his normal high-pitched voice even shriller and Titus looked over to see him moving as fast as his girth allowed, his expression one of almost panic. "Lord Eadwig! I offer my apologies! This boy…"

"This boy was able to saddle Hama in ten days when it took you six months, Dudda," Eadwig cut him off, and for an instant, Titus thought the obese stableman might drop dead, his face going deadly white as he came to a stop a few feet away.

"I…I did *not* give him permission to saddle Hama, Lord," Dudda managed to squeak. "I was on my way to the barn to do it, but I saw him here."

Eadwig turned to regard Titus coldly, who suddenly did not feel quite so confident.

"Is that true, boy?" the noble demanded. "That you took the liberty of your own accord? That he didn't give you permission?"

It was difficult for Titus to retain his composure, especially because, from where he was standing, he could see Dudda's malevolent smile, undoubtedly at the thought that Eadwig's ire was transferred to the youth.

"Y-yes, Lord," Titus answered, bowing his head as he did so. Thinking he needed to offer something, he added, "I just wanted to help Dudda, my Lord. He works so hard, and he's been so kind to me that I wanted to do something for him." He looked up at Eadwig and tried to sound as sincere as possible. "I swear it, Lord! I was just trying to repay his kindness!"

For a moment, the nobleman's expression remained harsh and unyielding; then, so faintly that he was not sure he saw it, Titus saw the corners of the Ealdorman's mouth lift, and when he spoke, it was with a sardonic, heavy humor.

"Well, then Dudda is truly blessed to have such a faithful stableboy working for him. Isn't that right, Dudda?"

Titus was slightly disappointed when Eadwig looked over at Dudda, and the fat man was able to alter his own expression in time as he nodded emphatically. "Oh, yes Lord Eadwig." He turned to look at Titus, giving him what Titus supposed was meant to be an appreciative smile. "I am truly blessed to have such a boy working for me."

Eadwig was not the most patient man under normal circumstances, and the truth was that he had exhausted the amount of time he wanted to spend on this curious affair, so he strode over, took the reins from Titus, and swung into the saddle, turning Hama so that he could ride past Dudda, stopping to lean down to speak to the stableman.

Titus was too far away, but Dudda certainly heard him say softly, "I've been looking for someone to replace you, Dudda, and this boy may be the one to do it."

Then he straightened up and kicked Hama, going to the trot, not bothering to look back as Dudda glared at Titus with a poisonous hatred.

Perhaps the best thing that could be said concerning Titus' situation was that the next day, Otha had announced the day that the fyrd would be marching, two days hence, meaning that both Dudda and the youth were too busy to engage in open hostilities. While it was tiring work, Titus did not mind it, because Lord Otha had essentially requisitioned him from Dudda to help with loading the lone wagon that would be transporting the heaviest of the necessary supplies to support a force that, once the various attendants, both free and slave, were counted would number well more than two hundred people, with the lighter items either being on pack animals or the half-dozen two-wheeled carts.

"You're stupid, but you're strong," Otha had growled when he came to the barn to inform Titus. "There are sacks of grain, the anvil and grindstone that need to be loaded onto the wagon." Titus missed the humorous glint in Otha's eye as he said conversationally, "Those things take muscles, not brains, which is why I picked you."

Since Titus did not know how to respond, he simply nodded, following the Thegn out into the yard, which was once again bustling with activity, with men, and some women, hurrying back and forth, each of them carrying something that was being loaded onto the carts, and the one wagon that Titus was loading. He picked up the anvil first, aware that he was being watched, which meant that he did his best to show that he was not struggling with the huge lump of iron, but while it *was* heavy, he felt a surge of pride that he did not have to pretend that it was not too heavy for him. He did have to catch his breath, and he spent the time watching as the men who were part of the fyrd were laboring in a manner that was in direct relation to their status in the hierarchy of Ealdorman Eadwig's force. Those men who were ostensibly of his class, the ceorls whose only armament was a round wooden shield and a stout spear, were clearly expected to help in the loading process, but it was Otha and the men with him, all of whom were clad in some sort of armor, albeit of varying quality and degree of repair, that Titus was most interested in, if only because they were uniformly lounging about, some seated at one of the tables, while others leaned against the hall as they watched and made idle conversation. To a fourteen year-old youth who dreamed of being a warrior, it was clear to Titus that *this* was the status to which he aspired, if only because it meant that you did not have to lug heavy sacks and things like anvils about. Once he was finished, Otha released him back to his normal duties, and he was in the barn carefully sorting the bits of tack that would be required for the mounted contingent of Ealdorman Eadwig's fyrd when young Eadward entered. Naturally, Titus had seen the young lordling about, and had even passed by him on two occasions, but Eadward had not even acknowledged him, which did not surprise Titus in the least. It had irritated him, however, which was why he regarded Eadward with a resigned expression, fully expecting to be ignored again, which Eadward noticed.

"What are you doing?" Eadward demanded, or at least tried to imbue his tone with the kind of authority that he heard his father use, but he was also going through that awkward time for a boy turning into a man, so his query began at one pitch and ended at another.

Titus' initial response was to laugh, but he did not, for a couple of reasons, not least of which was that it had not been long before when he had struggled with the same affliction, so instead, he answered simply, "Dudda has me sorting out which bridles still need mending and those that can be used immediately….Lord."

Titus was not particularly eager to use the term with a boy who was a year younger, or so he had been told, and was *much* smaller in every sense, but he decided it was the politic thing to do.

He was surprised when Eadward responded by wrinkling his nose, glancing over his shoulder, then saying conspiratorially, "He smells so *bad*! How can you stand it…?"

This prompted a laugh from Titus, and he correctly interpreted the unasked question, answering more easily, "Titus, Lord. My name is Titus."

Eadward frowned, but once again, Titus correctly guessed what was coming.

"That's a name that I've only heard with churchmen," Eadward commented, yet Titus heard no censure, or what was more common, the kind of leering suggestion that he was the bastard son of a wayward priest.

"It's a name that's been used on my mother's side of the family for generations, Lord," Titus explained. Then, also certain he knew what was coming, he still added, "It seems that every so often on my mother's side of the family, someone my size is born." Shrugging, he finished, "And we're always named Titus."

Eadward surprised Titus then, not making the kind of jest about how hard that must have been for his mother, returning instead to the subject that he had broached, "How can you stand the smell, Titus? Of Dudda, I mean?"

Again, Titus laughed. "I know what you meant, Lord." He actually thought for a moment, then admitted, "The worst is at the start of every day, Lord. But then?" He shrugged. "I suppose I just get used to it."

"I couldn't!" Eadward declared with an emphatic shake of his head. "He's revolting, and he never even cleans his beard!"

"That," Titus agreed fervently, "is the worst." They grinned at each other, sharing in their disgust, then before he thought better of it, he asked, "Are you staying here, Lord Eadward?"

"No." Eadward shook his head, and he suddenly looked down at the ground as he said tonelessly, "My Lord father has decided that I'm old enough to at least accompany him to King Alfred's fyrd, but he said I'll be staying in the camp." He looked up at Titus and asked, "What about you? What will you do? Are you staying here?"

It had not even occurred to Titus that he might not be accompanying Eadwig and his fyrd, and he had to fight down a sudden surge of panic at the thought that he had defied his father, come all this way, and he would not even be anywhere near a battle.

"I…I don't know, Lord," Titus admitted honestly, but before he could say anything else, Dudda entered, but because of where Eadward was standing, he did not see the lordling, and he snarled, "What are you standing there like a lump for, boy? There's work to be done, and…"

"I was talking to him, Dudda," Eadward interjected, causing the fat stableman to spin about so abruptly that it appeared he would topple over, forcing Titus to cover his laugh with a cough, although it was not successful, Dudda shooting him a look of fury over his shoulder before he responded to Eadward.

"My apologies, young Lord Eadward." When addressing his social superiors, Dudda's voice took on an oily, obsequious quality that Titus found nauseating, and it was on full display. "I did not realize that you were there." Bowing, or what passed for his version of a bow since he could barely bend over at the waist, Dudda asked, "Was there something you needed, my Lord? I can assure you that it's better to come to me than to approach this…boy. After all," Dudda pointed out, "he's been here barely two weeks."

Now it was Eadward's turn to struggle with his composure, because Titus was taking full advantage of Dudda's turned back to make a series of faces, along with grabbing his crotch in the manner he had seen some of Otha's men use when they were engaged in a mock argument, but unlike Titus, Eadward had more practice in controlling his facial expressions.

He also proved that he had a quick and sharp tongue because, without a discernible pause, he replied, "Yes, that's true, Dudda. And yet, he's already able to saddle Hama." The boy paused as if trying to think. "How long did it take you? Almost six months, wasn't it?"

Now Dudda was completely flustered, and while his back was to Titus, the youth was certain that the fat man was torn between embarrassment and rage that it was the young lordling who was the author of this indignity.

Somehow, he managed to splutter, "Yes, that's true, Lord, but there were other…problems." Before Eadward could reply, he said quickly, "Now, if you'll excuse me, I just remembered that there is a very important task I have to attend to outside."

"Then don't let me keep you, Dudda," Eadward replied blandly, but despite only having just met the young noble, Titus could see he was struggling mightily to retain his own composure. "Please, go attend to your business."

Dudda obeyed with an unmistakable haste, but despite knowing it was not a good idea, Titus could not stop himself from calling out, "Do you want me to continue sorting the bridles, Dudda? Or," he added cheerfully, "would you like me to come help you with whatever you're doing?"

The glare the stableman gave Titus was filled with such loathing and hatred that, despite being completely unafraid of the fat man physically, he had to fight the urge to reach up and grasp the wooden cross that was underneath his tunic.

"No," Dudda spat the word out then waddled out of the barn.

They did try, but there was no way that Dudda did not hear both boys burst out laughing, and soon they were so consumed with mirth that they had dropped to the ground, rolling as they held their stomachs.

Finally, Eadward recovered himself sufficiently to ask, as he wiped a tear away, “So, are you coming to the feast tonight?”

“Feast?” Titus repeated; he had been dimly aware that the cooking women had been busy all day, but nobody had mentioned a word to him.

Eadward looked embarrassed suddenly, and he began staring at the dirt floor of the barn again, although he did say awkwardly, “Yes, well, it’s apparently a tradition that there’s a feast the night before a fyrd marches, and a feast after the fyrd returns. I just assumed…” His voice trailed off, then in a clearly contrived manner, he slapped his forehead. “Oh no! I just remembered! I’m supposed to do something before the feast begins!”

“Yes, well, I have these bridles to finish sorting.” Titus pointed down at the piles that had actually already been separated, and without waiting for Eadward to leave, he bent down, pretending to work, only straightening back up after Eadward had gone.

He knew there was no reason he should have expected to be invited to the feast, but he still felt bitterly disappointed. Hadn’t he been working hard ever since he arrived, and at a job he had no interest in doing at all? However, as disappointing as the idea of being forced to hope for scraps from whatever was left over, the thought that he might not be going with the fyrd was terrifying, because he would have no reason not to return home, to his father and whatever awaited him there.

As night fell, Titus was tortured by a combination of things; as the day had progressed, the smell of roasting meat filled the air and was powerful enough that it overwhelmed the normal smells of the barn, making him salivate almost uncontrollably.

Worse than that was the agonizing uncertainty he experienced about whether he would be made to stay behind, and if he was, whether he would do so or return to the farm and Leofric. Because of the feast, the normal process for feeding the workers and slaves was nowhere in evidence, as the tables were now inside the hall, and he could hear the steadily increasing volume of mostly male voices as the ale and mead began flowing. Raucous laughter drifted out of the now-open doors of the hall, along with the smells of what Titus guessed was hog, beef, and fowl, along with the aroma of freshly baked bread, but Titus could not bear to be in a spot where he could see into the hall, so he had moved the thin blanket that he had been provided, grudgingly, by Dudda, away from his normal sleeping spot. What he could not escape were the sounds, and the smells, which was torture for him, his stomach loudly complaining and his mouth filling with saliva so often, he had to spit it out. He had never been in the vicinity of an event like this; the estate of Ealdorman Wulfhere was not only several miles from Titus' farm, the noble was notoriously stingy, although he did know that his father had been invited to attend one, mainly because Leofric boasted about it so often. Consequently, he was uncertain exactly how he would be fed this night; did he have to wait for after the feast was over? he wondered. As inexperienced as he was in such things, he was relatively sure that, judging from the noise, they were not anywhere close to being sated. So absorbed was he in his own misery that he did not hear the footfall of someone approaching, and since a light of any kind was strictly forbidden in the barn because of the risk of fire, the only illumination was what streamed out of the open doors of the hall.

"What are you doing, boy?"

Titus could not stop himself from yelping in surprise and, to his shame, a fair amount of fear, leaping to his feet as he did so, then stammered, "L-lord Otha?" Only then did his brain decipher that he had been asked a question, but he did not really know what to say, so he only offered, "Trying to sleep, Lord."

"What?" Otha actually sounded surprised. "You're too

good to come to the Ealdorman's feast?"

Again, Titus could not find the words, this time because he was so shocked, although he finally managed, "I…I wasn't invited, Lord."

"Who told you that?" Otha asked, but despite not being able to see the Thegn's expression, Titus sensed that he suspected the answer.

"Well, Lord Eadward mentioned the feast," Titus explained, "but he didn't know whether I would be allowed to attend, so I went and asked Dudda."

"And he told you that you weren't," Otha concluded, to which Titus nodded, not thinking that the gesture would be impossible to see given the dim lighting. Otha was silent for a moment, then said abruptly, "Follow me."

Naturally, Titus complied, following the Thegn as he strode into the hall, but to his relief, the youth saw that nobody took much notice, most of them clearly too absorbed in whatever tale or argument they were involved in at that moment. Otha did not have to walk far; the lowest ranking members of the Ealdorman's household had places at the table farthest away from where the Ealdorman was seated, at an ornately carved long table that was placed at the far end of the hall, positioned perpendicular to the other tables, which were aligned in three rows. It was smoky, although that was normal between the roaring fire in the center of the hall and the candles, and so loud that it made it hard for Titus to think, but he quickly saw that Otha was heading directly for the last table in the righthand corner of the hall. And, there was Dudda, what little of his face that showed shining in the firelight from the grease coating his exposed skin and completely absorbed in gnawing the last scraps of meat from a bone of roast pork so he did not immediately see Otha approaching, with Titus obediently behind him. When he did look up, Titus was in position to see the parade of emotions flash across the fat man's face; mild curiosity at the Thegn's approach, followed closely by concern, at least until his small, inset eyes moved to Titus, when the stableman's expression transformed into the same kind of blazing hatred he had witnessed when Eadward had belittled him.

"Lord Otha," Dudda called to the Thegn as he struggled to his feet, his huge belly shoving the table with enough force that it jostled the two men and woman on the opposite side to the point that all three cursed him. Once he was standing, although with a fair amount of weaving, he gave his version of a smile and in his oiliest manner began, "It's an honor that you would come speak with me, Lord! Especially on this…"

"Did you tell the boy he wasn't to attend the feast?" Otha demanded, his tone clipped and, as Titus would come to learn, was a sign that the Thegn's temper was aroused.

"No, Lord!" Dudda protested, but since he was facing the pair, he saw Titus opening his mouth, and he said quickly, "I mean, not exactly in those terms, Lord. I simply told him that it was important that someone remain in the barn, Lord! Surely," he said with an earnest tone that was so patently and obviously counterfeit that Titus could not contain his own snort, which Dudda ignored, "you approve of taking this kind of precaution, Lord! You're about to depart with Ealdorman Eadwig with the fyrd, and this is just being prudent! That's all I was trying to do, Lord Otha!"

Titus could not see Otha's expression, but there was no missing the sarcasm as the Thegn seemingly agreed.

"That is *very* commendable, Dudda, and yes, you're correct. That is a prudent step." Suddenly, he pointed down at the pile of bones that were the most potent sign of the stableman's gluttony, asking mildly, "How's the meat, Dudda?"

Dudda's smile, which had been plastered on his face longer than any other time Titus had seen during their short association, drooped slightly, and the youth could see the puzzlement, telling him that Dudda suspected some sort of trap but was unable to determine where it might lay.

"It's very good, Lord," he answered, readily enough. Then, he added, "The Dane slave Hild may not be much to look at, but," his smile returned, except this time with a leering quality, "she does know how to properly season and prepare meat…of all types."

"That she does," Otha agreed, then indicated the bones again, "and I can see that you've had your share. Maybe," the Thegn's voice hardened, "*more* than your share." Before Dudda could respond, he continued, "But now that you've had your fill, you can return to the barn and let the boy here have a chance to sample some of Hild's cooking. That's fair, isn't it?"

Dudda, his smile vanished and replaced by a dropped jaw, stood there uncertainly for a moment, as if he was unsure whether Otha was jesting, but he clearly saw something in the other man's expression that caused his mouth to snap shut.

"Yes, Lord Otha," he finally managed, something of an accomplishment given how tightly clenched his jaw was, "that's fair." With some difficulty, he stepped back and away from the bench, then with one pudgy hand that, like his face, was shining with grease, extended it towards his spot, although he refused to look at Titus.

Who, still uncertain about whether this was as it appeared, or an elaborate prank concocted by Otha and Dudda, stood there.

"Well?" Otha demanded. "You better sit down, boy. The longer you stand there, the less food there will be for you."

This got Titus moving, but to sit down, he had to push past Dudda, despite the fact that the fat man's back was against the side of the hall, and he could not help breathing in the mixed odors of the stableman, although what was most overpowering were the fumes from the mead, which was quite an achievement. He desperately wanted to look Dudda in the eye, but he was still young, and as confident as he may have been, such a display of defiance could evoke even further unpleasantness, and the truth was that he was hungrier than he was angry. Straddling the bench, Titus lowered himself, noticing for the first time that, either because of his girth or his stench, Dudda had had the bench to himself.

"All right, Dudda, hurry along now," Otha commanded, and the stableman complied as the Thegn stepped aside to let him pass, but he had gone less than a half-dozen paces when Otha called out, and despite the noise, it was louder than Titus thought necessary to be heard. "Oh, and Dudda!" When the stableman turned to face the Thegn, Otha said, "From everything I've heard, the boy here has done a good job as your helper. Would you agree with that?"

Dudda's reaction reminded Titus of a rat that he had trapped in the barn just the day before by driving it into a corner from which it could not escape.

"I…would, Lord," he finally answered cautiously, as if expecting there to be yet another barb in the offing.

Which, as Titus and all of the people at this end of the hall who had momentarily suspended their own exchanges to witness what appeared to be unusual, was a valid concern on Dudda's part.

"And have you told him that?" Otha asked, although it was clear he knew the answer.

"N-no, Lord," Dudda answered, then added, "but it's just that we've been so busy, Lord Otha!"

"Then what better time and place to do it, Dudda?"

Titus had only just become aware that the overall noise level in the hall had dramatically subsided, and when he tore his eyes away from the pair and glanced around him, he saw every attendee seemingly interested in what was happening here at this end of the hall, eliciting a combination of dismay and worry that he would be blamed for it. Nevertheless, he was every bit as interested in what the Thegn had in mind with this.

For a span of several heartbeats, it actually appeared that

Dudda would refuse, but whatever resolve was within the fat man crumbled quickly, although he did close his eyes as he said listlessly, "Titus, you have done a very good job helping me prepare for Ealdorman Eadwig's departure."

Titus was perfectly satisfied with this, but Otha was not done, except now he turned to face the youth.

"That is why I've decided that he's going to accompany us when we go to answer King Alfred's fyrd."

For a moment, Titus was certain that he had misheard, but as mystifying as this was, it was just the beginning of what would become an unforgettable night, as he learned just how much Dudda was universally loathed. It began with the three people at his table pounding it with their wooden cups, which he learned was their way of signaling their approval, and it quickly spread to the surrounding tables. Dudda did not stay after that, moving as quickly as his waddling gait allowed, disappearing out the doorway and into the night, heading for the barn, and despite the tumbling emotions that were battering Titus, he still worried about what he would be facing when he returned there himself. For his part, Otha turned back to Titus' table, his face expressionless, but as he did, he signaled to one of the women who had been tasked with carrying the steaming platters of meat, who immediately hurried over.

"Don't go getting a big head, boy," Otha growled at him as the woman—girl was more accurate—used a knife to drop several chunks of meat onto the wooden plate that had held Dudda's meal. "You're coming along because I think Dudda will drop dead being forced to walk that far, and we need someone who can saddle Hama."

Despite his deadpan expression, Titus had begun to understand Otha, and he grinned up at him just before he speared a piece of meat with his eating knife and shoved it into his mouth. Otha shook his head but said nothing else, then turned and walked back towards his own table, the nearest one to the Ealdorman's and in the center row, so it was natural that Titus followed his progress as he chewed his meat. In doing so, his eyes met those of young Eadward's, who was sitting two places down from his father, and while the lordling did not wave, he did nod his head, then held his nose, which caused Titus to almost choke on his meat as he laughed.

"Here, boy." One of the men across the table from him had snatched a wooden cup from one of the trays that were carried by serving girls in a seemingly endless procession, and he thrust it to Titus.

Who, naturally accepted it with a grateful nod, then took a deep swallow from the cup. That was his intention at least, but he had been expecting ale, all Titus had ever drunk, which meant the thick, sweet taste of the mead launched another coughing fit.

"This…is *mead*," he managed to gasp between coughs, but his table companions, even the woman, thought this was quite funny.

"Of course it's mead, boy!" the man who had handed the cup to him boomed. Then, leaning forward and in a slightly lower voice, he added, "Anyone who has to endure Dudda's stench and foulness is a man who deserves a man's drink!"

"If he grabs my ass one more time," the woman spoke up, "I swear by all that's holy I will claw the eyes out of his fat little face!"

She said it so fiercely that Titus was certain of her sincerity, but the other man, sitting on the opposite side of her, just laughed.

"You say that every time, Mildgyd, and you've never done it!" He glanced over and winked at Titus as he added with a leer, "I think you *like* him fondling you!"

"You," Mildgyd, tossing her head and tilting her nose, pronounced, "are a pig yourself, Osmund."

Osmund not only took no offense, he just laughed harder, as did the other man, who to Titus appeared to be his father's age, and with the same weather-beaten features that betrayed that the man was a ceorl. Mildgyd looked to be in her late twenties, with chapped, reddened hands and already with streaks of gray in her hair, but while she was rather plain, her smile shed years from her appearance. Osmund, Titus decided, bore the appearance of some sort of craftsman, but even with his size, and his companions' obvious delight in Dudda's comeuppance, he was too shy to ask. It was left to the ceorl, who thrust his hand across the table, and introduced himself.

"I'm Wulfric."

Somewhat awkwardly, Titus set his cup down and clasped hands with the ceorl, feeling the scaly hardness that reminded him of his father; when he thought about it later, he thought perhaps it was this association that caused Titus to tighten his grip, but rather than be offended, Wulfric grinned at him and returned the pressure until, by unspoken consent, they released their grip. The fact that they both instinctively flexed their hands brought another round of laughter, as Titus and Wulfric smiled at each other.

"That's a strong grip," Wulfric complimented Titus. "I think it's safe to say you've spent time behind a plow and with an ax."

Titus flushed with pleasure, although by this time, he had downed a half cup of mead, and he could already feel its effects, so he was unsure whether it was the compliment or the drink.

"I have," he confirmed.

"But," Wulfric's smile faded, and while he did not become unfriendly, Titus sensed the pointedness to his asking, "I don't remember ever seeing you before."

Realizing there was nothing to be gained in hiding his circumstances, Titus went on to explain how he had come to answer the fyrd for another Ealdorman, deciding on the fly to include his feelings about Ealdorman Wulfhere. At the mention of the noble's name, any sign of levity vanished, and Titus saw how Mildgyd actually glanced over her shoulder, although the girl passing by was paying no attention to them.

"Boy," Osmund spoke up, "I'm not saying that I disagree with you. Nor," he glanced over at the other two, who nodded, "do they. But Wulfhere is an important man, and he's a dangerous man, so you need to guard your tongue about him. Especially," he cautioned, "around Dudda."

While Titus knew it was sound advice in general, the specific mention of the stableman's name puzzled him.

"Why?" he asked.

"Because Dudda is a lying serpent," Mildgyd answered vehemently. "And I'm not talking about his habit of putting his filthy hands on good Christian women." She leaned across the table to place a hand on Titus' arm, locking eyes with him as she continued, "If Dudda thinks he can use a piece of information to his advantage, he'll do it, Titus. And he'll twist your words to do the most damage he can. *Never* trust Dudda!"

"She's telling it true," Wulfric added. "She works here on the Ealdorman's estate, while my holding is a few miles from here, but I've had enough dealings with Dudda to keep my hand on my coin purse and guard my tongue whenever I'm around him."

Titus' head had begun spinning from the mead, and there was a part of him that knew he should stop, but when Wulfric again stopped one of the girls passing by with a tray of full cups and he grabbed two, then reached across the table to hand one to Titus, to his surprise, he saw his hand, behaving as if it had a mind of its own, take it. And, he admitted, it did not taste as foul as it had the first sip, and he found he was laughing more than he normally did; in fact, he had a good sense of humor, but living with Leofric meant there was not much occasion for laughter, and he found he was enjoying himself immensely. Part of it was the mead, he knew, yet he also at least sensed it was due to the manner in which these three were treating him, and it pleased him to see them laugh when he said something they thought was witty. Only later, in the cold light of day and in the aftermath of his first hangover, would Titus recognize they had been laughing at the sight of an overgrown boy getting roaring drunk for the first time in his life, something he would recall with rueful amusement at himself in the years ahead.

As the night passed, the atmosphere in the hall became more boisterous, and bawdier, to the point that Osmund and Mildgyd began engaging in a session that started with kissing but quickly graduated to drunken fumbling with each other's bodies, to the point that Titus grew both uncomfortable and aroused at the same time. Wulfric did not seem the least bit discomfited, swinging one leg over the bench to watch with a grin, and in fact calling to Osmund to save some for himself. Titus, of course, knew the basics about sex, and he was quite proud of the fact that he had already touched the breasts of a village girl named Ebba, and she had even groped him, over his trousers, but now it seemed quite possible that Osmund and Mildgyd were going to start humping, right there on the bench. This seemed to be an appropriate occasion for another cup of mead; thankfully for him, both the couple and the rest of the hall were torn from whatever they were involved in by a sudden pounding from the head table. Like all the other attendees, Titus immediately turned his attention in that direction, but while he saw a figure standing up, it seemed to take his eyes longer to focus, then finally he determined that it was the Ealdorman himself, standing in an embroidered tunic, wearing a heavy gold chain that signified his status, waiting for the noise to subside. Which it did, gradually, yet Eadwig did not seem perturbed, which informed Titus this was not uncommon. Finally, he began speaking, not yelling necessarily, but projecting his voice loudly enough that anyone who happened to be outside the hall relieving themselves could hear that he was speaking.

"Friends," he began, "tomorrow we march to join our blessed King Alfred as part of the fyrd he has called to drive the Danes from our lands!" He clearly expected the sudden roar of voices, male and female, because he did not attempt to continue. After a span of heartbeats, he lifted a hand and the hall fell silent, more quickly this time. "I know that some of you," he still spoke in a ringing tone, but to Titus' ears, the quality changed, becoming more somber, "have already suffered loss at the hands of these pagan *dogs*." He thrust a pointing finger to a man who was seated at the row of tables along the opposite side, about halfway down the hall, a bearded, thickset man who by his dress was clearly a ceorl. "Hrothgar here had left his farm to come to Wiltun to sell some of his cattle, and while he was here, those savages descended on his farm and slaughtered his entire family." Titus examined this man more closely, and even through the smoke and from across the hall, he could see the drawn features and the grim set to his face that bespoke of an inner grief that, whether intentional or not, the Ealdorman had clearly stirred.

But Eadwig was not done, pivoting to point straight down the middle row as he continued, "And Isolde here, her cousin was part of the garrison at Cippinhamm who was slaughtered when the Dane Guthrum violated the truce and attacked our king, and forced him to flee!" The reference to this shameful act, the reason why they were all there, roused an angry muttering from the people, as they alternately cursed this vile act of treachery, or uttered an oath to avenge what was a painful and humiliating event for all Saxons in *Westseaxe*. It was, after all, why Titus was sitting there listening as intently as his condition would allow, although his eyes lingered on the now-named Isolde. It was not the first time he had looked her way, since she was seated on the row of benches facing his direction, and the more mead he consumed, the more convinced he had become that she was the most beautiful girl he had ever seen in his life. And, now that he had heard her tale of woe about losing her cousin, which had evoked enough pain that her eyes were now shining from the tears in them, he swore to himself, with all the passion of a drunken adolescent, that everything he did, every Dane he would slay once he was allowed to join the shield wall, would be done in her honor. So absorbed was he in his fantasy that he missed most of what Eadwig said, continuing to point out a handful of others who had suffered at the hands of the Danes, either with this latest incursion, or in the past, then moved on to calling on his thegns, beginning with Otha, who all stood and swore solemn oaths to fight to the death for their Ealdorman, and for their King.

As this was taking place, Titus' mind was roaming free, envisioning glorious scenes of battle, where he cut down bearded men who were even larger than he was, felling them left and right in a welter of blood and gore, while somehow, Isolde was always present, standing off to the side, watching him with shining eyes and a smile that bore a promise of a reward that he desperately wanted to experience. His pleasant dream was interrupted by another roar, but it was accompanied by everyone in the hall, except for him, leaping to their feet, facing the Ealdorman. He did react, or at least he tried to, but it took him two attempts to stand upright, and he had to reach out and grab the edge of the table to keep from falling backward, missing Wulfric's grin at the sight of the inebriated youth. Eadwig had moved from behind the table, and was now standing in the middle of the hall in front of the large central fire, receiving all who chose to come to him, greeting them not as Ealdorman and inferior, but as a fellow warrior, although the ceorls all still bowed their heads respectfully, before accepting the nobleman's outstretched hand. Titus wanted desperately to be part of this moment, and he actually briefly considered joining the line, but between his inebriation and his uncertain status, instead he turned and walked, unsteadily, towards the entrance of the hall. Before he reached it, a rough hand grabbed him from behind, and while he reacted quickly enough, the sudden change in orientation made his already spinning head and his feet have a disagreement, causing him to stagger back and land, hard, on his rear before falling back onto the rush-covered hardpacked dirt floor of the hall. And, as had happened on his first day, his vision was filled by the scowling visage of Otha, who stared down at him in what appeared to Titus to be disbelief.

"Boy," the Thegn growled, "I don't care how you do it, but you better be ready to leave with us in the morning."

"I…I'm going?" Titus managed, despite his tongue feeling thick and as if it was covered with wool and having completely forgotten Otha saying that very thing earlier.

"You *were* going, but now I'm not sure!" Otha snapped, which alarmed Titus enough to bring him to his feet, where he swayed unsteadily.

"I'll be fine, Lord!" Titus insisted, but even as he said it, he heard the slurring there, and he insisted, "I swear it, Lord! On the cross! I will *not* let you down!"

Otha continued to stare at him for a long moment, then grunted, "We'll see." He turned away, then repeated over his shoulder, "We'll see in the morning."

Titus stood, weaving on his feet, watching the Thegn stride away, and while he was thinking clearly enough, it just seemed that it was happening more slowly than he was accustomed to, but he did recognize he needed to return to the barn. It was not until he had exited the hall, the cooler air hitting him with an almost palpable force, that Otha's words actually registered. He was going! He was going to be marching with the fyrd! Yes, it was only as a lowly stableboy, but that was better than being left behind, wasn't it? The very thought did help in clearing away the fog in his mind, at least to the point where he could walk a relatively straight path to the barn, whereupon he learned that his travails were not over. Making his way to his sleeping spot, it was his nose that gave the first hint that all was not as it should be, the pungent odor of urine filling his nostrils, but when he bent down to feel for his blanket, it was missing. It took a fair amount of time before his benumbed mind worked out what had happened; someone had taken his blanket, then pissed all over the straw that covered his sleeping area.

"Dudda," he breathed.

There was no doubt in his mind, but although his first instinct was to go to Dudda's sleeping area, which, as the stableman, was actually an entire stall that was used for his own purposes, he thought better of it. That, he thought, is what he wants me to do, to make a fuss about it. So, sighing, he instead staggered a short distance away, collapsing in another spot, falling asleep quickly, despite the fact that the barn roof was spinning crazily above him.

Chapter Three

As Wulfric, Osmund, and every other person who had experienced the morning after a night of heavy drinking of mead could have told him, Titus awoke to a series of extremely unpleasant sensations, beginning with his realization that his cheek was wet and cold. When he opened his eyes and saw the cause, recognizing by the smell that it was his own vomit, his stomach immediately added to the slimy mess covering the straw around his head, or at least attempted to, bringing him to his hands and knees as he retched violently, although nothing much came out.

"Stop making that noise, boy!" Dudda's snarl pierced the darkness, the sound making Titus wince, certain that somehow an invisible being was plunging an awl into his ear and penetrating his brain.

While he managed to stop retching, he could not stifle the groan as he climbed unsteadily to his feet, but he was cautiously pleased that the barn was no longer spinning as it had been when he lay down in the pile of straw. It was before dawn, but Titus could hear voices outside the barn, and despite being upright, he could still smell the sour odor of the contents of his stomach, and he decided that he needed fresh air, recalling that it had made him feel better earlier. It was when he took his first step that he learned that even the jarring that came from a simple footstep sent a jagged bolt of pain through his head, and he could not stifle the gasp of pain that it elicited. Fortunately, this only prompted some muttering from the dark recesses of Dudda's sleeping spot, but since he had to walk past the stall, Titus was unable to avoid the stench that emanated from the stableman, so he was not particularly surprised when he felt his stomach roil again. It did serve to get him moving more quickly, and he shoved aside one of the doors and stepped outside, drinking in the fresh air, which made him feel a bit steadier on his feet. He leaned against the wall of the barn, content to watch as several figures were moving about the large open area between the hall, barn, and the buildings that served as the quarters for the Ealdorman's servants, although at the moment, the space was actually anything but open. The carts had all been loaded, as had the wagon; all that remained was to hitch the animals to each one, along with loading the horses that would serve as the pack animals. This last was one of the few things that neither Dudda nor Titus were responsible for, because these were for the men who fought for Ealdorman Eadwig and his thegns, carrying their personal belongings, spare weapons, and other items they considered essential, and they insisted on doing it themselves.

Resigning himself to the idea that he was simply going to be miserable for the foreseeable future, Titus considered what he should do now; normally, he would be lining up with the rest of the servants and slaves at the kitchen to grab whatever was left over from the feast the night before, but the very idea of food made him nauseous, so he decided to begin bringing the horses out that would be hauling the carts. Fortunately, he did not have to enter the barn to do so; the stalls inside the barn were reserved for the horses belonging to the Ealdorman, his family, and his thegns like Otha. The draft and spare horses were kept in an enclosure behind the barn, although there was a roof along the back of the barn to provide a modicum of shelter for the animals. The tack for each animal was hanging from a nail under the roofed area, and Titus began there, grabbing a harness, then walking over to one of the horses who, as usual, were huddled together. Titus' innate talent for calming horses was not confined to Hama, and whereas Dudda could expect to spend a fair amount of time trying to corner the first animal, which Titus believed was a game the horses liked to play with Dudda, certain that his smell was even more offensive to them than to humans, none of them did much more than blow, toss a head, and paw at the ground at his approach.

Murmuring softly, Titus selected a gray gelding that was not very tall, but with the wide chest and strong hindquarters that marked him as the kind of animal that could pull a load. Leading him by the bridle, Titus left the enclosure and went to the first cart, working quickly despite the darkness, this not being much different than hitching an ox to the plow, then tied the reins to one of the posts that were used for training. He was hitching the third horse when a rectangle of light appeared on the ground in front of him, causing him to glance up to see that one of the doors to the hall had opened to allow someone to exit. Framed by the light as he was, Titus immediately saw that it was Ealdorman Eadwig himself, and his stomach, which had actually settled somewhat, seemed to turn over when the nobleman turned slightly and headed directly for him. Whereas a moment before, his fingers had been working swiftly and surely, they suddenly seemed to forget how to obey his commands, so that he was still fumbling with the harness when Eadwig reached him.

"Who told you to hitch the animals, boy?" Eadwig demanded, and while his tone was not harsh, Titus sensed that he might become angry depending on how he answered.

Still, remembering to bow first, he answered honestly, "Nobody, my Lord. I just decided to get started."

"So Dudda didn't tell you to do this?" Eadwig asked sharply.

"No, Lord," Titus replied.

"Where is he now?"

Titus turned slightly and pointed to the barn, although he said nothing, which did not seem to bother Eadwig, who strode away, heading for it, leaving Titus in a quandary about whether he was expected to follow. Fortunately, his fingers suddenly remembered how to work, so he quickly finished harnessing this horse, and since he needed to head back to the barn, he decided that it would not be taken amiss if he did that very thing.

Only to himself would he admit that he was avidly hoping to hear the Ealdorman berating Dudda, and as he approached, while he could not hear the actual words, Lord Eadwig's tone confirmed that very thing was happening, especially when he heard Dudda's oily whine in response.

He was completely unprepared when, in a louder voice, Eadwig called out, "Come in here, boy! I know you're listening!"

For the span of a heartbeat, Titus thought about pretending that he was not there, then quickly realized it would be a foolish idea; simply put, he was more afraid of Ealdorman Eadwig than Dudda, so he meekly complied, stepping through the door. Since he had begun hitching the horses, the sky had lightened, so that while it was still two shadowy figures, there was enough light for Titus to distinguish the two just by their relative shapes.

"Yes, Lord?"

Titus sensed more than saw Eadwig turn to face him, but he was completely unprepared for the nobleman to ask bluntly, "Do you think you can carry out Dudda's duties on this march?"

Despite his shock, Titus' first instinct was to blurt out that of *course* he could, but as he was about to say as much, he stopped himself.

"No, Lord," he answered instead. "Not by myself anyway." Then, hating himself for it, he added, "And I still have things to learn that Dudda can teach me, Lord."

Eadwig's response was nothing more than a grunt, but while Titus did not know it, the Ealdorman had been testing the youth, expecting to hear the kind of braggadocio of an adolescent boy in a man's body who had been bigger and stronger than his peers his entire life.

Turning to Dudda, Eadwig said coldly, "This is the second time the boy here has proven to be a harder worker than you, Dudda. And," he continued, giving Titus a piece of information in the process, "if it hadn't been for your father and the sacrifice he made for me, you would have been out of a job long before." Eadwig extended an arm and poked Dudda in the chest as he warned, "There will *not* be a third time, Dudda. Do you understand?"

It was now just light enough for Titus to see that all three of Dudda's chins were quivering and his eyes were wider than he had ever seen them, but while nothing came out of his mouth, he nodded vigorously, prompting a snort of mild disgust from the Ealdorman.

"Get back to work, boy," he ordered Titus, then indicated Dudda with a wave, "and you as well, Dudda. We're leaving at sunrise."

Titus hurried past the stableman, but he could feel the hostile stare he was being given. It was not until he reached the enclosure that he realized something; he had assumed that by telling the truth about needing Dudda, it would at least partially appease the stableman. Unless, he thought suddenly, he didn't want to go. He could not stifle his groan as he realized this was almost undoubtedly the case. It was, he thought glumly, going to be a miserable day; he had no idea how the coming day would be so much more than that to young Titus of Cissanbyrig, where his problems with Dudda would be solved once and for all.

Despite his queasy stomach, his pounding head, and the worry about Dudda's wrath, there was one event that, at least for a moment, made Titus forget all of it.

It was as he was hitching the two oxen to the lone wagon when, from behind him, a voice called out, "Are you going with Lord Eadwig?"

His surprise was not just because he was startled, but that it was a feminine voice, and even in the instant it took for him to spin around, his ears told him that it was not Mildgyd, or Hild, the only other female he had spoken to during his time here. He was totally unprepared to see that it was Isolde, wearing the same smock she had been wearing the night before, and now that the rim of the sun was touching the horizon and providing light, Titus realized he had been in error the night before about how comely she was. She was even prettier than she had seemed in the hall, and his heart began pounding so hard that he could hear it in his ears, but when he opened his mouth to respond to what he knew was a question…nothing came out.

"Did you hear me?" she asked, then her eyes widened dramatically as she gasped, "Are you simple? Do you not understand my words?"

This served its purpose, nettling Titus to snap, "No, I'm not simple! I just…" His voice trailed off as he realized there was no way that he could explain why he had seemingly lost his wits, so he just shrugged, then said, "But yes, Lord Otha told me last night I was going."

"So is Lord Eadward," the girl replied, and there was something in the way she said it that made Titus bristle, and before he could stop himself, he muttered, "Yes, he's coming, but he won't be doing any fighting."

"Does that mean you are?" she asked him frankly, and he heard the doubt there.

"That hasn't been decided yet." He tried to sound as if it was a foregone conclusion, but he was honest enough to admit, "I haven't been trained to stand in the shield wall yet. But," he drew himself up and thrust his chest out, declaring, "I'm at least as strong as any man in this fyrd, and stronger than most!"

"Yes," she answered, her tone serious, but he thought he saw an amused glint in her eye, "and you can take a beating very well! I heard my father talking about it."

"Who's your father?" Titus demanded, thinking that at some point in the future, he would have something to say to this man.

"Why," she replied gaily, "Cenric is my father."

Titus could not stop himself from groaning aloud.

Then, without thinking, he replied ruefully, "Well, he would know."

This made her laugh, and he glared at her for a heartbeat, but then could not stop himself from joining in. From the front of the column that had formed up, a horn sounded, ending the moment between them.

Feeling awkward again, Titus mumbled, "I need to go now."

Rather than say anything, Isolde bent forward, and despite having to stand on her toes, gave Titus a light kiss on his cheek, then said softly in his ear, "I will pray for you every night, Titus of Cissanbyrig."

Before he could say anything, she turned and ran off, joining the small crowd of other women who had come to say goodbye, leaving him to wonder, How did she know my name and my village?

With the small crowd gathered there, those who were joined by blood or by bonds of marriage were easy for Titus to spot; they were all crying, but even the slaves, the women and some of the men who were left behind, while dry-eyed, looked solemn. Titus barely noticed any of this, his head still reeling, although this time it was not from mead but from the memory of soft lips on his cheek, and a smell that was far superior to sour vomit. Dudda was driving the wagon, if only because it took two oxen to haul the load and his bulk, while Titus was consigned to walking behind it, holding several long braided leather thongs that were attached to the bridles of the horses that would serve as spare mounts or draft animals. There were only a half-dozen of them, but Titus was very conscious of the responsibility; simply put, he knew that men like Ealdorman Eadwig and Lord Otha placed far more value on the life of one of these horses than they did a fourteen-year-old stableboy. Maybe, he thought with a flicker of excitement, some Danes will try to sneak up and steal them, and I'll fight them off! That would be *magnificent*! And there would be no way for Otha or Lord Eadwig to deny that he belonged in the shield wall, at the very least. After that, who knew? So absorbed was he in this flight of adolescent fancy that, when the wagon lurched into motion, it caught him by surprise, but he thought he recovered quickly enough that nobody noticed. As he led the animals by, he tried to find Isolde in the small crowd, but he was disappointed, not seeing her anywhere, and then he was outside the walls, the gates slamming shut behind him. He was dismayed to see that he was at the very end of the column, but this did not last long, as four men that Titus recognized as belonging to Thegn Ceadda, who was second in importance only to Otha, came trotting back towards him. They drew up, ignoring him as he led the horses past, then once the last animal was a few paces away, fell in behind them.

When they passed through the village of Wiltun, there was another crowd waiting, which puzzled Titus until he thought about it; of *course* the townspeople would know that their Ealdorman was on his way to meet with King Alfred! This was where most of the supplies and a fair number of the men who would be in the shield wall came from, although by the time Titus passed by, most of the people had already said their goodbyes and were dispersing. The pace set by Lord Eadwig was painfully slow as far as Titus was concerned, although much of his boredom was a result of his isolation at the rear of the column and his view being blocked by the wagon. His ancestor for whom he was named would have scoffed at what he would consider the slovenly, completely unmilitary fashion in which Eadwig's fyrd was moving, but given this was his namesake's first march, and this was actually how the Saxons went to war, the youth simply assumed that this was how it would always be.

They reached the ford at the River Wich (Wylye), where there was a small hamlet, although by this point in time, both men and women were busy in the fields or in their homes, and when it was time for Titus to cross, despite this being a relatively well-used ford, with a well-worn track, the opposite bank was now a morass of churned mud. It was precisely the kind of footing that Titus knew could prove treacherous to his charges, so he took extra care as he led them in a long single line, tethering one animal to the next before splashing through the water that came up to his mid-thigh. In fact, he was so intent on the horses that he did not take care with his own footing; perhaps the only grace was that he had turned to walk backward up the short but steep bank to watch the horses when his feet flew out from under him and he landed on his back before sliding down to the edge of the river. His back was soaked, and while he could not see it, he knew it was caked with slimy mud, but he scrambled quickly to his feet, ignoring the guffaws of the four men of the rearguard, and this time, he faced forward and pulled the tether on the lead horse, who scrambled up the bank, the others quickly following. All of whom, he noted with disgust, had less trouble than he had experienced.

"That's because you have four legs and I only have two," he muttered sourly, but when the lead horse, a chestnut, suddenly tossed its head as if agreeing, Titus' irritation faded. "At least they're the only ones who saw it." He indicated the four horsemen who were splashing through the river, while Titus actually went to a trot to catch up with Dudda and the wagon.

They stopped at noon, and Titus' guess was that they had covered barely five miles; it was this moment that Titus realized something. He had no idea where they were heading, and as a result, he did not know how long this march would take. The fyrd was marching in a northerly direction, and for a short period, he thought that they might actually be heading directly for Cippanhamm, which in turn would take them back through Cissanbyrig and into the heart of Ealdorman Wulfhere's shire, igniting a sense of foreboding in him at the thought. Fortunately, that worry did not last long, when, reaching a fork in the track, Lord Eadwig led the column along the left-hand branch, turning more west, and most importantly to Titus, away from Cippanhamm. When the horn sounded for the stop, Titus immediately led the horses over to the stream they had been paralleling that he assumed fed into the Wich, allowing the horses to water themselves. Dudda struggled off the wooden seat of the wagon, dropping to the ground with enough force that Titus was certain he felt the vibration under his feet, but while the stableman gave him a malevolent stare, to Titus' relief, he said nothing. Up the column, men were dismounting and leading their animals, both their mounts and packhorses to the stream as well, while the men on foot, almost all of them ceorls, walked away from the track to drop onto the grass strip between it and the stream, rummaging in the leather sacks they had slung over their shoulder that was their version of a pack.

Titus was more interested in Dudda and what he was doing, watching with a fair amount of nervousness as the fat man struggled up into the back of the wagon, hoping that the stableman would not find the small sack containing the food Titus had managed to squirrel away that he was looking forward to consuming during the stop. Not until Dudda emerged, dropped to the ground, and went waddling away did Titus breathe a sigh of relief; while the stableman had been carrying a sack, he recognized it as not belonging to him. Nevertheless, he made a wider circuit back to the wagon, leading the horses so that he could approach with the wagon between where Dudda was sitting in the grass and his path, noticing that he was sitting alone, not even the servants and slaves with the column seeking out his company. Securely tying the leads to the back of the wagon, Titus clambered in to move the large sacks of grain and retrieve his trove, then spent a few moments trying to decide how much he should consume of the round loaf of bread, four small cheeses, and a piece of pork that was more bone than meat. This was an everyday struggle for the youth; he lived in a state of perpetual hunger, not all that uncommon for a growing boy, but when his father owned just the bare minimum of one hide of land to qualify as a ceorl, and being his size, Titus was engaged in a constant battle between his appetite and his knowledge that the source of the next meal was not guaranteed. It was true that he had eaten better over the previous several days serving Ealdorman Eadwig than any period in his life before this, and in fact, it was this knowledge that convinced him to consume it all, gambling that when they stopped for the night, there would be more made available.

He had just emerged from the wagon carrying his sack when he heard approaching hoofbeats from the front of the column, although his view was blocked by the wagon itself. Expecting that it would be Thegn Ceadda coming to check on the four outriders, who were still mounted and looking on as their comrades rested, Titus was surprised when it was the young Lord Eadward who appeared, and who, Titus could see, was every bit as startled, pulling his horse's head, a smoke gray gelding that he knew the lordling had named Thunor, the Saxon name for the Norse god of thunder, with enough force to bring the horse to an abrupt stop, whereupon Titus learned why Eadward seemed so surprised.

"I didn't know you were coming!" he exclaimed, then added, "I asked my father at the feast and he said he was leaving it up to Otha to decide."

"Well," Titus could only think to say, "he did decide. And," he gestured towards himself, "here I am."

This made Eadward laugh.

"After last night, I didn't think I'd see you," Eadward said, but when Titus looked puzzled, his grin faded a bit, although he explained readily enough. "After you fell down, I saw Otha talking to you."

Titus might have bristled at this under other circumstances, but the vestige of his hangover was still sufficient for him to make a face as he admitted, "I had too much mead."

"You drank mead?" Eadward asked, clearly envious, and when Titus looked at him in surprise, he said glumly, "My father doesn't let me drink mead. I tried to last night, but he stopped me."

"Considering how I feel today," Titus answered honestly, "your father's right." He hesitated, then he admitted, "I woke up in a puddle of my own puke this morning." The face Eadward made conveyed his feelings on the matter, and they shared a laugh, but then Titus added impulsively, "And Isolde kissed me before we left."

Eadward's smile faded at this, which pleased Titus immensely.

"Isolde?"

"Yes," Titus answered. "Cenric's daughter." Then, less out of malice than a simple recognition of the world in which they lived, he added, "There's no reason you would know her, my Lord. Her father's a ceorl, not an Ealdorman or thegn."

"I know who she is," Eadward snapped, clearly nettled. "And I don't know why you'd think I wouldn't."

Titus was torn; he was pleased to see that he had rattled the lordling, who he instinctively viewed as a rival for the affections of the fair Isolde, yet he also had no desire to alienate the only person in this fyrd who was close to his age, and who would one day be the Ealdorman if God willed it to be so.

Despite this, it was still difficult for him to apologize, "I'm sorry, Lord. I didn't mean to imply anything." Slightly inspired, he said truthfully, "Since I'm not from anywhere near here, I don't know where Cenric lives, or if you had any reason to know him or his family."

He was pleased to see this mollified Eadward.

"That's true." The lordling nodded. "But yes, I do know Cenric and his family well; their farm is the nearest to my father's hall. Isolde and I grew up together, and we played as children."

This seemed to embarrass him, and Titus, feeling that he had scored enough of a victory, decided to move on to safer ground.

"Lord Eadward," he felt slightly silly addressing a younger boy in this manner, "may I ask a question?" Eadward nodded, and he asked, "Where are we heading? I haven't heard anyone talking about it."

"That's because my father ordered that it be kept secret until we left," Eadward explained. He paused, and Titus could see he was thinking about it. Finally, he shrugged and said, "And now that we're on the march, I don't see the harm in telling you. I know that everyone who was within my hearing until we stopped knows." Still, he did move his horse closer, and his voice dropped to just above a whisper. "We're meeting King Alfred at Egbert's Stone."

Like all Saxons, Titus knew of the place, although he had never been anywhere near it; from what he had been told, Cissanbyrig was more than fifteen miles away from the spot, and he had never been that far away from his home until he came to Wiltun.

"Have you ever been there?" Titus asked.

"No." Eadward shook his head. "My father has, but I've never seen it."

"It makes sense," Titus mused. "Since Egbert was Alfred's grandfather."

"That's what I thought as well," Eadward agreed.

Before either of them could say anything, the horn sounded the call that the rest period was over.

"I better get back," Eadward said, then grinned. "I don't want my father worried that I've fallen in the water and drowned." Before Titus could respond, Eadward had wheeled his horse, saying casually as he did so, "I'll come find you tonight after we make camp, and we can talk more then."

Titus acknowledged this with a wave, then watched as Eadward cantered back up the column, and despite his youth, Titus saw that he was clearly a skilled horseman, weaving through the men returning to their spots in the column. It was the sight of them doing so that reminded Titus of something, and he looked down at the sack with its untouched contents. Sighing, he resigned himself to remaining hungry, climbing into the wagon to replace the sack, completely unaware that, before much more time had passed, the state of his stomach would be the least of his concerns.

Titus had never seen a Dane with his own eyes, and everything he knew about them was secondhand, although not much of it came from his father; their communication was confined to usually monosyllabic commands, seasoned with curses and punctuated by slaps, kicks, and as he grew older, punches, although those had become increasingly infrequent as Titus had grown and made it clear that there would be a reckoning coming if his father continued. But something that Titus had accepted as an article of faith came from the fact that, along with their ferocity and shockingly bloodthirsty ways, the one thing that almost every person Titus had ever heard talking about the Danes mention was their rapidity of movement. Related to that was their skill at appearing seemingly out of nowhere as experts at ambush, in places where there was no indication they were anywhere in the vicinity. Knowing this, however, and experiencing it were two entirely different matters, but when it happened, it took a span of heartbeats before the sight of several dozen large, bearded men astride horses that looked absurdly small who suddenly materialized out of the edge of a thick stand of trees at the top of a low hill running parallel to the track on his left actually registered with Titus. He saw they were all wearing chain mail, waving axes in one hand with a large wooden shield strapped to their left forearm as they clutched the reins of their mounts. It was the sudden explosion of noise created by the roaring of the Danes as they rushed downslope at the gallop towards the column, and the shouts of alarm, along with what Titus understood were commands, that did as much to get him moving as the sight before him.

"God preserve us! The Danes! The Danes! They'll slaughter us all!"

Dudda's voice was the shrillest Titus had ever heard it, but it was the sight of the fat man leaping from the wagon with an agility that he had never exhibited before that Titus would have cause to remember, not only because he had never dreamed that the stableman could move so quickly, but in doing so, Dudda had understandably leapt down and headed in the opposite direction. By watching Dudda, Titus' gaze naturally fell on the right side of the column, so he was one of the first, if not the first Saxon who spotted a force of Danes crawling on all fours, their shields strapped to their backs, using the thick grass that grew waist high along this part of the track for cover.

What happened next would be a feature in Titus' dreams for some time to come, because while Dudda was not the only of the noncombatants to try and flee, somehow the fat man managed to be in the lead of the rest of the running Saxon servants and slaves, most of them out of their minds with fear, and it was Dudda's fate to be the first to die. Titus had the span of perhaps a full heartbeat to warn Dudda that he was, in effect, running directly towards the waiting Northmen, something that from his vantage point, Dudda either did not see or was too blinded by panic to do so, but the youth was frozen in place, unable to summon anything that could have saved the stableman. The first Dane to stand, with golden hair that was below his shoulders and tied into a single braid, did so in what seemed to Titus an almost leisurely fashion, as if he was just awakening from a nap, when Dudda was less than a half-dozen paces away. Titus knew that, even if Dudda had not been so obese, he would have been unable to either stop himself or dodge the ax that the Dane swung, horizontally and at about waist level. The blade was obviously sharp because the Northman's arm barely slowed, although once past the plane of the stableman's torso, there was a spray of blood and offal following behind it, whereupon he nimbly stepped aside as Dudda's momentum carried the fat man forward another couple of steps until his feet were tangled up in his own intestines. As Titus watched in fascinated horror, he saw that apparently the sight of the stableman being tripped up by his own guts amused the blonde Dane enormously, because he roared with laughter as Dudda toppled forward facedown atop his own intestines and internal organs. Titus had been so fixed on Dudda's fate that he was late in realizing that the Dane's companions had all leapt to their feet, and at least one of them had spotted him, pointing in his direction with an ax and shouting something over his shoulder as he began heading towards him. He *knew* he should run, but his feet seemed stuck to the ground, and he barely noticed that the leads had been jerked from his hand as the spare horses did what he should have done, bolting and moving at a gallop back in the direction from which they had come, away from these screaming demons now descending on the column from both sides.

"Get under the wagon, you fool, and stay there!"

The harsh shout, coming from one of the four mounted men who had come galloping up from their spot at the rear was what jerked Titus out of his daze, and he instantly spun about, sprinted to the wagon, and threw himself under it, panting from a terror he had never experienced before, even when he was a small child and fleeing from his father in one of his drunken rages. Safe for the instant, he watched as two of Ceadda's men galloped towards the Danes who had been creeping through the grass, the man he presumed had shouted the warning leading his comrade directly at the Northman who had slain Dudda. Who, Titus could see, did not look the least bit worried, and he saw why as, once more, with a timing that spoke of long practice, the blonde warrior leapt to one side, while at the same instant, brought his ax down in a brutal overhead blow, the edge striking the tender nose of the horse, causing the youth to wince at the spray of blood, while evoking an almost human shriek of pain from the horse. Not surprisingly, the animal lost all interest in heeding the commands of its rider, jerking its head instinctively away from the blow, the change in direction causing the Saxon warrior to go flying through the air. To Titus' surprise, Ceadda's warrior reacted quickly enough so that, although he hit the ground with a terrific force, he had ducked one shoulder so that his own momentum allowed him to roll, and while he did not come immediately to his feet, he was not only kneeling, but he had somehow managed to hold on to his shield, which he presented towards the oncoming enemy. More importantly, his comrade had been two lengths behind, and while the blonde Dane could evade and unseat one rider, he could not move quickly enough to avoid the slashing blow of the long, single-edged *seaxe* that cut deeply into the point where neck and shoulder met, slicing through the boiled leather jerkin as if it was cloth. Titus' view of the actual blow was blocked by the bulk of horse and rider, but they were past in an eyeblink so that he saw the result, the Dane still standing, but with his head tilted at an impossible angle, a spray of blood spurting up into the air. Then, he was gone, dropping out of sight in the grass, and Titus saw that the stalks in that spot were red, yet despite this, the pair of Ceadda's men were not out of danger by any means.

The mounted Saxon had drawn up next to his comrade, who had come to his feet, but they were quickly surrounded by what Titus guessed were more than a dozen Danes, leaving him to watch helplessly as the pair swung their weapons wildly about them, temporarily keeping their foes at bay, while the mounted Saxon used his horse's bulk as a weapon as well, giving it commands that swung its hindquarters side to side. Titus had never seen a wolf pack work, but he had heard stories, and he was certain that what he was watching here was essentially the same thing, and he wondered why the pair of men did not at least try and cut their way through. He got his answer when he became aware for the first time of the sound of beating hooves, coming from the front of the column, but since his view was partially blocked by the solid wheels of the wagon, he heard more than saw the sudden collision of mounted men slamming into the Danes' version of a shield wall, a hastily contrived one at that.

Screams of both men and animals, the deep, underlying thudding sound as the horses crashed into the round shields of the raiders, and the bright, harsh ringing sounds of metal hitting metal; all of these compelled Titus to move, despite his fear, out from under the wagon, although only after he checked the opposite side, where the mounted Danes had first appeared. Clearly, they had attacked the head of the column because there were no more enemy riders visible, prompting Titus to scramble out from under the wagon, although he crouched so that the right front wheel was at his back. The sight that greeted his eyes was hard for him to make any sense of, although over time, he would learn to read the signs of battle, and would even be able to tell the likely outcome long before the fighting was finally over. At this moment, however, to his eyes, it seemed to be a horribly disorganized mess, where small groups of mounted Saxons were clustered together, trying to either slash with swords or stab downward with spears at Danes who were using the cover of the grass to dash about, moving with an astonishing agility to seek an opening.

Even as he watched, Titus saw a man he recognized as belonging to Thegn Aelfnod suddenly reel in the saddle, turning his attention to him just in time to see a Dane suddenly appear, ax in hand, which he brought down on the man's right leg. Whether it was the wound itself or the horse rearing that caused the Saxon to fall from the saddle Titus could not tell, but he saw the ax rise up above the grass, blood already dripping from it, then swing down, cutting off the screaming of the Saxon whose name he did not know. So immersed was he in watching this drama, Titus was completely unprepared for the sudden appearance of a dozen mounted Danes from behind him, circling around the wagon, but while he was in plain sight, none of them gave so much as a glance in his direction, all of them intent on rushing to the aid of their comrades who had been creeping through the grass. To his inexperienced eyes, this seemed to be the culmination of this battle that he was now certain would be his last, as the mounted Danes charged directly for the knot of Saxon horsemen who had managed to force the Danes on foot into a compact circle.

"*Behind you! Danes behind you!*"

Titus only dimly recognized his own voice, but he could see that the Saxons facing in his direction on the opposite side of the circle of Danes on foot, which he saw included Otha and the Ealdorman himself, clearly saw the approaching horsemen as well, just by their gestures to their comrades. It was when those Saxons on his side wheeled their mounts around that Titus recognized, with a sense of profound shock, that one of them was the young lordling Eadward, his face white with the fear that he was certain was even more acute than Titus' own. Eadward was wearing helmet and mail, of course, and had a shield strapped to his arm and Titus recalled that he had had it attached to his saddle behind him in the custom of the Saxons, but before Eadward could do anything more than face this new threat, the horsemen on either side of him, both of them belonging to Otha, jabbed their spurs into their animals' flanks, causing them to leap forward in an obvious move to protect their Ealdorman's son. They were less than a horse's length in front of Eadward when the first of the mounted Danes arrived, barely slowing his animal down and clearly trying to split the pair; Titus recalled at that instant that the Saxon nearest him was Aelfwine, the Dane driving his horse in between him and Otha's other man in what, even as inexperienced as he was, Titus could see was either an extremely brave or incredibly foolish thing to do, since he effectively placed himself between two enemies. Well within the span of a normal heartbeat, Titus saw that it was not as foolish as it appeared; because of the opposite facing orientation, the Dane was now shield to shield with Aelfwine, putting the Saxon's sword out of position, while enabling the Northman to swing his ax at the Saxon to his right, his shield on the opposite side. Titus saw the Dane's weapon moving, but before he could see whether the second Saxon managed to parry the blow, the rest of the mounted Danes had arrived, completely obscuring his view in a maelstrom of movement.

Things were occurring so quickly that it was impossible for the youth to truly understand what was happening, still crouched next to the wagon and feeling as if he had lost the use of his limbs. Somehow, however, he instinctively grasped that the Danes were actually failing in this endeavor, because as far as he could tell, none of them had actually begun ransacking the baggage train, which would be their primary concern. Even as this thought occurred to him, he was alerted to a new development by another concerted roar of male voices, except they were distinct enough for him to recognize they were in his own tongue, coming from the opposite direction as the mounted Danes who had circled the rear, from the front of the column. It was this noise that prompted him to actually stand erect for the first time, and he experienced a surprise at how radically, and rapidly his perspective of what was going on changed. He saw that the roar he had just heard came from the other ceorls of the fyrd, as a triple row of spearmen came running in his direction, and while he could not be certain, he thought he glimpsed Cenric's face in the front rank, then they reached the fighting, but on the opposite side, where Eadwig, Otha, Ceadda, and the other mounted Saxons were located. The noise was still horrific, and the arrival of so many horses had churned up some dust as the tall grass was trampled down by the horses' hooves, partially obscuring Titus' vision along the ground. For the first time since Dudda's initial shriek of warning, the youth had managed to suppress his terror and gather his wits enough to actually observe this fight with some detachment, and he realized that the Danes were no longer trying to win; they were trying to extract themselves from their predicament.

The mounted Danes had somehow sensed that their comrades on foot had been stymied and were now in danger themselves, prompting the horsemen to try to chop a path back through the tall grass to the relative safety of the thick forest to the right of the column a couple hundred paces away. In between the forest and them was a mixed force of Saxon horsemen and some of the newly arrived ceorls of the shield wall; despite the fact that the fighting was still going on, Titus felt his body relax slightly as he actually began to think beyond the next few heartbeats. Then, over the sounds of the battle, there was a scream of mortal agony that, either because of the volume or the pitch, pierced the air, bringing Titus' attention back to the moment as he squinted in an attempt to discern the cause. He was just in time to see a horse topple over onto its side, a broken spear protruding from its chest as blood poured from the wound and from the animal's mouth, but to Titus' horror, he not only saw that its rider was now pinned with one leg underneath the dying horse, its hooves still thrashing feebly in its instinctive need to gallop to safety, he recognized not the rider, but the horse as Thunor, Lord Eadward's mount. And, before he had any conscious thought to do so, Titus of Cissanbyrig was running, unarmed and alone, directly into the fighting.

Chapter Four

Titus was not alone in seeing the horse carrying the heir to Ealdorman Eadwig fall and pin its rider; Eadwig and Otha saw it happen, but to Eadward's mortal danger, one of the mounted Northmen saw it too, as well as the Dane on foot who had been the one to snatch up a spear and thrust it deep into the animal's body. Eadward had already gotten himself in danger when, unknown to his father, after initially obeying Eadwig's initial command to stay put as the Ealdorman counterattacked the mounted Danes on the left side of the baggage train, which they determined later had been a feint designed to draw the Saxons' attention from the real threat, he could not resist the urge, and he had joined the contingent of mounted Saxons. When those mounted Danes had retreated, then turned about to dash down the train to swing around the opposite end where Titus and the wagon were located to reach their comrades on foot, however, although he made sure to stay to the rear of the group of horsemen as his father galloped to intercept them, Eadward was there with his fellow Saxons. So excited was he that he did not hear his father's command to split into two groups, with the second, led by another of Eadwig's thegns, Aelfnod, swinging around in the direction of the forest to encircle the Northmen acting as infantry, the young lordling followed the thegn instead of staying near Eadwig. He only realized his error when it was too late to return to where his father was; Thegn Aelfnod and his cousin Leofsige, who actually belonged to Thegn Ceadda, did realize who was with them, which was what prompted the pair to rush at the oncoming mounted Danes.

What happened next was a blur, that for Eadward, even after he had time to think about it, was a mixture of memories, of the contorted face of a Dane with hair the color of faded gold and long strings of spittle on either side of his mouth, glinting slightly silver in the bright sunshine, bringing an ax down, aiming directly at Eadward. He obviously had blocked the blow; simply put, he would not have lived another moment longer if he had not, yet for the rest of his days, he could never recall doing so, even after seeing the fresh gouge mark on his shield. What he did remember, to his shame, and was something he never told his father afterward, was that in the excitement, he had forgotten to draw his *seaxe*. This was why, he assumed later, he was able to do nothing more than watch helplessly as, from his right side, another Dane appeared, this one with black hair and a plaited beard, except that instead of an ax, he held a spear, which he drove unerringly into Thunor's chest. Eadward had an eyeblink's warning of his impending doom, feeling the convulsive shudder from his horse, who he had loved ever since his father had presented it to him on his tenth name day, but it was the heart-rending scream of pain that, even as he felt himself falling with Thunor, Eadward swore he felt as keenly as his horse, made worse by the knowledge that it was his fault.

The impact with the ground had been terrific; his head, even with the helmet he wore, slamming against the ground hard enough that he was temporarily blinded from what seemed like a sudden eruption of hundreds of tiny stars. Stunned as he was, Eadward had no idea how long he was in a befuddled state, but it was clearly long enough that, as if conjured by some sorcery, a figure appeared in his limited range of vision, standing in a semi-crouch but with his back to Eadward, who could only look up in bleary puzzlement. Why, he wondered, is his back covered with mud? Even when the figure turned slightly, Eadward could not see the face of what was clearly a man, and a good-sized one at that, but his mind had cleared enough for him to realize that his fate was being decided above him, although everything was auditory in nature because of his obscured vision. There was a shout that was clearly in the Danish tongue, followed by a sharp cracking sound that, from his training, Eadward knew meant a shield had been struck a mighty blow, but whoever his unknown champion was, the sounds he was making reminded Eadward of some sort of animal, more like the snarling of a wolf than a man. He heard another crack, but following so closely behind it that it could have been part of the same sound, there was a second, deeper thudding noise, punctuated by a snapping crunch of some sort. Eadward learned what it was when a man collapsed in front of him, the lower half of his body draped across Thunor's neck, while the upper half of the man's body was lying roughly parallel to Eadward and facing him so that he was suddenly looking into the wide open eyes of a man with black hair and a plaited beard. He instantly knew the identity of this Dane as the man who had slain Thunor, except now his skull was cleaved into two sections, almost perfectly down the middle to halfway down the bridge of his nose, and despite his own predicament, Eadward experienced a ferocious satisfaction at seeing that at least Thunor had been avenged.

The snarling sound had continued unabated, as did the shouting, yet even if he could not understand much of it, aside that most of them seemed to be cries to their gods Odin and Thor, Eadward was certain that there was now an alarmed quality there, as if these fierce Northmen were encountering something they were not prepared to face. Eadward began trying to pull himself free, but he quickly gave up, and between the helmet and the restriction caused by the hood of his mail shirt, he still could not twist his head to see anything that might give him an indication of what was happening. It was a feeling of such utter helplessness, one that would have a tremendous impact on young Eadward for the rest of his days, as he swore to Christ and all of His Saints that he would never be in this position again. He *was* able to determine that at least the location of the fighting had shifted, and that it was moving in the direction away from the baggage train, but it was the sudden revealing of his mysterious champion Eadward would have cause to remember, when a pair of legs suddenly appeared next to the corpse of the black-haired Dane, then before he could crane his neck to see, the figure dropped to his knees next to the young nobleman. Even then, it took perhaps three or four heartbeats for Eadward to recognize who it was, mostly because he seemed to be literally drenched in blood, his face looking as if someone had painted it red, making the whites of his eyes appear in startling and eerie juxtaposition.

"T-titus? Is that you?"

As little as Eadward saw of all that transpired, he still knew more than Titus would ever remember. His last clear memories were of his legs, despite his brain shrieking at them to stop, carrying him at a run in the wrong direction, not away from the danger but directly towards it, then slowing only long enough to bend down and snatch up the ax that had fallen from the hand of the Dane who had killed Dudda, whose corpse was just a matter of a couple paces away. He supposed that it was this movement that had prompted one of the Danes on foot to turn slightly, a man with black hair and a plaited beard, yet it was not what the Northman did, but the expression on his face that Titus knew ignited…whatever it was that fueled and protected him for what came next. It was the same kind of look his father Leofric gave him on an almost daily basis, of hatred and utter, sneering contempt, as if he was measuring Titus and seeing him as an insignificant threat and abject failure, so that when Titus lunged at this Dane, it was his father that he saw, his father he was striking down.

His next conscious memory was standing, a good distance away from the wagon, feeling as if his lungs were on fire, his legs trembling as they threatened to collapse from under him, and most strangely of all, with an ax in his hand that seemed glued to his hand because it and his hand were coated with a thick layer of blood, and other things he did not even want to think about, that he had no idea from where it had come. Following hard on this was his realization that his tunic was soaked, which he assumed was from sweat, but then he realized his face was wet as well, although he could immediately tell it was not from his perspiration. It was in this moment his legs decided they had done enough, and he fell to his knees, completely oblivious to the fact that he somehow managed to find the only spot in the area that was not already occupied by bodies of both man and horse or the detritus of a hard fight.

"T-titus? Is that you?"

He actually started in surprise, although his only meaningful reaction was to lift his head to look dully at Eadward; of the few things that Titus knew at this moment, the one bedrock certainty was that, even if the Danes returned and renewed their attack, he would not even have the strength to climb to his feet, and he would just meekly succumb to his fate. It was the sight of Thunor lying there that triggered the first fragment of recollection in Titus' mind.

"I saw," his voice sounded strange, but while he had intended to point at the corpse of the black-haired Dane, he could not lift his arm, so he just nodded in his direction, "that bastard kill your horse."

Hearing the cause for Titus' action ignited in Eadward a powerful range of emotions, and to his horror, he felt his eyes fill with tears at this reminder of why he was here.

More to cover his embarrassment, Eadward asked, "Could you help get me out from under him?"

Titus' only response was a shake of the head, which irritated Eadward; as grateful as he may have been to this ceorl, he was still the son of an Ealdorman, but it evaporated when Titus admitted, "I don't think I have the strength, Lord. I can barely keep my head up."

Before Eadward could respond, their little world was invaded, first by the sound of trotting hoofbeats, but while Titus could see the cause, Eadward could not, so when he heard his father's voice, he could not suppress a shudder.

"Are you hurt, Eadward?" Eadwig asked, but with the same kind of tone his son had heard him use with one of the ceorls or one of his Thegn's men: cool, dispassionate, and seemingly only mildly interested.

"I...I don't believe so, Father," Eadward replied honestly. "My leg hurts a bit, but I don't think it's broken."

Eadwig's response was a grunt, then two men appeared in Eadward's vision; one was Aelfnod, the other Otha, who commanded, "Lie still, Lord."

While Aelfnod moved to the feet of the dead Dane and roughly dragged the body off of Thunor's neck, Otha knelt down, ignoring Eadward's protests that he was fine as the Thegn poked and prodded him, grabbing one arm while watching the youth for signs of pain, then repeating it with the other.

This prompted Eadward to protest, "You don't have to do that, Otha. I'd tell you if I was hurt!"

"Considering that you got yourself in this predicament, you'll forgive me if I don't take your word for it, Lord," Otha said dryly, but he finished his examination. "Give me your arms," he commanded, then with Aelfnod's help, they dragged Eadward out from under his horse.

Understandably cautious, Eadward tested the leg that had been trapped under Thunor, but while it was with a limp, his smile of relief told the story. As all of this was taking place, Eadwig had been standing silently, arms crossed, but instead of being interested in his son and heir, his eyes were on Titus, who was still kneeling, head slumped.

Seeing where his father's attention was, Eadward cleared his throat and said nervously, "Father, I must tell you that…"

"Stop," Eadwig said, not loudly, but with a tone that his son had long before learned was a command that, by refusing to obey it, would unleash his father's wrath. "Not another word from you." Only then did he look away from Titus, regarding Eadward with what his son thought was the same coldness with which he had been looking at Titus. "In fact," he pointed towards the line of carts and wagons, "I want you to go over there. Check on how many slaves and servants we lost, how much of the stock is hurt, and wait there for me."

Under any other circumstances, Eadward would have practically sprinted away, but he did not do so now.

Trying to sound cool and calm, he said, "Before I do that, Father, I *must* tell you that…"

"*Get away from me*!" Eadwig roared, thrusting a finger towards the baggage train, his expression one of implacable anger.

Perhaps if Eadward had been a few years older, he would still have resisted, but he was a year younger than Titus, so with an apologetic glance at the other youth, who still seemed to be completely disinterested in what was happening, he limped away.

"Go with him," Eadgar commanded Aelfnod, who bowed his head and followed without a word.

Now it was just Eadwig, Otha, and Titus, the rest of the men of the fyrd either making sure the Danes had truly gone by pursuing them to the edge of the forest, checking the wounded and dead of both friend and foe, and, of course, looting the corpses of the Danes left behind. The two men stood staring down at the youth, the only sounds those common to the aftermath of a battle, the moans of the wounded being the most difficult to block out, yet Titus seemed oblivious to both the sound or their examination. Responding to a glance from Eadwig, Otha dropped to his haunches next to Titus, but while Titus did not lift his head, the Thegn saw the youth's eyes turn towards him in response to the movement.

"Well, boy?" Otha demanded. "Would you care to explain yourself?"

As he intended, this roused Titus from his stupor, and he lifted his head enough to look first to Otha, then up at Eadwig.

"Lord?" His voice was barely audible. "I don't understand."

For the first time, Otha's expression changed, though not

by much, just a slight upturn of the corner of his mouth framed by his beard, but Titus was in no condition to notice and be warned.

"Why didn't you tell us you were really a Dane?" Otha replied, then before Titus could respond, he added, "And one of their Berserkers at that."

Perhaps if he had had the time to gather his senses, Titus would have realized he was being teased, but he only frowned in confusion.

"But, I'm not a Dane, Lord!" he protested, shaking his head. "I swear it! I'm from…"

"Yes, I know," Otha interrupted. "You're Titus from Cissanbyrig." Otha stood up, thrusting his arm down, which Titus clasped and, with a fair amount of effort, pulled the youth to his feet.

He was unsteady, certainly, yet he managed to remain standing, and it was Eadwig who spoke next. Stepping in front of Titus, his expression still impassive, he said nothing for a long moment, seemingly content to examine the youth, who, under normal circumstances, would have averted his eyes. Not this time, however, choosing instead to look Eadwig in the eye, but with his face still covered in the blood that belonged to the Danes he had killed yet had no recollection of, and it was impossible for the Ealdorman to read what was there. Finally, Eadwig broke the silence.

"You," he said gravely, "saved the life of not just my son, but my heir…Titus of Cissanbyrig." He would never know for sure, but Titus guessed that the nobleman had been about to call him a "boy" again then thought better of it. He continued, "And for that, I owe you a debt. Tell me what it is I can do for you, and if it's in my power, I will grant it."

Even with a mind benumbed by an almost overwhelming fatigue, Titus did not hesitate.

"I want to be a warrior, my Lord. I want to fight for you in the shield wall." Then, before either man could respond, he thought to add, "At least to start with, but I want to be a thegn, Lord, and I know I have to earn that in battle."

Neither answered immediately, choosing instead to exchange a glance that communicated their amusement, and their surprise, at the youth's naked ambition, and perhaps most surprisingly, his willingness to express it. It was yet another trait that he shared with his namesake from centuries earlier, something that neither he nor the men standing before him would ever know.

Eadwig gave a slight nod, which Otha interpreted correctly, because it was the Thegn who said, "I believe you've proven yourself, so yes, on behalf of Ealdorman Eadwig, we agree to your request, Titus…the Berserker."

It was a moment that Titus would treasure only in retrospect, but in the moment, all he could offer was a mumbled, "Thank you, my Lord Eadwig. And," he bowed his head to Otha, "Lord Otha."

The pair turned away, leaving Titus standing there wondering, What am I supposed to do now?

Eadwig ordered that camp be made just a short distance away, upwind of the Danes whose bodies were left to rot and next to another stream. Hasty graves were dug by the surviving slaves, and aided by a fair number of ceorls, the Saxon dead were interred, including Dudda. By the Ealdorman's order, Titus had been excused from any tasks, but to his intense relief, the string of spare horses had been retrieved by Otha's men and returned to the baggage train. As far as Dudda was concerned, as Titus gradually emerged from the fog of whatever spell he had been under, he had decidedly mixed feelings. Certainly he had not liked the fat stableman, and if he had been asked just the day before, Titus would have sworn that he hated him with a passion. And yet, now, he realized that, while he certainly disliked the man, he still felt badly about his death, if only because of how it happened, and Titus was finding it difficult to suppress the manner in which he had perished, the image of his intestines sliding out from his greasy tunic and becoming entangled with his feet seemingly burned into his memory. He did wonder how many men it had taken to drag him to his grave, and how much bigger the grave had to be dug to accommodate the dead stableman's girth, but these were just fleeting thoughts.

More than anything, Titus could not get himself clean quickly enough, all of the blood and gore that had quickly dried and caked on seemingly every inch of his exposed skin so thick that he was forced to scrub with sand from the stream bottom. Worst of all was his tunic, although his trousers were only slightly better off, the former garment so thoroughly soaked with the blood of the man he had slain that when he stripped it off and dunked it into the water of the stream, it created a trail of red that he watched flowing downstream in the afternoon sun, yet no matter how hard he scrubbed it against the rocks lining the bank, there was still a dark stain that was so big, it essentially made the tunic another color, darker than the dull brown that it had been. The upper part of his trousers, like the tunic the only item of clothing of that type in his possession, were not quite as bad, yet he was certain that even those would be stained from the knees down. For some reason, this bothered him, and even after dunking himself and rubbing his skin raw, he still did not feel clean. This made him wonder whether it was his imagination, or if there was *something* that prevented him from truly washing away the blood of the man he had slain. More out of resignation that this was going to be the best he could do than any sense he had accomplished his goal, Titus wrung his trousers and tunic out as much as he could, not relishing the thought of putting on wet clothing, despite the temperature being relatively mild. He briefly considered letting both garments dry in the sun, but a quick glance upward informed him that this would accomplish nothing, so he resolved himself to being cold and miserable. And, he suddenly realized, hungry; this was the first moment he recalled that he had been unable to consume the food that he had hidden away in the wagon, so he began moving towards it, surprised to see that the oxen had been unhitched. He had not done it, nor had he done anything with any of the other stock pulling the carts, and while he recalled that he had been excused from his duties, he still felt a stab of anxiety at what Ealdorman Eadwig and Lord Otha might think of him. Would they think he was taking advantage? This thought consumed him so much that it was not until he actually reached the back of the wagon before he realized that he was the subject of scrutiny.

Fires had been built, several of them, around which were men of the fyrd, combatant and noncombatant alike, and to Titus, it seemed as if every single man squatting or sitting around those fires as they cooked their meal was looking at him. It was a quite peculiar sensation; yes, he was accustomed to being the object of attention because of his size, yet he was certain that this time it was for a different reason. His hunger overwhelmed his curiosity, and he hopped up into the wagon and retrieved the sack. When he dropped back to the ground, his first impulse was to head to the nearest fire, where he saw that the other men gathered around it were other noncombatant servants and slaves of Eadwig's fyrd, but for some reason, this repelled him. However, he did not feel right about walking over to where he saw Cenric, Heard, Wulfric, and some of the other men with whom he had become friendly were, so he simply dropped down and leaned against the wagon wheel as he opened the sack. So consumed with the idea of satiating his hunger, when Eadward cleared his throat, Titus was startled to the point that he let out a yelp, which embarrassed him yet seemed to make the young lordling feel better.

"May I join you, Titus?"

"Of course, Lord." Titus, out of a lifetime of habit, began to climb to his feet, but Eadward immediately waved him back down, choosing to drop to the ground himself.

For a long moment, neither youth said a word, but Titus had the excuse of stuffing the food he had managed to scrounge into his mouth.

"I just wanted to thank you, Titus." Eadward finally broke

the silence. "You saved my life, and I wanted to let you know that I'll never forget it."

Eadward would have been surprised to know that Titus' first thought was: I wish Leofflaed and Eadgyd were here right now!

Outwardly, Titus managed awkwardly, "It was my duty, Lord. I was only doing my duty."

"Why?" Eadward countered immediately. "Why do you say that? You're not one of my father's ceorls. In fact," the lordling pointed out, not in a contentious manner but as a matter of fact, "you're one of Ealdorman Wulfhere's. You really don't owe me or my father anything."

Titus had never considered the matter in this light, and the piece of bread hovered inches from his mouth as he frowned, thinking about it.

"I saw," he spoke slowly, "a man of *Westseaxe* in danger. So," he shrugged, "I suppose I just did what came naturally."

"What came naturally?" It was the manner in which Eadward asked this that arrested Titus' attention, and he glanced at the lordling to see Eadward looking at him with sharp interest. "Do you not know what you did?"

The fact was that Titus still had no idea; everything in his mind concerning that moment was still jumbled up, a series of disjointed images that even now made no real sense to him.

Nevertheless, he felt that he needed to offer something, so he answered slowly, "I saw Thunor take that spear." He stopped abruptly at the twist of pain on Eadward's face, and as awkward as it felt, he leaned forward to place a hand on the lordling's arm nonetheless. "And, I'm truly sorry for your loss, my Lord. He was a good horse. Not," he added hurriedly, "that I know all that much about them, but I'm learning." Returning to the topic, Titus thought for a moment, yet nothing more than the image of Thunor rearing, then toppling over on his side and trapping Eadward would come to him. Finally, all he could offer was another shrug. “I killed a Dane who was about to kill you. You would have done the same for me.” He said this with a confidence and, honestly, a complimentary tone that he hoped sounded sincere, which it was, to a point.

Eadward’s response was to say nothing, staring only at Titus’ face, giving Titus the feeling that the other youth was trying to determine something.

“You *really* don’t know, do you?” He said this in a questioning manner as if he was trying to test it out before making a declaration, and he obviously got his answer in Titus’ bewildered gaze. “Titus,” Eadward suddenly asked, “how many men do you think you killed?”

“Just the one who killed Thunor, Lord,” Titus answered honestly.

Eadward shook his head as he assured Titus, “That’s not true, Titus. I mean,” he modified, “yes, you *did* kill that Dane. But,” he took a breath, “you killed three more of them.”

This startled and alarmed Titus, but the mention of more foes also jarred another image from wherever it was hiding in his mind.

“You mean that I helped one of the others kill more Danes,” Titus mused, then admitted, “I don’t remember that, but if you saw it happen…”

“I didn’t see it happen because I was trapped under Thunor,” Eadward countered. “But everyone else did. Titus,” for the first time he showed some excitement, a reminder of how much youths on the edge of manhood hunger for glory, and when he thought about it later, Titus would realize that the emotion he was not able to place in the lordling’s voice in this moment was envy, “that’s all anyone is talking about! That’s why everyone is looking over here!”

This caused Titus to turn his attention back to the other fires, which were slowly becoming brighter as the daylight faded, but it was the manner in which some of the ceorls quickly looked away as his eyes fell on them that supported Eadward's assertion.

There was a silence, then Titus spoke slowly, "So what are they saying I did?"

Eadward's reply was immediate.

"That after you killed the bastard who killed Thunor, you picked up his ax and ran at the Danes, without a shield!" Eadward's voice betrayed the excitement as he related, "The second man you killed was carrying a sword, and a shield, but you split his shield with *one blow*, and when he tried to gut you with his sword, you jumped out of the way then cut him down. And," he added with a special kind of glee, "you almost took his head off with one stroke!" Now, thoroughly warmed to the subject, Eadward hurried on, "Another of those dogs saw you do it, and you had your back turned to him, but when he ran at you to put a spear through your back, you were already turning around as if you knew he was coming, and you started running at him the same way he was coming at you, so he missed with the spear." Eadward stopped then, but this time, it was to tease Titus.

Finally, Titus could not stand it any longer and demanded, "Well? What are they saying I did?"

"Oh not much," Eadward answered nonchalantly. "The Dane wasn't expecting you to react so quickly, and he certainly wasn't expecting you to go rushing at him, and because you got inside the point of his spear so quickly, you split his skull with the ax."

Eadward's words once more jarred something loose, except this time, it was the memory of a sensation, the feeling of a warm, sticky liquid spraying directly in Titus' face and chest, and how some of it had gotten into his mouth…and he had not cared. Indeed, Titus was realizing, in the moment, he had reveled in the salty taste, feeling a fierce, vicious joy at what it meant. Now, however, he felt his stomach lurch, and the cheese he had been about to shove into his mouth was dropped back into the sack.

"That's three," Titus reminded Eadward, who flushed slightly.

"Ah, yes. Right," Eadward mumbled. Frowning as he was, it seemed to Titus that he was trying to recall, but it was more because the young lord was having a hard time deciding which version to offer, because in his short period of time circulating the fires with his father, he had heard three versions that, while they all ended with Titus slaying his fourth Dane, the details varied. Deciding on partial honesty, he told Titus, "I heard from Cenric that right after you split that one's head, you looked around and saw that some of them had surrounded one of Ceadda's mounted men and they were about to unhorse him, so you drew their attention somehow."

He stopped, which prompted Titus' query. "How did I do it?"

"That," Eadward sighed, "depends on who you ask. Cenric said he heard you shout something at them that they seemed to understand."

This made no sense to Titus, who pointed out, "I don't know how to speak their tongue."

"I know, but Wigmund said he heard you curse their mothers in their tongue too," Eadward replied. "But what matters is that you drew two of them away, and when they came at you, you didn't move, you just stood there. This," Eadward admitted, "is where I've heard different things. Cenric says you dropped the ax, but it was to pick up a spear, and the Dane was running too fast to stop, and he ran himself onto the point. But Wigmund swears that you picked it up, but you threw it."

He stopped, and Titus considered for a moment, frowning in confusion before he shrugged and said, "Why does it matter whether I threw it or not?" He shook his head in frustration. "I don't remember it anyway."

"I suppose it doesn't," Eadward acknowledged.

Something occurred to Titus, and he asked, "You said two Danes came at me. What happened to the other one?"

"Aedelstan," Eadward answered. "He was Ceadda's man under attack. He cut the Northman down who was trying to kill him, then he ran the second Dane down from behind before he got to you. Not," he finished with a laugh, "that it sounds like you needed help."

Eadward had decided not to divulge the third version he had heard, although it was essentially a variation of Cenric's version, where the Dane ran himself onto Titus' spear, but where it differed was that more than one ceorl, and Aedelstan, had sworn that Titus had used the spear to pick the Dane up off the ground and flung him aside as if he was flicking a chunk of meat off of his eating knife, then had calmly bent down and picked the ax back up that he had been using. That, Eadward told himself, was impossible, so he did not mention it. They lapsed into silence, and Eadward was about to stand up and leave, not sure what else to say, when, from the growing darkness, a pair of figures approached that both youths quickly identified, causing them to scramble to their feet.

"Father," Eadward called out, then, "Otha."

Titus only mumbled the words; what was important to him was that he bowed his head, but this seemed to irritate the Ealdorman, who said gruffly, "No time for that…Titus."

Rather than say anything else, he turned his attention to Otha, which was when Titus noticed that the Thegn had his hands full, but he had not seen there was a third figure behind them until Otha stepped slightly to the side. It was this man who Titus saw was carrying a shield and spear, although not in a manner that suggested it was his. As he stepped next to Otha, only then did Titus recognize him as one of Ceadda's men, vaguely recalling him as one of the four who had been following behind him and the spare horses.

It was Otha who spoke next, but it was to turn to indicate the third man as he said, "Aedelstan has something to say to you."

For the first time, Titus noticed that this man at arms, who was no longer wearing his armor, was not all that much older than Titus, although he wore a full beard, and while he seemed embarrassed, he did not hesitate to say, "I owe you my life, Titus of Cissanbyrig. I was under attack by three of those savages when you appeared. Because two of them went after you, I was able to kill the one left with me." This was the moment his purpose in holding shield and spear became evident, because he extended them. "These belonged to the Dane I killed. While by right they're my spoils, I'd like you to have them as a token of my thanks."

This was completely outside of the youth's experience, and he looked first to Otha, and the Thegn gave a slight nod of encouragement, enough for Titus to take a step forward and tentatively reach out, taking the shield with his left hand and the spear with his right. Before he could stop himself, he felt a grin splitting his face, but when he gave a shy glance at the three adults, they were all smiling broadly, even Ealdorman Eadwig. Then it was Otha's turn to offer something, what turned out to be a boiled leather vest, but what made it unique was that it was larger than the average size, made of not one but two thicknesses of leather.

"We took this off the biggest bastard we could find," the Thegn said as he held it out. "It's not mail, but it's still better protection than your tunic."

Titus was at a temporary loss since his hands were full, but Eadward came to the rescue, relieving him of his burden as he said cheerfully, "I knew this was happening. I was supposed to keep you occupied until they got here."

The best, at least in Titus' mind, was yet to come, when Ealdorman Eadwig took a couple paces to stand in front of the youth, and while what he held in his hand was not nearly as large, nor in practical terms as valuable as armor, shield, and spear for a youth aspiring to stand in the shield wall, in their world, it mattered more than all of it combined.

"This arm ring," Eadgar spoke with a solemnity that was clearly transmitted to any man within hearing, "once belonged to a Dane. In fact, it belonged to a Dane who was slain by Titus of Cissanbyrig today. And, while by rights as Ealdorman, it is mine, I am bestowing this arm ring to its *rightful* owner, Titus of Cissanbyrig." With his free hand, Eadgar reached out to clasp Titus by the shoulder, squeezing it so hard that it was almost painful, which the youth correctly interpreted as the signal that this was not the time for humility, that the man he had sworn was his new lord expected him to look him in the eye, as a man. That he had to tilt his head downward did not lessen the gravity, nor the emotion surging through Titus as Eadwig spoke in ringing tones, loudly enough that every man around every fire could hear, "As of this moment, Titus of Cissanbyrig, you are no longer working in the stables. You have proven yourself to be worthy of standing in the shield wall of the fyrd marching for me, Ealdorman Eadwig of Wiltun!" As he placed the arm ring, which was made of silver and felt heavier than Titus would have thought into his palm, Eadgar raised his voice to a bellow as he proclaimed, "I believe these are just the first of *many* Danes who will be slain by Titus! Titus the *Berserker*!"

For the rest of his days, of all that was to come, with all the battles, all the dead, all the bleeding, suffering, and dying, this would stand as one of Titus' proudest moments, one to which he would refer back often in the coming time.

Chapter Five

While Ealdorman Eadwig had been sincere in his command that Titus was no longer a stableboy, it was the youth himself who approached the Ealdorman with what, at first, seemed to be an unusual request.

"Lord, I'd like to keep tending to the horses, at least for the next few days."

It was the next morning, and Eadwig was seated by the remnants of his fire, gnawing on a pork knuckle, and he looked up in surprise at the youth, although his tone passed for mild as he asked curiously, "Why?"

"Well," Titus explained, "with Dudda…dead," it still felt strange to say the word, "I'm the only one who has any experience with Hama."

"That," Eadgar allowed, "is true. But Hakon has experience with horses."

Hakon was one of the slaves that had been brought as part of the fyrd, and Titus pointed out, "He's a Danish slave, Lord. We're marching to fight the Danes. Do you trust him with your animals? Especially Hama?"

Titus instantly saw this resonated with the Ealdorman, who nodded thoughtfully.

Finally, he made his decision, standing up to deliver it, "You're right, Titus. I want you to tend to your normal duties at least until we join with Alfred at…"

He stopped himself, while Titus barely managed to escape without betraying Eadward's confidence by not blurting out their destination of King Egbert's Stone, which he managed to cover by saying hastily, "Yes, Lord. I'll do my best."

"That," Eadwig offered his version of a smile, "is something I do not doubt, boy."

Dismissed, Titus returned to the wagon, where Hakon was standing. While it was true that he was a Dane, Titus found it impossible to believe that he had been a warrior, and he reminded himself to ask Eadward what he knew about the man. In his mid-thirties, he was scrawny in build, although Titus was certain that some of this was due to the kind of diet that his type of captive received. He was not starving, certainly, but even through the thin tunic that was filthier than normal, when he leaned over, Titus could see the outlines of his ribs through the cloth. It was his demeanor that, somewhat oddly, actually put Titus on his guard, because Hakon behaved much like a dog who is expecting to be whipped for the slightest transgression, and his eyes were constantly roving around as if he was alert for an irate overseer to suddenly appear to beat him. Which, Titus recognized, was a real possibility.

Hakon eyed him uncertainly, while Titus suddenly realized, with some embarrassment, that he had not thought to ask the Ealdorman, so he posed his question to Hakon. "Do you speak our tongue?"

"Some…Lord," Hakon spoke hesitantly, licking his lips when he realized Titus was expecting more. "I…" he searched for the correct word, "…understand it more good than speak, Lord."

"That's all that matters, I suppose," Titus muttered to himself.

The pair stood there as Titus started to absorb the ramifications of his own request; he was, he realized, in effect now Dudda. It was an odd sensation, one that he would have cause to remember, the moment where for the first time in his life he was issuing orders and not just taking them.

With this in mind, he pointed to the picket enclosure that was nothing more than stakes pounded into the ground in a large circle, around each of which a long rope had been looped, the only security aside from the guards who had stood duty during the night that kept the spare horses from wandering off or being stolen, although after the events of the day before, it was deemed unlikely.

"Put the horses on their leads," he instructed. "We're going to be leaving soon."

Hakon nodded; more importantly, he did not hesitate, hurrying off to do as he had been instructed, while Titus walked over to where Hama had been staked to the ground, just a few paces away from where the Ealdorman had lain. Everyone was up, preparations underway, and the stallion was in his usual high spirits, giving Titus a bit more trouble than normal.

"You're lucky Dudda's dead," Titus said reprovingly, "or I'd have him come do it and see how you like it then!"

The animal's response was a snort that made Titus smile, even as he wondered if he should be feeling something for his lack of sorrow over the fat stableman's death. It was, he thought, a strange thing, what a difference a day could make in his life. At this time the day before, they had left the Ealdorman's hall, and all that Titus of Cissanbyrig had to look forward to was the prospect of tending the horses while enduring Dudda's foulness in temper and actions. These thoughts occupied his mind as his hands went through the familiar process of saddling Hama, then leading the animal to where the Ealdorman was involved in a discussion with Otha, Aelfnod, and Ceadda, while Eadward lingered just a few paces away.

Eadwig barely glanced at Titus, accepting the reins with a nod as he continued, "Barring another ambush, we should be there by late afternoon. But," his tone hardened, "I know I don't have to remind you to keep the men alert. We obviously know there are Danes skulking about, but if God favors us, they learned a hard lesson yesterday."

Titus was already walking away, although he managed to hear all of this, and he moved to the wagon next, his other major responsibility, leading the oxen, which had to be kept separately from the horses and staked to the ground like Hama because of their tendency to wander off, back to the wagon.

"Do you know how to drive the wagon?" Titus asked Hakon, who shook his head.

"By the blood," Titus groaned in dismay.

The problem was that he did not either, at least not anything as large as this wagon. Yes, his father had a ramshackle two-wheeled cart, but it was pulled by a horse that Leofric would have to borrow from another farmer, and Titus could count on one hand the times he had been allowed to drive it. This was entirely different, but he would not return to Ealdorman Eadwig to inform him of this deficiency, although it was not totally because of his youthful pride. He had been the one to propose remaining as the stableman for the time being, and he should have taken his lack of experience into consideration before he did so.

"Hopefully," he muttered to himself as he climbed up onto the seat in response to the blown horn command, "it's not that much different than walking behind a plow."

After some nervous moments, Titus grew more confident in his ability to drive the wagon. He was also acutely aware that it helped that they were moving in an essentially straight line, following what he could see was a well-traveled road, but early in the day, his stomach began clenching at the sight before him. Beginning as a dark green line, it slowly resolved itself into what Titus identified as trees, but clustered so thickly that he did not see how Ealdorman Eadwig would be able to penetrate what was the densest forest he had ever seen. Titus of Cissanbyrig, since this was how he still thought of himself despite the events of the day before, was the farthest he had been away from home in his life, but he knew what he was looking at, the eastern edge of the Selwood Forest. As inexperienced as Titus may have been in warfare, he instinctively knew that thick woods such as this were even better places for ambush, but he took comfort in the manner in which the men who were walking along in a shambling march ahead of him gradually subsided in their conversations. It certainly helped that this road was one of the best that the youth had ever traveled on; the fact that he was literally walking in the footsteps of ancestors, at least one of whom had actually labored on creating this road eight hundred years earlier as a Legionary of Rome would be something he would never know, and it would not be for a few years yet before he was even aware that the road network that was used by all who traveled through this land predated the coming of the Saxons.

The column briefly halted when Eadwig and his thegns sent four mounted men at arms forward, into the darkness of the forest, and there was a brief buzzing sound as the ceorls of the fyrd talked quietly among themselves. Titus took the opportunity to hop down from the wagon to relieve himself, then went to check on Hakon, who was standing uncertainly, holding the leads for the spare mounts, now two horses less because Eadward was riding one of them, and Ceadda's man, whose horse had been so grievously injured it had to be destroyed, the other. The rearguard this day was by Otha's men, who Titus knew better, albeit slightly, and one of them called out to him.

"The Ealdorman needs to send you in there first, Berserker! Those Danes won't stand a chance!"

The manner in which the man, his name Willmar, said this told Titus that he did not mean it in a mocking manner, while the other three men responded with laughs of their own.

"Next time, you need to save some for us, Berserker," the youngest of the four said. "My woman has expensive tastes, and I can't afford to keep her without loot."

His name was Uhtric, and he was a handsome man in his early twenties, with a growing reputation as a warrior. Most importantly, he had always been friendly towards Titus from his first days with Eadwig and was openly sympathetic of the youth's plight with Dudda.

Encouraged by their behavior, Titus grinned up at them and said, "I'll try to remember, Lord."

"Not Lord." Uhtric sighed. "I've told you before. Just Uhtric is fine."

"But he's not lying about Ealdgyd," the oldest warrior spoke up. He was formidable-looking, if only because of a diagonal scar that crossed from just above his left eye and down across his nose, leaving the left orb a milky white, but he was also thickly built. "Poor Uhtric here might have to kill twenty Danes all by himself to keep her happy!"

Ignoring the jibes from his other companions, Uhtric simply shrugged and said, "She's worth it, and you're all just jealous."

Before anything else could be said, the thin wail of the horn gave the warning that the march was about to resume, and immediately, all signs of levity were gone.

As Titus walked back to the wagon, Uhtric called out, "Stay alert, Titus. I don't think these bastards will try again after yesterday, not this close to Egbert's Stone at least, but it pays to be ready."

Lifting a hand in acknowledgment, Titus vaulted up onto the seat and picked up the reins just in time as the column resumed moving. Entering into the Selwood Forest would have been ominous even without a threat of Danes; the sun had been shining brightly from a partly cloudy sky, but within a matter of paces within the forest, the gloom was such that it was hard for Titus to make out any details, other than a thick screen of varying shades of green that culminated in the arcing trees above him that almost completely enclosed the track and only offered an occasional glimpse of the sky. For his part of the world, the track was wider than normal, another vestige that it had once been a Roman road; all that mattered to him was that there was space on either side of the wagon where there was no cover, if only a few paces. Not surprisingly, he was extremely tense, and despite his lack of experience, he could see just in the body language of the men walking ahead of him, both those leading the carts, and the spearmen of the rearmost ranks of the fyrd that they were as alert as he was. He did not know whether the spearmen had been ordered to do so, but Titus did notice that they were evenly divided across their four ranks, with a pair of men looking in one direction, and the other pair the opposite. Moreover, he saw that one man's attention was not on the ground level; instead, they were scanning the trees, something that had not occurred to Titus would be a possible source of trouble. Do Northmen hide up in the trees? he thought with some dismay, and immediately began trying to divide his attention between performing the relatively simple task of guiding the wagon and swiveling his head from one side to the other.

It was not until they were about halfway through the forest that Titus began to relax, and when they emerged into the sunshine unscathed, his tunic was soaked with perspiration that had nothing to do with the temperature. Only after they were away from the forest did Titus spot thin trails of smoke ahead on the horizon, and while it was not unusual to see, the number of them seemed to indicate to the youth that a town was up ahead, but as limited as his knowledge of the world more than a day's walk from his hamlet was, he did not think there was a town in the area. Before too much time had elapsed, the column drew near enough for him to be certain that up ahead was Egbert's Stone, where the king had called his fyrd! It must be, he thought with rising excitement, and even from his seat, Titus could see the tents dotting the crest of a low hill in the distance. When they were perhaps a mile off, he could make out that one tent was, by a substantial margin, the largest, but more than anything, it was its location in what Titus could now see was the rough center of the camp that told him that, almost certainly, this had to be the tent of the King! For the moment, all thoughts of battle slipped away at the thought that he, Titus of Cissanbyrig, was going to be in the presence of King Alfred himself! He had long before lost count of the number of times the thought, or more accurately, the wish that his sisters had been present had come to him, and this was just the latest. Following hard on the heels of that was another, far more unpleasant one; what if his father had gone through with it and answered the fyrd called by Ealdorman Wulfhere and that Wulfhere was actually loyal to King Alfred? He did not think it likely, given his absolute certainty that Wulfhere had gone over to the Dane Lord Guthrum, who Titus knew styled himself as King Guthrum, and of all the things Titus knew of Leofric, it was that his father was a coward and unlikely to put himself in danger, unless he had no other choice. Despite his youth and lack of any education, Titus had a quick mind, and while his faith in his conclusion was certainly influenced by his tender age and the confidence that is possessed by young men on the verge of manhood, his logic about Wulfhere's treachery was sound. Guthrum and his bands had been roving all over the lands that belonged to Ealdorman Wulfhere for months since they took Cippinhamm, and yet, despite some stories of rowdy, drunken Danes pawing at the local women, Wulfhere's holdings had been left almost completely untouched.

Indeed, prior to the day before, Titus had never actually seen a Northman with his own eyes, although his father had claimed to see a warband of them riding past their farm, a claim that he doubted, if only for the reason that he found it unlikely that these supposed Danes would not at least stop at their home, even as ramshackle as it was. Hidden deep within his mind, there was a conviction that, *if* Leofric had been telling it true, the reason the Danes had not descended on the farm was because, even from a distance, it was easy to see there was nothing of value there worth taking or even looking for. It was a thought that, whenever it managed to force itself out into the forefront of his mind, made him flush with the shame of it, although at the same time, he supposed he should be thankful, because Leofric's poverty meant that his sisters had not been subjected to the treatment he had heard men talking angrily about in Cissanbyrig. No, he told himself again, Leofric isn't here, because Wulfhere isn't going to be here, yet it was one of those nagging ideas that he could not seem to keep from forcing its way through.

So absorbed was he that, when he felt the wagon suddenly lurch as the oxen began straining to drag it up the slope, he almost lost his seat, just barely managing to grab the edge of the wooden bench to keep him in his spot. Glancing guiltily over his shoulder, he was relieved to see that Uhtric and the other outriders were nowhere to be seen, and only Hakon was behind him, and he was too busy paying attention to the spare horses to notice; it was not until he turned back around that he saw them cantering up the hill towards a cluster of men who, by their appearance, were waiting to welcome Eadwig and the men of his fyrd. Being the last to arrive, Titus missed most of the jocular, rough-edged humor that he would learn was standard behavior for warriors, as the men from the other noblemen's fyrds hailed Eadwig's men. It was probably a good thing, he realized, because for the first time, Titus was forced to actually do more to drive the wagon than just slapping and pulling on the double reins to start and stop, but guide the conveyance through the canvas tents arranged in a fashion that, like the marching column, would have enraged his Roman ancestors. Since this was his first military camp, Titus could make neither heads nor tails of any sort of order, but he would come to learn that there *was* an organization of sorts, based on the structure of his society. Moving slowly, he managed to maneuver the wagon to the spot Otha indicated, while Hakon obediently followed along with the spare mounts.

"Once you take care of the animals," Otha ordered him, "you help set up the tents."

"Yes, Lord," Titus replied, but then, even as he knew he should not, he blurted out, "Once I'm finished with that, will someone work with me?"

"Work with you?" Otha echoed, confused at first, then his face cleared, although the scowl was not encouraging. "You mean with handling a spear and shield, boy?" Titus nodded, and Otha's first inclination was to snap that this was not the time for such things, but then, remembering what Eadwig had decreed, realized that it was not unreasonable for the youth to ask.

"I'll have Uhtric spend some time with you," he said, somewhat grudgingly. "But only after I check on all that you were supposed to do and if I'm satisfied. Understood?"

He was not surprised when the youth nodded eagerly, but Otha had other things to do and was already turning away, missing the broad grin on Titus' face.

It took a great deal of effort on Titus' part not to rush through the tasks he had been given, although he was sufficiently experienced so he could work quickly when unhitching the animals, then leading them to the oxen enclosure, joining the more than two dozen other animals from the rest of what was, to Titus' eye, the largest group of people he had ever seen before. And, it seemed, nobody really seemed to know what to do, if the angry bellows of thegns was any indication. The slaves naturally bore the brunt of the ire, as the ceorls who were chastised by the thegns turned their wrath on the slaves, snarling at them, usually with a poorly aimed slap or kick that sent them scrambling.

"Here, help me unload the tent poles and headpieces," Titus commanded Hakon, who somewhat to Titus' surprise, obeyed readily.

The fact that Titus, having seen the high temper of the other men, had experienced a sense of protectiveness over the Danish slave was something that he would never divulge to anyone, not even Hakon, but the youth had an instinctive dislike of anyone who used their status as an excuse to bully others. It would only be over a period of time as he matured that he would understand this instinct more fully; in this moment, it was an unformed impulse.

The poles for all of the tents were carried in the wagon,

along with the large pieces of wood that served as the crown of each tent, in which holes were drilled at an angle the circumference of the poles so that it created a stable structure, around which sections of canvas were attached. The canvas was carried in the carts and on the packhorses, and one could see by the tent itself the relative rank of the occupants. Those designated for the use by ceorls were unpainted, and from what Titus could see, were constructed of a material that could only be charitably called canvas, providing a bare modicum of protection. Thegns like Otha, Aelfnod, and Ceadda possessed tents that were not only larger, but the canvas panels were painted, albeit in muted colors of a single shade that, Titus supposed, made them even more water and weatherproof. Ealdorman Eadwig's tent was, naturally, larger than Otha's, and while it was painted, it was in a dark blue, but each panel was adorned with a rearing stallion, in red, which Titus was informed Eadwig had adopted as the symbol of his status as Ealdorman of Wiltun. Not only wider around at the base, it was taller by at least two feet, so that even someone Titus' height could stand erect except for the area immediately next to the sides. Nevertheless, it was nothing compared to the tent of the King, which was almost twice the size of the other nobles', with the panels painted a rich red and with not one but three golden wyverns on each panel. Once Titus had a chance to walk around a bit, he saw that, despite appearances, there was an order of sorts. The camp itself was circular in nature, with Alfred's tent in the center, and as Otha led him and Hakon to an open area, the Thegn pointed to a pair of stakes.

"You need to put all of our tents up in between these stakes," he instructed. "Ealdorman Eadwig's tent will be set up closest to the King's tent. Then," he turned and paced off a distance, "you'll put my tent here. Lord Ceadda's tent will be next to mine, and Lord Aelfnod's will be on the other side of Ceadda's. The rest," he pointed downhill, "must be erected between the stakes down there. But you're only responsible for the Ealdorman's and our tents."

Otha did not specify who "our" tents were, but Titus

assumed, correctly, it was the three thegns, but even if he had been disposed to ask, Otha had already stalked off, leaving Titus and Hakon to stare at each other.

"Have you ever set up a tent before, Hakon?"

When the slave nodded, Titus made no attempt to hide his relief, nor did he feel awkward about saying, "Then I'll let you tell me what to do."

Titus only understood he had said something unusual by the manner in which Hakon eyed him, as if he was suspicious that Titus was playing a trick on him, but neither did he hesitate. They had dumped the pile of poles on the ground, most of which Hakon had carried, but only because Titus had, of his own accord and after testing the weight, grabbed the wooden headpieces as his own, stacking them on top of each other.

It only took a brief glance for Hakon to realize something, and he said tentatively, "We are missing pieces." Before Titus could ask what they were, the slave turned and moved at a trot, and because Titus hesitated, by the time he reached the wagon, Hakon had already retrieved what, to Titus' eye, appeared to be nothing more than short pieces of wood, also round, but he could tell they were larger than the tent poles. There were a dozen of them, but it was as Hakon handed some to Titus that the slave explained, "These are the sockets that connect the poles of Lord Eadwig's tent."

While the word "socket" had no meaning to Titus, he immediately saw that both ends of the pieces of wood had been hollowed out, although not for the entire length of the piece. Returning to where Eadwig's tent would go, they saw that the sections of canvas had been dumped on the ground, for the first time causing a reaction from the Danish slave that, frankly, Titus found curious.

"Those pigs," he heard the Dane mutter. "They do not treat the Ealdorman's property with enough respect."

Before Titus could query Hakon about why a slave would care, the Dane picked up a pole, then slid one of the shorter pieces of wood over one end, instantly demonstrating to Titus the purpose.

"That," he said admiringly as, on his own, he picked up a second pole to put it in the opposite end, "is clever."

"I know," Hakon agreed. Then, for the first time in their short association, the slave offered something that could almost pass for a smile as he said, "You Saxons copied us."

For the rest of his days, Titus would remember this moment where, for what would be the first but not the last time, he learned that these Northmen were not simply bloodthirsty savages who knew only rapine, looting, and slaughter.

Now that Titus knew what was expected, the pair worked quickly enough, and it was here that they both learned that Titus' height held some advantages, because it made sliding the connected poles into the holes of the headpiece easier. When they were finished with the frame, what Titus saw was a structure made up of four poles each along three sides, with two poles on one side that, as Titus would learn, would be where the flaps, or entrance into the tent would be. Naturally, the entrance faced inward, towards Alfred's tent. Next, Hakon showed Titus how to hang the pieces of canvas from the pegs protruding from the headpiece, then stretch each panel out, and using leather thongs tie the edge of each panel to a pole.

"You have to make the knot like this." Hakon showed him how to create a slip knot. "If you do not, and it rains, the water will swell the leather and make it impossible to untie."

The canvas had holes in it, at evenly spaced intervals along each edge, and as Titus worked, he answered his own question, seeing that the hole had been reinforced by sewing around the circumference of the hole. Naturally, it took the longest to erect the Ealdorman's tent, and Titus became so absorbed in the task that he was unaware that young Eadward had been standing watching, arms crossed.

Unfortunately, it was what Titus took to be a smirk on the lordling's face that Titus saw first, so he misinterpreted

Eadward's attempt at jocularity, which in turn, the youngster had decided was what was expected, given the nature of their arrival.

"It took you two long enough," he called out. "I'm tired and want to rest, but I have to stand here waiting!"

It was thoughtless, but it was also not meant in a mean-spirited way, something that Titus realized only later; in the moment, before he could stop himself, he snapped, "Have you ever set up a tent in your life…*Lord*?"

The instant the words were out, Titus had to resist the urge to groan aloud, but to his credit, Eadward, while he flushed and, if Titus was any judge, angered, replied evenly, "No, I haven't, Titus. And," he said stiffly, "I apologize for giving offense."

Before Titus could say anything, Eadward spun about and stalked off, leaving the youth to watch him walk off in self-recrimination, thinking, Titus, you fool. He's a good friend to have, and you let your pride get the better of you…again.

For his part, Hakon watched silently, but while his expression was blank, Titus was almost certain that the Dane had watched this with some amusement.

"Let's get the other tents done," Titus muttered, walking past his partner towards the wagon.

By the time they were finished, and thanks to their relatively early arrival, there was still a fair amount of daylight left, yet even in the relatively short amount of time they had spent erecting the tents, Titus had learned a great deal, and not just in how to erect them, but in how the Saxons arranged their camp. It was, he realized, much like a spoked wheel, where the King's tent was the hub, and each Ealdorman and his retainers occupied the space between the spokes, although it was not an even distribution by any means. Cuthred, the Ealdorman of Hampscir, for example, had a much larger fyrd than Ealdorman Eadwig, so his part of the wheel occupied more space. Most importantly, the social hierarchy of the Saxons could easily be determined, just by the proximity of a tent to the King's; Ealdormen were the closest, thegns were in the next ring, and the higher-ranking ceorls, sharing a tent, were in the next. Those of the lowest rank were the farthest away, but as Titus was about to learn, his own unusual status meant that no man of Eadwig's fyrd had given any thought to where Titus of Cissanbyrig belonged. For the most part, the slaves were left to shift for themselves, something that Titus could see Hakon understood, because he had quickly claimed a spot under the wagon as his sleeping spot.

Similarly to the placement of tents, the arrangement of cooking fires followed the same hierarchy, the only difference being the relative number of men around each one. From what Titus could see, there was one fire for the Ealdorman, his son, and his thegns; another for the men at arms who marched for each thegn, meaning that there were three outside each tent. From there, it appeared as if there was a fire for every other tent, the men from two tents gathered around it, although at this moment, none of them seemed to be doing anything other than lounging around it. There was quite a bit of movement still, which Titus observed for a bit, reaching the determination that there were men who marched from other fyrds who sought out a man or men they knew. This seemed to be confined to those men at arms who marched for each thegn, which naturally drew most of Titus' attention as he stood by the wagon, uncertain whether or not he was supposed to seek Uhtric out, or if the man at arms was going to come to him.

Cenric, Wulfric, Osmund, and the other ceorls were at a fire outside one of the tents in the outer ring, and Titus wondered if he was going to be allowed to share their tent and evening meal, although he was far more concerned with the food. It was early May, the weather growing mild as the days marched towards summer, so sleeping out in the open did not disturb him; going hungry did. Just as he was about to go in search of him, Titus spotted Uhtric making his way through the tents, gnawing on what was the last of the previous year's apple crop, and he tossed the core on the ground as he reached Titus. He was carrying what, to Titus, looked like a spear shaft with no spear point on it, and his shield was strapped to his back, but Titus' eyes were fixed on the *seaxe* hanging from his hip, the true sign that Uhtric was more than just a ceorl.

"Lord Otha told me to come work with you." Uhtric's tone communicated that he was, at the very least, unenthusiastic about the prospect. The young warrior's eyes narrowed, and he demanded, "Where are your spear and shield, boy?"

"In the wagon," Titus replied, and he made the mistake of taking his eyes off Uhtric because he had begun to turn towards the wagon to retrieve them, so he did not see the blow coming.

It did not hurt, exactly, although he felt the air whooshing out of his lungs when his back collided with the ground, and he stared up in a combination of bewilderment and shock at Uhtric, who was grinning broadly.

"Your first lesson, boy," he said cheerfully, "is to be ready for anything." The smile vanished as he continued, "Because those Danish sons of whores aren't going to wait for you to be ready. I thought," he added quietly, "you would have learned that yesterday." Before Titus could reply, he extended a hand to help the youth up, but when Titus refused it, eyeing him warily as he climbed to his feet, he laughed and said approvingly, "Don't trust me, eh? Good. Now," Uhtric actually moved a couple paces away in a signal to Titus he had no more mischief in mind, "get your weapons."

Titus hopped into the wagon, which was still almost full, picking up the shield and spear from where he had placed them immediately next to the bench. His eye was caught by the boiled leather vest, and he thought about putting it on, but he felt sufficiently chastened for not being ready as it was, and he hopped down onto the ground without it. As he waited, Uhtric had unstrapped his own shield, but in a surprise move, as Titus was fumbling to get his arm through the leather strap of his own shield, the warrior tossed the shaft to Titus. Because the youth had thrust his spear into the ground to strap on his shield, he caught the shaft deftly enough, although Uhtric did not seem impressed.

"First things first," he began. "I want to see how useless you are with a spear. So," he dropped into a crouch as he swung his shield in front of him, "I want you to hit me with your best thrust."

"With just the shaft, Lord?" Titus asked, confused. "That makes it shorter, doesn't it?"

"It does," Uhtric agreed, "and don't call me Lord. I'm just Uhtric. But you don't think I'm going to let you stab my shield, do you? Besides, by learning how to gauge the distance with just a shaft, once the point is added, you'll be actually punching *through* your target."

Once explained, both points made sense to Titus, and he dropped into the crouch that he had adopted after his days of watching Otha working with the ceorls of the fyrd who were only spearmen, placing his left foot forward as he held up his shield, which Uhtric noticed, although his face betrayed nothing. Titus paused, attempting to surprise Uhtric, then his arm shot forward, the thrust originating from the side of his own shield, the blunt end striking Uhtric's protection a matter of inches from the large metal boss, which on Uhtric's shield protruded several inches and came to a point. The hollow crack of wood striking wood was loud enough that it attracted the attention of the men around the closest fires, although Titus did not notice this, mainly because the jarring collision had sent a shock wave of pain up his arm that instantly turned his hand numb. It was, he was certain, a solid thrust, but it only earned a sneer from the warrior.

"If that's the best you can do boy," he said mockingly, "you better stay with the horses. Besides," he taunted, "with Dudda gone, the Ealdorman *does* need a stableboy."

It was no accident that Uhtric had said this loudly enough for the other men to hear, and Titus' face burned at the roar of laughter from around him, although he refused to acknowledge it. The truth, however, was far different; Uhtric had been shocked at the raw power behind the youth's thrust, but he had wisely braced himself, having a good idea that just because of his size and musculature, Titus would acquit himself well. Even more surprising to him was the speed; despite his size, and that Uhtric was expecting it, the shaft had been a blur of motion that Uhtric had rarely witnessed. Still, it always did a youngster good to learn humility first, and Uhtric, having witnessed part of Titus' exploit of the day before, had little doubt that the youth had the makings of a formidable warrior. He also knew, however, that overconfidence had killed more aspiring warriors in their first battle than any foe.

More quietly, he told Titus, "You're using just your arm. And," he said grudgingly, "you're not the weakest I've seen, but you still need to put more than just your arm into it. Here," he commanded, "toss me the shaft and I'll show you."

Naturally, Titus did as he was ordered, but Uhtric had more than one lesson in mind again because, in almost one motion, he snatched the shaft out of the air, catching it at the exact spot he intended and which allowed his arm to move back towards his body in the same direction the shaft had been traveling so that his hand was instantly behind him. Then, in one smooth motion, he tilted the shaft down with a twist of his wrist parallel to the ground, but it was already shooting back in Titus' direction, an even sharper crack signaling the strike against Titus' shield, which unlike Uhtric's, had a low, round boss that barely allowed Titus' hand to grasp the handle. The blow caused Titus to stagger a step backward, and he was disappointed in himself for it, but unknown to him, Uhtric was equally disappointed because he had expected to send the boy reeling backward several steps.

"Now, did you see what I did?" Uhtric asked, not expecting that Titus had been concerned with anything other than blocking his thrust, so he was surprised when Titus answered immediately, "You turned your hips at the last moment."

This time, Uhtric did not bother trying to appear

unimpressed, nodding with approval as he cried, "Exactly! That's the best way to add to your power, to get your body involved. But," he cautioned, "you also don't want to overextend or twist your body so much that you have to move your anchor foot for balance."

"Why?" Titus asked, but rather than being angered, Uhtric simply said, "Grab your spear. But," he grinned, "reverse the point, and I'll show you why." Once Titus was ready, Uhtric barked, "Thrust!"

Naturally, Titus complied, and as Uhtric had gambled he would since this was his first attempt, Titus put too much torsion into his thrust and, as Uhtric had warned, he was forced to bring his right foot forward in an unconscious effort to maintain his balance. And, Uhtric instantly launched his own thrust, but while it was done with the same amount of power as his first one, and struck Titus' shield squarely, this time, it did send the youth reeling backward because his right foot was no longer in position to brace him.

"That's why," Uhtric answered, and while Titus' cheeks flushed, he also gave a thoughtful nod. Resuming his position, Uhtric said, "Try again."

By the time they were through, Titus' arms ached, the sun was touching the horizon, he was soaked with sweat...and happier than he had been since he arrived to serve in Eadwig's fyrd. Uhtric had done his best to hide it from the youth, but Titus could see that the warrior was deeply impressed, and he also knew it was not just because of his strength. Titus had always learned quickly, and in fact picked up things with a rapidity that earned his father's ire, who would always slap or kick the boy as he snarled at him for thinking he was cleverer than his father. By the time Titus was ten, he knew this as a matter of fact, but he was also wise enough to not antagonize his father by letting Leofric know that he was aware of this. By his third thrust, Titus had learned to control his body sufficiently so that his feet did not move, and Uhtric found himself in a position where he had to fully concentrate in order to brace himself for Titus' thrusts which, he was certain, were not only more powerful, but seemed to be coming more quickly with every one. Indeed, the warrior began to worry about the condition of his shield, although this was not his best one and the one he would carry into battle, but his experienced ear picked up the telltale sound of a shield in danger of splintering, which was why he finally ended the session.

"That," he told Titus honestly, "wasn't bad. Not bad at all."

While he was clearly pleased, Titus was also disappointed, understanding that Uhtric had worked with him as much as he was willing on this day.

"Tomorrow, can you teach me how to use my shield better?" he asked, and before he could think about it, the warrior nodded, then thought to add, "If we have time. We might be fighting tomorrow for all I know. That," he turned and indicated Alfred's tent with a nod of his head, "is what the King and Ealdorman Eadwig and the others are discussing right now, I'll wager."

Uhtric's answer caused a strange sensation in Titus' stomach, but he thanked the warrior, who only answered with a grunt as he walked up the hill towards the tent he was sharing with Otha and his comrades. By this time, the cooking had begun in earnest, the air filling with the smells of cooking meat and baking bread, making Titus' stomach shift its attention from the worry about impending battle to the more immediate concern of being filled. Hakon had left his spot under the wagon, but while Titus could not see him, he was certain that he was around the fires that were just beyond the last ring of tents where the servants, both slave and free, were gathered. Their rations were provided, although they were nowhere near the same quantity or quality as those for the free ceorls, and certainly not for the thegns and men at arms. Perhaps the only advantage they had was that, because they received the remnants left from the two meals the day before, they did not have to waste much time in preparation, but as hungry as Titus was, he had no desire to eat moldy bread. Besides which, his pride would not allow him to wander over there, yet he honestly did not know what was expected of him. The night before had been different because of all that had transpired, and he had been accorded special treatment. Today, though, was he Titus the Berserker, a fully accepted member of the Ealdorman's fyrd and worthy of striding over to one of the fires and claim a place, and a portion of the meal? Or was he back to being the stableboy whose status was undetermined; more than slave, certainly, and even more than the freedmen servants? His dilemma was solved when, glancing up from the large pot hanging over their fire that was boiling meat, Cenric saw him standing by the wagon.

"Titus! What are you doing standing there gawking?" The ceorl made a beckoning gesture, and Titus was relieved that he had not been forgotten, immediately hurrying towards the fire. As he walked up, Wulfric joked, "What? Are you too good to eat with us?"

Titus did not bother trying to hide his pleasure at the invitation, and he was grinning as he dropped to the ground in an open spot. One of the ceorls whose name Titus had not learned yet tossed him a wooden bowl, watching as the others, using their eating knives, leaned over and stabbed a chunk of meat from the steaming cauldron to add to the broth they scooped up with their bowls. Somehow, he instinctively knew that he needed to be the last one to the cauldron, yet despite this, he could not fight the apprehension that when his turn would come, there would be nothing left but liquid. Finally, the last man served himself, and Titus climbed to his feet, approaching the cauldron cautiously as he braced himself for disappointment, but when he stared down into it, he was delighted to see a substantial portion of boiled beef floating amongst the smaller pieces of root vegetables that had been added.

It was Cenric who, seeing Titus' apprehension, correctly interpreted it, and he said jokingly, "You didn't think we'd let Titus the Berserker go hungry, do you?" The others chuckled as he added, "Because I know how hard you hit, and I don't want that to happen again."

For the second time in a short period of time, Titus felt his face flush at this sign of acceptance and respect. It was, he would reflect later, the kind of thing he only realized had been missing his entire life until it happened, because Leofric had never uttered a kind word to his only son.

Sensing he needed to say something as he scooped the last of the broth into his bowl before spearing the meat, he said honestly, "But I'm the one who took the beating. And," he felt proud of himself for admitting as much, "I was sore for a week!" The memory prompted him to notice something, and he asked, "Where is Heard?"

"Over there," Cenric jerked a thumb to the next fire. "He's sleeping with Ceolmund and that bunch."

It was an innocuous enough statement, but Titus instantly sensed two things; there was more to this than met the eye, since Titus had rarely seen Cenric without Heard in his company and vice versa, but the second thing was that Cenric clearly had no interest in being pressed about it. That was easily accomplished, since Titus was more hungry than curious, and he happily slurped from the bowl, this being the dominant sound as the men ate their meal. About halfway through, a slave appeared with two dark brown loaves of bread that were still warm, quickly torn into roughly even chunks by Cenric, who to Titus' eye, seemed to be the unofficial leader of this tent group. The chunks were used to soak up the broth, and while it was certainly filling, Titus was far from satisfied. This, however, was normal for him; he could not remember a day of his life when he had been full to the point he could not eat another bite, although the last couple of years, it seemed to have gotten worse. Titus was only dimly aware of the cause for this, that it was directly related to his growth, which even he knew had accelerated, given how often one of his sisters had to lower the hem of his trousers. He could not be certain, but it seemed to him that the pair he was wearing now, the only ones in his possession since he had left the farm with nothing, were shorter than they had been when he arrived at Eadwig's hall. With the meal finished, the talk turned, or probably returned to the subject that was certainly on Titus' mind, and it was a man named Deorwine, a sallow-faced man about a decade older than Titus who broke the silence.

"I wonder if the King has made up his mind?" he mused aloud.

"It depends," Cenric countered, "on whether our scouts have found those bastards. I heard from Willmar that when the Ealdorman told the King what happened to us yesterday, we're the only fyrd who's seen any sign of those savages."

"I heard that the main force is staying at Cippinhamm, and they're trying to lure us to try and retake it."

This came from another ceorl, Leofwine, who was about Cenric's age and someone who Titus did not care for very much; he was boastful and argumentative, but there was something about the way his eyes darted about that, to Titus, made it seem as if he was looking for something to steal. He had observed enough of their interactions to know that Cenric, Heard, and Wulfric, the ceorls he knew the best, felt similarly about the man.

Nevertheless, Cenric's tone was even as he allowed, "That would certainly make sense. But," he belched before continuing, "the one thing we know about the Danes is that they like being unpredictable."

There was no argument from Leofwine, although he did mutter something under his breath, but that was all he did.

"Whatever Alfred decides," Wulfric summed it up, "we need to drive these savages from Wessex. My farm can't go unattended, and I'm tired of having to strap my shield and spear to my plow. I can't even use little Wulfric for chores because he needs to be a lookout for poxed Northmen." He leaned over and spat into the grass next to him. "I just want it over with."

Heads nodded all around the circle, but while he wisely kept his own counsel, Titus was the only one who disagreed, certain as he was that he would be perfectly content to remain like this, free and away from the farm, with battle on the horizon. Isn't that what a warrior lives for? he asked himself. And I'm not a farmer like Wulfric, or Cenric; I'm a warrior.

Completely oblivious to the internal musings of a fourteen-year-old who, for the moment, Alfred of Wessex did not even know existed, the twenty-nine-year-old King was, as was his habit, pacing back and forth, hands behind his back and head bowed in what could have easily been in an attitude of prayer. That he was not praying at the moment was because, after hours of discussion with his assembled nobles, there was still no consensus as to the next course of action, forcing the monarch to retreat within himself as he thought. The tent, as large as it was, still was almost full, with only the Ealdormen seated in front of what was both desk and table for the King. The most senior thegns were present, but being more minor noblemen, whose holdings were confined to their own hall and the immediate area surrounding it, they were all standing, Otha, Ceadda, and Aelfnod among them. To this point, they had been mostly silent, although at one time or another, the Ealdormen present, Cuthred of Hampshire, Aelfstan of Dorsetshire, or one of the minor Ealdormen like Eadwig had asked a question of one of their men. The subject of discussion was whether it was better to remain here, at Egbert's Stone, taking the time to fortify the hill, upon which, as the name implied, was a stone monolith that was right outside the entrance to the King's tent, dedicated to the memory of Alfred's grandfather. Arguing against this was, of the Ealdormen present, Cuthred, but there were two other men who Eadwig understood were listened to by Alfred, although they held no official title. Mucel and Eardwulf were in their fifties, and had advised first Alfred's father Aethelwulf, then his older brother Aethelred when they had occupied the throne of Wessex. From Eadwig's viewpoint, their caution was a result more of their age than any other reason, but while he was opposed to the idea, the Ealdorman was wise enough to know that it was not without merit.

"The alternative is to try and force them from

Cippanhamm, which they've had months to strengthen, Lord King. With Ealdorman Odda holding the remnant of Ubba's army in place, we will at least have an advantage of numbers, but will it be enough?" Mucel, who had uttered this, held his hands out, palms up in a gesture they all understood. "That is why myself and Lord Eardwulf propose that we force the Danes from behind their walls by starving them out."

"That will take months, Lord Mucel," Ealdorman Cuthred pointed out, then turned and addressed his question to Alfred. "But can we afford to spend that much time?"

"No, Lord Cuthred, we cannot," Alfred answered without hesitation. "We must come to grips with Guthrum and his army as soon as possible. I already spent a wretched winter, hiding and skulking in Athelney, having to content myself with my men conducting raids like bandits, and I am done waiting and delaying." He extended an arm to point out of his tent, and one did not have to know the man well to hear the emotion. "The men of Wessex answered my call, my lords. Even those men of Wiltscir who came, ignoring their Ealdorman. Like," Alfred's hand moved to point directly where Eadwig was seated, "Lord Eadwig of Wiltun. He, at least, has remained loyal to his King."

Eadwig had to struggle to appear impassive, but he was glowing with the pride, and he wanted to glance over his shoulder to where he knew Eadward was among the men standing, albeit at the very back, but he did not because he felt it appropriate to respond, with a grave bow of his head, "You will never have any reason to question my loyalty, my King."

Alfred inclined his head in much the same manner, although he did smile at the older noble. Returning to the larger subject, he frowned down at the large sheepskin, inked upon which was a map, and as one might expect given the familiarity with his domains, he had had his scribes fill in with an enormous level of detail.

"No, I will not defend this hill, nor am I going to employ the stratagem you suggested, my Lords." If the two older men were disappointed, they were wise enough to not show it, and without glancing at them, Alfred continued, "Our scouts have reported that Guthrum had dispatched several bands out into the countryside, as," he glanced from the map to look at Eadwig again, "Lord Eadwig learned yesterday, to the detriment of the Danes. The reports I am receiving from those scouts is that Guthrum has either learned of Ubba's defeat at the hands of Lord Odda, our movement, or most likely in my mind, both, so he is recalling those bands to return to build his numbers. I have no intention of giving him that opportunity." Gazing down at the map, he tapped a tooth with a fingernail before, after a brief silence, he resumed, "The real question is what path we take on our approach to Cippinhamm. If," he indicated the inked blue line that marked the River Wich, "we stay south of the river, there are only two or three places where they can ford without much difficulty, and I will have scouts watching them." Finally, Alfred seemed to come to some decision, and when he spoke next, it was with a tone that every man recognized. "We are going to march tomorrow, for Cippinhamm. But," he offered a grim smile, "we will not be in a hurry. I am gambling that Guthrum's men are as heartily sick of being behind those walls as I am of having them there. Once they hear that we are approaching, I believe that Guthrum will be under so much pressure that he will come rushing to meet us, and when they do, we can lead them to ground of our choosing. And," he looked upward, "with the help of Almighty God, we will drive Guthrum and his Danes from Wessex."

Titus woke up quite sore, but he still managed to wake before the other men in the tent. It was something that he seemed to have an ability to do, setting an interval in his mind then waking, so when he sat up shortly before dawn, he was able to slip unobtrusively out into the predawn air, taking the threadbare, ragged blanket that Dudda had only grudgingly given him when he began working in the stables. He was hungry, of course, but his purpose was to go check on the animals, especially Hama, who had again been staked out separately from the rest of Lord Eadwig's animals, as were the other stallions belonging to the other nobility and thegns. Titus did feel a bit guilty because he had forgotten to save a chunk of bread for his lord's horse; fortunately, their relationship and the bond that came from it was substantial enough that the only sign of displeasure from Hama was a playful shove with his head before he allowed Titus to begin brushing him, using the implement he had retrieved from the wagon. It was a ritual that they both enjoyed, which had surprised Titus a great deal, at least as far as his own reaction; he had always been indifferent to caring for the cow and the pigs that were raised for a year before they were slaughtered. None of them, however, had been anywhere near as magnificent as Hama, who stood munching the oats and barley mixture that Lord Eadwig favored for his most valued animals.

It was not the first time that Titus muttered, "You eat better than I do, boy," but it was said without rancor, his tone more rueful than anything.

The rest of the camp was beginning to stir, and Titus saw dark shapes heading in his direction, which he assumed were part of the small army of slaves and servants who performed roughly the same duties for their respective lords that Titus did. When he had gotten the brush from the wagon, he had nudged Hakon, who was curled up on the ground next to the left front wheel, the Danish slave rising immediately and, without Titus saying a word, had headed to the larger enclosure. It was gradual, but soon enough, as the grayness faded, the camp began swarming with the same level and type of activity that had been a feature of the day before, but in reverse. Fires were stoked, although nothing was cooked in the mornings, but Titus was relieved to see that someone, he had no idea who, had arranged to hold back loaves of bread that had been baked the day before, and there were also some small, hard cheeses. He resolved not to eat until he was certain that not just his tasks were done but Hakon had done his part; to his surprise, he saw that not only had the Dane done his own, he had performed several of Titus' as well.

"Thank you, Hakon." Titus felt awkward thanking a slave,

but he could tell that the Dane was pleased, although he replied with a shrug, "You are welcome, Master."

It was, technically, true that this was how he should have been addressed, but the combination of his age and his uncomfortable recognition that the circumstances in real terms between this Dane and himself was almost razor-thin meant that Titus said nothing, but he gave a nod as an answer. Returning to the fire, where Cenric and the other ceorls had taken down the tent, he eagerly accepted the chunk of bread and three small, round cheeses, and without thinking, he began wolfing down his portion. All around them, some men were doing as he did, while others, either having already broken their fast or choosing to wait until later, hurried about, the air filled with shouted commands again.

"Does anyone know what comes next?" Titus asked, which he thought was a reasonable question, but Wulfric laughed.

"Does it matter?" he countered. "The King has decided to break the camp, so we go where he says we go, boy."

He could not argue this point, but he felt compelled to say, "So you're saying you don't know, Wulfric?"

The other men erupted in laughter, which, after a momentary scowl, Wulfric joined. And, as he always managed to do, Otha suddenly appeared.

"I'm happy to see that everyone is in such a good mood this morning," he commented sourly. "But you," he pointed to Titus, "need to take down the tents you put up last night."

Without hesitation, Titus moved away from the remnants of the fire, heading uphill to towards the tents that were his responsibility, but after a glance over his shoulder, where he saw Otha speaking to Cenric and the others, he took the risk of veering from his path, hurrying to where he had spotted Hakon.

"Here," he said abruptly as he thrust his hand out, "here's a cheese."

Hakon was understandably startled, but the manner in which he did not hesitate to snatch the small ball from Titus' palm was more informative than anything he could have said.

"Thank you, Master Titus," he did think to respond, but the Saxon youth was already moving at a brisk trot towards the tents, leaving the older slave in a state of bemused gratitude.

Pausing just long enough to shove the cheese into his mouth, he hurried after Titus, chewing as he went, arriving just in time to help remove the first panel from Lord Eadwig's tent. Somehow, the Dane knew better than to thank Titus again, or even mention the small kindness he had been shown, and the pair worked in silence, essentially reversing the process of the day before. Now that he knew what was required, the tents came down quickly, but so absorbed was Titus in his task that he did not notice Eadward, standing a short distance away, observing their work. Once the poles of Eadwig's tent had been disassembled, Hakon grabbed them and turned to head for the wagon, while Titus bent down to pick up the headpiece, deciding he would come for the sockets later.

Now it was his turn to be surprised at the sudden appearance of Eadward, who without a word, grabbed as many of the sockets as he could carry, prompting Titus to assure the lordling, "Thank you, Lord, but you don't need to do that."

"I know," Eadward said simply, but he was already moving towards the wagon, forcing Titus to hurry to catch up with him. Which, Titus recognized with some irritation, had been by design. Despite this, he also knew what he needed to do, and while the words came awkwardly, he meant them when he offered, "I want to apologize for yesterday, Lord Eadward. I..."

For his part, the lordling seemed as embarrassed as Titus, and he cut the other youth off, "That's all right, Titus. I'd forgotten all about it."

This, Titus was certain, was not true, though he said nothing more about it. Instead, he asked, "It's obvious we're marching, Lord, but do you know where?"

Eadward grinned suddenly, replying in a teasing tone, "I was wondering how long it would take you." He took a quick glance around, his smile vanishing at the sight of Hakon. When the Danish slave, who had reached the wagon to deposit the poles a few paces ahead of the pair, paused instead of returning back up the hill, to Titus, it seemed to be a natural thing to do since they were working as a pair. Eadward, however, clearly did not see it that way, and he snapped, "Stop loafing, *slave*." Pointing back to the tents, he ordered imperiously, "You know what you're supposed to be doing, so go do it!" This seemed unnecessarily harsh to Titus, but he wisely kept his own counsel, and once Hakon was out of earshot, Eadward muttered, "I don't trust him."

"Why?" Titus asked curiously.

Eadward's reaction was to stare at him incredulously, his mouth open in surprise.

"Because he's a *Dane*, of course!" Eadward's tone told Titus that the lordling considered this an absurd question, and it did make him feel a bit foolish, although all he did was nod in understanding. Satisfied his point had been made, Eadward returned to the original subject, still lowering his voice to just above a whisper to inform Titus, "We're going to try and lure the Danes out from Cippinhamm, and to do that, the King has us marching, but we're not going to go very far today, just long enough to see if we can get that bastard Guthrum to come out from behind those walls."

Titus' reaction was what he hoped passed for a thoughtful nod, then he realized Eadward was expecting something, so he asked, "Do you think it will work, Lord?"

It had not been a premeditated ploy on Titus' point, but it clearly pleased the younger noble to be asked for his opinion, even if it was from just a lowly ceorl barely older than himself.

"My father thinks it will," he replied, then added quickly, "and I agree with him."

For Titus, larger questions like this held very little

meaning, not as much from a lack of appreciation as his recognition that his opinion did not matter. What did was whether or not he would be allowed to stand in the shield wall; whether it was outside the walls of Cippinhamm or somewhere else really did not matter all that much. Still, he thought, it's better to have an idea than to not about what's coming. They had reached Otha's tent, where Hakon was waiting, and Eadward, having experienced enough manual labor for the time being, made a vague comment about his father needing him, and with a final glare at the Dane, strode off. Titus could tell that Hakon was curious about whatever Eadward might have said, but the slave also knew better than to ask, and in silence, they resumed their task. The lower rim of the sun had just cleared the horizon when the wailing of the horn sounded the signal for the day's march to begin.

Alfred's army covered just a bit less than four miles that day, and while the King had been in no hurry, he certainly had not anticipated that the progress would be so paltry. Simply put, the Saxons of Wessex had rarely gathered in such a large army, and when every Ealdorman was the supreme authority within his shire, and the minor Ealdormen like Eadwig were much the same, just over a smaller territory, it was inevitable that there would be a degree of chaos. It began when Ealdorman Cuthred took it upon himself to arbitrarily declare that it was the men of his fyrd who should take the pride of place by being in the vanguard, something that, surprising none of their subordinates on either side, Ealdorman Aelfstan objected to, strenuously. Indeed, the wagons, carts, and pack animals were loaded, each group clustered together in roughly the same spot they had been encamped, for the better part of an hour as the two noblemen bickered and argued. For someone like Titus, it was bewildering because it was a problem so easily solved; King Alfred should simply make the decision, and they would undoubtedly obey. This would be just the first of many examples for Titus of Cissanbyrig about how, in reality, the most important skill Alfred, King of Wessex possessed was his diplomacy. It was, he would come to learn through observation, an almost constant balancing act for Alfred as he sought to create a cohesive entity called Wessex, and not simply a confederation of the shires of Hampscir, Somersetscir, Dorsetscir, and Wiltscir, where the Ealdormen of each viewed themselves as petty kings themselves. Consequently, he sat on the bench of the wagon, staring uphill at the huge monolith, below which there was a cluster of men, but while they were too far away for him to recognize any of them, he understood that among them was the King, who he had yet to lay eyes on. Later, after he had, Titus would recall this day with some amusement, because when he had guessed which one of the men at the top of the hill was King Alfred, he had not even been close.

Once Alfred had soothed noble feelings sufficiently, the march began, with Ealdormen Cuthred and Aelfstan both having men in the vanguard representing their shires. Aside from the political problem, there was also the challenge posed by the sheer size of this newly gathered host; when Titus had observed he had never seen more people in one place in his life, this would remain the case for some time to come. Between the men of Dorsetscir and Hampscir alone, almost three thousand men had answered the fyrd; the only shire missing its full complement was Wiltscir, thanks to the minor Ealdormen and thegns who had either chosen to remain loyal to Wulfhere out of a sense of honor, or like their Ealdorman, had made the calculation that the Danes could not be defeated. Even so, there were still almost a thousand men from Wiltscir, the most senior among them Lord Eadwig of Wiltun, bringing the total number of men willing to fight to about four thousand. Of those, of course, Alfred knew that the vast majority was composed of farmers, craftsmen, and a relatively small number of free laborers whose status meant that their weaponry was confined to clubs, or perhaps sickles and billhooks. More prosperous ceorls were able to provide their own weapons, although their armor was practically non-existent, and none of them had helmets. Of his nobles, those who were as wealthy as Lord Eadwig possessed a mail shirt, a helmet with a mail fringe that protected the neck area, and favored the *seaxe* over the spear, while men of Otha's status wore a helmet, but many did not have the means to have a mail shirt forged, and instead, they often favored vests made of boiled leather, some of them with small iron rings sewn in or, as Otha and some of his men had done, taken mail from the bodies of their slain enemies. Of his army, Alfred had a bit less than a thousand men of the thegn class, and of those, less than a hundred were minor Ealdormen in Lord Eadwig's class. In its effect, a Saxon army would have been recognized by a Roman Legionary seven centuries earlier as being a typical barbarian Germanic horde. Practically speaking, however, there was one vital difference, and that was in how these men of Wessex viewed themselves. Indeed, it would have surprised the imaginary Romans to learn that, while they looked like Germans, they thought more like Romans in that they did not view themselves as individual warriors as much as part of a unit. Certainly, nobility, no matter what the age, tended to think along the same lines, as for them, the best way to advance their fortunes was through feats of arms, but with those of the ceorl class, these men were simple farmers and artisans who fought because they had no choice but to defend their own homes. In this respect, the Saxons of Wessex resembled the Roman Republic of a millennia before; none of which was in Alfred's mind as he sat his horse on a low rise, watching as his army rumbled past. Not only was Alfred only dimly aware of the parallels between his men and those of Rome, he was completely ignorant that he was the subject of intense scrutiny, and a fair amount of disbelief on the part of a large youth driving one of the dozen large wagons that was now part of the combined army.

It was prompted by Hakon, who was walking alongside the wagon after Titus had persuaded him to tie the leads of Eadwig's spare mounts to the back of the wagon. That it was more out of boredom and a desire to have someone to talk to than anything else was left unsaid. Like everyone else, they saw the small group of horsemen sitting on the top of a small hill that looked directly down on the track they were following that led, Titus had been informed, to a place called Iglea. There were nine men on horseback, but one of them was slightly separated from the others.

"There," Hakon nodded rather than pointed, "is King Alfred."

It was said casually, but the effect on Titus was dramatic as he suddenly stood upright from the bench, yet when he followed the Dane's gaze, although he saw the mounted men, he was unable to determine by sight which one was Alfred, prompting him to ask the slave to identify him.

"The one sitting off by himself," Hakon answered.

Titus' reaction was a dismissive snort, and he relaxed back onto his seat.

"That's not King Alfred," he declared.

Under normal circumstances, meaning that if it had been any member of Eadwig's fyrd besides Titus, Hakon would have simply remained silent, but he insisted to Titus, "Yes, it is, Master Titus. I promise you that is King Alfred." When Titus glanced down at Hakon, the Dane saw the doubt on the youth's face, so he explained, "Last year, the King came to Wiltun and stayed a night with Lord Eadwig. I saw him several times. I even," he added with a sound of pride that struck Titus, "filled his cup."

He was torn, remembering Eadward's admonition about the Danish slave that he was not to be trusted, but he could not immediately think of a reason why Hakon would lie about this. Still, it was hard to believe that the man Titus was examining could possibly be the King of Wessex. Despite being on horseback, Titus could see he was of an extremely slender build, although judging from where his head was in relation to that of his horse, Titus guessed that they might be the same height. Finally, just as their wagon drew even with the mounted party above them, Titus decided that there was no reason for Hakon to lie.

"Well, he doesn't much *look* like a king," he mumbled, but Hakon heard him and, for the first time in their brief association, the slave laughed.

"I overheard Lord Eadward say the same thing to his father," he said, which made Titus feel better.

Just as they were drawing past, he was struck by a sudden and horrible thought: was he supposed to stand up and bow to Alfred, or make some sort of sign of obeisance? A wave of what was close to panic surged through him, and he had actually begun to stand back up before, finally, a part of his mind pointed out that nobody in the column ahead of him had done anything of that nature. Dropping back down with some relief, Titus returned his attention to the track and the wagon ahead of him, musing about exactly why he had been surprised about Alfred's appearance. As he thought about it, he asked himself, What is a king supposed to look like? If he had been asked moments earlier, Titus understood he would have been unable to articulate anything that would resemble a description of what a king should look like in his mind, yet when he had first laid eyes on Alfred, he had been certain that the figure sitting on his horse at the top of that hill could not possibly have been the King himself. So, he wondered, why did I think that? It was, he decided, quite curious. This train of thought was something that Titus would have never dreamed of uttering aloud to anyone except Leofflaed; certainly, if Leofric had heard such views, he would dismiss them as nonsense and a sure sign that Titus was soft in the head, daydreaming about things that had no practical purpose, and just as certainly, this declaration would have been accompanied by a slap to the head. And, he admitted to himself, Leofric would have been right because, ultimately, Titus' opinion on what a king should look like mattered to nobody but himself. He was still ruminating about this matter when, to his complete surprise, from far ahead, the horn sounded a halt.

"It's too early for another rest stop," he called down to Hakon, standing up onto the bench to peer ahead, something he had begun doing regularly, in an attempt to know as much about what lay ahead as possible. Shading his eyes, he observed for a moment before adding, "It looks like we might be stopping for the day." Finally, he stepped down off the bench, frowning at the thought that had just occurred to him. "Since we've only gone about four miles, the only reason I can think of is that our scouts have spotted Guthrum and his army."

He reflexively glanced down at Hakon to see how the Dane took this news, and for a fraction of an instant, Titus was sure that he saw a look on the slave's face that could only be described as happy anticipation, but Hakon managed to smother it so quickly that he could not be certain.

Aloud, Hakon only said, "I suppose we will learn shortly one way or another, Master Titus."

Still suspicious, Titus' only response was a curt nod. No matter what Hakon's true thoughts may have been, Titus recognized that the slave was right, so he settled back onto the bench to wait.

"Guthrum has left Cippinhamm," Alfred announced in a hastily called meeting, a short distance away from the front of the column. He paused, then added quietly, "In force."

Not surprisingly, this created a small uproar, which forced Alfred to hiss a warning to his nobles.

"I have no intention of letting our men know before I'm ready, lords," he said sternly, only after they had subsided. Turning to indicate the mud-spattered man standing beside his lathered horse, Alfred continued, "This man rides with Wiglaf, who is the chief of my scouts. I sent them north to the escarpment that leads up to the Sarum plain, with orders to probe north across the plain. And," Alfred said calmly, "Wiglaf and his scouts saw Guthrum's advance guard about five miles north of Ethantun, and they are marching directly south."

"How does this Wiglaf know that it's Guthrum's army?" Mucel asked. "He and his men might have just spotted one of those bands Guthrum has sent roving about the countryside.

And," he was clearly warming to his subject as he insisted, "if we take a direct line of march to Ethantun, we will be on the Sarum plain, where there is no cover. Any Dane with eyes will be able to see our army in its entirety! And why?" He scanned the faces of the other lords. "Because we believe in one scout's report. No, Lord King," he shook his head dismissively, "I would advise that we do not take this as a matter of fact. Not yet."

Alfred had listened patiently, but when he replied, while his tone was polite, none of them mistook the message or the rebuke.

"While I appreciate your wise counsel, Lord Mucel," he began courteously, "I also trust Wiglaf implicitly. He has been with me since our victory at Ashdown, and I have learned that, if anything, he errs on the side of caution. Therefore," his tone turned flat, "I believe him, and we will plan accordingly."

Mucel was wise enough to know to desist, but anyone with eyes could see that he did not take what was an open chastisement from the normally mild-mannered Alfred well, something that Alfred wisely ignored. The ensuing discussion was brief, if only because the other nobles had read the mood of their King correctly in his treatment of Mucel, recognizing that he had already made his decision, which was to make camp. It was, strategically speaking, not a bad spot for a camp, because as the priests that were an integral part of Alfred's household would very quickly inform the men, the fact that the scout had returned to the army in a large clearing in the middle of what was otherwise a thickly forested area of mostly oak trees, what better sign that God's will had foreordained it? Whether the spot was divinely inspired or not, camp was made once again, and it was accomplished more quickly and a bit more smoothly than the day before.

Then, it was just past noon, and the army settled down to wait for whatever came next. A strong guard was set; as fortuitous as it was to be in a clearing, the woods on this May day completely surrounded it, and while it was unlikely, neither

Alfred, his Ealdormen, or his thegns were willing to bet their collective lives on the idea that, despite being about ten miles away and presumably doing the same thing the Saxons were doing in searching for the enemy, Guthrum and his horde would not suddenly appear from the surrounding woods. In recognition of the different terrain from the day before at Egbert's Stone, the carts, wagons, and livestock were actually placed more towards the center of the camp. Sitting atop the hill as they had been, and with the land around them devoid of heavy forest, it was next to impossible for anyone, Dane or bandit, to sneak up and steal a horse or loot a wagon or cart. Here, however, it was another story, and the practical effect for Titus of Cissanbyrig was that, for the first time in his life, he was at least near the center of their world in the form of King Alfred and his nobles. But never in his wildest dreams would he have foreseen what was about to happen to him, when one of Eadwig's other servants, a freeborn man named Beorhtic who was serving a period of indenture to pay off a debt his family had incurred, came to where he was busy unhitching the wagon.

"Lord Eadwig wants you to go get Hama from him, and I'll take care of the wagon," Beorhtic informed him. "He says that he needs to be rubbed down."

Titus' first inclination was to snap at the other man that he *always* rubbed Hama down, but he managed to refrain, handing the trace he had just unbuckled to him. While today's camp was configured differently, Titus knew roughly where Lord Eadwig would be, and he headed to where the King's tent was being erected. Just as it was the day before, it was a chaotic scene, and Titus had to weave his way through and around men involved in their particular tasks before he finally saw Eadwig. More accurately, he spotted the bulk of the large black stallion first, then saw Eadwig, with Eadward next to him but both with their backs turned as they were engaged in conversation with some unseen individual or group. Later, he would wonder if Hama had not blocked his vision, whether he would have simply turned and run, perhaps all the way back to Cissanbyrig.

Instead, he positioned himself just behind father and son, but he still could not see who Eadwig, who was the one talking, was addressing. It was Eadward who, sensing someone behind him, glanced over his shoulder, saw Titus, then without saying anything to the youth, instead reached out and touched his father's arm. Because of the other noise, Titus could not hear what Eadward said, but the meaning was obvious when Eadwig looked over his shoulder.

"Ah, so you're here," he had to raise his voice, saying gruffly, "and you took your time about it."

Titus had learned that this was not a real censure, but was just the manner in which Eadwig addressed those under him, but he also knew what was expected, so he offered an apology that was as artificial as the reprimand.

He was moving as he did so, reaching out to take the reins as he said, "Yes, Lord. I apologize, Lord."

To his surprise, Eadwig did not hand him Hama's reins, who was now tossing his head, the signal to Titus that he was ready for some sort of fun.

Instead, he beckoned to Titus with his free hand, "Yes, yes. I'll give him to you in a moment. First, there's someone I want you to meet."

Titus obediently stepped to the spot Eadwig pointed to, placing himself in between father and son, and in doing so, gave him his first opportunity to see who Eadwig had been talking to. Thankfully for Titus, the fact that his knees gave way worked to his advantage, since this was the behavior expected on one's first meeting with their King.

"This is the lad I was telling you about, my King," Eadwig said to Alfred, who gazed down at the youth's head, which was bowed with a mixture of curiosity and, frankly, doubt. "Two days ago when we were ambushed, he singlehandedly saved my son. And," Titus flinched involuntarily when Eadwig dropped a hand heavily on his shoulder, "he killed four Danes on his own."

Titus was in an agony unlike anything he had ever experienced before, and while he was flushing with pride, he still felt too afraid to lift his head, which Alfred noticed.

"You may rise," Alfred spoke quietly enough, "and tell me your name, boy."

Naturally, Titus obeyed, and he found the courage to lift his head to look directly into Alfred's eyes, which told him that his initial impression that they were the same height was correct. But it was the brilliant blue eyes that arrested the youth's attention, although he certainly noticed the dark blonde curly beard that framed a mouth that, while not smiling, seemed kindly.

"It's…it's Titus, Lord King," he managed to get out, then added, "Titus of Cissanbyrig, son of Leofric."

"That was before two days ago, my King," Eadwig put in. "Before he slaughtered four Danes. Now," he raised his voice so that it could be heard above the din, "my thegns call him Titus the Berserker!"

Just that quickly, Titus' feeling of an instant before was transformed into an ecstasy composed of equal parts embarrassment and pride, but he was emboldened to maintain his gaze on Alfred, who was smiling now.

"Is this true, Titus…the Berserker?" Alfred asked teasingly, but while he knew it was made in jest, Titus actually answered the question honestly.

"I…I don't really know, Lord King. But," he turned his head to indicate Eadward, "I know what Lord Eadward told me, and I believe him, as well as some other men who saw it." He searched for the right words, but all he could come up with was, "I just know that he's alive and that makes me happy."

He had certainly had no intention of sounding mawkish, but he was speaking honestly. However, Alfred's mind had latched on to something else, and the smile faded so quickly that Titus thought he might have imagined it.

"You just said you are from Cissanbyrig?" Alfred asked quietly. At Titus' nod, his tone turned cool. "So your lord is Owin, who serves Ealdorman Wulfhere, is it not?"

"Yes, Lord," Titus answered, feeling a bit queasy at yet another sudden change.

"So why are you marching as part of Lord Eadwig's fyrd? Wiltun is miles from Cissanbyrig," Alfred pointed out, needlessly in Titus' opinion, since he had walked it recently.

Even after Titus of Cissanbyrig reached manhood and had matured, he would have moments where he tended to speak without thinking, so it was not just because of his age that he blurted out, "Because I know that Ealdorman Wulfhere is a traitor, Lord King, and so is Lord Owin and anyone who follows him! He refused to call the fyrd himself! And," now, Titus had to swallow the lump that formed as his mind caught up with what his mouth was saying, "none of the farms anywhere around Cissanbyrig were raided by the Danes, Lord King, and I heard that holds true for almost all of northern Wiltscir. That's when I knew that Wulfhere was a traitor. I wouldn't march for someone like that, Lord King, I swear it by the rood!"

Titus had certainly heard of Alfred's piety, but he got an idea of how deep his convictions were by the disapproving frown that he gave Titus, making his knees, which had stopped shaking, to resume.

"Such oaths are not to be taken lightly, boy," Alfred counseled the youth, but his mind was still on the larger issue. "But I also appreciate your loyalty. Now," his tone hardened, "you mentioned your father? Leofric, I believe?"

"Yes, Lord King," Titus nodded.

Alfred made a show of leaning over slightly to scan the men all around them, giving Titus an idea of what was coming when the King returned his attention to the youth to ask, "Did he come with you to Wiltun as well? Is he as loyal to his King as you are?"

"No, Lord King, he's not here with me. He," Titus had to take a breath before he admitted, "told me that he wouldn't answer the fyrd for anyone but Ealdorman Wulfhere."

Alfred's expression did not alter much, but it was enough to ignite in Titus a pang of misgiving, wondering if he had just doomed his father, and he wondered if he should say...*something* that would paint Leofric in a more positive light.

Before he could, the moment was over, as Alfred, seemingly out of nowhere, asked him, "Do you pray every day, Titus?"

Once more, before he could stop himself, Titus answered honestly, "No, Lord King. I mean," he hurried to add, alarmed by the way Alfred's lips seemed to vanish into his beard, "I pray, Lord King. Just not every day."

"You must rectify that," Alfred said sternly. "If you are to be worthy of standing in our fyrd, you must have a relationship with God Almighty, and you should be thanking Him for all that He has given you."

"Yes, Lord King," Titus mumbled, but sensing the King wanted more, he said, "I promise, I will begin praying every day."

Then, with nothing more than a nod, Alfred, King of Wessex, dismissed Titus, which Eadwig correctly and immediately understood, thrusting the reins into Titus' hand. While Titus was aware that he had been dismissed, he did not know the proper manner in which he should excuse himself from the royal presence, but that problem was quickly solved when Alfred spun about on his heel and began striding towards his tent, which had just been erected, with a curt command to Eadwig to follow him. When Eadward moved to do the same, his father shook his head, and Titus saw the look of frustration flash across the lordling's face, but when he turned his attention to Titus, it was with a broad grin.

"So, how does it feel for King Alfred to know your name?"

Titus opened his mouth to answer, then hesitated as he thought about it.

"It feels," he finally allowed, "…strange, I suppose." A thought occurred to him. "But which name are you talking about? My first name? Or that…other one?"

Eadward laughingly admitted, "I'd forgotten about 'the Berserker' part. I was talking about your first name, not the other one."

"At least he didn't make a joke about whether my father was a priest," Titus observed with some relief.

He had not said it to be funny, but Eadward laughed again, prompting Titus to give him a quizzical glance.

"I'm laughing about you saying King Alfred might make a joke. I haven't been around him all that much, but I've never seen him laugh, and my father says that he doesn't jest at all, with anyone."

That, Titus thought, makes sense. How could any king have time for folly of some sort? And Alfred was facing the destruction of his kingdom.

After leaving Eadward, Titus worked quickly, giving Hama both a rubdown and a brushing as, all around them, a military camp materialized in the clearing, and by the time he was finished, the activity level was no longer as frenzied. Now it was time to gather wood to begin the fires, to secure the livestock, and prepare for the coming of night. In Titus' case, it was a time for training, except this time, Uhtric was not in as amiable a mood about it.

"Lord Eadwig told me he introduced you to King Alfred and made you out to be a real warrior, so he sent me here to make sure that you don't get yourself killed in your first battle."

This stung Titus, who retorted, "I've already been in battle, Uhtric."

Before he could say anything more, Uhtric cut him off with a curt, dismissive gesture as he countered, "That wasn't a battle, boy. That was a skirmish. No," he shook his head, "what's coming tomorrow, or maybe the next day is a *real* battle. Standing in the shield wall, shoulder to shoulder and close enough to those dogs to smell their breath and have their spit in your face, *that* is battle, boy. Now," he pointed to the wagon, "get your shield. We're going to work on your defense."

Titus quickly obeyed, but his feet had barely hit the ground when, instead of using the spear shaft he was carrying from the day before, Uhtric smashed his own shield into Titus', putting his weight behind the blow. As he intended, it sent Titus reeling back against the wagon, the impact sufficient to cause the youth to be distracted just enough that he temporarily forgot to keep his shield up high enough. Since Titus was not wearing his leather vest, Uhtric's thrust with the blunt end of the spear was something like a hard poke, just enough to elicit a yelp of pain from the youth who, belatedly, lifted his shield back to its proper position.

"That's what's going to happen to you if the Danes rush at the shield wall and you're not ready," the warrior said, not unkindly. "So that's your first lesson in defense."

He stepped away from the wagon then, giving Titus room to step away so that there was space behind him, and while he said nothing, Uhtric noted with approval that Titus kept his shield not only high enough, but between himself and the warrior.

"Since we don't have the time for it, and you weren't part of Lord Otha's training back in Wiltun, I'm not going to even try to teach you about how to be part of a shield wall," Uhtric explained. "Instead, I'm going to show you how to use your shield if you end up getting separated and are by yourself."

This certainly seemed straightforward to Titus, although he was slightly puzzled about exactly how complicated blocking a Dane's spear thrust could be; he quickly learned differently. Uhtric had Titus square himself, putting his shield in front of him with his elbow locked against his hip, resting the spear shaft on the top of the shield, the classic position for the Saxon spearman about to go into battle.

"Now," Uhtric instructed, "approach me. And remember to keep your feet far enough apart," he reminded the youth.

Titus did as instructed, using a shuffling step that kept both feet on the ground as he had been taught just the day before. And yet, despite anticipating that Uhtric would launch a thrust once he closed the distance, the speed that the blunt shaft of the warrior's spear struck his shield surprised him, although he cleanly blocked the thrust, feeling the impact of it through the wood just a matter of inches from his boss. He was completely unprepared for what came next when, while recovering the spear shaft back to its original position, Uhtric used the counter momentum to help him as, twisting at the hips, he shot his shield out. With unerring aim, the edge of Uhtric's round shield got behind and struck the inner edge of Titus' with enough force that Titus' left arm moved out from his body, taking the shield with it. And, as quickly as Uhtric's spear shaft had returned to its original position, it shot back out, again with perfect aim, shooting into the space just vacated by Titus' shield to strike him in the chest. The force of the blow wrenched a shout of pain from the youth that blended with the cracking sound of Titus' edge striking the shaft that would have sent the thrust wide, but just a fraction of an eyeblink too late. As had occurred the day before, Uhtric was actually deeply impressed at Titus' quick reflexes, not expecting his spear shaft to be touched by the youth's shield when he returned it to its proper position. The most impressive aspect was how quickly Titus responded with a counterattack of his own, even if it was clumsily executed, and while he used his shield to block the blow easily, he was reminded of the power behind this raw youth by the manner in which his left arm recoiled back towards his body. However, Uhtric realized that he had not made the point of his move obvious, and he paused for a moment to think. Titus' thrust was completely unexpected, the blunt point of his shaft striking the warrior in almost the identical spot, but unlike Titus, Uhtric actually had to move his feet to maintain his balance.

His initial reaction was to hurl a curse at the youth, but the fact that Titus was standing there, his face a mask of concentration, not gloating or celebrating in any way, caused him to say instead, "Drop your spear but keep your shield."

Titus' first reaction, understandably, was of suspicion, eyeing the warrior with clear skepticism that prompted Uhtric to drop his own on the ground. Only then did Titus relent and follow suit, his suspicion replaced by puzzlement.

"You need to use every weapon you can, Titus," he explained. Misunderstanding, Titus reached behind his back for his dagger that, while it could be used as a weapon, had so far only been used to spear pieces of meat from the cook pot, but Uhtric stopped him. "I'm not talking about your dagger or even a *seaxe*. I'm talking about," he tapped the shield with his free hand, "this."

"How can I use my shield as a weapon?" Titus asked with a frown that informed Uhtric the youth was unconvinced.

"Like I just did," Uhtric countered. "I used my shield to turn yours and give me an opening for my spear. If there had been a blade on the end, you'd be dead."

For his part, Titus opened his mouth to retort that he had just evened the score but almost instantly realized it would be a foolish thing to say, given that he would have been dead already.

Instead, he asked, "How do I use my shield as a weapon?"

Over a span of two hours, Uhtric showed Titus how he could use his shield as more than a defensive weapon, both of them unaware that this scene had been played out before, centuries earlier as an experienced warrior finally met a younger man who was every bit as committed to the pursuit of arms as he had been, when a scarred, one-eyed veteran of the Legions of Rome tutored an eager youth and the youth's best friend. Just as had happened the day before, there were many eyes on the pair, watching as Uhtric walked Titus through a movement then had him repeat it, and because of the configuration of this camp at Iglea, the onlookers were not just the ceorls of one lord's fyrd. The reason Uhtric called a halt had less to do with the time of day than the fact that he was exhausted, and he silently reminded himself, with rueful amusement, that being twenty-four was quite different from being fourteen. He had learned the day before what a quick study Titus was, but he was still astonished at the speed with which the youth had adapted to the idea of thinking of his shield as an extension of his hand. Almost immediately, Titus had determined that while the single leather strap made it more secure, it did not afford him the ability to use the shield to its full effect as an offensive weapon as Uhtric had shown him because it restricted the flexibility of his wrist. Once Titus was unencumbered, Uhtric found himself forced to rely on his own skills with every repetition as Titus quickly grasped the fundamentals of the idea behind using the shield as more than just a protection. It certainly helped that he was strong enough already that the speed with which he could move the shield compared to if he was unencumbered was barely noticeable. All that was missing, Uhtric recognized, was the dexterity that comes from practice, and the unthinking response that is perhaps the most essential skill that gives a warrior the best chance to see another sunrise. Titus was certainly fatigued, but when Uhtric declared the session over, despite the sweat dripping from the hem of his tunic and from his nose, he did not try to hide his disappointment, although he merely nodded. He watched as Uhtric strode away, only gradually becoming aware that Hakon had been watching the entire time, sitting and leaning against a wheel, but when Titus glanced at him, he had the impression that the Dane suddenly changed his expression to the blank appearance of all slaves, and he wondered why.

Impulsively, he asked, "Were you a warrior, Hakon?"

The change in the slave was subtle but unmistakable; although his features remained the same, Titus saw his body stiffen to the point he was sitting upright, away from the wheel.

Titus was beginning to think that the Dane would not answer when, with obvious reluctance, Hakon said, "No, Master Titus. I was not considered to be…worthy."

"Why?" Titus asked, genuinely curious.

Whether it was that Hakon sensed there was no malice intended, or he understood Titus would not be swayed, the youth would never know.

"I was born a slave, Master Titus," he answered, his voice toneless and his eyes on the ground in front of him. "The Danes do not allow slaves to learn how to fight."

"What?" Titus gasped. "You weren't captured in battle?"

The look that the Dane gave him, one of bitter amusement and the kind of rage that was more potent because it was helpless was something Titus would remember for some time.

"No, I was sold by my master to Lord Eadwig as part of a sale of cattle."

Titus' initial impulse was to call Hakon a liar, simply because it was inconceivable to him that Lord Eadwig would lower himself to sell the filthy Northmen cattle for any reason. They were the Saxons' mortal enemies! They were invaders! No loyal Saxon would do anything for the Danes! It was, Titus would come to learn, the view of an adolescent, and it was the first of what would become many lessons that matters between the two antagonists were far more complicated than he would have imagined.

Chapter Six

Shortly before sundown, Alfred's horn player sounded the series of notes that signaled the high-ranking nobles were to meet the King in his tent. Even before Eadwig, accompanied by Otha, Ceadda, and Aelfnod, reached the tent, they could tell that the Danes had been sighted, and the thegns broke into a near run, entering to an uproar, which Alfred was trying to quiet.

It took several moments before it was calm enough for the King to announce, "Wiglaf and his men have kept watch on Guthrum and his host. He's now camped about seven miles north of here, just north of Ethantun." He paused, as much to gauge the mood than for any other reason, and liking what he saw, he continued, "And we will march to meet these invaders and drive them from our lands." He did not attempt to say anything more, knowing that there would be no way to be heard over the sudden roaring of the dozens of voices, and he allowed the demonstration to continue for some time before finally raising a hand. This time, his nobles subsided almost immediately, and Alfred commented wryly, "I was going to tell you to inform your men, but I suspect there is no need now." There were some chuckles, but Alfred was already moving on. "We will break camp before dawn and march north, but we will leave the wagons and the noncombatants at the old fort on Battlesbury Hill, along with a force of one hundred men to stand guard. From the hill, we will march north across the plain."

"Lord King, Sarum Plain is completely open! The Danes will know we are coming."

If Alfred was irritated by this interruption by Eardwulf,

Eadwig thought, He's doing a good job of hiding it, and he watched carefully as Alfred responded, "I am aware of this, Lord Eardwulf. In fact, that is my intention. I want them to know that we are coming."

While Eadwig had reservations about the King's plan, it was not completely foolhardy, but now Eardwulf was joined by Mucel.

"Lord King, by doing this, aren't we allowing Guthrum to determine the best strategy to thwart us?"

"How so, Lord Mucel?" Alfred actually sounded interested, and Mucel was clearly happy to express himself.

"We forego the element of surprise, which we still hold." The nobleman held out a finger, and to Eadwig's ear, his tone was that of a tutor correcting a pupil. "Once we are spotted, Guthrum will have the opportunity to either pick his ground..." Another finger came out. "...or, he could even withdraw in good order back to Cippinhamm." This brought the third finger, which was accompanied by a grave shake of Mucel's iron-gray head. "Lord King, for those reasons, I ask you to reconsider."

"How would you have us go then, Lord Mucel?"

It was not Alfred who asked this, but Ealdorman Cuthred, and Eadwig had a suspicion this was not an accident, which was reinforced by the lack of hesitation on the other man's part.

"Skirt the edge of the plain to the west," Mucel answered. "If we stay at the base of that long escarpment, we can avoid detection, and it would give us the ability to put ourselves between Guthrum and Cippinhamm."

Eadwig was suddenly uncomfortable; it was, he thought, not a bad idea, and he could sense heads around him nodding. Alfred, however, registered no emotion, although he certainly seemed to be considering the suggestion.

This seemed confirmed when Alfred began, "There is merit in what you say, Lord Mucel. And," he allowed, "if we stay off the plain, we might be able to do what you suggest." There was a heartbeat's worth of silence before he continued, "But there is also a risk. If Guthrum's scouts spot us, and with the speed with which the Northmen move, they would then have the advantage of high ground, would they not? They could simply place themselves along the escarpment and wait for us to march past?"

"Well…yes, Lord King," Mucel admitted reluctantly, then before he could say anything else, Alfred pressed, "And if we are in column as we are marching, then they would have us flanked as well, would they not?"

By this point, Eadwig was thankful he had not even nodded his head, and he was amused at the manner in which the other men around him were suddenly interested in the dirt floor of the tent.

"Yes, Lord King," Mucel said quietly, and one did not need to know him to hear the defeat in his voice. "You are correct. And," he bowed his head, "I apologize for wasting your time."

"Your counsel is never a waste of time," Alfred assured him, and Eadwig almost believed the King was being sincere. With this disposed of, he returned to the business at hand. "Very well, we will be breaking camp two hours before dawn and deposit the baggage on Battlesbury Hill. From the hill, we will march north until we come in contact with Guthrum. And then," he spread his arms, turning his face to the heavens as he intoned, "with the help of Almighty God, we shall drive these heathens back to the bowels of Hell from where they came!"

It was unusual for Alfred to invoke the name of the Lord in direct connection with slaying his enemies, but Eadwig understood this was different. His King had been forced to skulk in the swamps of Athelney for months after being forced to flee, almost literally in the middle of the night. Now he had brought his fyrd to this place, and there was an air of implacable resolve about the King that Eadwig wondered if it had always been there but he had just never noticed, or if Alfred had been hardened by his ordeal. Whatever the truth was, they would find out if it would be enough, if not tomorrow then the next day.

The mood around Cenric's fire that night was much different than the previous evening, with not much of the jocularity and only desultory conversation, which suited Titus perfectly. He was still unaccustomed to the idea that he had been accepted by Cenric and the other men of this tent, and he was also preoccupied. In this, he was not alone; the reason, however, was starkly different between his concern and theirs. They *knew* where they would be the next morning, marching with the rest of the fyrd towards battle with the Danes. Titus, on the other hand, still had not been told anything by Lord Eadwig, or by Otha. Once the word had spread that there would likely be battle the next day, the camp had been in an uproar, and while the warriors had all been busy with their weapons and equipment the night before, now there was an intense quality to the sharpening of blades and checking of equipment, and Titus had been completely ignored. While he was sore from his work with Uhtric the previous two days, overall, he felt good, aside from the fluttering sensation in his stomach. Before the cooking fires were lit, and mimicking the more experienced warriors, Titus retrieved a spare whetstone from the wagon, then sat against the wagon, trying not to be obvious about watching Cenric as the ceorl sharpened his own weapon. Fairly quickly, he became absorbed in the task, actually finding the rhythmic motion soothing, and when he ran his thumb along the edge, he gave a small gasp of pain, then his face split in a grin as he saw the thin red line spread across the pad of his digit.

"You're going to bleed to death if you're not careful."

Looking up in surprise, he saw Eadward grinning down at him, but when Titus began to rise to his feet, the lordling stopped him, dropping down next to him instead.

"I take it that you've heard," he said blandly, and understanding Eadward was teasing him, Titus tried his best to appear mystified.

"Heard what?"

"About Guthrum," Eadward said, suddenly unsure if Titus was serious.

"What about him?"

"That King Alfred's scouts have found him," Eadward replied. "He's not far from here at Ethantun."

"Oh," Titus replied casually, dropping his head to hide his smile as he pretended to examine his spear. "Yes, I know."

Realizing Titus was teasing him in turn, he scowled at the other youth, but it was not in any seriousness. He contented himself with watching Titus as he turned the broad leaf blade over to begin working on the other edge, and the pair sat in silence for several moments.

"What do you think it's going to be like?" Eadward asked suddenly, which caught Titus by surprise.

"I don't know," he replied honestly, then asked curiously, "but haven't you asked your father about it? Battle, I mean?"

"I know what you mean," Eadward answered, then suddenly seemed to become interested in watching a pair of men hurrying past as he admitted, "and no, I haven't asked my father." He offered a thin smile. "He's been…busy."

Honestly, Titus was not certain this was true; from his perspective, Lord Eadwig did a lot of pointing and yelling commands at the men of his fyrd, who were the ones who did all the work, but he wisely kept this to himself.

Returning his mind back to Eadward's question, he recalled something, telling Eadward, "While I don't know what it will be like with the shield wall, I know that Uhtric told me it's nothing like what happened the day before yesterday."

For some reason, this caused Eadward to appear startled, but Titus quickly learned why.

"It's hard to believe that it was only two days ago,"

Eadward mused, and in this, Titus wholeheartedly agreed.

"Do you know where you'll be?" Titus asked, and now there was no way to mistake Eadward's embarrassment, although he did not hesitate in answering.

"I'm staying on Battlesbury Hill," the lordling said glumly. "With the baggage."

Since Titus was still unsure of his own status, he did not feel right making a comment one way or another, so he made a noise that he hoped would convey sympathy.

"Lord Eadward!" Both youths reacted as if they had been caught doing something wrong, which Otha noticed but said nothing about. "Your father wants to see you in your tent!"

Climbing to his feet, Eadward mumbled, "He's probably making sure I know what will happen to me if I try and sneak off to go with you tomorrow."

While Titus was certain that Eadward had used the word "you" in a general sense, his heart still quickened, though he simply bade the lordling a casual farewell before returning to his task.

Now, sitting at the fire, Titus had been working up the courage to ask Cenric if the ceorl was aware of his status, yet he could not seem to find the words, so he occupied himself with stuffing his mouth with food, more food than he had seen since the farewell feast.

As he would come to learn, one of the surest signs of impending battle was the sudden increase in food, but since this was his first experience, he was moved to ask, "Cenric, why are we each getting a loaf of bread? And," he held up his bowl, "four pieces of meat instead of two?"

This clearly surprised Cenric, but since his mouth was full, it was Leofwine who answered scornfully, "Because Lord Eadwig doesn't want us to die with an empty belly, boy." Nudging Deorwine, who was sitting next to him, he laughed.

"He may be strong, but the boy is a thick one, eh, Deorwine?"

Whether it was the moment or that it was Leofwine making the jibe, Deorwine barely glanced at Leofwine as he countered, "I'd rather have that boy next to me in the shield wall than some other men I know…"

Now the ceorl did turn his head to look directly at Leofwine, sending an unmistakable message, while Leofwine flushed, but rather than say anything, he stood abruptly, dropping his bowl onto the ground then tossed the half-eaten bread into it before he went stalking off. Judging by the manner in which the other men reacted, Titus deduced that this was not unusual behavior on Leofwine's part.

"You know that we're going to eat what you left behind," Osmund called out cheerfully to the other ceorl's retreating back, but Leofwine did not break stride. Leaning over, Osmund picked up the bowl, and while he kept the bread, he offered the bowl to Titus, grinning as he said, "He left because of you, so I think you deserve a reward."

For the first time, laughter rang out from the men around the fire, while Titus accepted the food gratefully. And, of all the memories he would hold of that time, Titus would fondly remember not only the feeling of acceptance, but of a completely full belly for one of the few times in his life.

As directed, the men of Alfred's fyrd rose earlier than normal, but before they began the process of breaking down the camp, Titus was surprised to see figures emerging from the darkness and heading in the general direction of Alfred's tent, which was still just a darker shape looming above the other tents surrounding it. Like the day before, Titus had risen a few minutes earlier than the others and headed for Hama, a chunk of what was almost a full loaf of bread in his hand, and that was where he was when the men began moving. He was extremely curious; no horn had been sounded, and he had not even heard anyone shouting an order to assemble, and he wondered if he was expected to follow along.

"What are you standing there for, boy?"

Even as he spun about, Titus recognized Otha's voice, which was good because the Thegn was barely distinguishable in the gloom.

"I was tending to Hama, Lord," he answered, although he thought it was obvious.

"While Father Aethelred is holding Mass?" Otha replied disapprovingly. "That's not a good idea, boy."

"Why aren't you there?" Titus countered before he could stop himself, and while it was too dark to make out the Thegn's features, Titus understood the tone all too well.

"That's none of your business," Otha shot back. Titus dimly made out that Otha was now pointing in the direction of the tent. "But King Alfred likes his men pious, so if you want to be in his favor, I suggest you hurry along."

Titus did turn to go, but he could not resist protesting, "King Alfred will never notice if someone like me isn't there."

The hand that grabbed his arm surprised Titus, while Otha was suddenly next to him, close enough that Titus could smell the ale on the man's breath.

"Don't ever think that King Alfred doesn't notice, Titus. He sees *everything*. Now," he gave the youth a shove, "go attend Mass."

Titus made it in time, barely, although he was among the rearmost row, but his attention was entirely on the dark figures standing just outside the entrance to the King's tent as he dropped to his knees, hoping that Otha was wrong. A figure detached himself from the small group who, Titus assumed, was Father Aethelred, confirmed when he began intoning what the youth recognized by the rhythm and words as the beginning of the Mass. It was in Latin, of course, which meant that neither Titus nor the vast majority of his comrades around him understood a word, but they had been a part of his life since his earliest memories, Leofric and his family attending the outdoor Mass held in Cissanbyrig. The village priest, Father Glaedwine, a scrawny man with a wandering eye of indeterminate age but who had been there for Titus' entire life, was a known drunkard, although Titus did like the priest's wife Frideswide, and Titus was almost certain that Glaedwine had no more idea the meaning of the words he intoned every Sunday than Titus himself. However, while Leofric could not be described as pious using any definition, the peer pressure and the power of the Church meant that he and his three children obediently walked into the village. Titus himself was not impious, strictly speaking; it was simply not something he thought about much. God was far away, and the few times he did think about Him and all that He was supposed to represent, Titus decided that for whatever reason, God was not all that interested in him or anyone else in his world. A King, however, was something else entirely, so as he mouthed the words in response to Father Aethelred's recitation of the Mass, he tried to sound sincere. And, he thought, it couldn't hurt to have Him on our side and not the Danes, although every fiber of his being rejected the idea that God would have anything to do with the pagan Northmen. They, he had been told, and he accepted without question, were all going to Hell for eternity.

With the last "Amen," he rose to his feet, aware that he could now dimly make out the King's features, the surest sign that dawn was approaching, and he momentarily debated taking a more circuitous route to the livestock enclosure, his first step in hitching the pair of oxen to the wagon so that the King would have a chance to see that he had attended the Mass, but he felt foolish for thinking of it. Hakon was already there, and they worked together, moving quickly as the army broke camp, knowing that Lord Eadwig insisted they not make him the last noble ready to march. Despite the darkness, Alfred's army broke camp more rapidly than the day before, and it was still dark when, again without the use of horns in the event that Guthrum's scouts were out early, Titus guided the wagon into the same spot it had occupied the day before. They began the march following a track, but when it began curving left off to the west, the vanguard continued in a northerly direction, forcing Titus and the others driving a wagon to take particular care as they continued over the rough ground.

Fortunately for Titus, since he was not the first wagon, he got a bit of warning when one of the wagons ahead of him suddenly lurched in one direction or another, or rocked over a bump, but it was still a rough ride. His first indication of their destination was when the hill grew close enough for him to see it, looming above them, but it was when they began climbing the slope that he began to understand what might be happening. Whoever was leading the way did not take the most direct route, choosing instead to lessen the grade by winding around the hill, but even so, there was a moment where Titus worried that his wagon would tip over. He did not, nor did the other wagons, while the carts had less of a challenge. The upper rim of the sun had just appeared, flooding the plain of Sarum below in the golden light, and under other circumstances, Titus would have savored the view of the vast, lush green expanse that was almost completely devoid of trees, but he was too busy once again guiding his wagon through the opening in the dirt wall of the hillfort to the spot that Otha was pointing to as his. Unlike the day before, or the day before that, the wagons and carts were arranged in a circle, mimicking the dirt wall but inside it, and this was where Titus' inexperience driving a wagon showed, so that Beorhtic was summoned by Otha to replace him, but when Titus began to jump down to the ground, Beorhtic stopped him.

"Sit next to me and watch," he said. "You may need to be able to do this on your own."

Of course Titus did so, and he was impressed at the skill with which the indentured man maneuvered the conveyance, although the animals had to be unhitched to move it into its final position, accomplished with the help of the other wagon drivers. The circle created by the wagons and carts was well more than a hundred paces across, but it was how the slaves, servants and other noncombatants, without being told, moved inside the circle that informed Titus what was happening. Then he spotted a handful of men in full armor standing in a knot where an older nobleman was standing, and Titus recalled that Eadward had told him this was Lord Mucel. Tying the oxen to the wagon for the first time, Titus had no idea what to do, so he stood there watching as, their orders issued, the fighting men around Mucel dispersed, and for the first time, he saw they were mostly men like Uhtric, the professional warriors who were loyal to thegns like Otha and Lord Eadwig. The fact that Mucel did not leave the inner circle also told Titus something, and his lip curled in disgust at what he was certain was the cowardice of the older nobleman. Since his attention was turned inward, he was completely oblivious to Otha drawing his horse up, observing the youth with a small smile. Uhtric and Willmar, also mounted, were with him, and Otha turned to Titus' tutor.

"Do you think he's ready?" he asked quietly. "Or should he stay here?"

Uhtric considered for a moment, then answered, "Honestly, Lord, with anyone else, I'd say of course not. But," he shook his head, "this boy is different."

"And," Willmar, who had grown fond of the youth as well, pointed out, "we'll make sure he's in the rear."

Otha did not respond to either of them, calling out instead, "Boy!" When Titus spun about, the Thegn asked gruffly, "Are you just going to stand there gawking? Why aren't you ready?"

It took a moment for the import to hit him, but not even Otha could fault the speed with which Titus ran to the wagon, leapt into the back to grab his spear and shield, then hesitated, but it was Uhtric who understood why.

"I know you haven't trained wearing that vest," he said, then indicated his own, although his had dozens of small iron rings sewn closely together, "but it's better to wear it, even if you're not used to it."

This was all Titus needed, and when he hopped down, Otha pointed to where the column of men on foot were waiting the order to resume the march.

"Go join Cenric," the Thegn ordered, but when Titus began to move, he stopped him. "You're going to be in the rear rank," he said sternly. "Do you understand? If I find out you tried to get anywhere near the shield wall, I'll flay you."

"Yes, Lord," Titus answered immediately, and Otha had to smother his smile until the youth had turned away and went running off.

"I remember what it was like, running off to my first battle," Uhtric sighed.

"So do I," Otha laughed, "and as I recall, you pissed yourself."

Not surprisingly, Willmar found this as amusing as Uhtric did not, and he protested, "That's not true! Yeorwic spread that rumor, and it wasn't true, Lord! I swear it!"

"Well," Otha countered, "since Yeorwic is dead now, I'll guess we'll never know."

"I told him he shouldn't try to bed Eorfwine's woman," Willmar commented. "Everyone knows what a bad temper he has."

"We could use him here," Uhtric allowed, and the other two agreed before they were quickly occupied with moving at a trot to take their place with Eadwig.

They left behind the men on foot, all of whom bore countenances that ranged from grim determination to apprehension…with one exception, as Titus was grinning ear to ear. He was doing it! He was marching to war!

Alfred's host remained in its marching column as it moved out onto the great chalk plain, which the King had decided to keep his army in until his scouts came back with detailed information about Guthrum. He had sounded confident in this strategy of announcing his army's presence to his lords, but the reality was far different; he was beset by doubts that were gnawing at his resolve and belief in this strategy. Mucel had been correct; by doing as he was, Alfred was handing Guthrum crucial time to array his forces, but what he had not divulged to any of his noblemen was that he was almost certain he knew where they would find the Danes. It was about two miles west and just a bit south of Ethantun, at spot where the escarpment that marked the end of the Sarum plain moved from its east/west axis to more of a north/south axis. The remains of an old hillfort like the one on Battlesbury Hill was located on a slight rise above the plain, and while the slope was gentle on its southern approach, there was a steep drop-off along the northern and western sides. This, Alfred felt certain, would be the anchor of the Danes' right flank, their line then stretching across the otherwise level ground a distance of perhaps a half-mile to where the escarpment fell off on the eastern side. The cause for his certainty was that this was ground he would have chosen in Guthrum's position, coming from the north from Cippinhamm, because it negated the very thing Mucel had proposed in trying to slip around to flank the Danes. Perhaps if the Northmen had not already been in Ethantun, Alfred might have tried to beat Guthrum to this ground, because then it would force the Dane to choose whether or not to try and assault the steep slope from the north, but once Wiglaf and his scouts had located the enemy, he decided this was the best alternative. It would be impossible for either force to flank each other, meaning that it would be a battle of numbers, shield wall to shield wall, and while Alfred had not lied to his nobles, he had withheld one other vital piece of information.

For the first time, Alfred and his Saxons held a numerical superiority to the Great Army of the Danes. Now, as he rode his horse at the head of the marching column at the same almost leisurely pace that they had held on their approach to the hill, there was little talk from his Ealdormen riding on either side, nor from his senior thegns behind them. They were all scanning the horizon continuously, watching for movement that would indicate that Wiglaf or one of his men was returning.

Further down the column, in the last ranks, Titus was

beginning to tire a bit, realizing that marching while carrying a shield and holding a spear was not quite as straightforward as he had assumed. He also felt conspicuous because, given where he was in the column, he was surrounded by unfamiliar faces, and was among the lowest-ranking ceorls that were as poor as his father, something that he had found hard to believe until he saw for himself. And, he also realized that at least his father had his own spear and a shield, although it was in even worse shape than the one Titus had been given. Most of the men around him did not even have shields, and their weapons, if they could be called that, were mostly billhooks, although a handful of men carried pitchforks, and none of them had any kind of protective equipment like Titus' boiled leather vest. It made him feel conspicuous, although these men, none of whom were from Eadwig's fyrd, seemed to accept him readily enough. Shortly after they started out, the man to his left in the shambling column spoke up.

"I saw you practicing yesterday," he said genially. "You gave the man who was training you all he could handle."

Titus looked over in surprise, realizing this was the first time he had actually examined a man who might possibly be standing next to him in battle. In many ways, the man resembled Titus' own father—about the same age, weathered features, and already missing several teeth— but what was most surprising to him was what the man had said, because he certainly had not felt that way.

Consequently, he was slightly suspicious that the man might be setting him up for some sort of jest, so he asked, "What makes you say that…?"

"Aedelstan," the man understood. "I'm part of Ealdorman Cuthred's fyrd. Although," he made a sour face, "I'm one of Lord Ceolmund's ceorls." Titus assumed that Ceolmund must be a thegn like Otha, but he did not ask. Aedelstan continued, "Anyway, I saw him after you were done, and," he grinned, and Titus saw that two of his missing teeth had been broken off, "he wasn't walking very well."

"Uhtric?" Titus responded instinctively, then understood the name would have no meaning to Aedelstan. "Really?" he asked doubtfully, then admitted, "It didn't feel like it to me."

"I saw him," Aedelstan repeated, "and I'd say that it was a draw at least." For the first time, he examined Titus more closely, and he asked suddenly, "How old are you anyway…?"

Just as Aedelstan had, Titus interpreted the unanswered part of the question, answering, "Titus. I'm from Cissanbyrig." Realizing that Aedelstan expected more, he spontaneously lied, "And I'm seventeen."

Aedelstan regarded Titus for several heartbeats, then either accepted Titus' lie or decided it was not worth pursuing and turned his mind to the first piece of information, which Titus anticipated from the man's frown, so he was prepared for the ceorl to ask, "Isn't Cissanbyrig part of Ealdorman Wulfhere's domain?"

"It is," Titus confirmed. "But I went to Wiltun to join Lord Eadwig because he's remained loyal to the King."

"I'd heard that not all of Wulfhere's nobles had followed him," Aedelstan said carefully.

"Wulfhere is a traitor," Titus answered firmly, both because he believed it and because he wanted to send a message to Aedelstan that he was loyal to their King. "And when I heard that he was with Guthrum and found out Lord Owin was with him, I left for Wiltun as soon as I could, because I heard that Lord Eadwig was standing loyal."

Aedelstan seemed to accept this, then asked innocently, "When you say that Wulfhere is with Guthrum, does that mean that the thegns and ceorls who stayed with him might be with these Danish bastards we're about to fight?"

In the span of three or four heartbeats that passed, Titus realized with a dull horror that he had deliberately shut this prospect from his mind. Aedelstan's reasonable question had opened the door in his mind where he had shoved the possibility that his father might be standing among the Danes. It was true that Leofric had said he was going to refuse the call put out by Ealdorman Wulfhere, but Titus also knew his father well; Leofric was a weak man who tried to appear to be strong, and he was susceptible to pressure from others. If Lord Owin, the thegn who held Cissanbyrig for Wulfhere had paid a visit to their farm after Titus' departure, he held little doubt that Leofric would have meekly picked up his shield and spear and followed obediently. What, Titus wondered, if I see him?

Aloud, he answered Aedelstan, "I suppose it's a possibility." He shrugged, doing his best to make it seem as if it did not matter. "We'll be finding out soon enough."

The ceorl sensed that there was something artificial about the large youth's indifference, but Aedelstan was by nature a kind man, and with the kind of commonsense logic that did not derive from any book, he deduced that it was likely that the lad's father might indeed be with the Danes. It had to be, the ceorl thought with sympathy, a terrible prospect for a son. Consequently, he decided to stop talking, and they walked in silence for some time.

Suddenly, the ceorl's face took on a look of dawning recognition, and he broke the silence by asking, "You said you were from Cissanbyrig?"

"Yes," Titus answered with a frown, wondering if perhaps Aedelstan was a bit soft in the head. "Why?"

"Because we heard about Lord Eadwig's fyrd being ambushed by a pack of Danes, and there was a ceorl with him who slew four Danes by himself! And," his tone turned almost accusing, "we heard that it wasn't a man from Wiltun, it was someone from Cissanbyrig! How many other men from Cissanbyrig came with you?"

Titus was flummoxed, torn equally between embarrassment and pride that, for the first time in his life, if not his name, then at least his deeds were known by strangers.

Nevertheless, he answered honestly, "None. I'm the only

one."

Aedelstan continued staring for a long moment, then signaled his acceptance by raising his voice to the men around them. "Lads, did you hear that? Remember we heard about the ceorl with Lord Eadwig's fyrd who singlehandedly killed four of those Danish bastards?" There was a ragged chorus of acknowledgement, and Aedelstan made an elaborate gesture towards Titus, "This is him! This is the one they call the Berserker!"

"But he's just a boy!" This came from behind Titus and towards the middle of the rank, and when Titus turned to scowl over his shoulder, his eyes met those of one man who, by the manner in which he looked away, he was certain was the one who had said it.

"Is it true?" the ceorl on the opposite side of Aedelstan asked, but in a more respectful tone. "Did you really kill four of them? By yourself?"

Despite a tendency to boast, Titus at heart was honest, not just with others but perhaps even more harshly with himself, so he answered simply, "That's what I was told. I…I don't remember much."

"I know Wigmund," another man spoke up. "He fights for Lord Ceadda. Aedelstan and I heard him talking about the…Titus here. If he says it happened, it happened. He said they call him the Berserker now."

To Titus' relief, this seemed to settle the matter, and there was a brief period where the only sound was the tromping of leather boots on the grassy surface of the plain.

"Have you ever fought in a battle like this?" Titus asked abruptly, as much to change the subject, but also with Uhtric's admonition that the ambush would be nothing like what was likely coming, and he winced at what could have been a challenging tone.

Fortunately for him, Aedelstan understood, and he replied,

"I was at Ashdown with King Alfred."

While Titus had queried men like Cenric and Uhtric about what battle was like, he understood that a man like Aedelstan, who did not even possess a shield and would be in the rearmost ranks, would have information that would be more valuable to him for this, his first battle.

Instead of asking him the question he had pestered other experienced men about what a battle was like, he asked Aedelstan, "What do we do? I mean," he added quickly, "here in the rear ranks?"

Aedelstan shrugged as he replied, "Mainly, we push the man in front of us, and if one of the men in front of us falls, we step into their place. But it's mostly the King and Ealdormen's men who will be in the front lines." Aedelstan completely missed the look of disappointment flash across Titus' face, but then he added casually, "Of course, the King will want anyone who knows how to throw a javelin to be a bit closer to the front." Suddenly, he looked over at Titus and asked, "Do you know how?"

"Yes," Titus lied immediately. "I practiced when I was in Wiltun with Lord Eadwig."

The truth was that he had watched the men who had been selected to hurl the lighter, shorter javelins, and had even been allowed to throw one himself, although he had badly missed the large wooden target. But, it had stuck in the ground, so he was not being totally dishonest, was he?

"Then when they hand out the javelins from those carts," he jerked his thumb over his shoulder at the pair of handcarts that were being pushed by slaves, "you need to grab a few."

"Then what?" Titus asked, and Aedelstan shrugged and replied, "Just follow everyone else. The lads will let you through to a spot close enough to the shield wall to throw them."

Nodding his thanks, Titus fell silent, as did Aedelstan, although other men were holding muttered conversations all around them, which Titus ignored to examine his surroundings. Because of his late arrival, he was on the outside file on the right side of the column, and since his view ahead was blocked by the men plodding across the green plain, he focused his attention to his right. The plain, he saw, was only flat in a general sense; there were seemingly endless undulations that, if he had ever seen it, would remind Titus of a rolling ocean. Although it was still sunny, there were clouds that briefly obscured the blazing orb as they drifted across the landscape, casting giant shadows on the plain as they did. So absorbed was he in his observation that when the single horn call sounded from the front of the column, Titus almost impaled himself on the tines of the pitchfork held over the shoulder of the man in front of him as he kept walking. Inexperienced he may have been, but Titus could instantly sense the change in the mood of the men around him, and he was almost certain there was a new and sudden odor in the air, one that he would come to know very well, the rank stench of fear sweat.

"There's only one reason we're stopping," Aedelstan commented grimly, and this was the last relatively calm moment as mounted men came galloping back down the column, stopping wherever the ceorls for whom they were responsible were located.

Somehow, amid all the shouting, Titus heard, "The Danes are waiting for us! We're forming for battle!"

Deciding not to wait to be told, he immediately headed for the pair of handcarts, although he was disappointed to see that the more experienced men, almost all of whom were barely older than he was, were already there, snatching up what Titus counted was four javelins apiece. He followed suit, briefly thinking of grabbing an extra before realizing that he was going to have difficulty holding four as it was. For a brief moment, he was on the verge of panic, thinking that he would have to discard his spear or his shield, and the idea of this mortified him so much that he forced himself to think, quickly determining that if he used the leather loop, his shield could dangle free from his grasp so that he could wrap his hand around the four slender shafts. Fortunately, the delay was not excessive, nor was his consternation even noticed by the others, all of them bearing more or less the same expression with features taut from the tension of what lay ahead. Doing as Aedelstan directed, he was moving with the other javelineers when he heard the ceorl call his name.

"God go with you, Titus the Berserker! Tonight I'll come looking for you and we can talk about all the heathens we slay today!"

Despite his own tension, Titus grinned and called back, "And to you, Aedelstan!" Then, before he could stop himself, he boasted, "I'll try and save some of them for you!"

Wiglaf himself had returned with the news for Alfred, and it took an effort for the King not to sag with relief as his scout confirmed that his guess had been a good one.

"When I left, they were just beginning to move into their shield wall to wait for us, Lord King," Wiglaf said, but he was pointing ahead where, barely visible, a dark straight line waited for them.

"Do they have any cavalry?" Alfred asked.

Wiglaf shook his head, but his answer was less than satisfactory.

"I do not know, Lord King. I sent a pair of men down off the plain to circle around just after dawn. But," his expression turned grim, "they should have been back by now."

"Lord King," Ealdorman Aelfstan spoke up, "I believe that Guthrum would keep their cavalry from our sight as long as possible."

While slightly irritated, Alfred agreed, and he mused aloud, "I would have them on the opposite slope, a short distance from the top." Addressing Wiglaf, he asked quietly, "You know those two men better than I do, Wiglaf. What do you think happened to them?"

"They're dead, Lord King," Wiglaf answered immediately. "Cynebald and Otho are," he corrected, "*were* two of my best. The only way they wouldn't complete their task is if they were killed. Or," he finished gloomily, "captured, which means if they're not dead now, they will be soon."

Alfred made the sign of the cross, which the men around him hastily copied, murmuring under their breath the kinds of things men said about those who are doomed.

"What are your orders, Lord King?" Ealdorman Cuthred broke the brief silence. "Should we move into our battle formation now?"

Alfred considered briefly, then shook his head. "Let's close the distance a bit more. They're too far away for the men to march in a shield wall. I want them to be fresh."

With that, they resumed the march, closing another mile, to a point where they were perhaps two miles away from the Danish host, which was now distinct enough to see the colors of the brightly painted shields. For their part, they seemed content to wait for the Saxons, and Alfred gave a curt nod to the horn player who was mounted and from this point forward would be next to the warrior bearing Alfred's personal standard, a golden wyvern, the mythical winged dragon with two legs and two claws and long tail on a red field, which had been adopted as the standard of the House of Wessex, who in turn would be immediately behind Alfred wherever he was. Licking his lips, he blew the series of notes that ordered the column to halt.

Alfred, spun his horse about, a chestnut stallion that was every bit the match of Eadwig's Hama, to face the noblemen who would bear the responsibility for what came next.

"Lords," he spoke in just a bit less than a full shout, "attend to your men. I want the men of Ealdorman Cuthred on the right wing, those of Ealdorman Aelfstan on the left, while I will occupy the center!" This had been expected by the Ealdormen, although there had been some quibbling the night before about who should have the honor of occupying which wing. What was unexpected was when Alfred, searching through the faces, found the one for which he was looking. "And, Lord Eadwig, while your Ealdorman Wulfhere has betrayed us, you and your thegns and the fyrd of Wiltun kept the faith with us. I ask that you and your fyrd do me the honor of occupying the center with me."

Eadwig, wearing a mail coif but still waiting to don his helmet, flushed with pleasure, answering immediately, "The honor is all mine, Lord King, and you can rest assured that the men of Wiltun will acquit themselves today!"

Alfred did not respond, for there was no need, the others understanding by his silence that he was expecting them to execute his orders, although there was nothing organized by the manner in which they all wheeled their mounts, crashing into each other as they hurled curses at the other nobleman they felt was at fault. It was unseemly, but Alfred said nothing, ascribing it to the nerves of the moment, and in fact, viewed their eagerness as a positive sign. The commander of his personal bodyguard, aptly named Cyneweard as a signal that he served in the same capacity as his father had, was among the others, but he did not have far to go since Alfred's household men were immediately behind their King. Alfred did turn to his standard bearer and order the man to follow him, and he walked his horse a short distance away, staring at the Danes who were now close enough that their shields were distinctly visible, an array of reds, blues, greens, and many of them multi-colored and with geometric designs. At this moment, they were all on the ground, resting against the legs of the front rank of Danes as they watched the Saxons arranging themselves. Alfred had done a perfect job of picking a distance that was just a bit too far away for the Danes to try and catch the Saxons unprepared with a sudden rush, even with their speed of movement. Aligning himself with what he was certain was Guthrum's personal banner, not because he could make out the design but because it was the largest, Alfred drew up, pointing to the spot to his immediate right, which his standard bearer quickly occupied.

From this point forward, everything that happened would be based on Alfred's position, marking the dead center of the line. Not, he knew, that there would not be adjustments made as they closed the distance, either because he saw that he had slightly miscalculated, or the Danes did something like either contract their lines or expand them. He did not think there was much risk of the former, simply because if the Danes did so, they might enable Alfred and his men just enough space between the Northmen's formation and the edge of the escarpment to get on their flank.

Alfred's men, all of them dismounted now, hurried to where their King was waiting, and Cyneweard began bellowing orders, and calling out specific men, the most experienced warriors belonging to Alfred. As befitted the bodyguard of the King of Wessex, every one of them wore a mail coat, their shields all decorated in the same manner, red with the wyvern emblazoned just above the boss. All of them had a helmet, but some also had a mail coif while others did not, a matter of personal preference that Alfred, somewhat grudgingly, allowed, if only because he appreciated uniformity. They all carried the *seaxe* on their belt, the single-edged long sword from which the name Saxon derived, but the day's fighting would begin with the spear. Once Alfred's personal bodyguard were arrayed to his satisfaction, they occupied a space more than a hundred paces across and five men deep, but unlike the Legions of Rome, there was literally no space between the men in the ranks, standing shoulder to shoulder so that, when they raised their shields, they would overlap. This was the shield wall, the method men used to try and kill each other for centuries now, and once the royal bodyguard was in place, those thegns and their retainers from around Hamtunscir who would have normally reported to Wintanceaster instead of Egbert's Stone as part of Alfred's personal fyrd, moved into place on either side, spreading across the green plain. Only then did Eadwig, Otha, Ceadda, and Aelfnod, and all of their household warriors move into the spot that Cyneweard designated, effectively forming the rightmost side of the center wing. Once this was done, Cuthred led his fyrd into their spot on the right wing, but in truth, there was barely the width of a man's distance between each wing, and was only used at this moment for organizational purposes, since even this small a gap could spell catastrophe once the fighting began.

While the Ealdormen like Cuthred and Aelfstan had banners of their own that the men of their fyrd could identify and assemble around, the minor Ealdormen like Eadwig had a standard that was a stout pole, atop which was a carving that represented their house. In Eadwig's case, it was, not surprisingly, a rearing stallion, painted black, that was a representation of Hama, which his bearer thrust high into the air so that the ceorls like Cenric who would be immediately behind the thegns and their men knew where to assemble. Once the shield wall was in place, it measured about six hundred paces across, which Alfred had calculated was the width of Guthrum's line. Finally, Alfred was satisfied, and he dismounted, handing the reins to one of his bodyguards, who led the horse away, and for the first time, the King of Wessex hefted his shield as he walked a couple of paces ahead of what was now an unbroken line of shields. It was far from silent, although the noise was more of a low buzzing sound as men said something to the man next to them, but it quickly died down at the sight of their King, wearing a helmet with a circlet of pointed stars made of iron welded to it, standing there in an obvious signal. He did not say anything; that would be coming shortly. Drawing his own *seaxe*, he held it aloft for a moment, then in a slow, careful motion lowered it until it was pointing directly at the waiting Danes. The attack was beginning.

Chapter Seven

For Titus, he was too busy trying to follow his newly found comrades to be scared, and as Aedelstan had predicted, the men closer to the rear simply moved aside as the javelineers pressed their way through the packed mass. If a thegn had given one of them the authority to give commands, Titus had not heard it, but there was a man of about twenty, with a patchy beard yet with an air of confidence that seemed to signal to the others, all of them young, that he was their leader.

Consequently, when he shouted to be heard, "Follow me! We need to be five ranks back from the shield wall!" Titus followed him obediently, as did the others. He had noticed that, while he was not the only one, he was one of the few who also had a spear and shield, but he was unique in wearing the boiled leather vest, which earned him several curious glances.

None of those who noticed said anything, and fairly quickly, he saw that their leader intended to array the javelineers with the center wing, and while he was never told, he quickly determined that his comrades were gravitating towards their own thegns. The problem for Titus was that, once amidst the crush of bodies, it was hard for him to make sense of anything. Then, out of the corner of his eye, he saw a rearing stallion, atop a pole, being thrust up into the air. Recognizing the standard, Titus felt his face split into a grin; he was well aware that Lord Eadwig had exchanged his previous symbol of a boar for this, representing Hama, and he felt a surge of pride that he had been entrusted with the care of the very stallion this standard represented. Maybe, he thought as he shoved his way in that direction, it's a sign from God. He was bolstered by the sight of familiar faces, although he did not really know any of the men from Eadwig's fyrd who were armed with javelins other than by sight, yet this still helped to settle his nerves.

"What are *you* doing here?" He turned in surprise at the accusatory tone, seeing someone just a few years older than himself, and while he recognized him, he did not know his name. Before Titus could respond, the other man said suspiciously, "I never saw you training with us! So," he pointed to the four javelins that Titus was holding in his left hand, "why are you with us?"

"Does it matter?" Titus countered, proud that his tone sounded cool.

He was surprised that this seemed to work, the other man, wearing a felt cap and without a shield or spear suddenly looking uncertain, then admitting, grudgingly, "I suppose not. But," he pointed to the javelins in Titus' left hand, "I hope you don't kill anyone but those Danes."

"I won't," Titus promised, although just the words uttered by the other Saxon ignited a flicker of doubt in his mind.

Before he could dwell on this, there was a ragged chorus bellowed by men in the front rank, and the compact group began moving forward. Very quickly, Titus learned that because of his longer legs, he had to be careful not to step on the heels of the man ahead of him, and he realized he was smelling the same stench he had noticed not long before. There was no talking, but all around him, he heard men muttering what he assumed were prayers to God, asking Him to watch over them, and he wondered why it had not occurred to him to do the same. Once he became accustomed to the pace, for the first time, Titus paid attention to more than his immediate surroundings, using his height to look at the waiting Northmen, now close enough to make out individual figures, although they still had not hefted their shields. He counted an even dozen banners spread along their line, but they were hanging limply because of the lack of breeze, but while this might have been the cause for Titus' tunic already being soaked with sweat, he understood the temperature had little to do with it, or the fact that he was wearing a leather vest, and just a glance around him at men who were only in tunics and seeing the dark patches confirmed this. He desperately wanted to ask one of the men around him what was coming next, but even if he tried, his mouth was so dry that his tongue was sticking to the roof of his mouth, and he cursed himself for not thinking to get a drink of water before leaving the wagon. Are we suddenly going to start running at them? he wondered. Or is King Alfred going to call a halt? When will we throw these javelins? Although, he acknowledged to himself, he had been foolish for wanting to be among the javelineers. While his shield was secure, because he was grasping the javelins, it was bouncing against his leg, and his hand was beginning to cramp from having to hold four of them. He was using his spear as a walking staff, noticing that while the slope was gradual, it was noticeable, both with his legs and how the Danes were slowly vanishing because of the men in front of him as they rose to roughly the same level.

Just when he thought that, in fact, King Alfred intended to go from the march to the run, the horn sounded somewhere off to his left front. This time, he was not caught by surprise, following the example of the other men, coming to an immediate halt that was surprisingly uniform. By leaning slightly to the side, Titus could catch glimpses of the men in the front rank, all of them wearing helmets, and he recognized Lord Eadwig by the device on his helmet, a copy of the rearing stallion, but he could not find Otha, Uhtric, or any other familiar face. The halt also marked the last moment of relative quiet, the men of Alfred's army suddenly erupting in a bellowing chorus that, as far as Titus could tell, began spontaneously. It was almost impossible to make out what the men around him were shouting, so he simply joined in by bellowing as loudly as he could. Within a matter of a couple heartbeats, a new sound added to the din, a competing sound that Titus was certain was coming from the Danes, and along with the roaring of men's voices, there was a rhythmic, clattering sound. With his view of the Danes obscured, Titus was left to guess what was happening, but he continued shouting, and even thrust his spear into the air when he saw the men ahead of him doing so. Another blast of the horn suddenly cut through the noise, and the compact formation began moving again, at a slightly faster pace, and still Titus could not see exactly how far away they were from the Danes. He moved with the others, even as he braced himself for the Northmen to suddenly come rushing at them, but there was nothing to indicate this was happening. Then, once more the horn sounded, and the formation stopped, while the noise was intensifying as men on both sides continued bellowing. Titus did not hear the command, but suddenly, the men around him swept their arms back, one of the javelins in their hands, and he was forced to hurry to switch his spear for one of his javelins to follow suit.

"Hurry up, you stupid oaf!" He recognized the voice as belonging to the javelineer who had challenged him, but unfortunately, this rattled him even more, and he actually fumbled, the javelin slipping out of his right hand, but the man snapped, "Don't bother with that one! Use one of your others!"

Somehow, he managed to do so just in time, and for the first time, he actually heard a voice over the other noise. "Release!"

If Titus was slower than the others, it was by an eyeblink, but it was enough that he did not copy the more experienced javelineers in hurling it seemingly skyward so that the missiles arced high in the air, as his javelin, trailing the others, was launched in a much flatter trajectory, skimming above the helmeted heads of the men in the front rank by no more than a foot.

His hope that nobody noticed was shattered when the same man snarled, "Are you trying to kill our own men, boy? Besides, we're too far away for you to throw it like that!"

That the others were now hurling their next missile, without any command this time, meant that Titus was once again slightly behind the others with the second volley, although this time, he did arc it higher in the air. It was just as the missile left his hand he heard a new sound, one that simultaneously made the hair on the back of his neck stand up yet filled his heart with a savage joy, screams of pain that needed no translation. For the next several heartbeats, Titus and the other javelineers sent waves of javelins over the heads of their comrades, the cries of pain also accompanied by a hollow cracking sound that he would come to learn was the sound of a hurled missile being blocked by a wooden shield. He managed to bend over and snatch up the javelin he had dropped, standing straight and throwing it in one motion, and he was secretly proud that he was not the last man to exhaust his supply. What he was completely unprepared for was what happened next, as the javelineer leader and the others immediately turned about and began pushing their way to the rear. It was not the man who had chastised him but one of the others who noticed that Titus was not moving.

"What are you doing, boy? We need to get out of the way now! Our part is over!"

However, Titus did not move, but the other javelineer was unwilling to waste time arguing with this overgrown boy who was clearly soft in the head, so he simply shrugged and turned back around, disappearing through the crush of men. Titus' intention was to push his way through the mass to get nearer to Cenric and the others of Eadwig's fyrd, having spotted the ceorl a few moments earlier, but his plan was literally swept away as, with a huge roar, the men of Alfred's army went rushing at the Danes, sweeping Titus along with them. He barely managed to snatch his spear out of the ground, and almost lost his footing; ironically, he was saved by the shield wall coming to a sudden stop as they collided with the Danes, and the fact that he smashed into the back of the man in front of him had been expected by the ceorl, but this knowledge did not extend to Titus. When the man behind him slammed into his back, he was completely unprepared, and he found himself suddenly struggling for breath as he felt crushed between an immovable object in the man in front of him and the irresistible pressure of the men behind him, their aggregate weight seeming to crush the very life from him. Very quickly, he was struggling not just for his breath, but against a rising panic as his senses struggled to make sense of what was ultimately a completely unfamiliar experience, and even as he tried to bring his arms up to push against the man's back, who had not even glanced over his shoulder, he had the fleeting thought, This is what a shield wall is like? Adding to his disorientation was something that just moments before he would have thought impossible, that it could actually be louder, but it was, and even with his inexperience, he heard the sharp metallic ringing of iron on iron, along with the deeper thudding as a blade struck the wood of a shield.

All around him, men were grunting from the effort of adding their weight to the mass of Saxons who, in simple but brutal terms, were trying to overpower the Danes through a combination of sheer weight and the collective will of men defending their homes and their lands. Finally, Titus was sufficiently separated to draw a breath, his head clearing and giving him the ability to do more than just respond instinctively. He quickly copied the men around him, placing his left hand on the back of the man in front of him and leaning into him, and he had the thought that it would help if there was something to grasp more than just the wool of the man's tunic, but his mind was immediately occupied with the sensation that was vibrating back through the bodies of the men in front of him and into his left arm. It took a bit of time, but he realized that he was actually *feeling* the fighting up there as whoever it was in the front rank of the shield wall either launched a thrust or blocked one from the Dane across from him. Inevitably, the shrill screams that Titus had heard with the volleys of javelins resumed, but now those cries were much closer, and while he had no idea how much time had elapsed, it was about a hundred heartbeats after the initial collision when he heard one of those screams to his direct front. Before his mind could register its possible meaning, he learned what it was by virtue of the fact that suddenly the man in front of him took a full step forward, but what caught his eye was movement down near the ground, and once he closed the distance and renewed his grip on a handful of tunic, he turned his attention to what he instantly saw was a man trying to crawl on hands and knees to the rear. His progress was hindered because he had one hand clasped to his face, covering his left eye, but although the rest of his face was obscured by blood that was dripping onto the trodden grass, Titus recognized him as one of Alfred's fyrd by his mail, and he wondered if this man was the first of the Saxons to fall. Hard on the heels of that thought was wondering how many men would have to fall before he got his chance to face the Danes, and he realized that he was no longer as eager for the chance as he had been just an hour before.

Whether it was on the express orders of Guthrum, or because of the inherent difficulty that came from men who only nominally recognized him as their commander resulting in a sort of paralysis, the Danes had chosen not to countercharge once the Saxons came rushing at them, choosing instead to stand their ground. What this meant in a practical sense was that the rearmost ranks of the Northmen, which were composed of men not all that dissimilar to the poorer ceorls on the far side of the Saxon shield wall, were already close to the edge of the steep escarpment that marked the northern edge of Sarum plain. Adding to their disadvantage was the factor that Alfred had counted on, that for one of the few times since the Northmen had arrived, the Saxons of Wessex had a substantial advantage in numbers. Since the Danes were aware of this, of course, it did stiffen their resolve, so that neither side could budge the other, and the sun, which had been almost at its zenith, began its downward arc over the struggle. The warfare of this era consisted of the most rudimentary of tactics, and when a pitched battle was fought, it was a contest of brute strength and willpower. Skill in arms, while useful, was not crucial, at least beyond the basics of being able to execute a killing thrust while not exposing oneself to a counterthrust from one's foe, and the ability to block an attack from that foe. Facing the Danes did mean that the Saxons faced more axmen, but the Danes had been here in Wessex for almost four decades, and they had learned how to handle the threat offered by this particular weapon.

Essentially, standing in a shield wall required endurance, and perhaps somewhat confusingly, patience as a warrior waited for an opportunity stemming from the exchange of thrusts and counterthrusts, as spear points flicked out at the Danes all along the shield wall. Most of the time, especially early in the contest, these attacks were blocked, either by a shield or by blade, but this was also when men had the most energy and were in full voice, roaring their defiance, their exultation at killing or wounding the man across from them, or in agony as the strand of their life was cut short. And, in the middle of it all was King Alfred, shield in hand, standing in the front rank, for this was what the Saxons expected from their kings, and while he did not particularly care for battle, and was not infused with the bloodlust as so many of his warriors were, he understood perfectly well what he had to do. Today, however, was also slightly different, because Alfred sensed a real opportunity here to not only deal Guthrum and his Danes a resounding defeat, but to avenge the indignity of being forced to flee from Cippinhamm, something that only his wife Eahlswith knew had scorched his pride in a way that nothing else had, or could. On this day at Ethantun, Alfred was as close to the battle fury as he had ever been, and it was his example that kept his men fully committed to victory. He had refused to relinquish his spot, and this *was* unusual for a king; normally, while he would be in the front rank of the shield wall when battle was joined, once honor had been satisfied, he would remove himself at least one spot, although it was usually several ranks back, depending on the courage of the monarch.

Despite his example, and despite the numerical advantage, the Danes were standing fast, and the casualties were beginning to mount. A glance to either side of him told Alfred that a disturbing number of his personal bodyguards had fallen, although he would not know how many of them were dead or wounded until after the battle, but Cyneweard was still with him, his spear point covered with blood, as was his face and front of his mail, although he had assured his King that it was not his own. The time for the sword was not yet; that was reserved for the moment when the enemy cracked and a gap opened in the shield wall, when a less cumbersome weapon than a spear was necessary. No, Alfred thought with a touch of worry, it was not time yet because these stubborn Danes were not budging. As soon as one of them fell, just as with the Saxons, another Northman would immediately move into the spot, before the gap in the shield wall could be exploited. Alfred knew, as did the other veteran warriors in the fyrd, that the chance for exploitation required more than one man falling at close enough to the same time to create a gap more than a single shield's width, and that had not happened yet anywhere along the six hundred pace-long shield wall. Alfred blocked another thrust from the Dane he had been facing for a fair amount of time, a burly man older than Alfred with a plaited red beard who wore an ornate helmet that Alfred suspected had come from a dead Saxon, perhaps from Northumbria by the look of it. Not surprisingly, he had been very energetic, almost frantic in his attacks on Alfred, but this was something that Alfred was prepared for and expecting; this was what it meant to be a king, after all. Killing a king would not only enhance a warrior's prestige, no matter whether they were Dane, Saxon, or Frankish, but it would make him a wealthy man, and he had already weathered three Northmen who were every bit as committed to killing him as this red bearded, ax-wielding warrior. But Alfred had an advantage; unlike a Dane who was trying to kill a king, he did not feel the need to slay his foe singlehandedly, and he had understood Cyneweard's nudge in the immediate aftermath of blocking this last attack. He knew what to do because it was a maneuver they had not only practiced, but had used at Ashdown, and now Alfred launched a counterthrust just as the Dane was pulling his arm back to prepare for another blow. The Dane moved his shield, offering a contemptuous laugh as he did so, never seeing the spear thrust that came from Cyneweard, the point unerringly cutting through the space that had been occupied by the Dane's shield a fraction of an eyeblink before to punch into the man's throat just below his jaw, unleashing a fantastic spray of blood that briefly obscured the man's face. Before Alfred could blink, the Dane had collapsed onto his knees, but when he began to topple forward, the King used his spear, not to inflict a wound but to shove the dying man's upper torso back towards the next Northman, also wielding an ax, who was rushing forward to shove his shield into the newly opened gap. As satisfying as it was seeing another enemy vanquished, Alfred was disappointed that the gap was plugged too quickly to exploit it, and he also realized he was growing fatigued.

"Lord King!" Alfred did not turn his attention away, simply nodding that he had heard Cyneweard's call. "I think you have done enough for now, Lord King. Let Theobald have his chance. That way, you can be fresh for when these heathens break!"

Alfred nodded again, but he was raising his shield slightly to block the overhand blow launched by the red-bearded Dane's replacement, this man with hair like summer wheat, although his beard was full and flowing, and he was younger than Alfred. Feeling Theobald's hand patting him in the signal he was ready to step in, Alfred executed a thrust of his own, hard enough to force the Dane to defend himself but without his full weight behind it, enabling him to take a quick step back and to the side, Theobald moving immediately into the gap, just in time to block the Dane's next attack. Removed from immediate danger, Alfred's next act was to accept a leather flask filled with water, handed to him by one of his bodyguards, forcing himself not to drain it despite his raging thirst. The sun had been making intermittent appearances through the scudding clouds, but it was not excessively hot, and he was thankful for that. His thirst temporarily slaked, he turned his attention towards trying to ascertain how his fyrd was faring, and Titus would have been distressed to learn that even a King who fought in the shield wall had an extremely limited view of the fighting, something that Alfred hated. If it was not for the expectations of him, he would have preferred to remain on horseback, and at enough of a remove where he could have a view of the entire battle, but he had learned how to track the progress of a fight by listening to the sounds around him. The roaring of curses and challenges was practically nonexistent by this point; the noise coming from men's throats were almost exclusively grunts, although there was the sudden shout of exultation that was usually in concert with a scream, the shriller ones being an almost certain indication that the wound was mortal. Sometimes there was a gurgling quality when a man took a thrust to the throat, or the blade penetrated a lung, although in the time Alfred was thusly occupied, he did not hear anything like that. As he listened, he looked to either side, searching for the banners of his Ealdormen, both of them still flying, along with the standard poles of his senior nobles like Eadwig's horse, which was still visible just above the heads of his men. No, this battle was nowhere near its end, unless something unexpected happened, and Alfred began what, to him at least, was as important as the things he had just done. He began to pray to God for a sign of His favor, in the form of the Danes breaking.

It happened so gradually that Titus hardly noticed, and to him, it seemed as if one moment he was at least ten men back from the warriors in the shield wall and then he was the sixth man from the front. What puzzled him was that only one other man had left his spot in the front rank, although he was essentially dragged backward by his comrades, being passed from one row to the next. Because of the tangle of legs and bodies, it took Titus a moment to see why this warrior was unable to move under his own power; both of his blood-covered hands were clutching his abdomen, but they were not pressed flat against the man's stomach, and while he was conscious, he was out of his mind with pain, moaning and repeating something that was unintelligible to Titus' ears. Then he was at Titus' feet, and he saw that the man was actually trying to keep his intestines from falling out of the huge gash in the man's armor, which like Titus' was a boiled leather vest, except that it was more similar to Uhtric's, with dozens of smaller iron rings. And, he thought grimly even as he grabbed the back of the vest as he had seen the other men do, it didn't help him at all. He was strong enough to drag the man a few feet further back without using anything but his arm, and when he leaned over slightly as he twisted his torso, while he refused to look at it, he got close enough to the wound to catch the stench of shit, the sign that the man's bowels had been punctured. The bile came rushing up, and he had to clamp his jaws tightly to keep from adding to this poor soul's agony by vomiting on him, but he managed to force it down, and he felt slightly ashamed at the haste with which he turned away from the sight, trying to shut the image out. Fortunately, his mind was quickly occupied with another matter, namely the probable cause for men who were no longer in the shield wall that required him to move closer to the front rank, but had not shown up. They have to be lying up there, he thought, and they're either dead or they're even worse off than the man I just helped. It was a grim thought, but he also chastised himself for thinking that the only men who would die were Danes, and somehow the Saxons might be wounded but not killed, and he resolved that he would never think such childish thoughts again. Now that he was closer to the fighting, the sensations he was experiencing through the body of his comrade intensified as well, and once he lost his grasp on the man's tunic when he recoiled backward, earning him a snarled curse over the man's shoulder. He had no idea who this ceorl was, only that he was not part of Eadwig's fyrd, but once he had finally spotted Cenric, several men over to his right, he had begun trying to think of a way to make his way over so that he would at least be with men he knew. It was not a conscious decision, really, yet before he could stop himself, he looked over his shoulder at the man who was doing the same thing he was, except that he was forced to hold on to the collar of Titus' leather vest.

"I'm going to join my fyrd over there," Titus used his head to indicate the direction, "so you need to move up when I step over."

He waited only long enough to determine that the man heard and understood, then he stepped aside, ignoring the curse of the man, although he moved quickly into Titus' spot. Now, he was forced to shove his way through the men between himself and Cenric, and he was roundly cursed, all of which he wisely ignored. Finally, he was next to Cenric, who, as might be expected, was paying attention to what was going on along the front rank, but he did cast a quick glance at the movement to his left.

Even with all that was going on, Titus laughed at the way the ceorl's eyes widened in surprise, but Cenric recovered quickly, demanding, "What are you doing up here, Titus? I saw you throwing javelins! You should be in the rear now!"

In answer, Titus raised his spear, but Cenric was unimpressed, and he opened his mouth to essentially order the youth to move to the rear when there was a sudden renewal of the bellowing, although it was localized and off to their left. Every man in the area turned their attention to that part of the battle, including Titus and Cenric, and they were just in time to see the sudden movement, but it was Cenric who understood the meaning.

"We've broken through!" He shouted this then immediately returned his attention back to their direct front, then nudged Titus with his shield to get his attention, and when Titus tore his gaze from what he could now see were Saxon warriors moving forward off to their left, he turned to see that the Danes in front of them were now fleeing as well.

"What do we do now?" Titus had to shout for Cenric to hear him, as all of the men around them were suddenly infused with energy, but he received a partial answer when the men to their front suddenly surged forward like their comrades who had created the initial breach.

This time, Titus was somewhat prepared, so he began moving as well, as Cenric replied with a grin, "Why, now we kill as many of these heathen bastards as we can! But," he warned, although he was moving just as rapidly as everyone else around them, "be careful! These savages might suddenly decide to stop and fight!"

It was, Titus realized, sound advice, and he resolved to himself to heed it, yet within a few paces, the youth had pulled ahead of Cenric and his other comrades, mainly because he recognized Uhtric from behind, the warrior having discarded his spear for his *seaxe*. Titus was slowed when he reached where the front ranks had joined, not only from the practical problem of hurdling the bodies of both Danes and Saxons, but from the gruesome evidence of what battle, a *real* battle was like.

"It's not pretty, is it?"

Cenric's voice served to yank Titus out of his horrified examination of the carnage, yet all he could summon was a nod as he followed Cenric's example as the ceorl hopped over the bodies, some of them still moving. The last of the fleeing Danes were just a handful of heartbeats from reaching the escarpment, but from Titus' viewpoint, a disturbingly large number of Saxons seemed to be more interested in looting the Danish bodies, and presumably, helping those comrades and friends who had fallen but had not been able to make their way to the rear. There were certainly Saxons engaging in the pursuit, and he saw small knots of men along the length of the shield wall engaged in the kind of smaller struggles that were reminiscent of the ambush a few days earlier, while a ragged line of Saxons were still intent on pursuing the vanquished foe. Where, Titus thought, is Alfred? Why hasn't he taken control? He was moving again as he thought this, and his intention was to reach those Saxons who still seemed interested in killing Danes, so he quickly picked up speed, intent on participating in this battle because hurling javelins simply had not been enough to satisfy him. A warrior needed to face an enemy, and this was, after all, what he had wanted. He was still about thirty paces short of the escarpment when Uhtric and the other pursuers of Eadwig's fyrd vanished as they went plunging downhill after the Danes, although they had managed to cut down a half-dozen fleeing Northmen. His lungs were burning, but he forced himself to lengthen his stride even further, keeping his shield, which he was now holding in the proper manner, out from his body to allow him to achieve full speed. In the back of his mind was the recognition that he was essentially defenseless in this posture, and at the speed he was running, if he reached the edge of the escarpment and there was a Dane who had done as Cenric warned and decided to fight, he would essentially kill himself by running right onto the point of a Northman's spear or sword. This did not slow him; afterward, as he thought about it, he convinced himself that he had known that Uhtric and the others would be between him and any foe who had tired of running.

Reaching the edge of the escarpment, as determined as he was to catch up, this time, he did falter in his stride as he gaped at the sight of hundreds, no, thousands of men streaming down the hillside, the difference between pursued and pursuer a narrow strip of the slope separating them. It would be a sight that would stick with him, and while it seemed longer, his hesitation was only a heartbeat or two before he was moving again. The angle of the slope was steepest near the top, and he came very close to careening out of control, but after a few stumbling steps and a sickening eyeblink where he was certain he would pitch face first into the chalk slope, he got his feet back under him. With the extra speed, his longer legs drew him closer to Uhtric and the others, but his eyes were on the thin line of Danes now no more than ten paces ahead of the pursuing Saxons. If I could just get to face one of them, he thought, then it will be worth it! It was only later as he pieced things together that he recalled this was also the moment where he noticed something that had struck him when he had briefly paused, how many of these particular Danes were practically indistinguishable from Saxon ceorls. The same tunics, the same trousers, same leather boots, same shields and spears, but it was a passing thought that he quickly shoved aside because, whether they were already exhausted or wanted to die fighting, three of the fleeing enemy suddenly stopped and spun about, raising their shields as they did so. This was his chance! Uhtric, and Willmar, who Titus had just picked out from the other pursuing Saxons, slid to a stop, just out of reach of the Danish spears, while the other nearby Saxon warriors ignored them, continuing their own pursuit, something Titus did not understand but welcomed. His arrival would even the numbers, and he was now less than fifteen paces away when it happened. It was an inconsequential thing, and it was only an accident that Titus was looking beyond the trio of Danes, trying to determine if they were buying time for the others to coalesce, when he saw one of the fleeing men glance over his shoulder. Even at almost a hundred paces, it was a face that Titus would recognize, a face that had been part of his everyday existence, and a fair number of his dreams, or more commonly, nightmares.

Leofric had obviously decided to fight for Wulfhere, and the sight of his fleeing father filled him with a rage that swept away any idea of helping Uhtric and Willmar, neither of whom were aware he was anywhere near them. In fact, when he suddenly veered to his left, cutting across the slope to pass by what was about to be just one of the smaller battles, the movement startled Uhtric to the point that he turned his attention away from the three enemies. Fortunately, it did not cost him his life, and it was more from his startlement than any idea of warning as he shouted Titus' name, but the youth made no indication he had heard, because he had not. This was all the attention the warrior could pay to his young pupil, and the distraction was no more than a couple of normal heartbeats before he and Willmar focused their attention on killing these foolish Danes who had stopped running. Uhtric's last thought about Titus the Berserker was in the form of prayer that the boy did not do something stupid; he had such potential.

For Titus, it was as if every other man within his range of vision, both friend and enemy, had vanished, with one exception: his father, and his prey. Leofric had only looked back once, so that Titus was not certain at first that his father had even seen him in the line of pursuing Saxons, but there was something desperate in Leofric's churning legs and pumping arms that told Titus that he had. Titus did not shout his name; even if he had had the air to do so, he would not have called to Leofric. Ahead of them, perhaps two hundred paces from the bottom of the slope that marked the end of the Sarum Plain was the leading edge of a forest, and Titus could see men vanishing into the trees. That's where he's trying to get, he thought grimly, and that's not happening. It was almost as if Leofric divined

Titus' thoughts, because he chose that moment to discard his shield, and it did enable him to pull away, opening the gap perhaps an extra pace, but while Titus was tiring, he was young, and Leofric was exhausted, the only thing propelling him now his abject fear. Suddenly, one of his feet caught a furrow, and while he kept his feet, his stride was broken, and Titus was on him within a heartbeat, using his shield to slam it into his father's back to send him flying and colliding with the ground so quickly, he could not get his hands out to break his fall. The impact sent Leofric's spear flying, while Titus' own momentum took him past his father, who rolled over several times, so that by the time Titus stopped and spun about, his father had just come to rest on his back. He was conscious, and most of the skin was scraped from his forehead and chin where he had smashed into the ground, but it was his eyes that Titus was looking into, wide and wild with fear. Good, he thought with a grim pleasure as he strode to stand over his father's body, and he did wonder what Leofric was seeing in his son's face. Judging from the terror, it was not pleasant, and yet, Titus was suddenly torn and completely at a loss at what to do. In fact, any of the other Danes still running past could have struck him down, but they were more intent on escaping than striking down a lone Saxon who was standing over a man who was no Dane himself. If any of them had possessed even a fleeting curiosity, it was not enough to stop, either to watch or to intervene.

"W…what are you going to do with that, boy?"

This was the first moment that Titus realized that he was not just holding his spear, he had drawn it back for an overhand thrust, which startled him, though not enough to cause him to lower it.

"I'm trying to make up my mind."

It was not the words, it was the tone that Titus heard in his voice that made him certain that someone else had spoken, because it was a grown voice, a cold voice that belonged to a much older man.

"You…you wouldn't kill your own father, would you,

boy?" Leofric was getting his breath back and his composure, the blood dripping down from his forehead and chin. Still terrified, certainly, but his mind was beginning to work, which was why he added, "You know you'd go to Hell everlasting for killing me, right, boy?"

"My name," his son replied coldly, "is Titus." Without thought, he blurted, "Why don't you ever call me by my name?"

"*Because I hate that name! And I hate you!*" Leofric howled, temporarily forgetting his fear enough to point a shaking finger in his son's face. "*You killed the only thing I ever loved!*"

Without any conscious thought, Titus drew his arm further back, his gaze never leaving his father's face, who in turn was staring up at him with a hatred that, under other circumstances, would have shaken Titus, but that was before. Before he had killed, before he had tasted from the cup of battle, and this reminded him of the ambush and all that he had been told he had done to save Lord Eadward.

Consequently, he informed Leofric, "You won't be the first man I've killed…Father." He spat the name as an epithet, and he was pleased to see the look of surprise and the renewal of the fear, but it was the doubt he noticed, and he assured him, "Oh, yes. I saved Lord Eadwig's son Eadward, and I killed four Danes in single combat four days ago…Father."

"You?" Leofric's lip curled, and Titus realized that his father's nerve was coming back, but even worse, he could feel his own will weakening as the habit formed over fourteen years, developed out of necessity to survive, began reasserting itself. Then Leofric laughed, his confidence returning to the point that he sneered, "I don't believe you, boy. You were always squeamish about slaughtering the pig! And you expect me to believe you killed four *Danes*?"

"You should believe it, because I saw it happen."

Titus could not stop the gasp of surprise, and he turned his head to see that Uhtric and Willmar were standing there, although as distracted as he was, Titus noticed that they were holding their *seaxes*, and they were both still dripping with blood.

"Who is this, Titus?" Willmar asked.

For a brief instant, Titus considered lying, not wanting to acknowledge that his father was fighting for the Danes, but he admitted, "This is my father."

The lack of surprise on Uhtric's face was telling, and the warrior walked over slowly to stand over the ceorl, and as quickly as it had come back, any sign of defiance vanished.

"You," Uhtric's voice was cold, "are a Saxon who chose to fight for the Danes."

"I…I was obeying Ealdorman Wulfhere and Lord Owin." Leofric's voice had suddenly assumed the whining quality that his son had heard before with social superiors, and despised. "That's what I was supposed to do, Lord!"

"I'm not a Lord," Uhtric cut him off. "And no, you are supposed to be loyal to your *King*. Like," he suddenly raised his sword and pointed to Titus, "your son." Uhtric turned and addressed Titus quietly. "I know it's a hard thing to strike down your father, even if he is a traitor, Titus. But," he returned his attention to Leofric, "I'm not his son."

This elicited a moan of fear from Leofric, igniting the queerest sensation Titus had ever experienced, because there was no denying the thrill of a fierce, ruthless joy, yet at the same time, his most immediate thought was, What will happen to Leofflaed and Eadgyd? Instantly following that thought was the same older voice he had heard himself utter; you'll have to return to Cissanbyrig, of course. They'll need you, at least until they're married, but alone, they'll be in great danger, not from any Danes but from our own people. It was, Titus realized, an impossible choice.

"What do you want me to do, Titus?" Uhtric asked quietly, then reminded him, "Whatever it is, we need to do it now, because we're not through running these dogs down."

Titus was in an agony of indecision, yet outwardly, he barely hesitated, saying, "Let him go."

Leofric's sudden exhalation of breath was not surprising, but the dark stain that Titus noticed on his trousers made the youth wonder if he had done the right thing.

"Get up…Leofric," Titus commanded, and his father scrambled to his feet, but when he bent down to pick up his spear, Titus said sharply, "If you touch that spear, *I* will kill you." Inspired, Titus walked over to it, picking it up as he said, "This is mine now. And so is your shield. Now," he made sure to use the spear to point towards the woods, "run, Leofric. And keep running. If you're wise, you'll go back to Cissanbyrig and forget this ever happened. Because," he finished flatly, "if I ever see you again, I *will* kill you."

To his credit, Leofric did not attempt to get the last word in, turning and loping off, while from behind them, for the first time in hours, Titus heard a long note sounding.

Titus still watched for a moment, then turned and asked, "What now? What does that horn mean? Is the battle over?"

"Yes," Uhtric replied, then his face split into a grin, "and now we better get back to grab what we can."

Before Titus could respond, both warriors turned and began trotting back towards the escarpment, leaving him to stand there uncertainly, unsure if Uhtric was including him.

He got his answer when the warrior called over his shoulder, "You better hurry up or you're not going to find anything worth keeping."

Not surprisingly, Titus followed them.

Uhtric's assessment had not been entirely correct; while the battle was over, Alfred was not content to allow his entire army to revel in what was a resounding victory. In fact, anyone who saw him would think that he was not the victor, but the cause for Alfred's consternation was based in the simple fact that, after a search of the Danish bodies, it was determined that Guthrum had escaped. If men like Cyneweard had been asked, they would have assured their King that the chances of catching up with Guthrum, who was undoubtedly mounted, were next to nothing. More importantly, while Wiglaf's assessment that the small band of Danish cavalry had been kept out of sight on the reverse slope was confirmed, if only because of the large number of horse droppings, when Alfred's personal bodyguard broke the Danes and pursued them to the edge and over the escarpment, there was no sign of horses anywhere. To experienced warriors like Cyneweard, the shire Ealdormen, and minor Ealdormen like Lord Eadwig, this was virtually concrete proof that Guthrum had sensed the tide of battle shifting, and had not been present for the final breakthrough. Alfred, however, did not ask Cyneweard, nor the Ealdormen or anyone else. Instead, he snapped out orders for every man who could mount a horse do so, and he had already sent a rider back to Battlesbury Hill with orders for men to bring all the spare mounts in order to bolster his forces. Titus was aware of none of this; all he knew at the moment was that not only had he been robbed of the chance to actually fight in a real battle, while he was generally accepted as part of Eadwig's fyrd and despite Uhtric's invitation, this did not extend to the idea that he had a right to a share of the spoils with the rest of the more experienced ceorls. In fact, it had been Heard, who he had considered a friend since their first meeting weeks earlier, who snarled at him in much the same way one wolf will warn off another around the carcass of a deer when Titus had bent over to search a Dane nobody else had looted. He was quite put out, but he was also wise enough not to argue, which meant he was at loose ends and wandering around when, from the south, his eye caught movement that was too large to be just a single rider. It took a few more heartbeats, but he recognized that what he was seeing was a handful of mounted men, leading or driving a few dozen horses, and as they drew nearer, he began to suspect he knew the identity of at least one rider. Consequently, he stayed where he was easily seen so that it was actually Eadward who, leading the four remaining spare horses belonging to his father, all of them saddled, veered towards Titus, looking down at the youth with a questioning expression that Titus instantly understood.

"No," he called out when Eadward was still about twenty paces away, "I didn't get into the fight. But," he added, "I did throw javelins."

Eadward's obvious pleasure at Titus' admission that he had not tasted battle irritated the youth, but in his heart, he could not fault the lordling, honest enough with himself that he knew he would have had the same reaction if the roles had been reversed.

Instead, he asked, "What are you doing here? What's happening?"

Eadward had reached Titus, and he explained as he swung down, "The King sent for every spare horse. He wants to mount as many men as possible to go after Guthrum!" Once on the ground, he thrust the reins of his horse that had replaced Thunor into Titus' hands as he commanded, "Stay here with the horses while I go find my father and see what he wants me to do." The younger lordling's peremptory tone deeply irritated Titus, but he resolved to keep his mouth shut, which was a good thing because, after moving a few paces away, Eadward spun about and asked with some obvious chagrin, "Do you know where I might find him, Titus?"

With his free hand, Titus pointed towards where Alfred's banner had now been planted in the ground, and there was a large and rapidly growing knot of men, most of them mounted.

"My guess would be over there…Lord."

Titus' tone clearly caught Eadward by surprise, judging from his expression, and Titus thought he saw a look of abashment flash across his features, but the lordling simply nodded and went trotting away. Left to his own devices, Titus returned his attention to what seemed to be almost a festival as the Saxons thoroughly searched then stripped the Danish dead, then immediately began bargaining with each other for items they had looted from one of the corpses. As he watched in glum silence, he saw Cenric and Heard, the feud that had developed shortly before the march from Wiltun nowhere in evidence now as they bickered back and forth over a pair of leather boots. Boots, he saw dismally, that were almost exactly his size, and after a few more exchanges of good-natured insults, Cenric tossed them to Heard, while Heard tossed over a sheathed dagger. Similar transactions were being made all around him, and he was so absorbed in this and feeling sorry for himself that he did not notice Eadward come running back.

"Titus!" Eadward called out when he was still a half-dozen paces away, and when Titus turned, he saw the broad smile on the lording's face, but he was completely unprepared to hear, "I asked my father, and he said that we can accompany him and the King! He said you can ride one of the spare horses!" Eadward's face suddenly changed, and he asked hesitantly, "You *can* ride, can't you?"

"Yes."

It wasn't a lie, Titus told himself, not exactly. In fact, he *had* taken the opportunity to ride the horses who belonged to Lord Eadwig's wife and daughter, and he had even ridden Thunor once. True, it had only been around the barn and up to the hall, but there was no way that he was going to pass up this opportunity.

The important thing was that Eadward believed him.

"Good," he said with obvious relief. "Pick one of the spares. They're already saddled."

Titus managed to comment that he had noticed that, and actually his choice was easy. Aside from Hama, there had been another horse who seemed to have a deeper connection with Titus than the others, a gelding with a deep golden coat and a black mane and tail, and he headed immediately for it, trying to appear confident as he swung into the saddle. The change in perspective was dramatic, but things began moving so quickly that he barely had time to appreciate what a few feet of elevation gave him. Eadward had mounted as well, and he immediately began moving towards Alfred's standard, which had become the gathering point for all the mounted men. Titus spotted Lord Eadwig, and he wanted to thank him for including him, but he was in the circle around King Alfred, identified by the helmet with the iron circlet, so Titus contented himself with guiding his horse to a spot along the outer fringe of the mass of horsemen, while Eadward was content to do the same.

"Titus!" Uhtric seemed to materialize out of the crowd, but it was what he held in his hand that Titus' eye was drawn to, which was good, because in one motion, the warrior tossed a scabbarded sword to him.

Somehow—he had no idea how—he managed to catch it as if he had done such a thing dozens of times.

"Strap that on," Uhtric commanded. "I doubt you'll need it, but it's better to have it. And using a spear on horseback takes a lot of training." Titus obediently unwrapped the leather belt from around the scabbard then strapped it around his waist, and he was certain that this was a moment he would remember for the rest of his days, when Uhtric had signaled his acceptance of him as a fellow warrior. It was a feeling destined to last as long as it took Uhtric to command, "As soon as this is over, I want it back."

Fortunately for Titus, Uhtric wheeled his horse about so quickly that he missed the look of disappointment on the youth's face, and Titus studiously ignored Eadward as he adjusted the scabbard so that it hung comfortably and did not impede his riding. Alfred's horn player blew a long note, then after a pause of perhaps five heartbeats, played three shorter notes in a row, and Titus learned that it was the signal to begin moving. He was careful to allow almost the entirety of the mounted force to pass by before he nudged his horse forward; Eadward had either been allowed to or had taken it upon himself to place himself at his father's side, so he resigned himself to being surrounded by strangers. This belief did not last long.

"*Oy*! Look, lads! It's the Berserker himself!" Titus looked over in surprise to see Wigmund grinning at him, and the warrior pointed down at Titus' hip. "And he's got a sword now! No need for worry anymore!"

The words could have been meant as mockery, but Wigmund's tone told Titus that this was just the normal jocularity, and he flushed with pleasure. He wanted to say something witty in return, but he could not think of anything, so he sat astride the horse, bouncing along and grinning like a fool as Alfred tried to run down Guthrum.

Chapter Eight

Before an hour had passed, the thought crossed Titus' mind that perhaps it might have been better that he had stayed behind; by the second hour, this was a conviction, but he was determined to suffer in silence. It was not the pace necessarily, but the very act of using the muscles of his inner thighs in a manner that he had never used them for such a prolonged period that was proving to be beyond uncomfortable. However, even if he had been accustomed to riding for a longer period than it took from the barn to the hall, he had resolved to himself that he would keep his mouth shut, but the chatter lasted only long enough to enter the forest. Every man rode with one hand on the reins and the other on the hilt of their sword, or with the relatively few men who were still carrying it, their spear, and Titus copied them in every detail, scanning the undergrowth.

They had gone barely a hundred paces into the forest when he saw a ripple of movement further up the column, as some of the horses shied away from something, but he saw that none of their riders appeared perturbed. He saw the cause lying on the side of the track they were using, a dead Dane who had obviously succumbed to his wounds, lying facedown on the bed of small plants, the leaves looking as if they had been painted with the dead man's blood. It was the first but would not be the last of such sights, but this first corpse sent Titus' mind in another direction. The last sight of his father had been of him dashing into this very forest, so while he appeared to be as vigilant as the other warriors scanning the area for some threat, he was searching for one and only one man. His imagination immediately took flight upon this realization, to the point that he convinced himself that he would see his father lurking behind every bush. Not for the first time since the event, and it would be far from the last, he began to question his decision to spare Leofric, the inbred horror at the idea of a son killing his own father, for any reason, slowly fading as his rational mind took over, asking the cold question; if the situation had been reversed, did Titus hold any doubt that Leofric would have plunged his spear into the chest of his only son? The answer to this question, no matter how many times he asked himself, was always immediate and delivered without any doubt from within his own mind. His father would not have hesitated, and would in all likelihood have enjoyed the prospect of killing the thing that he hated with such a passion. Titus had always known that Leofric despised him, but the virulence of that hatred that he had witnessed earlier in the day had profoundly shaken him, something that he would never utter aloud, even when he saw his sisters again. I was childish, he thought grimly, and sentimental. I don't care what the Church says, I should have killed Leofric because he'd certainly kill me. As grim as these thoughts were, they did help to pass the time, and as they emerged from the northern edge of the forest, the tension among the party clearly eased. They had moved through the forest at a walk, but once in the open again, the King had immediately ordered the party to go to a brisk trot, which as Titus was learning, was the most jarring pace a horse could maintain…and as he was discovering, they could maintain that pace for a long time. Adding to his discomfort, he had not thought to adjust the stirrups for his longer legs, so he could not use his legs to ease the impact as effectively as the other riders. The subsequent bouncing in the saddle was not only uncomfortable, it signaled to the men around him that he was an inexperienced rider.

It was Aedelstan, Wigmund's friend who served Ceadda as well, who asked casually, "Have you done much riding, Berserker?"

There was no way for Titus to miss the chuckles from the men around them, but he tried to block them out as he answered honestly, "No, Aedelstan, I haven't."

This seemed to surprise Aedelstan, making Titus think that the man at arms had been trying to get some sort of rise out of him, and he partially confirmed this by commenting, "I was expecting you to blame your stirrups being too short, Bers…"

"It's Titus," he snapped before he could stop, even as he admonished himself that these experienced warriors were offering him a compliment. This was why, in a softer tone, he said, "I prefer just Titus, Aedelstan. I," he shook his head, "haven't really earned any kind of name like that. It happened one time. And," he concluded glumly, "all I did today was throw four javelins."

Aedlestan and Wigmund exchanged a startled glance that shared their surprise at a youth on the cusp of manhood trying to downplay what he had done, and while they did not speak about it, they both arrived at the same conclusion; this lad still did not fully comprehend what he had done during the ambush. They were not the first to observe this, and unknown to Titus, it was one reason that, at Otha's urging, Eadwig had agreed to include him in this desperate and probably fruitless attempt to run Guthrum down. As experienced warriors, they knew how deadly overconfidence was in a young warrior, but to their surprise, if anything, Titus was erring in the assessment of his natural skills. This was why Eadwig did not feel he was wasting a horse, although if he thought there was any likelihood of cornering Guthrum and the remnants of his army, he would have insisted on a more experienced man in his place. As it would turn out, Cyneweard, Eadwig, and all those of their mind were only partially right; they did not catch Guthrum, but they certainly ran into Danes.

Titus never learned who spotted who first. From his viewpoint, they just suddenly went from the trot to a canter, and the men in the rear had to rely on what was shouted back over the shoulders of the men ahead of them.

"Danes! On foot! They're running!"

Things happened very quickly after that, which proved to be to Titus' advantage because he had no time to think, and he simply copied what the men around him were doing, which included drawing his sword.

"Titus!" Wigmund had to shout now to be heard over the hooves and the whistling wind. "Don't hold your reins, hold the saddle!" When Titus' reaction was to gape in disbelief, the warrior forced himself to be as patient as the circumstances allowed. "Your horse is going to follow the others, and if you want him to turn, use your knees. You're going to need to have a grip on something solid!"

Titus desperately wanted to ask why, but he did shift his grip from the reins to the front edge of his saddle, and he was encouraged by the fact that the horse did not even seem to notice. It was not destined to last long because someone, presumably Alfred, shouted an order to change from a column to a line to account for the Danes scattering as they tried to escape. He was almost unhorsed when the animal, reacting to the sudden movement to the right by the rider directly ahead of them, followed suit, but he was saved because of his grip on the saddle. More importantly, by spreading out, he saw the reason for the command, as what he guessed had to be at least three hundred Danish warriors, all of them on foot, had scattered in three directions.

"Use your edge!" Wigmund shouted. "Don't try to stab any of these savages because you'll be unhorsed! Pick a man and aim for the neck!"

It helped Titus immensely because he was able to actually see the technique Wigmund was trying to instruct him in when the men ahead of them reached the first of their quarry. Over the wind, Titus heard the beginning of the screams, but it was what he saw that was most informative, as one of Alfred's bodyguards, barely slowing, almost decapitated a Dane who was attempting to escape to the east. Using his left knee as Wigmund had advised, he felt the horse shifting its own weight, but he quickly learned that he had clearly pressed too hard because, instead of a gradual curve to the right, the horse veered so sharply that, even with his grip on the saddle, he was afraid that he would fall off. By this time, Wigmund, Aedelstan, and every other man was too busy to offer Titus any advice, and he quickly found himself the outermost Saxon to the right of the track they had been following. What this meant in a practical sense was that none of the Danes who had chosen east as their preferred direction of escape had reached his spot, which in turn meant that he would not be running anyone down from behind like the others were doing. Nevertheless, Titus was determined to participate in this battle, even if it was in the aftermath, and his choice was essentially made for him as the Dane who had been the fleetest of foot in breaking to the east seemed to realize Titus' intention. More likely, he saw a beardless youth who was clearly uncomfortable on his horse, and he calculated this was the most vulnerable of these mounted Saxons, thereby providing the best chance for escape into the trees a hundred paces away that, while not thick enough to be called a forest, still provided more opportunity for escape.

From Titus' viewpoint, he saw a man who was actually a bit larger than he was, wearing a helmet and mail shirt, also carrying a sword, but it was sheathed. In his left hand was his shield, which he was actually holding out to his side just as Titus had done in his pursuit of Leofric, and a spear that he was holding out from his body as well. Without any forethought, Titus kicked his horse to go to the gallop as he aimed the animal's nose to the Dane's right, understanding that he was too unskilled to try and approach from the other side to perform the kind of slash Wigmund had suggested, but across his body. The idea that he was outmatched and should have waited for help never occurred to him, nor did he see coming what every experienced warrior knew was inevitable in this situation. It was a case of one moment he was on his horse, beginning to lean over to extend his reach to slash down at the Dane, certain that he would have to dodge a spear thrust but equally certain he could do so, then he felt himself flying through the air because, as if by some form of sorcery, his horse disappeared out from under him. In the eyeblink of time he had before he slammed into the ground, he heard the same screech of pain he had heard when Thunor had been impaled, then his world seemed to explode, the impact with the ground igniting a sharp pain in his left shoulder, but it was the series of images that flashed between sky, ground, then sky again, repeating several times in a way that was as disorienting as the pain. When he came to a stop, he was on his back, gasping for the breath that had been explosively forced from his lungs, and while he was conscious, he was puzzled as to how there could be stars above him, yet somehow be below the clouds. Once again, Titus astonished the men who had seen it happen by his relatively quick reaction of rolling over onto his hands and knees, although it yanked a shout of pain from his lips. From Titus' perspective, what prompted his recovery was the sudden panic at the thought he had lost his grip on his sword, and the certainty that the Dane would be upon him within a span of the next couple of heartbeats. To his intense relief, he immediately spotted it, and it was when he began to crawl over to it and put his weight on his left hand that wrenched the shout of agony, but he ignored it to snatch up the sword and scramble to his feet. Weaving, dizzy, and with a left arm that seemed useless at least for the moment, but on his feet nonetheless.

It took an extra moment for him to realize that the Dane was not interested in finishing him off and was back at the run, heading for the cover of the trees. The sight of his foe escaping served to clear Titus' head almost immediately, and with a bellow of rage, he broke into a sprint after the Dane. Later, he would understand why this had the effect that it did, that his brooding over allowing his father to escape had become intermingled with this Danish warrior who had taken advantage of his inexperience. He did have a pang of concern about his horse, recalling the scream of pain from the animal, but it did not cause him to falter, and instantly, all other sounds and cries of pain, alarm, or as he would learn later, warning aimed at him, once more ceased to exist. In his mind, there was one, and only one, thought; kill. Only one thing mattered, and only one thing existed in his world at this moment, killing this Dane who had humiliated him. The pain that had been so agonizing seemed to have vanished, although a detached part of him noticed that he was unable to pump his left arm to help his speed, but this was of little matter because he was rapidly gaining on the man.

With his spear gone, the Dane had drawn his sword, although it must have been before Titus began his chase, but he still had his shield while Titus had none, and even if he had, it was unlikely he could have used it. The Dane, either hearing or sensing a pursuer was closing, glanced over his shoulder, but whereas what Titus had seen in his father's face not long before was terror, when this warrior saw that it was the beardless youth, Titus saw nothing but contempt in the man's face. It was the penultimate mistake in the Dane's life; the final one, while understandable, was related to the first, the Dane assuming that this youngster was undoubtedly a novice warrior eager to make his first kill. Consequently, he chose to come to a sudden stop and not at least make an evasive move to give himself a chance to get set, certain that the sight of an experienced warrior turning to face him would be enough to halt this boy.

For Titus, he would always relish the memory of this bearded warrior's blue eyes going wide with shock at how quickly Titus was inside of both his sword and his shield because he had not done what the Dane had counted on. Consequently, Titus was at full speed when he slammed into the Northman, sending the man flying backward off his feet, and while he did not roll over from the impact as Titus had when thrown from the horse, it would have been better if he did, although it would have only bought him perhaps another couple of heartbeats. Landing flat on his back, he was still trying to regain his senses when his vision filled with the contorted face of what he had been sure was nothing more than an overgrown boy, but his last thought, as the blade of Titus' borrowed sword thrust down into his throat, right in the hollow above his mail was why this youth had called him "Leofric."

Titus was completely unaware that he was snarling his father's name as he drove the point of the blade down through the soft tissue of the Dane's throat, then the bones in the neck before plunging into the soil, and he relished the quivering he felt transmitted up through his blade as he stared down into the man's eyes. Although he did not know he had been verbalizing his father's name, he was acutely aware that when he was looking down at the dying Dane, it was his father's face he was seeing; only later would this give him pause. It took an extra effort to withdraw his sword, the grating sensation as the bone stubbornly kept the blade trapped causing an odd sensation, but when he did free it, following it was a spray of blood and he was unable to straighten up before it spattered all over his face and tunic. His natural instinct was to wipe it away, yet for some reason, he resisted the urge, standing erect as he heard the sound of more than one horse approaching at the canter. He was straddling the Dane's corpse, and he stepped over it as he turned to see who was coming; he was not sure whether he should feel better or worse, because while Wigmund and Aedelstan were closest, Titus saw not far behind were three other riders, recognizing Lord Eadwig, Lord Otha, and Eadward coming at the canter.

Wigmund and Aedelstan drew up, and it was Wigmund who broke the silence. "We were coming to help, but you clearly don't need it."

Since he was unsure whether this was meant to be answered, Titus said nothing, offering a shrug instead because, frankly, he was more concerned with the arrival of Eadwig. Drawing up next to the pair of warriors, Eadwig regarded Titus with an impassive expression, which was matched by Otha, who was next to Lord Eadwig. Eadward, however, was easy to read, although he had chosen to stop a short distance behind his father and Otha, and to Titus, it seemed as if the lordling he was beginning to think of as a friend, while certainly envious, was also proud.

"It seems," Eadwig broke the silence, "that you have a talent for killing Danes…Titus."

"Yes, Lord." What was he supposed to say, he wondered. If he agreed, it would sound boastful, but he could not bring himself to say that it was just a happy accident. So he answered with at least partial honesty, "I was…angry, Lord." He dreaded it, but he asked, "What happened to my horse?"

"*Your* horse?" Eadwig countered, raising an eyebrow, yet while he was not smiling, Titus sensed that he was more amused than irritated. "I thought it was *my* horse."

"Yes, Lord," Titus mumbled. "I apologize." Taking a breath, he forced himself to say, "It's dead, isn't it?"

To Titus' surprise, it was Wigmund who answered, "No, it's not dead. It's got a bad cut on the right shoulder. But," he shook his head, "that horse has some sort of protector looking out for it. Maybe," he joked, "it's the same angel who's watching out for you."

"Don't blaspheme," Eadwig growled, but again the nobleman did not seem all that irritated. "Horses don't have guardian angels. This boy," he turned his attention back to Titus, "is another matter altogether." Drawing Hama's head around in a signal that he had seen enough, just before he started away, he casually called over his shoulder, "Hurry and take your spoils, boy."

Titus did not move, certain that he had either heard incorrectly or Lord Eadwig was having some fun at his expense, but then Otha barked, "Don't take all day, boy. Strip him and take what you want."

The Thegn spun his horse to follow Lord Eadwig, yet Titus still could not seem to make his feet move.

"If you're not going to take them," Wigmund said, kicking his horse to move towards the Dane, "then I will."

This got him moving, and he bent over, trying to ignore the Dane's sightless stare and the hole in his throat with the pool of blood around his head that was still soaking into the ground.

"Do you want some help?"

Titus looked up in surprise to see Eadward, and he did not try and hide his relief, nodding quickly.

"I've never done this before," he confessed to the lordling, which seemed to startle Eadward, if only for a moment.

"Ah, yes," he nodded, "that's right. You...weren't yourself the other day."

With Wigmund and Aedelstan offering advice, the pair unbelted the Dane's sword, pulled his mail shirt off, which would have satisfied Titus, but when it became obvious that he believed he had thoroughly searched the body, with a sigh that could be heard from where they were standing, Wigmund swung down.

"I have to show you everything." He shook his head as he strode to the two youths, but the fact that he was grinning as he said this was a signal to Titus no malice was intended. Dropping to his haunches, Wigmund offered a lesson in the finer points of looting the dead. "First," he was saying as he untied the leather thongs that wrapped around the soft leather boots all the way to mid-calf, "you need to check his boots."

"To see if they fit?" Eadward asked curiously.

"Yes, Lord," Wigmund agreed, "but there's more." Once the first boot was off, he thrust his hand down into it, frowning as his fingers searched for something. He tossed the first aside with a disappointed grunt, but almost as soon as his hand began its search with the second, his expression changed, and he gave the two a wide grin, and he dramatically removed his hand as he said triumphantly, "Like this."

Titus felt his jaw dropping at the three large gold coins in Wigmund's palm; it was more money than Titus of Cissanbyrig had ever seen in his entire life, and even Eadward let out a small gasp.

However, when Wigmund extended his hand, Titus hesitated, his sense of justice warring with his greed, and at least for a moment, justice won, and he shook his head.

"You found them," he said, but he was completely unprepared for Wigmund to seem angry about it.

He learned why when the warrior said sharply, "Lord Eadwig ordered that all of the spoils belong to you. I'm not going to anger him by going against his orders, so take these cursed coins, boy!"

When put that way, it allowed Titus to console himself that he was following the Ealdorman's order, and he leaned over and took the coins from Wigmund's hand, savoring the heavy feel of them in his palm as he calculated that these coins would certainly provide for his sisters; the question was how long. That, he understood, he could find out about later, and when Wigmund commanded Titus to help flip the Dane over, he hastily complied, but doing so prompted a muttered curse from Wigmund, while Titus and Eadward exchanged a glance, their noses wrinkled in identical fashion.

"I was afraid of that," Wigmund growled. "He's already shit himself. So," he straightened up with a sigh, "I won't be taking his trousers." This puzzled Titus, but Wigmund understood, and he pointed down at them and said, "They're made of leather, not cloth. They're more durable, but I'm not going to clean another man's shit out of them to wear them." He ran his hands along each side of the Dane's body, explaining, "Sometimes, they sew secret pockets in their tunics and put coins or jewels in them." As had happened with the boot, his left hand suddenly stopped, as his right drew his dagger from behind his back, slitting the cloth that, to Titus' eye, appeared to be of no better or worse quality than his own tunic. Wigmund fumbled for a moment, then withdrew what had been contained in the pocket, holding it out for Titus and Eadward to see. "That bastard," Wigmund spat, "probably took this from a nun! He's going to be roasting in Hellfire everlasting for being a heathen, but I hope the Devil has special plans for this son of a whore!"

It was a crucifix, and Titus immediately saw that by its size it would be the type of thing worn by a woman, but it was made of solid gold and was finely worked, while the thin golden chain exhibited the same exquisite craftsmanship. It is, Titus thought, one of the most beautiful things I've ever seen, and this time, he did not hesitate to take it from Wigmund's hand, holding it up for a moment, letting the sun catch the gold and offer a tiny display of winking fire.

"Put it in the purse you took," Eadward suggested, and Titus realized that he had absentmindedly tucked it into his own belt, so he withdrew it and opened the drawstrings, dropping it in with the gold coins.

Eadward leaned over, and the pair peered down as Titus shook the contents around, slightly disappointed that there was no more gold, but only silver. Coins, certainly, only a couple of which he had ever seen before, but there were also small hunks of silver that he assumed had been chopped off from something larger.

"Finished," Wigmund announced, and his surly attitude about the trousers was nowhere in evidence as he said with a grin, "Now *that* is how you search a corpse."

Titus opened his mouth to thank him, but then the horn sounded, drawing their attention back to the point where Alfred and the majority of the horsemen had gathered. Scattered all around were bodies whose torsos and legs were a stark white in contrast to the faces that had been exposed to the sun, although most of them had blood partially obscuring parts of their bodies.

"We need to get back to the others," Wigmund said, but he was already striding back to his horse as he did so.

And, Titus realized, he was on foot, and as far as he knew, his horse, while alive, was maimed.

"Here," Eadward commanded, "give me the mail. I'll carry it with me. You can wear the helmet and carry the rest."

Titus gratefully surrendered the armor, and he was surprised that, when he put the helmet on, it fit perfectly. Wrapping the belt around the scabbard, he picked up the shield, which was in much better condition than the one he had been given after the ambush, but it was emblazoned with a series of designs that Titus was certain were pagan in nature that gave him a moment's pause. They could be painted over, however, and Titus left the corpse after one final glance at him. This one, he thought to himself, is different. This one I remember.

Eadward and the others had naturally pulled ahead and he ran to catch up, but to Titus' astonishment, as he approached, he saw his horse, reins trailing on the ground and with its head down, cropping grass as if nothing had happened. It was true there was an ugly gash, high on its right shoulder where the Dane's spear had glanced off the animal's side, and blood streamed down almost to its hoof, but when he approached, he was greeted with pricked ears.

"I'm sorry," he murmured as he picked up the reins. "I should have known better."

It was as he was swinging back into the saddle that he was stopped, by Otha, who called his name instead of using his normal "boy."

"We have prisoners," he called to the youth. "You're part of the group staying behind to guard them."

It should not have been unexpected, Titus recognized, yet he was disappointed nevertheless, although he answered simply, "Yes, Lord."

However, when Eadward nudged his horse to head towards Alfred, Otha stopped him, saying politely but firmly, "You're going to remain behind as well, Lord Eadward. By your father's command."

Titus had to smother his smile as Eadward obediently turned back about, scowling as he did so, and for a brief instant, the lordling opened his mouth and Titus thought he would try to overrule the Thegn. It was the flat stare by Otha, who had forgotten more about cowing men than Eadward would ever learn, that convinced the lordling to at least attempt not to appear displeased.

Guiding his horse over to Titus, he said sourly, "Since we're going to be left behind, you might as well wear this in case the Danes try anything."

He had draped the mail shirt across the back of his saddle, and he pulled it off and dropped it into Titus' waiting, and eager, arms. The horn sounded again, and the pair were left, along with twenty other men, as Alfred resumed his pursuit of Guthrum, and it was beginning to dawn on Titus that he was on the way to being a warrior.

"You know," Eadward spoke casually, but Titus had learned to pay attention to his friend, "my father giving you the spoils was a test."

The pair were dismounted, as were all but five of the other Saxons, surrounding about a hundred Danes, the remnant that had been unable to escape but managed to survive. They were not naked, but all of their weapons and armor had been stripped, and whatever had not been claimed was in a pile which, as Titus would learn, was the best indication that there was nothing worth taking. Alfred's orders had been simple; they were told to wait for the rest of the army to arrive, where Ealdorman Cuthred had been left in command, but it was becoming increasingly clear that they would not be arriving any time soon. A thegn loyal to Ealdorman Aelfstan, named Hereweald, had been left in command, and even Titus could see his youth as he relentlessly circled the prisoners, constantly checking that the men watching them were alert.

Titus considered Eadward's statement, yet he could not discern why Eadwig's son seemed so certain, which prompted him to ask bluntly, "How so?"

Eadward looked a bit surprised, as if he had expected Titus to understand immediately, but he did not hesitate to answer, "Because it's customary for a warrior to give some of the proceeds of whatever loot he takes to his lord. He wants to see if you'll honor the custom."

Now it was Titus' turn to be surprised, though not for the reason Eadward assumed.

"You mean," Titus countered, "I'm one of Lord Eadwig's men?"

Without thinking, Eadward laughed. "By the rood, no! Titus, I'm talking about Lord Otha. He's your Thegn. And," he finished matter-of-factly, "Otha is my father's sworn man."

It was not really Eadward's fault, but the unthinking manner in which he had responded, something he would have never dreamed to do once he was more experienced, understanding the touchy pride of other Saxons when it came to their status, had aroused Titus' ire. Yet, he managed to maintain his composure and even forced himself to nod thoughtfully.

"So," he countered, "how much should I give to Lord Otha? And," he added before Eadward could respond, "how are you so sure that I'm now one of Lord Otha's men?"

The other youth looked uncomfortable; it was as if, Titus suddenly thought, he's betrayed a confidence. Which, as it turned out, was exactly what had happened.

Lowering his voice, Eadward prefaced his statement, "Before I tell you, swear to me on the rood that you'll act surprised when Otha tells you."

"I swear it," Titus answered immediately, without hesitation or reservation, feeling his heart quickening. Could I really be so close? he wondered.

"Even before today, I happen to know that Otha approached my father to ask permission to take you into his service and have you become one of his men," Eadward said confidentially. "And," he added, "my father hadn't made up his mind. Until today."

Titus truly did not know how he should respond; simply put, it was exactly what he had dreamed of happening, but he had not foreseen this thing that Eadward was talking about, although he did not doubt his friend's sincerity.

"That," he spoke slowly, "is good news. And," he assured

Eadward, "I'll pretend to be surprised." He had to smile at the lordling's obvious relief, but his mind was working through the practicalities of what was being discussed, which prompted him to ask, "How much should I offer Otha?"

"Two of those gold coins," Eadward answered immediately. "Although," he added helpfully, "all three would be even better."

It was in that moment that a quiet but insistent voice began whispering in Titus' mind, and he quickly realized something. There's a reason why Eadward is saying it should be at least two gold coins, he thought to himself, although he did his best to appear impassive and keep his eyes on the huddled Danes. Then, it hit him; one of the coins would be going to Eadwig, he was certain, and the instant the thought came, he knew that he was correct.

Aloud, however, he said firmly, "I'll offer Otha two of the gold coins, but I'm keeping the third one for myself."

If Eadward was disappointed, he did a good job of hiding it, although the most he would allow was, "That will probably work."

They fell silent then, waiting for the rest of Alfred's army to arrive, leaving Titus to ponder just what all of these dramatic changes might mean.

The army arrived, along with the baggage train, shortly before dark, but rather than stop, Ealdorman Cuthred ordered that they press on the six miles remaining to Cippinhamm. Certainly, the men were all tired, but there was a sense of urgency created by their knowledge that their King was hard in pursuit with a force of barely four hundred mounted men. And, while Guthrum's army had been shattered, a substantial number left dead on the field, veterans knew that more men ran than stood and fought to the death, even Danes, so there was no real way to know exactly how many warriors Guthrum still had.

While it was unlikely, it was not impossible that he might rally his men before they made it to Cippinhamm and, seeing Alfred's small force of horsemen, decide to risk all by standing and fighting. The risk to the King was such that, while there was some inevitable grumbling, it was muted, and isolated. As far as Titus was concerned, the arrival of the baggage train meant that Beorhtic brought Eadwig's wagon, with supplies in it that could be used to tend to the wound on his horse's shoulder. Shortly after the King left them behind, Titus had dismounted, and he refused to ride the horse as the army continued on, not wanting his weight to hamper the healing of the wound. Beohtric had helped him clean the caked blood from the gash, which had already started to attract flies, the servant holding the bridle of the horse as Titus, as gently as he could, scrubbed the gore with a relatively clean piece of cloth. Once that was done, Beohtric pulled out a small jar of a thick, black substance.

"I saw Dudda use this after Ashdown with some of the wounded animals," he explained to Titus.

"Did it work?"

Beohtric nodded, although he did allow, "With all but one, but I heard Dudda say that it probably wouldn't be enough because the muscle was cut too deep and wide. This," he indicated the now cleaned wound, "isn't as bad as a couple of the ones that healed just fine."

This relieved Titus immensely, because he had been brooding about Lord Eadwig's comment about it being his horse, and he was worried that he would end up having to offer up the third gold coin if the horse was injured badly enough it had to be put down. It was limping slightly, but otherwise did not seem in any discomfort, although it did drink deeply from the stream they crossed shortly before full darkness. Eadward had started out walking as well, but he grew tired of this, although he was content to ride alongside Titus, who had chosen to be just ahead of the baggage. The composition of the men at this part of the column had changed, neither Eadward or

Titus recognizing any of the ceorls. The Danish prisoners had been roped together and were surrounded by their original guards behind the column, and there was not much talking, which suited Titus fine, given his preoccupation. It was not only about the health of his horse; just as he had learned earlier that day that marching while carrying a spear and shield was not as easy as it might have seemed, wearing a mail shirt and helmet was taking some getting used to as well. He had thought the helmet was a perfect fit, but as he walked, the slight jarring with each step made the helmet move, and the rivets on the inside were catching on his hair, while his neck was beginning to get sore. The mail did not bother him as much as he thought it would, but that was because Eadward showed him how, by bunching the mail just above his sword belt, it helped distribute the weight. His new shield was heavier than the one he had left behind at the battle site, the pieces of wood a bit thicker, but the most weight came from the boss which, unlike his first one, protruded several inches and was in a cone shape. It was the sword, however, that he had been most interested in, finding that it was not a *seaxe*, but a double-edged blade with a deep blood groove that came to a needle point about a foot longer than the *seaxe*. It was, he decided, the most beautiful thing he had ever seen, and he had to resist the urge to keep drawing it to examine it. He had shown it to Eadward, of course, but he had not seemed nearly as impressed as Titus thought he should, and he decided that it must be jealousy.

Once it became dark, torches were lit, but even with the artificial light, the pace inevitably slowed, and it was shortly before midnight that, looming ahead in the darkness and outlined by the moon, the walls of Cippinhamm came into view. Between the town and the head of the column were more lights, but it took a bit of time before Titus could make out that they were not torches but campfires. A horn sounded, the column stopped, and out of the gloom, riders came trotting up, and it quickly became clear that they were the thegns who had continued with Alfred, with orders from the King to call the men of their particular fyrd for further orders.

Titus heard Otha's voice before he recognized him among the riders, the Thegn forced to bellow over the shouted orders of the other nobles, "All of Lord Eadwig's fyrd, follow me! We're going to be positioned on the northern side of Cippanhamm on the other side of the Afon! (Avon)"

It was confusing, as it immediately became clear nobody had given any thought about deploying the army to surround the town in any organized manner, and it would have been difficult even without the darkness. As it was, it was another full hour before Titus, Eadward, and the rest of Eadwig's fyrd were sufficiently settled to start fires, while by unspoken consent, erecting the tents would wait until the morning, except for the King and highest-ranking nobles, of course, but Titus' name was not called for the task, which he silently relished as a sign that he was no longer a stableboy. Eadward quickly disappeared into his father's tent, and by the time Titus had unsaddled his horse, taking care not to rub against the wound, then filched some of Hama's oats from the wagon to feed the animal, he was staggering with exhaustion. A quick search of the faces sitting on the ground around each fire led him to Cenric and the others, but his fatigue was such that he had completely forgotten that simply dropping down onto the ground while still wearing a sword and in mail took some forethought. The tip of the scabbard struck the ground first, throwing him off balance so that it appeared as if he had just collapsed to his right side, but it was also Leofwine's misfortune because Titus partially fell into him, and the older man was far from happy about it.

"Watch yourself, *boy*," the ceorl snarled, and while Titus might have apologized, all chance of it happening vanished with, "or I'll thrash you worse than your traitor father ever did."

Titus' next memory was of an immense weight on his back, while a burly, hardened arm was around his throat, although he sensed that whoever it was on top of him was not trying to choke him as much as trying to pull him away. But it took both Cenric and Heard to pry loose Titus' grasp from around Leofwine's throat, the ceorl's eyes already rolling back in his head and his face purple in the firelight. They finally managed to wrench his hand from Leofwine's neck, but Cenric sensed it was as much because Titus had come to his senses than they had overpowered him. For a brief moment, everyone around the fire, most of them now on their feet or at least kneeling, had their eyes on Leofwine, and for an awful span of heartbeats, Titus was certain that he had killed the ceorl, which in turn triggered a train of thoughts that, ultimately, led to his death, unless he could pay Lord Eadwig Leofwine's *wergild*. Then the ceorl's mouth yawned wide as he took in a huge, gasping breath, while the colored parts of his eyes became visible again, and he sat upright, both hands around his throat as he sucked in as much air as he could.

His eyes went to Titus, who, now that he had been pulled off of Leofwine, was being held by one arm by someone, and he rasped, "I'm going to…"

"You're going to keep your mouth shut, Leofwine," Cenric cut him off coldly, and it at least told Titus who was holding him by the arm. "You insulted Titus' father." When Leofwine opened his mouth, clearly about to protest, Cenric added, "And if you haven't heard, Titus is now serving Lord Otha. Whose side do you think Lord Otha will take? Especially," the ceorl glanced around at the others meaningfully, "after he asks us why he attacked you?"

This immediately deflated the other ceorl, but rather than endure the humiliation, he stomped off into the darkness, although Titus was happy to see he was still massaging his throat. Now that he had learned the hard way, Titus hitched his sword to a different position as he sat down, and his ass had barely hit the ground when the talking began.

"Where did you get that mail?"

"Is that sword yours to keep?"

"How did you get them?"

The questions came all at once, and Titus started laughing, once more experiencing the warm glow that came from the acceptance, and yes, the added element of envy that he heard in the others.

Rather than answer them, Titus turned to Cenric to ask, "How did you know about Lord Otha?"

"Lord Eadward told me," Cenric replied, then grinned and said, "but don't change the subject."

So Titus told the story of the Dane that he slew, and he left nothing out, not sparing himself at all, telling them how his inexperience almost cost him not only the death of his horse, but of himself. The others listened intently, although the youth barely noticed as he stared into the flames and described everything.

Once he was finished, there was a silence, then Heard asked, "You said you didn't slow down when the Dane turned around?" When Titus affirmed this, he scratched his beard thoughtfully before asking, "How did you know that would work? Couldn't you have just run yourself onto his sword?"

"I didn't," Titus admitted honestly, then added, "and yes, I could have, I suppose."

"Clearly," Deorwine spoke up, "God has favored you."

This elicited a murmured chorus of agreement, and of crossing themselves, and while Titus naturally did as well, he was not so certain. If God is suddenly favoring me, he wondered, why did He start now? Why couldn't He have turned His face on me before this? It was a troubling thought, but he kept it to himself, content to let the conversation flow around him as, unaware, his chin kept dropping to his chest. Finally, he began snoring softly, and the older men grinned at each other.

"He's had a busy day," Cenric chuckled, and with help

from Heard, they leaned the youth over next to the fire, and he did not stir.

"Should we take off his mail?" Heard whispered, but Cenric shook his head.

"Do you want to risk waking him up after what he did to Leofwine?"

This, Heard agreed, was a good point. Not much later, they also curled up around their fire, falling asleep on the night after the Battle of Ethantun.

Chapter Nine

What Titus and the rest of the men awoke to the next morning was the first day of a siege as King Alfred hurried to seal the Danes inside the walls. From what Titus could tell, nobody really knew how many Danes were left, but his exploit of the day before clearly meant nothing because, like most of the other ceorls, he was handed a shovel and told to start digging. Very quickly, Titus' muscles reminded him that, not only was this work he had done most of his life, it had been weeks since he had done so. It did help that he was far from alone, and he found that he actually enjoyed listening to the men around him talking as they worked, particularly since it was almost entirely about the battle the day before. More specifically, they alternated between boasting about their actions, or bemoaning the fact that the Dane they looted had been as poor as they were. What was not mentioned were the men missing, and while Titus was curious, he also did not feel confident enough about what the proper behavior after a battle was to ask the others. He did know that Osric, one of Otha's men, had lost his right arm at the elbow, although he was expected to survive as long as corruption did not set in, and he assumed that this was why he had been promised to Otha by Lord Eadwig. The fact that Titus was still not technically bound to Lord Eadwig's household and, by Saxon law, was still part of the fyrd of the Thegn of Cissanbyrig, Owin, was certainly a concern, but while King Alfred had made no official decree, it was widely assumed that Wulfhere would be stripped of his title and lands, and if that happened, the same would extend to all those thegns who chose a traitor to the Danes over remaining loyal to the King.

The night before when the army gathered back together, he had heard that of Lord Eadwig's fyrd, twelve men had died, but Titus had not heard any names mentioned, and he only knew about Osric because he had noticed he was missing and asked Uhtric. Because of his limited perspective, it was hard for Titus to tell what the overall plan was, although he had gathered it included cutting off access to Cippinhamm from the south with a deep trench, using the dirt from the trench to act as a dirt wall with a flat top on the side opposite from the town. Now that it was light, he also saw that the ditch was at least five hundred paces away from the outer town wall, which was also made of dirt, and Cenric had informed him was a new addition made by the Danes. Speaking of the enemy, they were standing in plain sight on the outer wall that had a crude wooden parapet so they were only visible from the waist up. What Titus noticed was how they were watching silently, with none of the boasting, curses, and challenges that he had mostly heard the day before. The ditch and dirt wall was only on the southern side because Cippinhamm was situated in a loop of the Afon, which meant that it was constructed before midday, but if Titus and his comrades thought their labors were over, they were disabused when the King ordered that a makeshift breastworks be constructed along the riverbank. What this meant was that working parties were sent out to find deadfalls that could be dragged back to create a crude but effective barricade that would force any Danes trying to escape to negotiate it after crossing the river, and because of his strength, Titus was ordered to do this as well. Once completed, Titus' namesakes who once marched for Rome would have found the efforts of their descendant and his comrades to be laughable, but the art of siegecraft as practiced by Rome was, like so many other things, lost in the mist of the ages. Regardless, what mattered was that the Danes inside Cippinhamm were effectively cut off from any hope of resupply. Despite his initial resentment that, even with his new status as a man at arms, he was expected to labor while Uhtric and the others who fought for Otha joined the men at arms of the other thegns, supposedly to stand watch as the work progressed, he resigned himself quickly enough to his fate. And, while he was using neglected muscles that he knew would be aching the next day, he found that he enjoyed being part of the laborers because it reminded him of planting and harvest time when the men of Cissanbyrig helped each other on their own farms. Within a matter of days, he would be looking back at that time with rueful amusement, because Titus was about to learn something about sieges, and that was just how dreadfully boring they were.

While Lord Eadwig and his fyrd had been honored to share the center wing with King Alfred, now that the battle was over, his status as a man of only middling importance was reestablished, not by Alfred but by the senior Ealdormen and their high-ranking thegns who prevailed on the King to place the Ealdorman of Wiltun on the northern side since it was the least likely direction for any breakout by the Danes. Consequently, Eadwig's men were left with little to do but lounge about outside their tents in the late spring sunshine, playing at dice, challenging each other with riddles, and while neither Titus nor any other of his comrades knew it, playing the game of *tafi*, which was identical to the game played by Romans, and from whom the game came. Titus did not participate in the dicing, not wanting to risk any of his small hoard of silver, and he did not know how to play *tafi,* so he was content to watch, although he did like the riddles. Despite their different stations, it was natural that young Eadward and Titus gravitated towards each other, even though there was still awkwardness between them. Eadward had offered to teach Titus *tafi*, and while he was tempted, the idea that he would have to be either inside or just outside Eadwig's tent made him decline the offer, which Eadward accepted without rancor, hinting to Titus that the lordling had just been polite. Otherwise, there was precious little to do, and while this suited the men of Alfred's army at first, since many of them needed to recover from the brutal exertions of battle, the stiffness and soreness inevitably disappeared, and wounds healed, so that by the fifth day, there was an atmosphere of restlessness that permeated every man, noble or basely born. However, the Danes trapped in Cippinhamm not only had the issue of boredom, they had the prospect of starvation because Alfred's encirclement was complete. There had been skirmishes as bands of Danes who had been sent out by Guthrum before he departed Cippinhamm with orders to forage the countryside blundered into Alfred's mounted patrols on their return. It was a triple blow to the Danish cause, as without exception, the returning Danes were killed and not taken prisoner, but more than the manpower loss, it was the supplies they had looted from the countryside to the north of the town that hurt the most; the fact that it in turn kept Alfred's army fed was not just an insult to Danish pride, but weakened them while providing Alfred and his men succor. It was on the third day that, as had been his habit, Uhtric wandered over to Cenric's tent, but this time, instead of talking or engaging in a dice game, he approached Titus, who, as had become his habit, was sitting on the ground alternately wiping down and sharpening his new sword. Glancing up when the shadow appeared in his lap, Titus was surprised that it was Uhtric, since he had barely offered him a word since the siege began.

"I'm bored," Uhtric said bluntly. "And I'm tired of playing dice and *tafi*. So," he continued in an offhand tone, "I might as well waste my time trying to show you how to keep you from stabbing yourself with that thing."

Titus needed no more invitation than that, leaping to his feet, but he hesitated when Uhtric turned to walk away.

"Should I put on my mail?" he asked, and when Uhtric turned back around, he saw the warrior's chagrin.

"Yes," he nodded, then called to Titus as he ducked into the tent, "and bring your helmet and shield."

Rather than take the time of donning the mail, Titus snatched everything up, emerging from the tent, determined that the broad grin on his face was nowhere in evidence when Uhtric glanced over his shoulder.

Certainly, Uhtric's training sessions helped pass the time, but Titus quickly learned that it was a mixed blessing as he came limping back to the tent shortly before the evening meal. Not surprisingly, the first two days were the hardest on him physically, but it got infinitely more difficult when the other men who belonged to Otha decided to alleviate their boredom as well, with Titus quickly learning that facing the same man, while valuable, was not the best training. Willmar, for example, was the quickest-moving man, forcing Titus to sharpen his reflexes to reduce his reaction time, although just as Uhtric had been, Willmar was deeply impressed with the youth's raw ability. The price for that lesson was bruised ribs when Willmar got behind his shield before he could respond, making every breath painful for the next two days. Hrothgar, who was the largest man fighting for Otha, and was a couple inches taller and perhaps thirty pounds heavier than Titus, did not move as quickly, but his blows, even when Titus blocked them, turned his arm numb all the way to the shoulder, and more than once had buckled his knees. Ealdwolf was the most skilled with a spear, handling it with a dexterity and deftness that enabled him to use both ends as a weapon, something that Titus discovered when, with a seemingly simple flip of the wrist, Ealdwolf had bashed Titus' helmet, denting it so that it had to be hammered out. It was the headache that Titus remembered from that lesson, but he was also determined not to make the same mistake twice, and in this, he was largely successful, earning him quiet commentary from the other men when they gathered for the evening meal.

And, always making an appearance at least once a day but never talking to him, or participating in the training, there would be Lord Otha, arms crossed and watching impassively as

Titus gamely took the bumps and bruises that came with becoming a Saxon warrior. Titus understood why this was the case; Otha was still Eadward's primary tutor, and they were not far away, just beyond the last line of tents, training every day much like Titus. Another difference was that Otha had gotten a tree trunk to use as a post, while Titus' opponents were flesh and blood, and he quickly recognized that, in his own way, Otha was paying him a compliment, since sparring was usually reserved for men who had proven that they were fundamentally sound. A painful compliment, to be sure, but Titus was as happy as he had been when he learned he was included in the fyrd, so he accepted every bruise as a badge of honor. More importantly, he could tell he was getting better, and he knew this was true not just because of his own judgement, but by the manner in which the others treated him, as it seemed that on a daily basis, the rigor of the training increased and they added different tactics to their attacks and to their defenses. Titus fervently hoped that he would get the chance to test his new skills in combat again, but it seemed to be an article of faith that the Danes inside Cippinhamm were defeated and simply hoping for a miracle. They were not; they were waiting for the slightest chance to make one last attempt to change their fate.

That opportunity came on Wednesday, ten days after the battle, when Titus and Alfred's army awoke to a steady rain that kept up throughout the entire day, confining the men to their tents. Not surprisingly, it did not take long for tempers to grow short, but Leofwine had learned just how unpopular he was, and somewhat surprisingly, wisely removed himself from the tent to spend time with other ceorls who were at least willing to tolerate his company. Otherwise, not that much was changed; the games continued, as did the talk, just the conditions were more cramped. Titus mostly watched, although he participated in the conversations, contributing when he felt it was appropriate. As much as he had progressed physically, Titus was more surprised at the growing confidence he was feeling just being in the presence of grown men. Naturally, it helped that he had been accepted, and he implicitly understood that the major reason for that acceptance stemmed from the fact that he had killed men in battle, but it was still quite a pleasing feeling. While it was certainly boring in many ways, the patter of the rain on the canvas created a soothing backdrop that helped Titus relax, and he was actually dozing when the flap was suddenly thrust aside and Uhtric appeared, dripping wet but with an expression that Titus could not recall seeing on the warrior's face.

"Lord Otha has ordered his household men to put on their armor now that it's dark," he said peremptorily. When Titus, who had jerked awake at the noise, only looked at him blankly, the warrior added impatiently, "That means you, Titus." Either missing or ignoring the sudden look of happiness on the youth's face, as much as for the others as Titus, he explained, "Lord Otha thinks the Danes might use the rain to sneak past us. He wants us to be ready for something."

Titus moved immediately, prompting some protests and good-natured cursing as he shrugged into his mail and strapped on his sword belt, inwardly pleased at his foresight; he had been practicing donning his armor in secret a few times a day, something that the others knew very well and were amused by, although they said nothing to him. Snatching up his helmet, he suddenly realized he was not sure what he was supposed to do, but he had been so absorbed in getting ready, he had not noticed that Uhtric had disappeared.

"Am I supposed to go after him?" he asked aloud. "Should I be outside?"

"Only if you want to get wet and cold," Cenric answered equably. "And," he added, "if you want to spend all day tomorrow getting that mail scrubbed so it doesn't rust."

"I wish he had told me that," Titus grumbled, then sat back down on his blanket, without incident now that he had learned how to sit on the ground with a sword.

"Titus!" Uhtric's voice was muffled by the rain and the

tent, but his irritation was unmistakable. "What's taking you so long, boy? Get out here!"

Scrambling to his feet, Titus glared at Cenric as he walked out of the tent, but the ceorl's grin was unapologetic, and very quickly, Titus forgot all about it as he immediately became soaked.

"Where's your cloak?" Uhtric demanded.

It was too dark for him to see Titus' embarrassment, who mumbled, "I don't have one."

"What are you sleeping on?" Uhtric asked.

"The blanket Dudda gave me when I began working in the stable," Titus explained.

Uhtric cursed under his breath, but louder, he said only, "Come with me."

Titus did as he was told, although when Uhtric ducked into the tent he shared with Willmar and the other men of Otha's household he stayed outside. The warrior returned quickly, thrusting a cloak at Titus.

"This is my spare," he said curtly. "Put it on. You can use it until you get one for yourself. But," he warned, "I want it back."

Titus nodded his promise, and while he was grateful, there was a part of him that thought sourly, I'm already soaked to the skin, so Cenric was right about what I'm going to be doing tomorrow. Naturally, he kept this to himself. He was about to ask what Uhtric expected of him, but the warrior was already moving towards the river, which was a hundred paces from the tents of Eadwig's fyrd. As he approached the makeshift barricade, he dropped into a crouch, and Titus copied him, but between the darkness and the rain, they were almost to it before

Titus made out a dark shape that was not part of the barricade.

"You're going to be with Ealdwolf," Uhtric spoke at just above a whisper because of the rain.

Ealdwolf was crouched down, and he did not even glance at Titus, keeping his eyes towards the river, and without another word, Uhtric vanished into the night.

Finally, after several long moments, Titus could not restrain himself, and he whispered, "What are we looking for, Ealdwolf?"

This did prompt the other man to take his gaze away from the river, and even in the gloom, Titus could see the look of scorn on the man's face.

"What do you think we're looking for, oaf? We're looking for Danes!"

Titus felt his face grow warm, but he was not satisfied, and he pressed, "But why does Lord Otha think they might try to cross here?"

Ealdwolf's expression changed, and Titus got the strong sense that the older man had not even considered why this might be, which was confirmed when he snapped, "How should I know? Lord Otha told us to watch, and that's what we're going to do!"

This was certainly true, but while Titus did not say anything, he did consider why Otha seemed to believe this was possible. And, as he thought about it, he started to see why, or at least he believed he did.

"Maybe," he whispered, "it's because it makes no sense that they would try here."

Ealdwolf looked over at him in surprise.

"What makes you say that?"

"Because if they want to use the river and swim downstream, this is the worst spot," Titus pointed out, and his confidence grew as he thought about it. "Remember that the King ordered trees felled across the river on both sides of the horseshoe?" He used the term the men had adopted to refer to the large loop of the Afon. "And he always has a guard on the downstream side, on both sides of the river." This got Ealdwolf's head nodding, slowly, but nodding nonetheless, and encouraged by this, Titus mused, "So, if I'm Guthrum, I don't really have much choice but to try the place that offers the only chance to get across, even if it's a bad one."

Ealdwolf's only response was a grunt, and he returned his attention to the river that was barely visible as the rain kept falling.

Once the initial excitement of being summoned wore off, Titus found it difficult to stay awake, even with the relative discomfort of being in a kneeling position as the water streamed off his helmet. Now that he had Uhtric's spare cloak, his body heat had dried out his tunic, but he occupied his mind with worrying about how his new mail shirt was undoubtedly rusting, his imagination such that he resigned himself to the moment he doffed the cloak, he would find the mail covered with orange spots of rust. He had leaned his shield against his body then covered it with the cloak, copying Ealdwolf, so that the wood did not soak up the rain and become waterlogged. With no moon or stars, it was impossible to tell how much time had elapsed, and Titus was beginning to think that perhaps time had managed to stand still. And yet, even with his mind wandering, his young ears heard a sound that was different than the hissing noise to which he had become accustomed, but when he glanced over at Ealdwolf, the warrior did not seem to have noticed. I'm probably hearing things, he told himself, but he was certain that he had heard *something*.

Screwing up his courage, he elbowed his companion as he pointed off to his left and whispered, "I heard something over there."

He was not particularly surprised when Ealdwolf's reply was a quiet snort and shake of his head.

"I didn't," he said flatly. "And if I did…"

He got no further because, from the exact spot where Titus was pointing, there came what was, unmistakably, a splash. As if, he thought with a suddenly racing heart, something big is getting into the river. Ealdwolf did not hesitate, hissing an order to follow him as he crawled on all fours, paralleling the riverbank and using the brush barricade for cover, although it took a heartbeat longer because Titus fumbled getting his shield out from under his cloak, but he moved quickly and caught up so that the other warrior's feet were within arm's reach even as he hoped his more rapid movement did not draw a Danish eye. He had no idea what Ealdwolf had in mind; he was about to learn that neither did Ealdwolf, not really. From Titus' perspective, Ealdwolf's shout was one of surprise, as if he was unaware of the likelihood that the splashing they had both heard was connected to the likelihood of Danes suddenly lunging up out of the gloom. Regardless, Ealdwolf certainly reacted quickly, leaping to his feet, and Titus heard a sharp cracking sound that his ears informed him was some sort of blade striking a shield that was instantly drowned out by male voices roaring at the top of their lungs. This was the last relatively quiet moment, as from either side of him along the barricade, Otha's men leapt to their feet to come rushing towards the sound of the fighting, while what was later counted as a dozen Danes emerged, water streaming from their tunics, none of them wearing even a leather vest that would have weighed them down, and without shields, rushing for a single spot along the barricade that, as the Saxons were discovering, was actually weaker than it had appeared from their side.

By the time Titus reached Ealdwolf's side, the Dane who had initiated the attack had been joined by three other men on the Saxon side of the barricade, and in the eyeblink of time he had as one of them turned his attention to Titus, he could just make out that this man was wielding an ax. He would never know how he did it; none of Otha's men favored the ax, so he had never trained against it, yet he managed to lift his shield, and most importantly, tilt it slightly so that when the blade slashed down and struck, the force was evenly distributed. Nevertheless, the impact was terrific, yet even in the moment, Titus determined that it was not as strong as Hrothgar's blows, but while he had not trained to defend against an axman yet, he had been working with the spear, and despite the darkness, he saw that this Dane had neither armor nor shield. Consequently, when he launched his thrust, holding the spear shaft about midway, somehow the warrior managed to recover his ax and parry the thrust with a wild swing that did serve to knock Titus' spearpoint away so that it punched harmlessly into the air. And, as Uhtric and the others had learned, even if it had been daylight and full visibility, it was unlikely that the Dane would have anticipated the speed with which Titus' shield moved as he used it as an extension of his hand to punch his foe. Because of the dark, his aim was off, so that instead of striking the Dane in the face as he intended, the pointed end of the cone-shaped boss struck the man in the breastbone, just below the hollow of his throat. Titus felt as much as heard the sound as the hard plate of the man's breastbone snapped, accompanied by an explosive gasp of breath that robbed the Dane of the ability to shout from the pain. He did not drop his ax, but his left hand went instinctively towards the concave hole in his chest, and it was unlikely he had even a presentiment of what was coming as Titus recovered his spear then made another thrust. This time, it struck true, the point driving into the Dane's body just underneath the ribs, and Titus felt the sudden involuntary spasm through the spear shaft, the Dane falling away from him.

By this moment, the rest of the Danes had emerged from

the river, although even now only the now-dead Dane and three of his comrades had managed to get on the opposite of the barricade, and they had been surrounded, with Ealdwolf standing so the barricade was against his right hip, with Titus to his left. Titus thought that it was Willmar next to him on his shield side, but he could not afford a glance to see, as one of the surviving Danes roared what had to be some sort of curse and, using the dead man as a platform, launched himself directly into Titus. Undoubtedly as he intended, the Dane's move caught him completely by surprise so that he was unable to interpose his shield between his body and his enemy. As he fell backward, in the back of Titus' mind was the recognition that this was exactly what he had done to the Dane he had slain the week before, and he was in the process of wondering if this was God's way of punishing him for his pride when the thought was driven from his mind by his impact with the ground. It did not feel like it in the moment, but the day of rain had softened the soil to the point that, while it was jarring, it did not drive the wind from his lungs.

A hand grabbed at his throat, causing Titus to instinctively let go of the shield so that he could grasp the man's right hand with his left, but he was too slow to stop the fingers from clenching around his windpipe, whereupon Titus of Cissanbyrig, the Berserker, learned another valuable lesson. As strong as he was, there were still men stronger than he was, and faster than he would have believed possible, he felt his body weakening, while even in the darkness, as his eyes, which he could feel bulging out of their sockets, stared up into the snarling face of the Dane who was killing him, it was as if he was falling down a well, the circular walls closing in on his vision. Then, from somewhere in the recesses of his mind, he remembered one of the stories that he had heard during the stories told around the campfires, when Heard had talked about a brawl he had witnessed. Before he could think about it, Titus shot his right hand up with his fingers extended, splayed out and like a claw, aiming for the Dane's forehead before raking his nails downward. His reward was his second and third fingers striking the Dane in his eyes, whereupon he shoved forward to drive deep into the sockets; although the shrill scream of pain felt like someone shoved an awl into both of his ears, most importantly, the crushing pressure was instantly gone, the Dane suddenly recoiling backward and off of Titus, both hands clutched to his eyes.

Despite knowing that he had to follow up his advantage, Titus was unable to move for a crucial number of heartbeats as he struggled to get air past his bruised throat and subsequently confined to listening to the fighting and resisting the urge to vomit at the thought of what the sticky substance covering two fingers was. *Get up! You have to get up or you're dead!* It was not the words themselves that spurred Titus, it was the voice that he heard in his mind, and it would be something that puzzled him for some time to come. Certainly, this voice was speaking the truth; of all the things that Uhtric and the other men of Otha's household had stressed to him, it was that losing one's feet in a fight was the best way to an early death. Why it would be Isolde's voice that he heard would remain a mystery, but it had the desired effect. Snatching up his shield as he climbed to his feet, he fumbled for his spear but could not find it, drawing his sword instead, and despite the pain from his throat, he felt a rush of excitement at the prospect of being able to use what had instantly become the most prized possession of his young life. From what he could tell, pairs of men were now struggling with each other, but with the darkness, it was difficult for him to tell who was who, and even with those he identified, like Ealdwolf, who was still furiously engaged with another ax-wielding Dane, they were moving about to the point where he was not willing to strike for fear he would hit a friend instead of foe. As he was trying to determine what he should do, he sensed movement almost literally at his feet, and when he looked down, he recognized the Dane who had almost choked him to death, rolling on the ground as he clutched his ruined eyes. Titus did not hesitate, taking a single step forward to plunge the point of his sword down into the Dane's chest, wrenching a gurgling scream from the Northman who, for the next handful of his last heartbeats, forgot all about his eyes. From his perspective, the brief moment he had been occupied in stabbing this Dane was all the time it took to finish the fight, because when he returned his attention to the larger scene, the predominant sound now was once again the rain, although it was punctuated by the harsh panting of the men around him, along with some low-pitched moaning.

"Is it over?" Titus asked of nobody in particular, but there was no immediate answer.

Instead, a dark shape that he identified as Hrothgar walked over to one of the prone bodies, and Titus saw his arm raise for an eyeblink of time, then thrust down, eliciting a shriek of mortal agony from the Dane.

"Now it's over," Hrothgar declared.

Naturally, Titus was inclined to accept this statement as fact, but he also heard that there was at least one more man moaning, and he strained his eyes to try and identify the source, deciding it had to be coming from a dark figure sitting on the ground with his back against the barricade.

"Is that a Dane we're keeping as a prisoner?" he asked.

Titus' blood froze in his body when Hrothgar replied in a flat monotone, "That's not a Dane. It's Uhtric."

The rain stopped shortly before dawn, and when the sun began poking over the horizon, the clouds that had delivered the downpour were nowhere in sight. Titus had not slept a wink, unable to do so due to a combination of the normal case of nerves after a fight that he was still trying to become accustomed to, but mostly out of concern for Uhtric. Fortunately, while his tutor's wound was gruesome in nature, it was not life-threatening, and in fact, he was alert and talking when Titus hurried to his tent after shedding his armor, so distracted that he completely forgot to wipe the water from it.

"It was just the tip of that bastard's sword, but it was enough to do this."

Uhtric indicated the new bandage that covered his left eye; in the light from the single candle that had been lit to enable Willmar to tend to Uhtric's wound, Titus could see the bright splotch of blood that had soaked through the fresh bandage already.

"I hope you gutted him for it."

"He didn't, but I did," Leofsige interjected cheerfully. Pointing at Uhtric, he said laughingly, "He was too busy rolling around on the ground crying like a little girl."

This elicited a laugh from all but Uhtric, who glowered at him with his good eye, but Titus sensed that it was not with any real ire. For his part, he was just relieved to see that the wound had not been mortal or would spell the end of Uhtric's fighting days. Otherwise, he was mildly astonished to see that, aside from a couple of slashing wounds, the ten remaining men of Otha's household were unharmed, while the Danes had been slaughtered to a man, although two of them were now presumably tangled up in the downriver treefall. Titus had not seen it, but he quickly learned that those two Danes, realizing they had been defeated, had plunged back into the river, and Willmar had used his spear and another that he snatched off the ground to hurl, hitting both men. Not surprisingly, this was a topic of conversation; while the Saxon war spear could be thrown, not many men had the skill to hit two moving men, in the dark, although there was some bickering between Willmar and his comrades about whether he had mortally wounded both men.

"How could you see?" Hrothgar shook his head. "I could barely see my hand in front of me, and those two bastards were already a dozen paces away and in the river."

"I'll wager you a shilling that those two are fished out by

one of the others downstream and they'll both be dead," Willmar countered.

Titus had learned that, for all his ferocity, Hrothgar was an inherently cautious man, and Willmar's challenge caused him to stroke his beard, suddenly uncertain. However, another aspect of Hrothgar's character was his stubbornness, and it was on full display now.

"That doesn't mean you killed them, necessarily," he insisted. "So maybe they were just wounded and they drowned. How would we know the difference?" he asked triumphantly.

"Even if that's true, they drowned because I hit them," Willmar countered, but then gave an elaborate shrug that told Titus what was coming. "But if you're too afraid to lose a shilling, I understand."

"I'm not afraid of anything!" Hrothgar took the bait, just as Willmar, and everyone else who was watching with amusement, had known. Now that his pride was involved, Hrothgar challenged, "How about we make it *two* shillings?"

"Done." Willmar did not hesitate. Then, addressing the others, "You're all witness. Hrothgar is going to be losing two shillings."

Titus was most amused by watching Hrothgar's expression slowly change as he realized that he had been goaded into something he really did not want to do. He also noticed the air was growing close, the tent crammed full of men who had just participated in a fight, and while he did not want to, he decided it was time to return to Cenric's tent, but he felt compelled to say something to Uhtric, who was now being largely ignored as the other men began recounting their own version of the battle.

Sidling up to the warrior, who was sitting on his cloak and bolstered by his pack, Titus crouched next to him and asked awkwardly, "Is there anything you need, Uhtric?"

Without thinking, Titus had approached Uhtric from his left, which meant that the warrior had to twist his head even further to meet Titus' gaze.

"How about a new eye?" he asked, and while he said it lightly, Titus heard the bitterness, and he felt horrible for reminding Uhtric of his loss, however inadvertently it had been done.

Not knowing what else to say, he mumbled, "I…I'm sorry, Uhtric. I…"

It was Uhtric's turn to be embarrassed, and he cut Titus off with a gentle squeeze of the youth's arm.

"No, *I'm* the one who should apologize, Titus. This wasn't your fault." For the first time, a smile played across his lips as he said, "But since you're asking, if you could find a woman to send my way, I'd have a bard write a song in your praises!"

This made Titus laugh, as Uhtric had intended, but Titus saw an opportunity, and he asked innocently, "But what about Ealdgyd? She wouldn't be happy hearing about that, would she?"

Uhtric shuddered, and it was only partially in jest.

"She wouldn't need to know about it," he said fervently.

Having had his fun, Titus patted Uhtric's shoulder, promising, "If I happen to stumble across a comely wench…I'll save her for myself."

"As if you'd know what to do with one." Uhtric laughed, giving Titus a playful shove that was also permission to leave.

Titus, as Uhtric had intended, flushed deeply, and he grumbled, "I never should have told you that."

"Don't worry," Uhtric assured him, "once we get back to Wiltscir, we'll take care of that problem."

Titus had already begun moving to the tent flap, so the warrior did not see the broad grin across the youth's face.

It came as no surprise that this night attack was the last effort by Guthrum to save himself and his fellow Danes from starvation. In the months after their surprise assault on Cippinhamm, most of the Saxons who called the town their home had fled, or they had been butchered for some action that Guthrum deemed worthy of execution. Those women within the walls were not there by choice, and their presence would be a source of shame for those with husbands who had chosen to flee rather than die trying to protect their wives. That, however, was in the future. In the aftermath of their breakout attempt, Guthrum was faced with the grim arithmetic that came from too many mouths to feed, and that was even if he put not just the women but all the noncombatants to the sword in order to win what his advisers assured him would be less than another week before, not one Danish warrior would be strong enough to put up a fight of any kind. Therefore, on a sunny morning two weeks after the Whitsunday battle of Ethantun, a large white cloth attached to a spear was lofted into the air from the Danish outer defenses. From the perspective of Titus and the men of Lord Eadwig's fyrd, they had no idea the cause of the sudden eruption of noise created by thousands of voices, although it did not take long for them to guess.

It was Cenric, who, glancing up from the *tafi* board, cocked his head to listen for a moment, then with a broad grin on his face, announced, "I think we're going home."

Lord Eadwig had made it a habit of visiting the King twice a day, once in the morning and once shortly before dark, so he was gone, which forced the men to wait for his return before Cenric's announcement was confirmed. It had become a habit for Titus and Eadward to find each other in the morning, before their respective tutoring sessions began, and without any kind of plan, they alternated their meeting places, one day in front of Cenric's tent and the next in front of Lord Eadwig's. On this day, they were standing in front of Eadward's tent when the Lord came at the canter, which was his normal pace, but most unusually, he was wearing a broad smile, something that Titus was certain he had never seen in the weeks of his association.

"Guthrum is surrendering!" Eadwig boomed as he swung out of the saddle, dropping Hama's reins, the black stallion immediately trotting up to Titus and thrusting his nose into his tunic. Titus tensed, certain that the Ealdorman would not appreciate this show of affection by the animal that he treasured almost as much as his children, but the nobleman was in an ebullient mood, so his response was to laughingly say, "He knows where to go for something special, eh, boy?"

"Yes, Lord." Titus grinned, more pleased at Eadwig's good mood and less irritated at being called a boy. "He knows me too well."

"What happens now, Father?" Eadward asked. "Are we going home?"

"Soon, lad, soon," Eadwig assured his son. "There are some…details that need to be worked out, but the important thing is that at noon, Guthrum and his men will leave the town and surrender their armor and weapons." Turning to address Titus, he ordered, "Take Hama to water and get him some oats from the wagon. We'll be returning to Alfred and the rest of the army to watch the surrender."

By this time, Otha, Ceadda, and Aelfnod had arrived at the tent, but Titus did not stop to hear what Eadwig was ordering, leading the stallion away towards the wagon, and he was more than happy to be the first person to inform those men out of earshot the cause for the commotion on his way. By the time he reached the wagon, he was quite pleased with himself, but when

Hakon crawled out from under it, which had become his semi-permanent spot, Titus suddenly felt guilty for being so happy. Whether the slave sensed this or not, Titus could not tell, his demeanor the same as it always was, with the carefully blank expression that the Dane had learned to cultivate as a way to avoid the random beatings that were the lot of those slaves who were unable to hide their feelings.

Titus did not know it, but Hakon was less reserved around Titus than anyone else, yet he still was cautious, simply asking, "Has Guthrum surrendered, Master Titus?" Titus had stopped trying to get Hakon from calling him Master when the slave explained, "You may not like being called Master, but if I forget with another Saxon, he will very likely beat me."

Consequently, Titus only nodded, but quickly realized he needed to expand, so he explained what was happening.

"And then we can go home?"

There was a wistful quality in the Danish slave's voice that sounded much like Eadward, but he understood why Eadwig's son would be homesick, while hearing an echo of that with Hakon surprised him. He was about to ask why, then thought better of it, replying, "I think so. That's what it sounds like at least."

"That would be nice," Hakon murmured, and Titus could not resist the urge to ask, "Why do you want to go back to Wiltun so badly, Hakon? Is your life really that different wherever you are?"

He did not really have any expectation of what Hakon would say, but he was flabbergasted when the Dane answered without hesitation, "My wife and son are in Wiltun."

"Your *wife*?" Titus gasped, and for the first time, Hakon showed a glimmer of amusement as he added, "And son."

"But…but you're a slave!" Titus exclaimed, then immediately regretted it, but Hakon had discovered that this overgrown youth did not view him with the same kind of disdain other Saxons did, so he answered with amusement and not rancor.

"I am aware of that, Master Titus," he answered dryly.

"So you were married when you were captured," Titus said, thinking he had solved this tiny riddle.

"No, I was not." Hakon shook his head. With a streak of mischief, he added, "My wife's name is Enflaed."

"Enflaed!" Titus started, then he scowled suspiciously at Hakon, certain that the Dane was having fun at his expense, and he said accusingly, "That's a Saxon name!"

"It is," Hakon replied blandly, then said nothing more.

Titus glared at Hakon for a long moment, expecting the Dane to finally admit the truth, but when he simply gazed back at the youth, Titus finally asked in exasperation, "Is she a Saxon or not?"

"She is a Saxon," Hakon assured him. "And I met her after I was sold to Lord Eadwig."

"And he let you marry her?" Titus was thoroughly confused, but before he could pursue this any further, he heard Otha bellowing for his household men, and this time, Titus remembered this included him.

After unstrapping the feed bag, Titus led Hama back towards Eadwig's tent.

As he passed Otha, the Thegn ordered, "As soon as you take Hama to Lord Eadwig, hurry and go get your armor and weapons. King Alfred wants the entire army turned out and armed in case that Danish scum has any ideas."

Once he returned the horse to Eadwig, Titus hurried to his tent, donning his mail and helmet, which he had spent the entire day after the night battle scrubbing with a stiff brush and some oil that Hakon had supplied, with the quiet word that it had been taken from Lord Eadwig's supply without permission. Now it gleamed, which he thought was appropriate given the circumstances. When he had examined his shield the next day and seen that it now had a fresh gouge in it, he had been unhappy, until Heard had pointed out that it showed that, despite his youth, he had seen battle, which immediately made him regret that it was not as scarred as Uhtric's and the other men's of Otha's household. He had to hurry to join the rest of Eadwig's fyrd, but while he expected at least Otha to growl at him, when nothing was said about him being the last one, he guessed that it was because the Thegn had seen that Eadwig had given him extra duty. There was a reprimand coming, but it was when Titus had hurried to the spot to which he had become accustomed, next to Cenric in the rough formation. Seeing this, Otha jerked his horse around and came trotting down the column, coming to a stop to scowl down at Titus.

"What are you doing back here, oaf?" Without waiting for an answer, the Thegn pointed to where Otha's household men were standing, "You belong up there now."

It took an effort for Titus not to grin, but there was no hiding his pleasure as he went jogging up to where the others were waiting, including Uhtric; the fact that Otha pointed to the last row of four did not bother him in the slightest. Without any more fanfare, Eadwig put his horse in motion, and they moved from their camp. Being on the opposite side of the river, it meant a march of a bit more than a mile because the ford across the Afon was below the horseshoe. It was something of an odd sensation, at least to Titus, as they appeared to be marching away from Cippinhamm, where he could see the rest of Alfred's army in the process of assembling, and just as Eadwig had ordered, fully armed and armored. Reaching the ford, which was up to Titus' upper thighs, he took care to hitch even more of the mail above his belt, not wanting to spend the time cleaning it again, proud of himself for thinking about it. Only Eadwig, Eadward, and the thegns were mounted, but Eadwig set a quick pace that required the men on foot to break into a slow trot to keep up.

"He doesn't want to be late and make the King angry," Titus heard a man behind him, one of Ceadda's, mutter.

"The King does like his lords to be prompt," another voice agreed.

This time, Titus and the men of Eadwig's fyrd were relegated to a spot on the far end of the long single line, although it was several ranks deep. As it happened, now that he was part of Otha's household, he was in the second rank of the men on foot when arrayed in other than a marching column, his view only slightly obscured by the horses in front of them, one of which bore Eadward, who, as they were waiting, glanced over his shoulder and with a smile, stuck his tongue out at Titus. It was the kind of thing boys do, and yet, while Titus desperately wanted to be considered a man, he could not resist responding in kind, then adding a gesture towards his crotch, and Eadward laughed. Which, of course, prompted a snapped rebuke by his father for this sign of levity at such a solemn occasion, and forced Titus to cough as a cover to hide his own laugh. Attention quickly shifted when the outer gate the Danes had constructed in their earthen barrier opened, and for the first time, Titus got a good look at Guthrum, self-styled King of the Danes of East Anglia, which by this time had become more commonly referred to as the Danelaw.

"He's not as tall as I thought he would be," Willmar commented, to which Titus wholeheartedly agreed, secretly relieved that he was obviously taller than the Dane.

In every other way, however, Titus was impressed at what

he saw. Despite being of average height, Guthrum, identifiable by wearing a helmet with a pointed circlet similar in style to Alfred's own, which the King was wearing again, was broad across the chest, with huge bare arms that were adorned with so many rings of both gold and silver, it was hard to see his skin. He was bearded, of course, and Titus was close enough to see the streaks of gray in the black, which was when Titus realized that he had assumed Guthrum would have the yellow or red hair that was more often associated with the Danes. There was a heavy silence in the air as, without being told, all the men who had been murmuring to each other stopped, their collective attention now on the moment when, slowly, Guthrum dismounted. With the same slow pace, which Titus was certain was a sign of the Dane's reluctance, he approached Alfred, who at that moment was still mounted, and when Guthrum drew his sword, despite him doing it with the same rhythm as his approach, Titus felt himself tense nonetheless, and he could see he was far from alone. Maybe, he thought, this is all a trick, so that instead of watching what was coming between his King and Guthrum, Titus turned his attention to the gate, which was still open. Just inside, he could see what he assumed was the entirety of Guthrum's army, although he could only see a relatively small number of them, and while it made sense they were all armed, given they would be surrendering their arms and armor, as a Saxon, Titus accepted the duplicity of the Danes as a matter of fact. The consequence of this was that he was completely unprepared for the sudden, spontaneous roar from thousands of Saxon throats, and when he returned his attention to Alfred and Guthrum, the moment was over. All he saw was Guthrum kneeling, while Alfred, after dismounting, was holding a sword aloft, which Titus recognized as having been in the Dane's hand an instant before. It was, he thought with a mixture of feelings, truly over. King Alfred had been victorious against the Great Army of the Danish King Guthrum…and Titus of Cissanbyrig, Titus the Berserker, had been a part of it.

Chapter Ten

When Titus returned to Cissanbyrig, he did not come alone. He was accompanied by Uhtric, who was now wearing an eyepatch that covered his missing eye, although the scar tissue along his left temple was still an angry pink, while part of his eyebrow had been sliced off and would never grow back. Nobody should have been surprised that Titus was wearing his new armor and helmet, with his Danish sword strapped to his waist, but the fact that he was mounted, on a horse with a dull golden coat, black mane and tail, and a scar on its right shoulder was a potent sign that the youth who had sneaked out of his father's house now these three months before was no more. The village was nestled in between two low hills, along the Afon just as Cippinhamm was, with the remains of an old hillfort on the highest hill a bit less than a mile to the east, but the pair were not approaching from the direction of Cippinhamm, but of Wiltun. Which, as far as Titus was concerned, was his new home.

The month after Guthrum's surrender had seen many changes, not just in Titus' life, but with the entire Kingdom of Wessex. Alfred's victory terms had been, in the eyes of all but a few, generous, perhaps exceedingly so, with some even going so far as to mutter the word "foolish," although it was always into a cup of ale and only loud enough for perhaps one other person to hear. Titus had certainly not been consulted, but if he had been, he would have leaned towards the latter sentiment.

Allowing the Danish army to retreat back to East Anglia was certainly understandable; if they had been held captive, they would have to have either been ransomed, and there was no other Danish noble with either the resources or the motivation to pay it since Guthrum was still alive and in command of these warriors, or they would have to be fed and guarded, neither of which was a viable option. This much Titus comprehended, if only because he accepted the judgement of the more experienced men around him, but like many of his counterparts in the lower class, he was having a hard time understanding Alfred's decision to allow Guthrum to retain the title of King of East Anglia in exchange for being baptized as a Christian. Since he was part of Otha's household now, he had been required to attend to the christening ceremony, which was held, not in Cippinhamm or even Wintanceaster, but in a small church in the village of Aller, which before he saw it with his own eyes, Titus had never even heard of. The fact that it was fifty miles from Cippinhamm meant that this was the farthest he had ever traveled in his life, but it was its location that was significant. In reality, the village was nothing more than a raised spot in the surrounding marshland, and while they did not visit, Eadward had informed him that the village was barely three miles from the floating island of Athelney, where Alfred had been forced to flee and take refuge through the winter before.

"It makes sense in a couple ways," Eadward had explained as they rode together on the journey. "First, it's far to the east of the nearest Danes, and it has symbolic significance."

Titus' vocabulary did not include words like "symbolic," but he impressed Eadward both by his admission he did not know the meaning of the word, but with the fact that, before Eadward could explain, he deduced, "You mean that the fact that Alfred is taking Guthrum to the spot he was forced to run to is a way to remind Guthrum of how he may have made Alfred run, but he didn't make Alfred quit?"

"Exactly." Eadward nodded, and Titus was pleased with himself.

The ceremony itself had been conducted in the small church, while the Saxon men at arms remained outside, talking quietly, but although Titus did not really know what to expect, when the King emerged from the church, followed by Guthrum, dripping wet and wearing the traditional white baptismal gown, it took an effort for him not to snicker. He looks like a wet white puppy following the King, he thought, but if Guthrum was humiliated, he certainly hid it well, and Titus was now less than fifty paces away from both men, although once again, he was in the rearmost rank.

"I, King Alfred, *Anglorum Saxonum Rex*," he spoke with a ringing quality to his voice, but to Titus, what was most important was that he was speaking English and not Latin, "do hereby accept this man, formerly known as Guthrum, self-styled King of the Danelaw and East Anglia, into the company of all of us who have been baptized into Holy Church, and who have accepted our Lord God and Savior, Jesus Christ into his heart and mind! From henceforth, this man," he turned and indicated Guthrum, who was standing there with a somber expression, "shall be known not as Guthrum the Dane, but Aethelstan, who I have adopted as my son!"

This was the last quiet moment, which to Titus seemed to be equally divided between the kind of shouted support one might expect from any proclamation by the King, and consternation, and it was not lost on Titus that the men cheering were the lower class like him, and the men who seemed upset were men like Lord Eadwig. Not that it mattered to him; he was now wholly Lord Otha's man, and Lord Otha had sworn fealty to Lord Eadwig, and he believed that his opinion did not matter, Lord Eadwig's did, so if Lord Eadwig was upset, then he probably should be as well. He was not, but he decided that he should at least pretend he was, although all he did was scowl in the general direction of the King, knowing he was safe in the rear of the group.

Once the ceremony was over, Alfred and Guthrum went to one of Alfred's estates, Wedmore, while, at last, the remaining part of the fyrd of King Alfred was released. The ceorls like Cenric had been allowed to return to their homes once it was determined that the remnant of the Danish army had safely returned to East Anglia, while the thegns and their households had stayed with Alfred until this last moment. Their return to Wiltun had been leisurely, and Lord Eadwig ensured that they spent their nights under a roof whenever possible, and it was during this progress that Titus, who was now referred to as Berserker by his comrades, received another part of his education that was, if not quite as important, was certainly more enjoyable, at least for the most part. It was during their return to Wiltun that Titus experienced both the pleasure that comes from lying with a woman, and a repeat of the anguish of a ferocious hangover, courtesy of mead once again, and not just one but three in succession before Titus swore he would never touch another drop of the stuff. And both of these vices had been introduced to him by Uhtric, although it was with the eager cooperation of the other men of Lord Otha's household, and while he never had it confirmed by any of them, he suspected that the Thegn himself had contributed his silver to the cause of introducing Titus to the world of men. Nevertheless, as momentous as this was, it was what happened at Aller on the day of their departure that he would remember for the rest of his days, if only because he was certain at the time that nothing like it would ever happen again.

The sun had just risen when, once the tents had been packed onto the wagon, which was now being driven by Beorhtic permanently, the King arrived on horseback, accompanied by the Ealdormen Cuthred and Aelfstan, having also been joined at Aller by the Ealdorman of Dorsetscir, and the hero of the battle against Ivar the Boneless and his brother Halfdan, Odda. As the Ealdormen watched with what, to Titus, appeared to be a wary interest, the King made a show of personally thanking first Lord Eadwig, then Otha, Ceadda, and Aelfnod, but it was when he stepped in front of Otha, who dropped to one knee as Lord Eadwig had done, that Alfred's eyes were on the ranks of the Thegn's men, and they stopped on the tall youth who stood almost a full head above his comrades in the front rank. Once again, Titus had the most peculiar sensation when, before he could stop himself, he met Alfred's gaze, feeling as if he had suddenly been run through, albeit painlessly, before dropping his eyes in horror that he had been so brazen.

"Ah," Alfred spoke only a bit more loudly than he had been an instant before, "I see that you have taken on a new household warrior, Otha."

"Yes, Lord King." Otha's voice was muffled because he was kneeling and his face was turned from Titus. When Alfred did not say anything in reply, he added hurriedly, "He acquitted himself well at Ethantun, Lord King."

Alfred nodded in a manner that suggested to Titus that he had already been aware of this, reminding him of the warning from Otha himself that the King of Wessex heard and saw all.

"You have clearly been favored by God…" Alfred looked embarrassed, and Titus heard Otha whisper his name, "…Titus of Cissanbyrig. " His expression remained the same, but there was a slightly harder inflection when he asked, "Do you remember what I told you when we first met?"

"Y-yes, Lord King," Titus replied, but Alfred regarded him steadily, and Titus realized that he was expecting more than this, so he added hastily, "That I should pray every day, Lord King, to keep God's favor."

He thought he had supplied the right answer, but Alfred frowned and he shook his head in a clear rebuke.

"That is *not* why one prays, Titus. God's favor is bestowed not because you ask it of Him, but because you prove you are *worthy* of His favor, even as you know that you will fail in that endeavor. What you should be doing in your prayers is asking Him, 'How better can I serve you, Lord?' That," Alfred said severely, "is what you should be praying for."

"Y-yes, Lord King." Titus imbued his tone with as much sincerity as he thought he could get away with while not making it ring false. "I will do that, I swear it."

As suddenly as it had appeared, the scowl left Alfred's lips, and while he did not say anything more, he rewarded Titus with an approving nod before he turned and stepped over to Ceadda and his household men, leaving the youth hoping that nobody noticed how his knees were shaking. And, Titus would think whenever he recalled that moment, at least I've *tried* to do as King Alfred commanded; most of the time.

Their return to Wiltun was a cause for celebration, and on their arrival, Lord Eadwig announced that a feast would be held to celebrate the victory, and the role of Eadwig's fyrd in it. It was held three days after their return, and in that interim time, Titus had accompanied Otha and his men to the Thegn's estate, which was about three miles northwest of Wiltun. Naturally, Otha's holding was not nearly the size of Lord Eadwig's, but Uhtric had informed him that Otha's estate was fifteen hides, which to Titus meant that his new lord was extraordinarily wealthy. Naturally, Otha's hall was the largest building, but like Eadwig, he had a detached barn, and a low, long building where the slaves lived. As Titus learned, being a member of Otha's household was meant literally; the Thegn personally showed Titus a spot at the left front corner of the hall.

"This is where you'll sleep," Otha informed him, and Titus learned there was more to his placement than just his junior status. "That means you're responsible for making sure the doors are shut and secured every night, and if anyone goes out during the night to piss or shit, you have to make sure that the door is barred after they come back inside. Is that understood?"

"Yes, Lord," Titus answered, trying not to betray his happiness, choosing to see this duty as a sign of trust rather than a task assigned to the lowest man of Otha's household.

And, he quickly grasped when he saw that there were actually markings that Otha informed him outlined the boundary of his personal space that he now had more room than he had ever had in Leofric's miserable shack. Not, he felt a sudden stab of homesickness, that he had minded sharing space with Leofflaed and Eadgyd, at least most of the time, and hard on that thought was a pang of guilt that he had not really given them much thought for several days. This was the moment he decided to ask Otha for permission to visit Cissanbyrig; after the feast, of course. His thoughts about his sisters inevitably led to their father, and on this subject, his sentiment was decidedly less charitable, and it actually gave him pause about asking Otha for permission to go to Cissanbyrig. What, he wondered, if Leofric is there? I swore the next time I saw him, I'd kill him, and what kind of man would I be if I went back on my word? Fortunately, there were other things to distract him, and one of them was the thought of seeing Isolde at the feast, although he kept this to himself.

The next day was spent in performing a more thorough inventory of the loot that had been taken by Otha and the others, as well as spreading the tents out to dry before they were put into the small storage shed. Titus was introduced to Otha's wife, Wulfgifu, a woman who Titus was certain had once been beautiful, but now in her mid-thirties, time had worn her down so that, while a handsome woman, she was not what she had been. What became obvious very quickly was that Otha loved her well, and this was returned by her. The couple had two children, Sunngifu, a vivacious girl of nine with hair the color of gold and a mischievous air about her that reminded Titus of his oldest sister, and Wistan, seven, who was every bit as solemn as his sister was gay. Like most thegns of his status, Otha was ostensibly a farmer, although he was better known as a horse breeder, and he had one of the larger cattle herds in Wiltscir, something that Titus learned when two days after his arrival, he was awakened by a kick in the foot even before the sun had come up. Looking up blearily, he saw Otha holding a candle, staring down at him with an impassive expression.

"The stables need mucking out," he told Titus, then turned to walk away as if that was all that was needed.

Afterward, Titus blamed just being awakened for blurting out, "Why me? I thought I was…" He could not think of the correct term, so all he came up with was, "…done with mucking out stables."

Otha stopped, turning back and crossing to Titus, and there was something in the manner in which he moved that got Titus scrambling to his feet.

The Thegn did not strike him, but despite being at least four inches shorter than the youth, it was Titus who was thoroughly cowed by the manner in which Otha thrust his face directly up at Titus, and he felt himself leaning back away from the Thegn.

"So," Otha spoke quietly, but there was no mistaking the menace, "you think now that you're a warrior, you don't have to do anything but fight, drink, and fuck? Is that it?"

This, in fact, was exactly what Titus had been expecting, and it was not altogether without cause, which he explained, "But that's all your men did when the fyrd was gathering, Lord! They didn't do any of the work to get ready!"

Otha did not reply immediately, and if his expression altered a bit, Titus could have been excused for thinking it was his imagination, but Otha was, above all things, an honest man.

Which led him to allow, in a slightly gentler tone, "That's true, Titus. When we were at Lord Eadwig's, my household men didn't participate in the work. That's customary for household warriors at times like this. But here," he said firmly, "everyone works." He paused for a moment, internally debating what he was about to offer because, frankly, he had not made up his mind, but then acting on impulse, he said, "I've seen the way you have with horses. Anyone," he did offer a slight smile, "who can do what you've done with Hama is someone that I can use…and," he added, "…train."

It took a moment for the import to register, but Titus' mind had latched on to something else, and it took him a moment to make the connection.

"Lord," he spoke slowly, "are you the one who…?"

"Who foaled Hama and raised him, then gave him to Lord Eadwig?" Otha finished for him, nodding as he did. "Yes."

"Why would you give up such a magnificent animal?" Titus gasped.

"Why do you think?" Otha laughed, and for a moment, there was no gulf between them. "I couldn't handle him, and Lord Eadwig was the only horseman I knew who had what it takes to earn his trust. Until," he said, "I saw you do it."

It was, and would remain one of the greatest compliments Titus was ever given, and in response, he said humbly, "I'll go immediately, Lord." He grinned. "As long as I don't have to answer to Dudda, I don't mind shoveling shit."

The day of the feast, Titus was in an agony of anticipation, but after seeing how the other men treated one of their comrades who was unwise enough to declare his love for a certain woman, he had kept his feelings about Isolde to himself. In fact, he spent most of his waking hours trying to talk himself out of setting his expectations too high, and on the morning of the feast, he had resolved to himself to expect that Isolde had been somehow betrothed to another ceorl. He had briefly thought of Eadward as a potential suitor, despite his age, but quickly discarded that; the sons of thegns did not marry the daughters of ceorls in their world, let alone the son of a minor Ealdorman. Besides matters of the heart, he was also still trying to decide whether or not he would follow Eadward's counsel about handing over at least one gold piece to the Ealdorman of Wiltun. He had already surrendered one to Otha, and his fear was that, given the hierarchy and customs, it was not out of the realm of possibility that Lord Eadwig would expect the other two as a sign of fealty to not just Otha, but to him, Otha's overlord. Granted, it still left him an amount of silver that he had certainly never possessed, and he was sure that neither had Leofric, but he had plans for it. At this moment, he was the only member of Otha's household who did not own a horse, and he was acutely aware that, when Otha, his family, and men departed for the feast, he was the only one riding a borrowed mount. His tunic was at least clean, and had been patched by Wulfgifu, with the help of Sunngifu; at least, this had been her claim as she presented the freshly laundered and repaired tunic to Titus, who was blushing furiously. He had wanted to wear his armor, but this was something he wisely kept to himself, although he was happy to see that his new comrades were all wearing their swords. They rode at a leisurely pace, the bottom rim of the sun touching the horizon, while Titus' heart was beating in a manner with which he was still relatively inexperienced but had only happened right before Ethantun began. The sensation in his stomach was eerily similar as well, although it was also subtly different, perhaps not as intense as before going into battle. As he rode into the yard, the celebrations had already started, and Lord Eadwig was standing outside the hall, with Eadward, his sister Eadburga, and Lady Leofe, Eadwig's wife, receiving the guests.

"Remember, you kiss Lady Leofe's hand, and you bow to Lady Eadburga," Uhtric whispered in Titus' ear, who offered a grateful nod in return.

Then he was standing in front of Lord Eadwig, dressed in an embroidered tunic with the heavy gold chain that was a mark of his status, but Titus also knew that it was new, having been given to Lord Eadwig by the King after the battle, and was even larger and more ornate than the one he had been wearing at the first feast before their departure, and now had a heavy pendant attached. The Ealdorman did not smile, but his tone was, if not friendly, cordial, but what mattered was how, once Titus had bowed, he offered his hand.

"Here's the lad I was telling you about, Lady." He was looking at Titus as he addressed his wife. "I had planned on having him replace Dudda because of his way of handling Hama, but it turned out he's a more formidable warrior, and Lord Otha convinced me that it would be a waste of his talents to confine him to the care of the horses."

Titus was confused, but Otha had already moved past and into the hall; fortunately, he was distracted by the Lady Leofe, who exclaimed as she extended her hand, "But you are so *young* to be a warrior! Why, you can't be more than sixteen?"

Titus felt foolish, bent over like he was, and he just touched his lips to the back of her hand, which was what he had seen Willmar do, who was just ahead of him, but her exclamation made him respond shyly, and truthfully, "I'm not sixteen, my Lady. I'm fourteen."

Leofe stared at him in astonishment, and Eadwig looked amused, remarking dryly, "That was my reaction as well when Otha told me, my dear."

"Well," the Lady did recover quickly, "whatever your age, it is good to know that you are a man that my Lord husband may count on in the future."

Now Titus was flushing again, but this time with pleasure, although he could only mumble as he moved in front of Eadward, who was looking up at him with a grin, knowing how Titus felt about what was expected of him. Titus had decided to make something of a game of it, and he gave an even deeper bow than he had with his father.

"Lord Eadward," he did his best imitation of an educated noble, "it is my great honor to greet you again on this…" Now he fumbled, not knowing what word to use, coming up with, "…important occasion."

As both Eadwig and Leofe watched with amusement, Eadward performed a slow bob of his head, trying to imitate what he had seen King Alfred do, as he answered with a mock gravity, "And I welcome you, Titus…the Berserker."

This elicited a gasp of shock from Lady Leofe as she glanced at Eadwig.

"I'll explain later," he told her, but it was the reaction of young Lady Eadburga that drew the most attention, because along with her own small noise, she clapped her hands in delight.

"Why are you behaving like that?" Eadward asked her, with an indulgent smile.

"Because it must mean that he…" she glanced shyly up at Titus, who was trying to decide whether he was going to burst with pride or embarrassment, "…must have fought like a Berserker. Which," Eadburga sniffed, giving her brother a look that communicated her displeasure that she was being treated as if she was simple, or young, "means that he must have killed many Danes." Turning back to Titus, she asked eagerly, "Did you, Titus the Berserker? Did you slay many Danes?"

Before Titus could say anything, Lady Leofe interjected, "That is *not* the kind of thing a lady discusses, Eadburga. And," she added severely, "we have discussed this before, have we not?"

"Yes, Mama," Eadburga murmured, turning her attention to her feet, which were just barely visible underneath a gown that Titus could only imagine its cost. Tonelessly, she addressed Titus. "I apologize, Titus."

He was about to assure her there was no need, but he correctly interpreted the warning glare from Lord Eadwig, so he just nodded his acceptance. Now, Otha, having sensed there was a delay in what was a ritual that had its own rhythm, had paused at the open double doors and was watching with narrowed eyes, making Titus feel even more self-conscious as he hurried to join the others, who seemed to be waiting for their entire party to finish their greetings to their host.

"What was that about?" Otha demanded.

Rather than answer directly, Titus instead countered, "Does Lord Eadwig know that I'm going to be working with the horses?"

As Titus would learn, Otha was hard to catch by surprise, but this was one of those times, and he asked quickly, "Why? What did he say to you?"

Titus explained Eadwig's comment about the idea of his replacing Dudda, and Otha relaxed slightly, but his tone was serious as he said quietly, "I would prefer that you didn't make that known tonight, Titus."

The youth did not hesitate to assure him that he would not utter a word, but he was intensely curious and wanted to know more. Uhtric, however, the last of Otha's household, joined them, interpreting Otha's raised eyebrow correctly.

"The Lady Leofe fussed over this." He pointed to the bandage that still covered the wound, although it at least was no longer bloody.

This evoked laughter from the other men, while Wulfgifu gave a small shake of her head at this display of what she thought was an indifferent attitude towards the suffering of one of their own, and Otha entered the hall, followed by his household. Immediately, Titus' eyes started to roam the interior, but he did not see Isolde anywhere, although he did see Cenric, seated at the same table in the center about halfway down the row of tables as he had been at the departure feast. Instinctively, Titus began to move towards the table that he had occupied the last time, but he was stopped by Uhtric, who grabbed his arm.

"What are you going over there for?" he demanded, then pulled Titus in the direction to where Otha was now standing, an impatient look on his face. "Lord Otha likes us all to sit down together to show the other thegns that we act as one."

To Titus' utter horror at the attention drawn to him by his error, which competed with the delight at the thought of being included, he allowed Uhtric to guide him to the table in the center row that was directly below Lord Eadwig's long table, putting him at the very end of Otha's table and directly next to Cenric, who greeted him with a broad smile.

"There he is!" Cenric boomed, and Titus could smell the ale on his breath, reminding him that Cenric did love his ale and had clearly gotten an early start. "Titus the Berserker!"

His voice was immediately joined by the others, who Titus had already seen were the men with whom he had shared the same tent, along with their families, of course, and this time, he was keenly disappointed that Isolde was nowhere to be seen. Before he was fully seated, a large wooden cup was thrust into his hand, and for the next few moments, the babble of voices made things hard to understand. Immediately, Titus had sensed a quite different mood in the hall from the first time; there was an absence of tension that he only appreciated now that it was missing. Very quickly, he was laughing at something Heard had said, while Cenric slapped him on the back for what he was certain was the tenth time, and it was almost impossible to hear anything. The sign that all of the invited guests had arrived was signaled by Eadwig leading his family up to the long, perpendicular table, as Titus realized two things; he was much closer to Eadward than he had been the first time, and he was well on his way to being drunk. The idea that he might be babbling if Isolde did show up convinced him to shake his head the next time one of the slaves with the trays passed by.

Waiting for Cenric to finish what he was saying to

Osmund, who was across the table from the other ceorl, he tried to sound casual as he asked, "Where is Isolde? Is she coming?"

He was relieved to see that Cenric was not alerted by the question, probably because he was more interesting in draining his cup, so he did not answer immediately.

With a smack of his lips, he wiped them with his sleeve as he answered indifferently, "She's helping in the kitchen tonight." A frown creased his face, and he turned his head to glare at the occupants of one of the tables in the row nearest the wall on the left side of the hall. "And that bastard Hygebald's offer is an insult, so I don't want her out here any more than she needs to be!"

"Offer?" Titus asked, and while he was confused, he felt a sudden sinking in his gut that he knew the answer. "Offer for what?"

Now Cenric looked over at him in bleary surprise, and Titus realized that, in all likelihood, Cenric had started celebrating even earlier than everyone else.

"Why, for Isolde, of course," he responded as if the answer was obvious.

Titus did not know Hygebald very well, but he knew him by sight, and before he could stop himself, he gasped, "But he's so *old*! Surely you won't agree to it!"

For a span of a couple heartbeats, Cenric's only response was to stare at him, blinking several times, then Titus' words apparently registered, although his reaction was to burst out in roaring laughter, to the point he began rocking back and forth.

Finally, he managed to reply, wiping an eye as he did, "Not for Hygebald, you fool! For his son!"

"Who's his son?" Titus frowned, trying to recall whether

he had seen anyone around Hygebald who might be his offspring. "Was he in the fyrd?"

Cenric laughed. "By the rood, no! Swithbehrt's only fourteen!" As soon as it came out, despite his advancing intoxication, Cenric clearly understood who he was talking to, and he looked embarrassed. Reaching out a hand, he gave Titus an awkward pat as he offered, "I meant no offense, lad, I truly didn't. It's just that you're…you," he finished lamely.

Fortunately, Titus took this as the compliment that it was intended to be, although he was not much happier about the subject at hand.

Deciding to do his best to sound disinterested, he asked, "And how much is Hygebald asking?"

"Asking?" Cenric frowned. "What do you mean?"

"I thought it was customary for the father of the…bride to provide the *brydgifu* (bride gift)," Titus explained.

Cenric gave him a look of scornful amusement, but he agreed, "It is. But," he shook a finger, "what about the *morgengifu* (morning gift), eh? And that's not even talking about the *handgeld*!"

"*Handgeld*?" Titus shook his head at the unfamiliar word. "What's that?"

"I thought you said you had two sisters who are older than you," Cenric countered. When Titus assured him that this was the truth, for the first time, the ceorl began thinking of the other things he knew about Titus' father. Suddenly, his expression softened as he realized just how deficient Leofric of Cissanbyrig was as a father, and a teacher. "The morning gift," he explained, "is from the groom, and it gives the bride…Isolde," he offered, needlessly, "in this case, some independence in the event that the groom is a fool or a drunk or he dies and she's left to support the family."

Titus considered this for a moment, then asked, "And what's the *handgeld*?"

"That," Cenric answered, "is the most important, because it shows the bride's family that the family of the groom has the ability to make sure the bride..." for the first time, Cenric showed some emotion, blinking rapidly, "...Isolde, will be cared for, for the rest of her days."

"Why," a new voice interjected, and in a demanding tone, "are you talking about me?"

Both of them had essentially the same reaction, as if they were children who had been caught sneaking a meat pie from the table, while Isolde stood there, hands on both hips, glaring down at them.

"Nothing!" Titus squawked, immediately realizing this was a nonsensical answer, although Cenric's was not much better.

"No reason!"

She stood there, completely disbelieving, and Titus was certain that she was, without a doubt, the most beautiful thing in the world, and if he had been able to pick Swithbehrt out of the faces around them, he would have happily killed him right then. For a long moment, Isolde continued to stare from one to the other, but in this, Cenric and Titus were of a like mind, neither of them willing to betray the other.

Finally, she shook her head, resigned to this being a mystery, and she informed Cenric, "I was just coming to tell you that the meat is about to be served...*Father*." Somehow, she managed to imbue this with what sounded like disapproval, but Titus understood when she pointed down to Cenric's cup. "So you might want to leave some room and not fill your belly with ale."

Then, without waiting for a response, she spun about and, with her head held erect, walked towards the rear of the hall, towards the door that led to the kitchen, and Titus was acutely aware that it was not just his eyes that were following her.

The arrival of the food occupied everyone's attention, including Titus who, for a brief moment, forgot Isolde, although he was displeased to see that she had either been assigned or chosen to serve the third row where Hygebald was seated. He did feel better when, finally, the empty spot on the opposite side of a woman with a pock-marked face and lank brown hair streaked with gray who Cenric had confirmed was Hygebald's wife was filled by a youth who could only be Swithbehrt. He's so scrawny, Titus thought with amused contempt, although he felt a stab of shame at his violent thoughts of earlier, that I could just push him over and he probably couldn't get up. It did explain why the boy, which was how Titus thought of him, had not been with the fyrd. It was perhaps the third time he glanced over that he saw Swithbehrt looking at him, and even in the smoking torchlight, Titus saw the boy blushing as he looked away, and for the first time, it hit Titus that he might be better known than he had thought. Consequently, the next time he saw Swithbehrt glancing in his direction, he made it a point to pick up his cup in a way that allowed him to flex his bicep, and he sat up a bit taller and pulled his shoulders back.

"Why are you doing that?"

He had not seen her because she had approached him from behind, and he almost spewed the mouthful of ale out, which would have hit Hrothgar, who was seated across from him, and that would have been a bad thing.

Twisting around, he looked up at her as she gazed at him curiously, and he decided his best course of action was to ask innocently, "What do you mean? Doing what?"

This amused her, telling him she was not fooled, and she opened her mouth to say something, but then her eye was caught by something, across the room. Naturally, Titus' gaze followed her, whereupon he saw that both Swithbehrt and his father were now watching them with undisguised interest, and, judging from Hygebald's expression, a fair amount of hostility. He did not want to, not really, but Titus could not seem to stop his head from turning back to look up at Isolde, but fortunately for him, she did not even notice because she was staring down at Cenric, who was oblivious, talking to Heard now, who was roaring with laughter.

While he had no idea what was coming next, he was certainly unprepared for Isolde to lean down and, while she whispered in Cenric's ear, Titus clearly heard her hiss, "You told *Titus*, Father?"

Cenric was obviously shocked, but his reaction was delayed by his inebriation, so that by the time he opened his mouth to say something, she had stomped away, quickly disappearing through the double doors, which were open to allow some ventilation.

"If you don't go after her, you're a bigger fool than I thought."

Titus was as shocked as Cenric had been, though not because of the words as much as who had said them, and he spun in his seat to Uhtric, who was seated to his right and regarding him steadily.

"But…how did you know?"

It was all Titus could think to say, which caused Uhtric to give a short, barking laugh that contained a note of bitterness.

"I may only have one eye, boy, but I'm not blind." Then he

nudged Titus, nodding his head towards the door as he urged, "Now, go into battle. And," now his grin was reminiscent of the Uhtric before he had lost his eye, "go with God. She looked pretty angry."

Before Titus rose, he glanced over at Cenric, but he had returned his attention to his conversation with Heard, allowing Titus to get up and step over the bench and head for the doors. He had just reached the doorway when, from behind him came the sharp rapping sound that Titus knew was meant as a signal, having heard it at the last feast, and he stopped, afraid to look over his shoulder. Nevertheless, he did so, and despite expecting it, the sight of Eadwig standing up, one hand on the table as his eyes scanned the room wrenched a groan of frustration from his lips. For a moment, he considered just continuing, but then Eadwig's gaze fell on him, and while the Ealdorman said nothing, the manner in which he dipped his head in the direction of Titus' vacated seat was unmistakable. Nodding his understanding, Titus returned to his seat, ignoring Uhtric's look of sympathy as he dropped back down on the bench.

"There's still time," Uhtric consoled him. "We just have to listen to Lord Eadwig for..." he cocked his head as he grinned, "...the rest of the night, I suspect."

Titus shot him a sour look, not amused in the slightest, but fairly quickly, Isolde was forgotten for the moment.

In many ways, what Lord Eadwig said was identical to the words he had spoken at the previous feast, the main difference being his confirmation that the men he had singled out during the departure feast had fulfilled their duties to him and to their King. The other major difference was that, this time, when Eadwig called the names of his thegns, each one came to him, as before, but instead of offering an oath, they received a gift from Eadwig, as the Lord of Wiltun described the deeds of the thegn in what was already called the Battle of Ethantun. What struck Titus as odd was that Eadwig did not start with Otha, making him wonder if his new Thegn had somehow fallen out of favor, although he was sure that he would have heard of it from Uhtric and the others. In another change, once Eadwig was done speaking, he offered Ceadda, who had been the first of his thegns to be called, a nod, whereupon Ceadda called out one of his men, who stood and walked up the aisle to where the other two men were standing. Naturally, Titus recognized all of them, although some of their names he learned that night, but he listened as Ceadda described the man's actions in the battle, and at the end of the recitation, the hall erupted in a roar composed of both voices and cups being slammed onto the table as the man at arms stood, receiving the acclaim of his comrades, and their families. It was, Titus thought with a lump in his throat, a powerful thing, to be hailed by your comrades, and his voice was raised as he bashed his cup onto the table, sloshing the ale everywhere. Once the tumult died down, Ceadda reached into his pouch and withdrew a large silver ring, which he ceremoniously handed to the warrior, which marked the end of his participation, and he returned to the table to the congratulations of his comrades. Ceadda did not recognize every man of his household, but Titus was pleased to see that one he did was Wigmund, and as Titus suspected, Ceadda commended the warrior for his actions at the ambush as well as the battle. Titus was aware that, as Ceadda described that day, there were dozens of pairs of eyes on him, including Eadward and his father, but he did not think anything of it, and once Ceadda was done, Titus once again raised his voice and banged his cup on the table, extremely pleased when Wigmund turned and acknowledged Titus personally by pointing to him with a nod of his head. Once Ceadda was done, it was Aelfnod's turn, but when Titus turned to Uhtric to ask why, the older warrior had anticipated the question.

"Lord Eadwig is saving Lord Otha and us," he said in Titus' ear, adding, "because he's saving the best for last."

This pleased Titus, who did not even think to doubt Uhtric;

after all, it made sense now that he thought about it. He sat listening as Eadwig praised Aelfnod, presented him with a gift, then Aelfnod called out some of his warriors for commendation, and the other celebrants roared their acclaim. Then, it was Otha's turn, and with his usual impassive expression, the Thegn went to stand in front of Eadwig, as the Lord of Wiltun extolled all that Otha had done, and as might be expected, Eadwig spoke longer and in more glowing terms. It had been Otha who had trained the ceorls of the fyrd, after all; it had been Otha who had been responsible for organizing it, and, as Titus had learned the night after the battle, Otha had personally slain five Danes in defense of Lord Eadwig. The gift Eadwig presented Otha with was a gold chain, similar to but smaller than the one Alfred had given to Eadwig that Titus was almost certain had been the one Lord Eadwig had been wearing at the first feast, and whereas the households of Ceadda and Aelfnod had been boisterous in their acclamation of their lord, Otha's men, Titus included, spontaneously came to their feet, bellowing and slamming their cups down on the table. It took a few heartbeats before Otha shouted them back down into their seats, but Titus could see that he was pleased. Now that it was Otha's turn, he began by speaking of Osric, which slightly marred the mood; the man at arms' wound had become corrupt, and he had died of a fever a week after the battle so that it was his widow who was there representing him. He did not have a gift for her, at least in the form of a ring or necklace, but he announced that he would care for her and their three children for the rest of her days, or until she wed again. This was met with a similar demonstration, but while it was muted, Titus could tell it was more heartfelt, and he also observed that the most enthusiastic response came not from the men, but from the women in the hall. Which, once he gave it a moment's thought, made sense. Next was Hrothgar, and the mood returned to its raucous air as the warrior walked slowly over to Otha and Eadwig.

"He looks like he's expecting a scolding from his father," Uhtric remarked, and Titus laughed because he had been thinking the same thing.

Hrothgar's gift was also a ring, but this one was of gold, the first such, and Titus glanced over to Ceadda and Aelfnod, and it was easy to see they were unhappy, although whether it was the thought of being upstaged or that Otha was wealthy enough to offer gold to his men, he had no idea. Willmar was next, and he also received a ring, then it was Uhtric's turn, and Titus was pleased to see that his popularity extended to more than just Otha's household, and Cenric almost ruptured his eardrum with his bellowed cheer, but Titus was just as loud in his appreciation.

"Uhtric, son of Wiglaf, companion of my childhood and comrade in battle," Otha began, "who fell at my side in the Battle of Reading, your father is looking down on you, proud of the warrior you have become." Turning his attention to the hall, Otha continued, "In the Battle of Ethantun, I saw Uhtric cut two Danes down in single combat, both of them with many arm rings." This elicited the same roar that had preceded the recounting of the other warriors, and Titus joined in. Then, Otha pointed to Uhtric's eye, which Titus sensed made his friend uncomfortable. "And, Uhtric was there with Hrothgar and Willmar during the night attack after the battle as well when the Danes tried one last time to escape, which is where he lost his eye. But," Otha raised his voice, "he continued fighting, even after receiving this wound!"

The roaring resumed, with Titus joining in of course, although he found it curious that Uhtric had not mentioned that he had continued fighting that night. Before the tumult subsided, Otha withdrew another gold ring, but even from a distance, Titus could see that this one was more intricate, with a flat surface that indicated there would be some sort of figure incised on it. Uhtric accepted it, naturally, then stood for a moment next to Otha, shuffling his feet and looking embarrassed yet pleased at the same time. As Uhtric made his way back to the table, Titus scanned the hall once more, except this time, he was not looking for Isolde, but Ealdgyd, Uhtric's woman, and he realized that he had not seen her at all this night. She should be here for this, he thought with disapproval, and he was going to ask Uhtric where she was, but before he could, he saw Otha make a gesture in their direction. Titus, assuming that Otha intended to call one of the others, was more interested in seeing who it might be, leaning back to look down the table to see who stood up. It took Uhtric, who had just dropped back down onto the bench to elbow him hard enough in the ribs, causing Titus to yelp in pain, to get his attention.

"What did you do that for?" he demanded, but instead of saying anything, Uhtric simply pointed.

Following his finger, Titus saw Otha standing there, glowering at him, while the cheering had turned to laughter. With his face feeling as if it was on fire, Titus leapt to his feet, and to his mortification, tripped as he swung a leg over the bench, and while he did not fall, he stumbled and had to be caught by one of Ceadda's men seated behind him. He could not bear to look at Otha, or anyone for that matter, and to his ears, the laughter he heard was mocking and derisive, and not the good-natured amusement that it actually was. Somehow, he managed to make it to stand in front of Otha with his back to the crowd, and only then did he raise his head to look his Thegn in the eye, yet rather than angry, Otha's eyes were alight with amusement. But then, in a change from what he had done with the others, he grasped Titus by the shoulder to turn him around, while drawing him back to his side, and as he did so, the noise in the hall subsided so that he only had to raise his voice to be heard.

He began saying, "When this boy showed up in Wiltun and said he was from Cissanbyrig but wanted to fight for Lord Eadwig, I thought he was a spy sent by either Lord Owin, his thegn, or Ealdorman Wulfhere…" He had to stop because the men in the crowd immediately launched into a spontaneous chorus of growls and curses, and even their women hissed at the mention of the former Ealdorman who had been stripped of his land and title by a victorious King. Holding up a hand to lower the noise, Otha continued, "And, I even had him beaten, thinking that this would drive him away. But," Otha turned to grin at Titus, "I learned that he could at least take a beating. And," now, he looked directly at Cenric and Heard, "two men here learned that he could give as good as he got."

"My jaw is still sore!" Cenric called out, and again the hall filled with laughter, while Titus exchanged a grin with the ceorl who, in his secret dreams, he hoped would be his father-in-law one day.

"But he also proved something else to me," Otha went on, and now his tone became more sober. "He proved that he was speaking truly, and he was sincere in his desire to fight our enemy." For the first time with any of his men, Otha reached out and placed his hand on Titus' shoulder as he continued, "So, I decided to take a risk and allowed him to join the fyrd." Otha suddenly turned almost all the way around, and since Titus did not follow his gaze, he only saw the Thegn nod for some reason.

The voice that began speaking was enough to get him to turn about, eyes wide in surprise at the sight of Eadward, standing behind the table, and while Titus heard the quaver, the lordling's voice was strong and loud enough to be heard.

"As all of you know," he began, "when we were marching to Egbert's Stone to join with King Alfred's fyrd, we were ambushed by a band of Danes." This was met by a ragged chorus, with the men of the fyrd nodding their heads at the memory. Eadward paused for a long moment, and when Titus glanced over his shoulder again, he could tell his friend was struggling to continue, but it was not for the reason he thought, his grief over Thunor, because at last he said, "I disobeyed my Lord father and did not stay where I was told to stay as he and the others rushed to stop the attack." Eadward's eyes shifted over to where his father, who was still seated, was watching impassively, and Titus now understood that this was the punishment Eadwig was meting out to his son for his disobedience, a public confession before the assembled fyrd. "I was attacked by a Dane, who rushed at me and Thunor. Thunor," he explained, "was my horse." He paused again, and now Titus heard the emotion in his voice as Eadward continued, "The Dane tried to kill me with his spear, but Thunor reared to protect me, and he took the spear meant for me."

The hall had fallen silent, and there was a rustling murmur at this, while Titus tried to recall whether he had heard this version before, certain this was new. Not that he would ever say as much; after all, he thought, it's certainly possible.

"When Thunor fell, I was trapped underneath him, and the Dane who killed Thunor was standing over me. That," for the first time, Eadward turned and indicated Titus, "is when Titus, who had been tending the horses along with Dudda, showed up. I didn't see everything," Eadward said honestly, "but I know that if Titus hadn't come to my side, I would not be here today." He paused again, and their eyes met as Eadward said, strongly and simply, "I owe you my life, Titus. Which," now he smiled, "with my father's permission, I am offering you a gift, of any horse that you may choose from my father's horses."

Titus gasped, his eyes lighting up, but Eadwig suddenly intervened, "With one exception, boy!"

The fact that Eadwig was smiling as he said this meant there was a roar of laughter, since everyone present knew how much he doted on Hama, but despite the smile, Titus also knew that Lord Eadwig was deadly serious; in fact, it had not even occurred to Titus to try, though he did his best to make a show of being disappointed.

Eadward signaled his part was done by sitting back down, leaving Otha to continue, "All of you who were there saw what happened at the ambush. This…young Saxon warrior," Titus was certain if he died at this moment, he would never be happier hearing himself described this way, "as untrained as he was, still singlehandedly slew four Danes."

This raised another roar of approbation, and it was all Titus could do to keep from squirming in such an ecstasy of discomfiture and pride, trying to portray an impassive demeanor as he stood there, but while he managed to stand still, his eyes were roaming the hall because, for him, there was only one set of ears he wanted to hear this.

It was Uhtric who started it by bellowing, "Titus the *Berserker*!"

Before anyone could have counted to three, the men in the hall began repeating Uhtric, but then fairly quickly it became a chant.

"*Ber-ser-KER! Ber-ser-KER!*"

As the men, and some of the women, roared this chant, they were slamming their cups in rhythm as Titus stood there, completely flummoxed about what he was supposed to do, with part of him hoping they would stop, yet another part wishing they would do this for the rest of the feast, but most of all, that Isolde would hear him being acclaimed in this manner, wherever she was at the moment. Finally, Otha raised both hands up, making a patting gesture in a signal for quiet, and it died down fairly quickly.

Resuming, Otha said, "That is why I don't have a ring for this young warrior, because I don't think it suits the occasion. Instead," he reached down into his pouch and extracted an arm ring, made of gold wires that were twisted around each other, with what looked like two golden acorns on the ends, "I am presenting him with a Danish arm ring, as a mark of not only my favor, but as a sign to all who face him that they are facing Titus the Berserker!" The tumult began anew, and Otha leaned over to say in Titus' ear, "I know it's not our custom to wear arm rings, but Lord Eadwig already gave you one after the ambush, and I couldn't think of a better way to reward you than this." Placing his hand on Titus' shoulder once more, he squeezed it to the point it was almost painful, which Titus correctly took as a sign that Otha wanted Titus' attention, and he met the Thegn's gaze as the older man said, "I'm proud of you, boy, and I'm happy that you'll be at my side."

"I'll never fail you, Lord," Titus answered fervently, temporarily forgetting everyone else.

"I know you won't." Otha smiled, then gave the youth a gentle shove. "Now go sit down and let people toast you the rest of the night."

The rest of Otha's household were standing and, copying what he had seen the others do, Titus made sure to walk past each of the others and accept their congratulations. When he sat down next to Uhtric, the older man straddled the bench and helped Titus adjust the arm ring to fit his bicep, and it pleased Titus to see that it had to be widened slightly.

"I wonder who this belonged to," he mused, unable to take his eyes off it, thinking that his sword had been replaced as the most beautiful thing he had ever seen. "Maybe it even belonged to a Danish lord!"

Uhtric smiled, but he agreed, "That's possible." Then, since he was facing in Titus' direction he spotted someone, and he gave Titus a nudge. When he looked up questioningly, Uhtric used his head, nodding in the direction of the doors. "I can think of someone who might be interested to see it."

Naturally, Titus swiveled his head, immediately seeing Isolde standing at the entrance, but she seemed to change her mind about returning to the hall, spinning about and exiting into the darkness. This time, Uhtric's shove was less gentle.

"Go after her, idiot," he told Titus. "That's what she wants."

"She does?" Titus could not help feeling doubtful. "How do you know?"

"Because she was staring at you until you turned around,"

Uhtric explained patiently. "Then when you saw her, she left again."

He was not entirely convinced, yet he did get up and began heading for the doors, but he found his progress was hampered by the men who wanted to offer their congratulations, standing and offering their hands, slapping him on the back, and offering some words, all of which he tried to acknowledge. Finally, he broke free of the grasp of the last ceorl, stumbling out into the night, his head spinning, not from ale but from yet another sudden change in his life. He stood in the light spilling through the doorway, but Isolde was not immediately visible; then, he caught movement out of the corner of his eye, and when he looked in that direction, he made out a shadowy form standing at the corner of the hall. With his heart pounding wildly, he walked slowly over towards her, part of him hoping that it was someone else, but he saw quickly enough that it was Isolde, except she was turned away from him, hugging herself as she seemed to be staring up at the night sky, which was cloudless, offering a sparkling carpet of stars. He debated with himself about whether to approach quietly, then decided against it, scuffling his feet, then when that did not seem to alert her, giving a small cough.

She did glance over her shoulder at this, and the light from the doorway illuminated her face, but Titus could not determine what her expression meant, although she said politely enough, "Congratulations, Titus."

This caught him by surprise, and he realized that he had not come up with anything to say, yet somehow he managed to reply with, "Thank you." He glanced down at the arm ring, which felt strange, and he wondered whether he would become accustomed to it.

"Why do you want to marry Swithbehrt?"

The words were out before he could stop them, and he heard the harsh tone of his own voice, and he could not stop from cringing at himself; certainly, he had wanted to know, but not like this! If he was hoping for a reaction, he got one, as Isolde spun about to face him for the first time, her cheeks flushed with what he could immediately tell was anger.

"That's none of your business!" she snapped angrily. "And my father had no right to tell anyone!"

Titus was almost overwhelmed with dismay, but while he did his best to disguise it, he still heard the plaintive note in his voice.

"But why do you want to marry *him*?"

"I don't!" Isolde's answer was immediate, causing Titus' heart to soar, for as long as it took her to add, "I don't want to marry *anyone*!" Titus gaped at her, certain that she had misspoken, but while her anger seemed to be dissipating, she continued fervently, "I don't want to be the property of *any* man, Titus! My father knows this!"

"But," Titus interjected with some apprehension, yet he thought that he had logic on his side, "that's the Saxon way. And," he pointed out, "you'll have the *morgengifu* and your *handgeld*."

She gave him a look of scorn that was impossible to misinterpret, even for an inexperienced youth.

"Is that what you and my father were talking about? How much money I'll have?" She scoffed. "I love my father, but he knows *nothing* about me!"

Sensing that he had an opportunity, although he had no idea why, Titus asked, "What *about* you?" When she looked over at him sharply, he amended, "What doesn't he know about you that he should?"

Now it was her turn to be startled, and she regarded Titus

thoughtfully, while he gazed back, trying to maintain his concentration on anything other than the sprinkling of freckles and how blue her eyes were, although somewhat unusually, her hair was actually black, which made them even more striking.

"That I don't want to be anyone's property," she answered quietly. Before he could interrupt, she correctly anticipated his objection. "Just because I'll have my own money, that doesn't mean I'm free, Titus." She paused, biting her lip, then went on, "I want to be with a man who doesn't view me as *his* but as a partner. Someone who will listen to me and take my advice. Not," she added quickly, "all the time."

Hoping this might help his cause, Titus replied, "I listen to my sister." Suddenly, he felt compelled to add honestly, "Well, most of the time."

To his utter delight, this made her laugh, and she asked teasingly, "When's the last time you didn't take her advice? And," she added mischievously, "was she right?"

He was smiling, but he answered honestly, "She didn't think I should come to Wiltun to join Lord Eadwig's fyrd."

"Why?" she asked, and despite not wanting to talk about it, Titus did, telling her everything, about his shame at Leofric's actions, and then seeing his father at Ethantun, leaving nothing out, even his mixed feelings about letting Leofric live, all of it, including his dreams of being more than some ceorl with one hide of land, growing old before his time without ever tasting life, not really. And, she listened, without interruption, until he was finished. After a silence, she said, "Well, I think that this was one time that your sister was wrong." This made Titus laugh, but she was not smiling, and he understood why when she asked shyly, "Is my father speaking the truth? I mean," she hurried on, "about what happened when the Danes attacked you?" When he did not respond right away, she pressed gently, "Did you really kill four Danes like he says you did?"

Titus suddenly realized that he and Cenric had never spoken of it, so he asked, "What did he say I did?"

She stared at him, puzzled.

"You don't remember?"

He did not reply immediately, but then, in the recesses of his mind, he reminded himself about what Isolde had said about wanting a man to treat her as an equal partner, so he decided to be honest, thinking that this would be the first step in being what she wanted.

"Not much of it," he admitted, then shrugged. "I only remember bits and pieces. I remember seeing Eadward and Thunor falling. Then," he sighed, "the next thing I remember is standing there, and I was…covered in blood." In the moment, he decided that he would be honest, but only to a point, not wanting to disturb her with his memory of the gore dripping from him, the way things smelled, and the sight of a body hacked into bits…and how he reveled in it all. He did think to assure her, "None of it was mine, though."

She considered this, and while she did not say as much, he got the sense that she decided that this was as far as she would press, but she still had other things on her mind.

"Why do you like battle so much?"

Titus instantly recognized that it was a good question, so he thought about it seriously for a moment, before he finally answered hesitantly, "I suppose that I've always felt like I was born to be a warrior. But," he shrugged, "I don't know why, exactly. Besides," he made a face, "I don't want to be anything like Leofric. And I've always hated being a farmer." They lapsed into a silence then, and Titus found that it was not uncomfortable, both of them content to simply stand there, staring off into the darkness, oblivious to the sound of the music that was now coming from inside the hall. Finally, Titus glanced over at her, and asked, "So…you're not marrying Swithbehrt?"

"No," she answered immediately, although she did not look up at him. "I am not marrying Swithbehrt."

"Good," he answered simply.

He was surprised when he felt her hand slip into his, while they continued looking off into the darkness, in a world of their own.

Chapter Eleven

Titus only saw Isolde once after that before he left for Cissanbyrig, and while he thought he had worked up the nerve to tell her how he felt, when they ran into each other in Wiltun, where Titus had gone to pick out his gift horse, all the things he had come up with to say fled his mind, leaving him standing there feeling like an oaf. She did not seem to notice, yet somehow Titus sensed that she was acutely aware of the effect she had on him, and moreover, that she enjoyed it. He was not wearing his mail, but only because Uhtric had been merciless in his derision at the sight of him dressing for battle to go into the town, but he was wearing his sword, and the arm rings, of course. Somewhat ironically, his detour to the market had not been with Isolde in mind; he had planned to stop at Cenric's farm after he selected his horse, thinking that her seeing him with what was a status symbol and sign of favor would impress her even further.

It had been Uhtric who suggested, "Now that you have some money, you need to buy new clothes. That," he pointed to Titus' ragged and patched tunic, "stinks." Titus knew Uhtric was right, yet it was embarrassing to have it pointed out nonetheless, but Uhtric suggested, "And you should get at least one tunic in the Danish style."

"The Danish style?" Titus frowned, then grasped what Uhtric was saying. "Do you mean a tunic with short sleeves?"

"Sleeveless would be better," Uhtric replied, but while Titus now knew what he meant, he was still unclear as to why, and he asked Uhtric to explain. "Because," Uhtric tapped Titus' arm rings, "if you're going to act like a Dane, you should look like a Dane. Those rings looks silly with a long sleeved tunic. This way," he grinned, "the women will see your arms. And," he nudged Titus, his smile turning lascivious, "women love men with big arms. They think it means they have big…"

"All right," Titus cut him off, embarrassed. "I know what you mean."

This was why he was in the market when he ran into Isolde, but to his disappointment, the lone merchant who dealt in clothing, buying the excess cloth from the nearby farms after it had been spun and woven by local women, did not have anything suitable immediately available. Isolde was there because she had taken on the role of her mother, who had died two years previously, and Cenric had not remarried, leaving her to care for the home and her two surviving siblings, both younger and both boys, and she needed to barter for some fresh vegetables, bringing eggs in trade.

"What brings you into town?" Isolde asked, and he explained, "I've come to pick out the horse Lord Eadward gave me."

"But Lord Eadwig's estate is that way." She pointed back over her shoulder. "And coming from Lord Otha's, this is out of your way."

Titus flushed, but he replied honestly, telling her about his plan to purchase two new tunics and two new pairs of trousers; he had already purchased a cloak, used but in good condition.

"That," she said with a smile, "is a good idea."

He knew she had not meant it unkindly, but this reminder of his poverty, even by the modest standards of Saxon ceorls, made him flush.

Even worse, it made him say stiffly, "Yes, well now that I've done that, I must be going to Lord Eadwig's. It was nice seeing you again."

With an abrupt turn, he strode away, leaving Isolde to stare at his retreating back, mouth open and wanting to call him back to her, yet not knowing what to say. She had hurt his feelings, she knew, and the knowledge of this dampened the rest of her time in the town, so that when she returned to Cenric's farm, she was in a thoughtful mood, wondering why she found that so unsettling.

When Titus arrived at Lord Eadwig's estate, Otha was already there, and he was standing behind Eadward at the scarred stake, which Titus took care to approach from a direction where his friend would not see him. He tried not to feel smug as he watched, but at the same time, he forced himself to be fair; Eadward had markedly improved just in the barely two months of time since Titus had first walked through the gates, and, he was honest enough with himself to know that he still had a long way to go, even if he was better than Eadward already. Otha glanced over, and seeing Titus standing there, tapped Eadward on the shoulder, signaling him to stop. When Eadward straightened up and looked inquiringly at Otha, he saw Titus approaching, his face splitting into a grin, but in his excitement, he committed a cardinal error, tossing the sword into the dirt, which earned him a slap across the head from Otha.

Eadward yelped, while Titus winced in sympathy; he had learned just how hard Otha could hit, and the Thegn growled at the lordling, "I've told you more than once. You treat your training weapons like your real weapons. That way, you don't get any bad habits."

"Yes, Lord," Eadward mumbled, picking the sword up and

leaning it point down against the stake.

Titus could not stop from laughing as Eadward rubbed the side of his head, and the lordling glared at him.

"I'm only laughing because I know how much it hurts." Titus at least tried to sound sincere, but Eadward was not fooled.

"Oh, lick my arse," he grumbled, but he was not someone who could stay angry long, and the excitement of the moment was such that he was grinning again as he led Titus to the barn.

"I'll get your Lord father," Otha announced. Then, as he was walking away, he said over his shoulder, "He said he doesn't trust Berserker here and he knows he'll try and steal Hama."

The youths laughed at this, but Titus said cheerfully, "If I thought I could get away with it, I would, Lord."

They entered the barn, keeping the doors open so that there was some light, but it was Titus' smell that was all Hama needed, the black horse's head suddenly appearing from its stall, ears pricked, blowing with his huge nostrils, taking in the scent of the youth who had earned his trust and affection.

"He certainly remembers you," Eadward remarked, and Titus was sure there was a note of envy in his friend's voice.

Before he could respond, the stallion began pawing at the dirt floor and tossing his head, which Titus knew was the most potent sign that the animal was losing patience; he had learned the hard way about the danger of that happening, so he hurried across the space, reaching into his tunic to withdraw the piece of bread he had brought with him, holding it flat in his palm. It immediately became apparent that Hama was falling back into the routine they had developed, as he allowed Titus to scratch the white blaze on his broad forehead as he snatched the bread and began munching on it.

"I knew I needed to be keeping an eye on you," Eadwig called out with heavy humor as he and Otha entered the barn. "But," he joined Titus and began stroking the stallion's neck, speaking to it with a severe tone, "I'm even more disappointed in you. I think you'd be perfectly happy to run off with the boy here."

When, Titus thought sourly, will I stop being a boy to him and to Otha? He said nothing of course, simply smiling, then Eadwig stepped away and said briskly, "So, have you thought about your choice? You know these horses well, so I suspect you've been thinking about it a great deal."

"I have, Lord," Titus admitted, but then he shocked the others when, instead of moving along the double line of stalls where the most valuable animals were kept, he turned and walked out the side door that led out to the large enclosure.

He paused long enough for the others to catch up, then without hesitation, he walked directly to the gelding with the dull golden coat, black mane and tail, and a freshly healed scar on its right shoulder. While the horse's reaction was more subdued than Hama at Titus' approach, he did come walking towards the youth, lowering his head and stretching out his neck.

"Him?" Eadward asked in surprise.

Eadwig, however, smiled, silently saluting Titus for his shrewd choice, and when he exchanged a glance at Otha, the Thegn returned the smile, along with a slight nod of approval. No, the horse was not much to look at, and it did not have the same high spirit as Hama, although this was natural with a gelding, but the animal was in its own way as sound as Hama. It was, he reflected, a very good choice, and it was yet another example for the Lord of Wiltun that this raw youth possessed...*something* that marked him as unusual. In some ways, he thought, it's a shame that he's the son of a traitorous ceorl; that will haunt him for the rest of his days. Although, he allowed as soon as the thought came, that's not necessarily a bad thing because it will fuel his ambition to erase that stain, and a man with a grudge can be a valuable tool.

Aloud, he said gruffly, "You might as well have that one since you're why he's marked. I," he gave a shrug that was patently false, and he meant it to be, "was thinking of hitching him to a wagon. Or maybe slaughtering him for meat."

Despite the dire words, Titus was not fooled, and his broad smile made that clear, but then it faded, and to the surprise of the two lords, it was Eadward Titus addressed next.

"Lord Eadward," he said hesitantly, "I have a request."

"Oh?" Eadward responded in surprise, uncertain what Titus could want from him when his father was standing there. "What is it?"

"With your permission, I'd like to name him Thunor," Titus said quietly, then added needlessly, "after your Thunor."

The only thing that saved young Lord Eadward from the shame of bursting into tears in front of his father and Otha was that both men were moved. Not, of course, to the point of tears, but Eadwig offered Titus a solemn nod of understanding, grateful to the youth for this gesture towards his son.

Eadward did his best, and while he could not keep tears from forming, he retained his composure to reply gravely, "I would be honored, Titus. Yes, I'd like that very much."

Titus was astride Thunor, with Uhtric beside him, as the pair rode into Cissanbyrig, from the south. They had ridden past the great stone ruins of Stonehenge, and while Titus certainly knew of the massive stones, it was the first time he had laid eyes on them, and it engendered a spirited debate between him and Uhtric as to its origin.

"Fairies," Uhtric announced emphatically. "Many, many years ago. They moved the stones and put them here in a circle like that."

"Fairies?" Titus repeated with an incredulous laugh. "How is that possible? Fairies are *tiny*! Everyone knows that!"

"That doesn't matter," Uhtric snorted. "They have magic! You don't need to be big if you have magic powers!"

To Titus, it was obvious that the answer was almost literally the opposite, and he shook his head as he pronounced, "No. It was giants. They're the only ones who would be strong enough to carry stones that size and set them up."

"Giants," Uhtric scoffed contemptuously. "There's no way it was giants! Everyone knows that they're too dim-witted to do anything like that! Now," he allowed with a shrug, "*maybe* the fairies cast a spell on the giants and they carried the stones here from wherever, but then the fairies used their magic to put them in the ground and put them on top of each other like that."

While Titus was still skeptical, he was also of an age where he instinctively deferred to someone older than him, especially someone he trusted implicitly like Uhtric.

"Well," he finally said doubtfully, "it would take a lot of magic for fairies to do something like that."

They had dismounted and were walking around the huge stones, and even as casual as Titus was about his faith, he crossed himself, surreptitiously so Uhtric did not see him, his mind struggling to comprehend how something as massive as these stones could have been thrust into the ground, and if it *was* magic, whether that was some sort of offense to God. After all, what little he knew of the stories of the Bible, the only giant he knew of was Goliath, slain by David, and he could not recall ever hearing any priest speak of fairies. If he had been aware that fully two-thirds of the sarsen stones were buried in the ground and what he was seeing was just the top third, and that the stone itself did not come from anywhere nearby, he might have fled in terror and vowed never to come back. As it would turn out, Titus would find himself strangely drawn to the place, and would return to it several times over his life.

They covered the last few miles to Cissanbyrig in relative silence, and when they saw the thin trails of smoke from the homes in the village, they drew up so that Titus could don his armor. He was now wearing one of his new tunics, in the Danish style with very short sleeves, as was his plundered mail vest, the Danes favoring a shorter length of sleeve because it allowed more freedom of movement. It made sense once Titus thought about it, particularly since the Danes favored the ax, which was not a thrusting weapon, which meant it required greater freedom of movement. The arm rings were now around his bare skin, one on each arm, and to his eyes, it made his biceps, which were already larger than most grown men's, look even larger, and he was struck by the thought that Uhtric had been right about this much at least. Once he donned the helmet, he knew he looked formidable, and Uhtric nodded in approval at what he saw. Titus' shield was lashed to the back of his saddle, lying flat across Thunor's hindquarters, but he had left the spear back at Otha's estate. This was about making an impression, his way of announcing that he was a man now, so it was not surprising that he took the most confidence from the sword hanging from his left hip. He also appreciated that, while Uhtric was armed with his *seaxe*, he had chosen not to wear his armor, not wanting to detract from the impression his young friend was intent on making.

"Have you decided what you're going to do if he's there?"

It was the question that had been lingering there, unspoken, for the entire journey, and Titus knew that, despite Uhtric's joking announcement that he wanted to see the sights of Cissanbyrig, he understood why the one-eyed warrior was with him. And, while he would never say it, he appreciated it deeply.

Titus considered for a few paces, the horses now at a walk, then sighed, "No, I haven't."

"Well, you *did* tell him that you'd kill him the next time you saw him," Uhtric pointed out, and Titus did not try and dispute this since it was true, but Uhtric was not through. "And a warrior's honor is the most important thing he has, Titus. If you give your word or offer an oath, then you *must* keep it. Otherwise," he held both hands out in an empty gesture, "you're nothing."

It was the way of their world; Titus was acutely aware of this, but as much as he hated the man, Leofric was his *father*. However, there was a practical consideration, which Titus pointed out now.

"If I kill him, and if Leofflaed or Eadgyd haven't married yet, there's nobody to protect them."

"And," Uhtric countered, "what are the chances of your sisters getting married over the last three months?"

"Not very good," Titus admitted.

Uhtric was silent, but it was because he was searching for a tactful way to ask, and knowing she was older, he began with, "How old is Leofflaed now?"

"She just turned nineteen," Titus answered, which seemed to confirm to Uhtric his suspicion, although he was not about to offer his judgement.

Instead, he tried to sidle up to the subject by asking casually, "So why do you suppose she hasn't married yet? Has nobody asked her?"

This did get Titus' attention, and he looked over at Uhtric, but rather than be irritated or defensive, he answered with dry amusement, "No, that's not the problem. My fath…Leofric says it's because she's too choosy and she has ideas in her head."

"So she's not…plain," Uhtric said cautiously.

This made Titus laugh, and he assured his companion, "Judging from all the lads sniffing around her the last few years, no, I don't think you could call her plain. But," he shrugged, "to me, she's just my sister, and I never really thought about it." He was silent for a moment, then finally, he finished, "Yes, actually, I think she's quite pretty. So is Eadgyd, for that matter."

As Uhtric got to know Titus better, he would learn that he rarely was prone to understatement, but he was about to learn that there were exceptions. Before that happened, however, they encountered a knot of people, all men, standing in the large open area that was used for market days, the traditional gathering place during daylight hours for men who found a way to escape from their toils during that time before the lone alehouse opened. And, as anyone who dwelled in a small village in Wessex during those days knew, there were always men who would rather loaf than work, which was why Titus was so tense as they approached. If Leofric *is* here, he thought grimly, this would be the spot. Since they were huddled together, it was natural for one of them to glance over their shoulder at the sound of approaching horsemen. The pair was too far away to hear what was said, but the reaction of the villagers was something that, of the two of them, Uhtric was accustomed to, the sudden shift of the group's attention to these two strangers, and warriors, every man now watching them warily. And, Titus saw with some irritation, suspicion and veiled hostility, as if they did not recognize…

"They don't know it's me," he murmured, the understanding igniting a queer feeling in him, one of equal parts satisfaction that he had transformed to a degree he was no longer recognizable to men he had last seen a matter of a couple months before, and a sense of apprehension that he had now entered new territory.

Outwardly, he untied the thongs of his helmet, pulling it off, and this was sufficient for one of the men, a young one with a patchy beard and a nose that seemed to have decided to go in a different direction than originally intended about halfway down its length to gasp, "*Titus*? Is that you?"

"*Wes hal*, Oswiu," Titus answered, using the formal greeting of the Saxon people, secretly proud that he managed to sound so cool. He had intended to behave himself, but the sight of his former nemesis swept that resolve away, and while he was smiling, there was nothing friendly in it as he said, "I see that the beating I gave you improved your looks."

Oswiu reacted as if he had been struck again; the fact that three of the other men burst into mocking laughter made the moment even better for Titus, but it was the look of impotent rage on Oswiu's face that was most satisfying. Both of them knew that, because of the sword on his hip, Titus held an insurmountable advantage, and the stories of disrespectful ceorls being run through by enraged men at arms were too numerous to count. The recognition of this fact actually caused Titus a twinge of shame, which surprised him; he had been more than able to beat Oswiu with his fists, but now he was the one who looked like the bully by taunting the other youth while knowing that Oswiu could do nothing about it.

"Why are you wearing armor, Titus?"

The questioner was a ceorl about Leofric's age, his name Cuthwine, but what mattered to Titus was that he was one of the few men his father was on friendly terms with, so he answered with barely disguised hostility, "Because I'm a part of the household of Lord Otha, Cuthwine."

"Lord Otha? Who's that?"

Since it was another ceorl, and one who Titus knew and actually liked who asked this, Titus answered in a softer tone, "His estate is outside Wiltun, Godstan. He's a thegn of Ealdorman Eadwig of Wiltun."

"Did your father give his permission?" Cuthwine interjected. In response, Titus nudged Thunor, guiding the horse into the group so that he effectively separated the ceorl from his companions, then stared down at the man with a cold expression. Still, one reason Cuthwine and Leofric were on friendly terms was because of their similar character, so Cuthwine said stubbornly, "You know that's the law!"

Rather than reply directly, Titus instead asked abruptly, "Did you answer Lord Owin's call to the fyrd to fight for Ealdorman Wulfhere?"

Cuthwine swallowed hard, but he shook his head.

"I don't believe you," Titus snapped.

"It's true, Titus," Godstan spoke up, and when Titus glanced over to where he was standing with the others, they were all nodding their agreement. "Cuthwine didn't answer, nor did I. Nor," he turned and indicated the others, including Oswiu, "did anyone else here."

"But my father did." Titus frowned; something did not seem right with this. "Are you saying that he was the only one from the village?"

"No," Godstan admitted. "There were a half-dozen who went with Lord Owin to Cippinhamm. None," he finished grimly, "have come back."

"If they're wise, they won't," Uhtric spoke up for the first time. Even without the armor and with just a *seaxe* on his hip, now that Uhtric had discarded the bandage and was wearing an eyepatch, he was even more formidable, especially to simple villagers. "In the event you haven't heard, King Alfred has stripped Wulfhere of all his lands and titles, and that includes any thegn who followed him. Now," he shrugged, "whether that extends to those ceorls who followed their thegn, I haven't heard."

Titus had been dreading it, but despite Godstan's claim that none of them had returned, he still felt compelled to ask, "Are you saying that Leofric isn't here?"

"No, Titus," Godstan answered immediately, but Titus was watching Cuthwine, and he was certain that there was something in the ceorl's demeanor that made him suspicious. Regardless of this, he decided that there was no point in pressing the matter; if Cuthwine knew something, such as Leofric being somewhere in the area, he was certain that Leofflaed would know more.

He nudged Thunor with his knee, and it caused the animal to sidestep. By doing so, he sent Cuthwine staggering back several steps, although the ceorl wisely kept his mouth shut. Titus was not through, turning Thunor so that it brought him next to Oswiu, and he stared down at him, wondering why he had ever been scared by this boy, for that was how Titus viewed him now. Then, without another word, he kicked the horse into a trot, leaving the village by the road that traveled up the shoulder of the hill between Cissanbyrig and Leofric's farm.

He knew that it was inevitable, but Titus still dreaded the moment when they rounded the gentle bend in the track and Leofric's shack first came into view. Despite the change in his circumstances, even wearing armor he had won in battle and riding a horse that he had been given as a reward for his bravery, he experienced the same twisting sensation in his stomach that he always did, even with a pouch full of silver and two gold coins. That, at least, had gone better than he had hoped; when he offered Lord Eadwig one of them at the feast, he had flatly refused it, which had confused Titus.

When he confronted Eadward, his friend had laughed and said, "I told you it was a test. I didn't say that he would take it, just that you should offer it. And," he assured Titus, "I heard him tell my mother that he was impressed that you did."

Nevertheless, despite all this, the sight of his farm created the same twisting sensation in his stomach that it had for his entire life, and it was only exacerbated because of Uhtric's presence, which reminded him of when one of his few childhood friends had sought him out and they saw his poverty with their own eyes. And, he could see, in a glance, that Uhtric was embarrassed for him as they rode into the yard in front of the ramshackle house.

"It's very…clean," Uhtric offered, and while this was certainly true, it was thanks to the efforts of his sisters, which was another source of shame for Titus, remembering all the times he had sullenly refused to pitch in, declaring that he did more than his share out in the fields.

Before he could say anything, a shadow crossed the open doorway, then Eadgyd appeared, drying her hands on a cloth as she squinted from the gloom of the house. Titus felt his face splitting into a grin, but his sister's response was a suspicious frown, and he realized that he had put the helmet back on so that its nose piece blocked a clear view of his face. He had not tied it back on, so he pulled it off, completely forgetting his embarrassment, relishing the sight of her jaw dropping as a hand flew to her mouth.

"*T-Titus?*"

It came out a squawked whisper, and from inside, he heard Leofflaed say irritably, "What? What about Titus?"

"He's here," Eadgyd replied, her eyes not leaving her brother as he swung down from the saddle.

"That's not funny, Eadgyd!" he heard Leofflaed snap, but before Eadgyd could say anything, he put a finger to his lips, giving her a grin that signaled his intentions.

She stepped aside and he crept to the doorway, while Leofflaed, puzzled by her sister's lack of response, came out of the house, colliding directly with her brother.

Her shriek of fear transformed into one of happiness as Titus swept her up in his arms, roaring with laughter as he assured her, "I think it's *very* funny!"

Uhtric was temporarily forgotten as he witnessed the three reunited siblings expressing their joy at seeing each other again, and the sight affected him, though perhaps not for the reason Titus might have assumed, his good eye fixed on one figure and one only.

"You're strangling me!" Titus kept saying, albeit with a laugh as the sisters both threw their arms around his neck and refused to let go.

"You deserve to be strangled!" Leofflaed countered, and while she was smiling, even Uhtric could see that her anger was only partially feigned. "The battle was almost two months ago and this is the first we're seeing you?"

"I know," Titus mumbled, and now Uhtric had to cough to cover his laugh at the sight of this large, young, mail-clad man at arms suddenly cowed by someone whose head did not even reach his chin as he suddenly began studying the ground, kicking at it with one boot-clad toe.

It was Eadgyd who noticed Uhtric first, and she asked politely, "Brother? Who is this?"

Titus was secretly relieved to have the subject shift, and he replied instantly, "This is Uhtric, son of Wiglaf, who was of Lord Eadwig's household. Uhtric serves the household of Lord

Otha." He turned back to his sisters and said quietly, "As do I."

Leofflaed's smile faded, but she murmured so that only Titus and Eadgyd could hear, "We'll talk about this later." Louder, she addressed Uhtric. "Welcome, Uhtric, son of Wiglaf. Please, accept our hospitality. We don't have much, but we are happy to share it with you. Anyone who is a friend of Titus' is our friend as well."

Uhtric did as she bade, swinging down from the saddle to approach the other three, but to Titus' eyes, this was not the Uhtric he knew. The warrior had developed a well-earned reputation for his success with the fairer sex, something that Titus secretly, or so he supposed, studied every opportunity he got, and now that the mystery about Eadgyd had been cleared up, Uhtric had seemingly resumed his campaign of conquest without a pause.

When Titus had finally worked up the courage to ask Uhtric the day after the feast, the one-eyed warrior had shrugged and replied in an offhand manner, "She thinks I'm ugly now. She doesn't like being with ugly men."

At first, Titus was certain that his friend was only pretending to be indifferent, but he quickly determined otherwise as Uhtric resumed his amorous conquests, turning his attention to one of the daughters of the smith in Wiltun.

This Uhtric was nowhere to be seen, however, as he offered a nervous bow to first Leofflaed, then Eadgyd before looking back to Leofflaed.

"Thank you," he replied. "The honor is mine."

Titus was so bemused by his friend's suddenly shy demeanor that he completely missed the expression on his sister's face, but then the four of them entered the house, and he thought no more about it.

By the time Uhtric and Titus left his farm two days later, the young warrior was aware that he was faced with yet another dramatic shift in his circumstances, and he had a decision to make, or, at least he believed he did. Perhaps it was a blessing then that there were other things he learned from his sisters that at least partially diverted his attention. Eadgyd had wasted no time, broaching the subject as soon as Leofflaed had filled their cups, with water and not ale, another sign of their dire poverty, although perhaps the one redeeming quality of Leofric's farm was the well, which provided clean, cold water.

"Leofric showed up a week after the battle," Eadgyd said bluntly, but it was the look she gave Leofflaed that was most informative as she continued, "and Leofflaed gave him four shillings. The four shillings," she added bitterly, "that *I* had earned spinning, for almost an entire year!"

"He is our father, Eadgyd," Leofflaed countered, but while she sounded calm, Titus heard the tension there, and he was certain that this was not the first time his sisters had had this argument.

Consequently, while he certainly wanted to learn more about Leofric, he thought it the appropriate time to interject, and he was sure this would lighten the mood.

"Neither of you will have to worry about money anymore." Reaching down to his belt, he unfastened the purse, then made a point of dropping it onto the table so they could hear the clinking of coins.

As Titus hoped, this had the desired effect, forestalling the coming quarrel between his sisters, and he enjoyed their look of astonishment, yet neither of them seemed willing to touch the pouch and open it up.

"Go ahead." He laughed. "There's nothing in there that will

bite you."

As she usually did in such moments, Eadgyd silently deferred to Leofflaed, who reached out with a visibly shaking hand, loosened the strings, then upended the pouch onto the table. Not surprisingly, it was the gold coins that elicited small gasps from both sisters, but the dozen silver coins and the chunks of silver that actually weighed more than the coins alone represented more money than any of Leofric's children could expect to see in at least two years.

"How did you get this much money?"

It was less the question than the tone Leofflaed used, one that told Titus that, as usual, his sister knew or suspected there was more to the story.

He was trying to frame his answer, when Uhtric, who had been completely silent up to this moment, saved him from a conversation Titus had been dreading.

"Your brother slew several Danes in single combat," Uhtric said quietly.

"'Single combat'?" Eadgyd frowned. "What does that mean?"

"It means," Leofflaed cut in, "that our brother put himself in even greater danger than he needed to!"

This was said with a disapproving glare, causing Titus to flush, which in turn caused Uhtric to laugh at the sight of his young friend being cowed by his oldest sister, not even attempting to try and hide his amusement.

Still, he felt compelled to defend Titus, and he continued, "It wasn't like that. At least," he amended, "not exactly."

For the next several moments, only Uhtric talked, and while he took care to omit some of the details, he also did not downplay what he saw Titus do on the day of the ambush.

"Before that day," he said frankly, "all I, or anyone else, for that matter, knew, Titus was just the stableboy who was helping Dudda."

"Dudda?" Eadgyd asked.

"He was Lord Eadwig's stableman," Titus explained. "He was killed in the ambush."

As he said this, Titus realized with some surprise that his hostility towards the fat man had more or less died with Dudda himself, and while he could not bring himself to feel much sympathy for the man when he lived, he no longer cursed his name.

Uhtric continued, "But when Lord Eadwig's son Eadward had his horse killed from under him and had one leg trapped under the animal, it was Titus who moved faster than any of us could. And," he shook his head at the memory, "none of us have ever seen anything like what he did that day, and I know that because we all talked about it. Not even Lord Otha had seen anything like it, and he's seen more battle than any man I know."

There was a silence that lasted for several heartbeats, then Leofflaed addressed Titus, asking him with a direct gaze, "Was this like what happened with Oswiu?"

Titus' initial reaction was one of surprise, but almost as quickly, he recognized that he should not have been; there was nobody in his life who knew him better than Leofflaed.

Still, he hesitated before answering haltingly, "Yes…at least, I *think* so." Having been forced to relive the moment, he said, "It was the same as far as that I didn't remember anything afterward. With Oswiu, I saw him hurting Merwenna's puppy, and I remember running at him. After that?" He shrugged. "Godstan and some of the other men were dragging me off him."

"Oswiu?" Uhtric broke in, trying to place the name. His expression cleared, and he pointed to his nose. "Was that the lad whose nose decided to try and run away from his face halfway down?"

As he hoped, this lightened the mood, the girls giggling and Titus laughing as he nodded.

"Yes, that's Oswiu. But," his smile faded. "I wish I could remember that much at least with him." Returning to the ambush, he looked directly at Leofflaed, continuing, "And it was almost the same when I saw Lord Eadward trapped under Thunor. That was his horse's name," he explained, but when he said no more, his sister was not fooled.

"You said almost," Leofflaed pointed out. "What was different this time?"

"I remember running from the wagon," Titus explained. "And I remember seeing an ax lying on the ground, and I picked it up. And," he swallowed the sudden rush of bile as the image came roaring back into his conscious mind, "I used it to kill the Dane who was about to stab Lord Eadward while he was trapped, which I do remember. Then…?" His voice trailed off, and he finished honestly, looking Leofflaed in the eye as he did. "I don't remember anything about the other men. I mean, besides what Uhtric and the others told me."

He could see that his sister was not satisfied, but in turn, she saw that this was all Titus was willing to volunteer, so by unspoken consent, she turned back to Uhtric.

"What…" she began, then faltered, her cheeks reddening. "When were you wounded, Uhtric?"

His good eye went wide with surprise that, while feigned, completely fooled Leofflaed.

"What?" He shook his head in apparent bafflement, but while Leofflaed did not know Uhtric, Titus did, and he quickly lifted his cup to hide his grin as his friend cried, "Are you saying I was wounded?" He looked over at Titus, demanding severely, "Why didn't you tell me I was wounded, Titus? What kind of friend are you?"

Titus had every intention of prolonging this teasing of his sister, but he could not keep his composure at the sight of Leofflaed's face, and he began roaring with laughter. Eadgyd quickly joined in, leaving Leofflaed flushing with embarrassment, and Titus felt a twinge of regret at his role, but then to his immense relief, she chose to see the humor and, if not quite as heartfelt, it made Titus feel better to see her laugh. He was shocked when, displaying a playfulness that to this moment his sister had only shown with her family, she reached over and gave Uhtric a light slap on the hand.

"I see that I'll have to watch you carefully," she warned him. "You like to tease!"

Shockingly, to Titus at least, Uhtric's reaction imitated his sister's of a moment before, as his tanned face darkened.

"Only with certain people," he answered quietly.

Suddenly, Titus became acutely uncomfortable, but when he looked over at Eadgyd in order to reassure himself he was imagining things, one glance at her face told him that she was as nonplussed as he was.

By noon the next day, Titus could not deny that he was facing a situation for which he was totally unprepared; Uhtric and his sister were falling in love, right in front of him and

Eadgyd.

"It's like they don't even know we're there!" Eadgyd had whispered when Uhtric had volunteered to help Leofflaed gather eggs from the handful of chickens they kept.

"I know," Titus agreed miserably. They were seated at the table, listening to the couple laughing outside. "But I don't know what to do about it."

This was when he learned something, that while Eadgyd was similarly nonplussed, it was for an entirely different reason.

"He didn't even look in my direction!" she fumed, crossing her arms in a pose that Titus knew all too well, and he braced himself for what he knew was coming. "Am I not as pretty as Leofflaed?" she demanded, and even knowing this was inevitable, Titus could not stop a groan from escaping his lips.

"Why are you asking me that?" he said plaintively. "You know I don't look at you like that. *Either* of you," he added quickly. Then, knowing it was a bad idea, he still felt compelled to point out, "Besides, Leofflaed is older than you are."

"So?" Eadgyd sniffed. "What does that matter?"

Then, before either of them could say anything else, they were warned by the sound of the pair returning, and Titus' mood was not helped in the slightest by the flush on Leofflaed's cheeks, but it was the broad smile on Uhtric's face that was the most alarming. However, Titus noticed something else that, in its own way was the most unsettling. He had seen Uhtric smiling in the presence of a woman whose favors he had won, if only for a night, but the one he was wearing in Leofric's dim shack was nothing like that. He looks, Titus realized miserably, like a man who's truly in love. He inadvertently made matters worse by broaching another subject that had been bothering him through the night.

"What are you going to do if Leofric comes back?"

As he had hoped, this immediately wiped the happy expression off his sister's face, and he did feel a stab of shame about it, but his concern was justified as far as he was concerned.

"What do you mean?" Leofflaed asked cautiously, but Titus countered, "You know what I mean. That," he pointed to the pouch, which had been sitting on the table since the day before, "is yours, not his. I gave it to you and Eadgyd, not him. So," he demanded, "what happens if he hears that you've suddenly got money and comes back? Because you know that he *will* find out, the moment you go into town and spend a single shilling."

The sisters glanced at each other, but it was Eadgyd who answered, "What Leofflaed did was because he caught us by surprise. We won't make the same mistake again."

Ignoring Leofflaed's look of gratitude towards her sister, Titus said flatly, "That's not good enough."

"What are you looking for, then?" Leofflaed snapped.

It was, Titus realized, not only a good question, he also understood that his sisters were working at a disadvantage; they had not seen the real Leofric like he had.

Once more, it was Uhtric who came to the rescue, because he broke the tense silence, speaking gently, "Leofflaed, Eadgyd, may I tell you something?" Of course, they both nodded, while Titus was mystified as to where his friend was heading. He learned quickly enough, when Uhtric said, "I was there when your brother and father met at Ethantun."

For a long moment, neither of his sisters could speak, Leofflaed staring at Uhtric, while Eadgyd stared at Titus, but it was his older sister who addressed the warrior.

"Are you saying that Titus and our father met in battle?"

"Not exactly," Uhtric said quickly. "It was actually after the worst of the fighting, and the Danes were running. Titus," he nodded to their brother, "saw Leofric running away from the battle. He went after him, and I caught up to them after Titus caught him. What your father said, the things he threatened to do, not just to Titus, but to the two of you, is something that no father should say about his children," he said grimly. He took a breath then, and Titus understood why, but again, Uhtric was speaking not to him but to Leofflaed. "The things he said were so vile, Leofflaed, that I told Titus that I would kill your father so that he wouldn't have to. My father," his voice grew hoarse from a surge of emotion, "was a good man, a *great* man, and he loved me and he loved my sisters well. Leofric," he shook his head, "is not a father."

"Is this true, Titus?" Leofflaed asked her brother, and he did not hesitate.

"It is," he nodded gravely, although he could not recall Leofric saying anything about his sisters, reserving his hatred for his only son, but he decided that, if this was a lie, it was for a good purpose. Recognizing that he needed to say more, he went on, "I didn't want to tell you about it, either of you. He…said horrible things, and I wanted to kill him." Saying it aloud was a relief, and the words came out in a rush. "I swear on the rood that I did! I wanted to plunge my spear through his black heart so that none of us had to worry about him ever again. And," he leaned over and put a hand on each of his sister's arms, "as long as he's alive, you're going to be in danger!"

Leofflaed looked down at Titus' hand, then reached out and put one of hers on his as she nodded acceptance of what her brother was saying, but she was also the practical one of the family.

"But this is our home, Titus," she said quietly. "Without it, we have no place else to go."

"I might have an idea about that."

They all turned to stare at Uhtric, but with three decidedly distinct, and different, emotions.

"Are you sure about this?"

Titus had addressed both of his sisters, but he was looking at Leofflaed, who understood that there was more to her brother's question than what might appear on the surface.

Nevertheless, she did not hesitate, nor did Eadgyd, although it was the younger sister who spoke for the two of them. "I don't think we have any other choice. Besides," she offered her siblings a mischievous grin, "I want to see Leofric's face when he does come slinking back."

It had taken an extra day for Titus to make the arrangements once everything was decided, but he was actually aided by the state of flux created in the aftermath of Ethantun in the lands of the deposed Ealdorman and those thegns who had thrown their lot in with the Danes, specifically with matters of property that belonged to those declared traitorous by King Alfred.

This, at least, had been how Titus, with Uhtric's help, had expressed it to Godstan when Titus approached him about buying Leofric's hide of land. It made sense, Titus had argued, on a number of levels; Godstan's land adjoined Leofric's, and as land went, it was not bad. The lack of production from it had been more from Leofric's sloth than because of the soil. Titus was actually working from an advantage because he was aware that Cuthwine, whose land abutted Leofric's on the side opposite from Godstan's, had also coveted the land, and the two ceorls detested each other. Even better, the year before, Godstan had made what, to Titus and his children, was a generous offer for Leofric's holding, but the problem was that this hide of land was all that gave Leofric the status of a free Saxon, so none of them had been surprised when Leofric flatly rejected it. Now Titus was offering Godstan the hide for far below the full pound of silver he had offered for it originally, but the money was a secondary consideration; depriving Leofric was by far a happier prospect than the money. The deal was concluded, as was the custom, in the square of Cissanbyrig, with a very unhappy Cuthwine watching, Titus accepting a purse bulging with silver pennies, while handing the lead rope to their cow to Godstan. Immediately after this, Titus and Uhtric exchanged a pile of those silver pennies for three horses, one of which was barely suitable as a packhorse, along with a pair of saddles, and they came trotting around the bend of the road to find that, as planned, Leofflaed and Eadgyd were waiting in the yard with what, by any measure, was a pitifully small pile of possessions.

Seeing them standing there, Titus asked for what Uhtric was certain was at least the tenth time, "So you're sure that your sister won't have any trouble with them staying with her and her family? I mean," he assured Uhtric, "it won't be for long. I'm going to find something for them in Wiltun."

"I'm sure," Uhtric assured him, albeit with more confidence than he actually felt.

He had not said as much, but the truth was that Leofflaed and his oldest sister Leofgifu had more in common than similar names, and he was at least certain that she would provide for anyone her older brother asked of her. Nevertheless, being certain here in Cissanbyrig was not exactly the same as standing in front of his sister at her and her husband's home, although he did not really consider Wigstan as being the decision maker. If Leofgifu said it was all right, it was all right; all he could do was hope that he knew his sister as well as he thought he did. Working quickly, they loaded the pack animal, then Leofflaed turned to go back into the home that was all the sisters had ever known, never spending a night under any other roof.

Titus sensed more than realized what Leofflaed was doing,

although he called out to her to be sure, "What are you going to do?"

In answer, she indicated the small trail of smoke rising through the hole in the roof.

"I need to smother the fire," she answered, but Titus shook his head, saying flatly, "You don't need to do that."

"Why?" She frowned. "Is Godstan going to be here so soon?"

"No," Titus replied, but when Leofflaed demanded to know what he had in mind, he said only, "You'll see."

She opened her mouth to press him, then decided it was unnecessary, since her last time in Leofric's house was about the severing of the last tie to her father and all that he represented more than snuffing out a fire. Eadgyd came and joined her, standing next to the scarred table, the sisters not speaking, each of them absorbed in their own thoughts to the point they did not notice Titus standing there in the doorway. Once more, he was wearing his mail, although this was mainly because he did not want to load the packhorse down, which was clearly on its last legs, but he had been unwilling to spend a penny more than he had to. He watched his sisters, noticing that Eadgyd had reached out for Leofflaed's hand as the pair surveyed what, by any measure, was a pathetic sight, the sum total of what their lives had been to this point, their only fault being who their father was. The love Titus experienced in this moment, silently watching his sisters from behind them, was so strong in its ferocity, so overwhelming, that he felt the tears forming, and he was forced to blink several times before he cleared his throat.

"It's time to go," he said quietly, and his sisters obediently walked to the doorway, but when Titus made no move to follow them as they stepped out into the yard, Leofflaed stopped, giving him a questioning glance.

"I'll be along in a moment," he assured her.

Leofflaed's eyes narrowed, and Titus braced himself for a confrontation; when she glanced over at the smoldering fire then back to him with a knowing expression, he was certain she would try and intervene. To his astonishment, he saw her lip lift in a faint smile, then offered a barely perceptible nod before she turned away.

He rejoined the three when they were about a half-mile from the farm, Thunor moving at a canter, and while Eadgyd gave him a questioning glance, for whatever reason, she chose to say nothing. Unusually, Titus then led them around Cissanbyrig instead of through it, moving at a fast walk, but this time when Eadgyd opened her mouth to protest, wanting to say goodbye to two of her friends, it was Leofflaed who reached out and touched her on the shoulder, giving her younger sister a shake of the head. All was explained when Titus, without any warning, suddenly led them off the track to climb the side of a low hill, then turned Thunor to face back to the north. Eadgyd inexpertly guided her mount up the slope behind Leofflaed, who was having similar troubles, and as soon as she oriented her animal in the same direction as her brother, she let out a small gasp.

"Is that…?" She did not finish, but there was no need.

"It is," Titus confirmed, his eyes fixed on the thin but unmistakable black line of smoke that rose above the hill that shielded what had been Leofric's house from Cissanbyrig.

They were content to sit there then, none of them speaking, as they watched the evidence of their childhood home being consumed by flames. When Leofflaed gave a surreptitious glance at her brother, wondering what his thoughts were at this moment, she was unsettled at what she saw. Gone was any hint of the boy who had declared that he was going to leave their farm, and their father, to join the fyrd held by an Ealdorman he knew only by name, miles away. Instead, what she saw there was a hardened warrior; young, but somehow not, at least not anymore. He has, she thought sadly, gone from boyhood to manhood in a matter of months, faster than normal, and probably faster than was good for him. Hard on the heels of that thought came another one, and this caused Leofflaed to smile; her brother had never been normal, not from the day he was born, a day that she had steadfastly lied to Titus about, claiming that she had no memory of it. The truth was quite different; her memories of that day were not only vivid, so was the recollection of the feelings she had experienced, and it was to Leofflaed's undying shame that, for several months, she had shared their father's hatred of her new brother, both because of her own grief and the desperate need to do something about which her father approved. It would be a secret she would take to her grave, the shame of it so palpable that on those few occasions she did think about it, she wanted to weep.

"Since we got such a late start," Titus broke the silence, "I think we're going to sleep at Stonehenge."

"Stonehenge!" the sisters exclaimed at the same time, exchanging an alarmed look, while Uhtric hid his smile.

"Stonehenge is cursed with spirits! Everyone knows that!" Eadgyd insisted, but Titus knew his sisters very well.

Behind the protests, he saw they were every bit as curious as he had been, so he only offered a bland reply as he led them back down the hill, knowing that they would talk themselves into it. Nothing more was said, but when Titus nudged Thunor to a trot to move a distance ahead of the others and Uhtric made to follow, he was restrained by Leofflaed's hand on his arm, which caused them both to flush.

"I think he wants to be alone," she said quietly.

"Yes, my Lady," Uhtric answered gravely, causing her to flush even more deeply.

As she usually was, Leofflaed was right. Over the course of the next couple of miles, Titus took the last steps in shedding the skin of Titus of Cissanbyrig, son of Leofric, and becoming the man he at least aspired to be. From this moment forward, he became Titus, of Lord Otha's household, called The Berserker by some, although it still made him uncomfortable hearing the title because it reminded him of *why* he had earned this name; not the act itself, but what had fueled it, his blind, all-consuming rage that, if he was honest, frightened him as much as it did those who were the targets of that wrath. More than that, however, was his conviction that he had not done enough to earn such a reputation, but in this, he was determined to add to it. There was still one nagging uncertainty: Leofric lived, and while he still felt conflicted about killing his own father, Titus also understood that his transformation would not be complete, and his future would not be truly secure as long as his father lived. Nevertheless, Titus was happier than he had been in his entire life, and he looked forward to whatever challenge God placed in the path of Titus, whether he was the Berserker or not. And, while he did not, nor would he ever know it, he was doing nothing more than fulfilling a destiny that had been set for him almost a thousand years earlier, on a ramshackle farm far from Wessex, by another youth named Titus, and he would be doing what he had been born to do.

Made in the USA
Coppell, TX
20 January 2022

71976776R00184